LUSTS OF THE BORGIAS

LUSTS OF THE BORGIAS

MARCUS
VAN HELLER

Carroll & Graf Publishers, Inc.
New York

LUSTS OF THE BORGIAS

LUSTS OF THE BORGIAS

VOLUME ONE

CHAPTER 1

When she was only ten years old Cardinal Roderigo had doted on the remarkable physical development of his daughter and now, at the age of eleven, he thought of her as a fresh, young woman with her breasts and buttocks as full as cannonballs.

But it was not only her voluptuous dimensions which produced the burning erection under Roderigo Borgia's robes every time he watched her playing in her little girl's shift which seemed so unsuitable. It was the deep, knowing look in those bright blue eyes, which seemed to look past his apparent paternal smile and see the incestuous desire beyond. And in the look was the hint of a smile, as if she were daring him to translate his desire to action.

Of course, Cardinal Roderigo was aware that his own feelings interfered with his objectivity of vision. It was hardly likely that his daughter, raised in a true God-fearing way, could really have the faintest inkling of the lustful labyrinths of men's minds. And yet there was a definite sexual aura about her which he could not reconcile with his imagination, nor with her youth.

He sat on a log in the grounds of their house near St. Peter's watching her playing now with her brother Cesare. Cesare pushed the swing while she, with her shift above her knees and her legs apart as she urged it to greater heights, sat on the wooden platform as if on a horse.

The paternal smile was fixed on Cardinal Roderigo's face. Any observer would have felt his heart stirred at the sight of the busiest, most important cardinal in Rome, relaxing with his children. But through that smile, the

Cardinal's eyes dwelt on the uplifted breasts as she reached upwards, holding the ropes of the swing. Their outline was forceful; they seemed to spring out towards his eyes. It suddenly occurred to him that she hadn't put on her undergarments today.

"Higher, higher," she urged her brother.

Even the voice, he mused, was that of a woman; it had body and modulation. It had a soft, caressing warmth, the way her flesh would be if it nestled nakedly against one.

The swing was mounting. Back and then forward toward him. His eyes dropped to her well-formed legs. She squirmed her bottom on the swing, exhorting it with passionate fondlings to fly up and up. The Cardinal found the movement exciting. He imagined, tried to imagine, the feel of that bottom against his loins. He stared at her hips. His face colored slightly. He could see right up those delicious, milky thighs to the darkness of their junction. Oh those thighs! He raised his eyes guiltily, with an effort, and saw that hers were on him, lids slightly lowered, suggesting a smile. He started. The little minx. She was positively inviting him. He was convinced of it.

"Lucrezia, my child," he said. "Have you no warm clothes under your shift?"

She squirmed her bottom and kicked her legs forward, urging her mount on.

"No father. It's so warm, today."

"It's not a question of warmth, my sweet one. It's unladylike to be naked under such a thin garment. It shows off too much of your body."

He enjoyed this sort of conversation. It was fatherly because he was, after all, speaking to his little daughter for her own good; it was also rousing because he was speaking to an unknown woman about her raw beauty. It could be indulged in with safety.

"I thought it wouldn't matter," Lucrezia purred. "There is nobody to see me but you and Cesare."

"Paternity and fraternity, my dear, do not turn men into marble statues."

He continued to look at her, suddenly, overwhelmingly aware that he was talking to no child at all. He was talking to some strange, instinctive essence of woman which needed no experience to know about the effect of the apple. She looked back at him, unspeaking, her eyes sphinxlike, her thighs still wide, her arms relaxed a little on the ropes so that her breasts jogged slightly as she jerked forward.

Roderigo glanced past her to Cesare. His son was two years older and as beautiful as his sister. But he was not so aware. Even now, he seemed not to have followed the conversation. He concentrated, grinning, on his job of hurtling Lucrezia up to a horizontal sweep. His secret ambition was to see her swoop right up and over the bar.

"You must always wear underclothes in the Orsini Palace," the Cardinal said, determined to keep the conversation going. "It would be unbecoming to your tutors to treat them like suitors."

She stared at him for a few seconds as the swing flowed forward and back. He knew she was working over his words, but she was clever enough to make it appear that she understood.

"Passion is a poor accompaniment to scholarly disinterest," he pursued, reveling in the train of his thought, the sequence of images—of tutors mixing Greek with French in confusion, while his daughter calmly surveyed their discomfiture with deep eyes and a half-shown bosom.

"Will study make me scholarly and disinterested?"

You precocious little bitch, he thought. I ought to spank you—but I should ejaculate over your flushed buttocks even as my hand lashed them.

"You are too bursting with the good things of life," he answered.

"Cesare," Lucrezia said, "I want to come down."

Reluctantly Cesare caught the swing, moved back and forth with it, slowing it. With the courtesy he'd always been taught, he moved around and lifted his sister down. She slipped down him, still watching her father. Her limbs seemed to cling to her brother's like slowly relaxing rubber. As her feet reached the ground she looked up at his face suddenly and her round mouth parted in a smile to which her brother responded.

Her father saw the smile and sensed the desire behind it. But his son, he saw, was not awakened to his young sister's potentialities.

He looked at Cesare. The boy was already tall and sturdy. He must have had sexual desire, must experience it often, but it did not focus on his sister. A pity, the Cardinal decided. The little witch needed to know what it was like and she had a bit of a crush on her brother —that he had noticed in years gone by.

Cesare would be more or less of a handsome stranger to her of course, away as he was most of the time, studying at Perugia. An idea occurred to him and he smiled at it. He would open Cesare's eyes to the little fruit that his

14

sister was. She would, surely, do the rest without any encouragement. Then, when she had been deflowered by Cesare's growing manhood, the way would be prepared for his own full organ to enjoy an hour or two of passion with her.

"Why don't you go and bathe in the pool," he suggested. "Take off all your clothes and let the sun fill you with goodness."

Lucrezia looked quickly at her brother. Cesare looked at his father. A number of unuttered questions clouded, uncomfortably, in his eyes.

"Oh, don't worry," the Cardinal said paternally. "There will be nobody to see you and you are well sheltered by the pergola."

Cesare continued to look uncomfortable and his sister caught his hand.

"Poor Cesare. I think he's embarrassed," she said innocently. "Why are you embarrassed, my darling brother?"

Cardinal Roderigo heard the innocent-sounding words mincing provocatively from her pretty lips and smiled inwardly. He wondered just how far her mind went, how much of the next hour or two she anticipated.

"Embarrassed," he roared, with mock impatience. "Of course Cesare's not embarrassed. He has too fine and athletic a frame to be embarrassed to let his little sister see it. Give her a spanking Cesare when there's nothing to protect her—and then duck her head in the pool."

Cesare smiled. He was still embarrassed, but now he dared not show it. His father's praise of his body had pleased him.

"I'll make her scream for mercy," he boasted.

"Mind she doesn't make you scream for

15

mercy," the Cardinal muttered more to himself than to his son.

"Off you go now," he urged. "I have some work to do."

He watched them run off in the direction of the pool, Lucrezia leading, her buttocks straining against the shift as she moved, laughing over her shoulder at Cesare, who followed, smiling, superior in the knowledge that he could overtake her as he wished.

The Cardinal waited for several minutes before he followed them slowly through the grounds, stepping quietly toward the pool.

The pool was surrounded by a covered walk with a single entrance at one end. The Cardinal pushed his way gently through the trees and bushes bolstering the trelliswork. He crouched and peered through the rose-twined woodwork to where the clear, blue pool glittered in the sunlight.

Cesare was immersed in the pool, keeping to its edge, obviously still embarrassed at his sister's presence. She, however, was standing on the marble surround brazenly drawing her shift over her head.

Cardinal Roderigo's eyes became transfixed. She threw the shift down on a wooden seat and stretched, looking down invitingly at Cesare. The curves of her body were generous, her waist tight and slim, breasts opening out like an enormous flower above, hips vying with breasts for roundness and maturity below. The sun, which turned her golden hair almost silver, made her pink flesh shine with an almost luminous whiteness. The large red nipples stood out astonishingly dark against the white background and the down at the solid triangle

16

between her thighs was another quick flash of silver.

If I had been more thoughtful, Cardinal Roderigo told himself, I would have got rid of her nanny and her maids and enjoyed the sight of her womanly body often before.

Lucrezia was walking along the edge of the pool away from Cesare, staring up into the sun, opening her arms to it like a lover. Her buttocks bulged under the slimness of her waist, stretching one against the other as she moved, her legs tautened, hard and slim and then relaxed as each swept forward with her step.

Cardinal Roderigo was hot all over, and sweating between his thighs. His eyes gloated over the fullness of her body, the movement in it as she moved, little eddies of shadow, ripples of half-formed muscle. He watched her parading for Cesare's benefit as if she were an experienced harlot and he was amazed. The little bitch really needed it good and hard and deep enough to make her tremble from her toes to her golden plaits.

Cesare, too, watched her every movement. His own nakedness had suddenly made him aware of hers—as a woman, not as his sister. He clung to the edge of the pool whose water was so clear that if he moved out into the middle she'd be able to see him just as he could now see her.

Lucrezia turned and walked back toward Cesare.

"Isn't it lovely not to have any clothes on?" she called out. "I feel like a nymph."

"Hurry up and come in," Cesare answered gruffly. "The water's warm."

"Why do you sound so cross?" she pouted. And with a quick movement she swept her little

17

foot down into the water beside him and shot a spout of water into his eyes. Cesare gasped, released his hold on the side and plunged out into the center of the pool. The shock of the attack robbed him of his embarrassment.

"I'll get you for that," he called, laughing.

You'll get her anyway, the Cardinal chuckled to himself. He was envying his son the view he must have had of Lucrezia's soft, little vagina as she stretched her foot down to splash him.

"I don't care. I'm not afraid of you," she cried, laughing too. And with that she gave a neat little dive down into the pool, out of sight of both father and son.

Leaning forward, the better to see, Cardinal Roderigo heard his son shout and saw him begin to flail his arms as he disappeared under the water. In another second Lucrezia shot to the surface and broke into peals of laughter at her skill in ducking her brother from underneath.

Cesare came to the surface, furious now at the impudence of the trick. He began to race toward his retreating sister.

"I'm going to spank you as father said," he cried. "And then I may kill you as well."

Shrieking insults, Lucrezia turned her back on him and swam with all her strength to the edge of the pool. She reached up, gripped the edge and hauled herself out, lying along the marble and wriggling herself out of the water.

Cardinal Roderigo could feel the painful pressure of his rigid penis against his clothes as he devoured the back view of her wriggling escape. Her buttocks stretched out, her thighs pushed and flailed in the air. He could see the slim walls of flesh between her legs. She would be the most beautiful, the most voluptuous woman in Italy in a very short time.

Cesare reached the pool's edge and grabbed at one of his sister's feet, but all he succeeded in doing was getting a hearty kick in the shoulder as she swung clear, climbed to her feet and began to run.

Her father's eyes followed lustfully. Her buttocks swayed like helpless jellies as she fled; her breasts sprang up and flopped back within their small range of movement. She laughed as she ran and glanced over her shoulder to where Cesare had quickly pulled himself up to the marble surround and was getting to his feet. Her eyes took in the water-cooled limpness of his organ, the dark hair around it. She wondered fleetingly what it was like to touch that thing which performed the functions of which she'd read vague descriptions in some of the best literature of the times. Then Cesare was on his feet and running dangerously fast after her and she turned her head frontwards again, racing breathlessly around the pool's perimeter.

Cardinal Roderigo drew back a little as her rippling, trembling figure turned the end of the bath and came towards him. He looked back at his son and was proud of him. Slim, strong body. He could have been eighteen or nineteen and his penis was a good specimen, a worthy initiator for Lucrezia.

Cesare was overhauling his sister with ease. She glanced back again and began to laugh with that breathless hysteria of someone in desperation.

She was practically opposite the point where her father was hidden in the mass of foliage when Cesare caught her. She turned away from the pool onto the soft bank of grass next to the inside trelliswork, trying to dodge, to double back. But it was too late, Cesare's muscular young arms had fastened, one around her neck, the other across her breasts, and all she could do was kick and struggle and laugh and pant helplessly.

The battle between their fine young bodies, his lean, muscular, hers ripe, voluptuous, took place about six feet from the unseen Cardinal, who moved forward again, so unlikely were they to see him in the concentration of their struggle.

"Now I shall spank you," Cesare shouted, flinging her down on the grass, falling with her.

"Oh Cesare, how rude and brutish," his sister laughed.

Cardinal Roderigo looked down at her close, fleshful body so near to him and felt a fierce gripping in his rod, so that he longed to burst through the flimsy trellis and the roses and sink himself into the soothing well of relief she promised. He watched their struggle on the ground. Cesare had forced her down on her belly and she had caught one arm and held it firmly gripped under her breasts. He had twined one leg around hers while he raised the other hand and gave her the first sharp-sounding slap across her rearing buttocks.

The Cardinal watched the hand descend, saw her squirm and cry out, half laughing, half startled, saw the pink mark on the white mounds as the hand rose again.

Lucrezia struggled again, desperately, and managed to throw Cesare's leg off her. The Cardinal grinned avidly as he saw that his son's penis had stiffened out, was cleaving the air alongside his daughter's buttock.

Cesare was flushed; he looked a little confused. He noticed, too, that Lucrezia was trembling.

With a sharp movement of his strong arms, Cesare gripped her shoulders, holding her flat on the ground, only her legs kicking wildly in the air. Again he lifted his hand and it lashed down across her behind, and again. His erection had expanded to the limit of its capacity as he half lay, half knelt beside his sister and administered punishment to her darkly blushing bottom.

Watching closely the Cardinal saw Lucrezia's mouth open, was aware that she was pressing her body into the grass as she smarted under her spanking.

"Oh, Cesare!" she gasped out at last.

Her brother eased up, wondering at last if perhaps he hadn't been too harsh. Lucrezia stayed still, her shoulders trembling, her face against the fresh grass.

Cesare lay down alongside her, concerned, and tried to turn her over.

"I didn't hurt you really, did I?" he asked.

Lucrezia turned over at this, edging half under him. She smiled.

"You didn't hurt me at all," she said.

"Well don't be too cocky or I'll give you another," Cesare warned, a little put out.

Lucrezia trembled against him, her soft flesh moving against his. She put an arm over his shoulders.

"Don't spank me any more, Cesare," she begged. "It's made me feel all funny."

Cesare looked down at her. Her flesh against his was an undreamed of torment all of a sudden. His penis felt tight, ready to snap. He knew what went on, but had never seriously considered it. But here was his sister's body all naked and exciting curiosity and a pent-up emotion.

She wriggled under him again, her face close to his and suddenly the other arm had gone around his neck.

"Oh, Cesare!" she said once more. And then she pressed her lips against his.

"Great God," the Cardinal was muttering. "Great God! Eleven years old and with all the wiles of woman born in her! Cesare my son, consider yourself seduced and your father as a serious rival." He was hot as a furnace around his loins and his head was tight with lustful concentration.

Cesare kissed her back. He was flushed in a way he hardly understood. Just the touch of her flesh, her lips, her breasts, the round, nude hips against which his prick was pressed, made him feel almost nauseous with desire.

She took her mouth away from his and looked at him with her deep eyes, half-lidded and deeper looking than he'd ever seen them before. She ran her tongue around her lips and wriggled her body against him.

He bent his head and kissed her lips again and ran his mouth violently over her face. He was afraid at the heat inside him and where it would end.

Get in, Cesare, for the Lord's sake, his father was urging through his will. The little minx wants it so much she'll bite off your prick out of spite if you don't manage it.

He watched her wriggling her hips under her brother's and he wished with a great prayer-like wish that he were lying on her now, poising his hot penis beside that soft little crack ready to pump out his life in love of her.

22

"Oh, Cesare!" he heard her say more softly. Her arms were hugging him, her hands moving gently over his lean shoulders. Her eyes were closed. The Cardinal could see the slightly crushed globes of her breasts prodding up into Cesare's chest, heaving against him like a sea washing the hull of a ship. Her hips were washing like waves against his loins, too.

"Cesare, dear—do you know how to?" she asked breathlessly after a while in which they pressed against each other and kissed, and he felt afraid.

"Have you read about it in books?" she whispered.

"Yes—yes," he said brokenly.

"Let's do it, Cesare, darling. I feel all tight and it must be the time to do it."

My God, my God, the Cardinal thought. Listen to my daughter. She might be her mother for the way she's talking and acting. Her tutors would be shocked out of their wits.

Lucrezia pushed her hands down Cesare's back, tentatively, letting the palms run over the long, lean curve until she felt the sudden hard jut of his buttocks. She caressed his buttocks and pushed them at her gently with an inspired instinct. She could feel the heavy heat of his penis on her loins and she wanted him, so desperately, to do what it was they did. Deep in her belly, deep in her being she needed it.

Gently she pressed her face against his and bit him on the neck. He uttered a little gasp and his hands tightened on her shoulders, squeezing them until they hurt. His loins pressed against hers with a new pressure. She felt them slither around against her skin.

Perhaps I should really go out and show

23

them exactly what to do, Cardinal Roderigo was thinking. If he doesn't shove it in and blast her for all he's worth she's likely to turn into a man-hater. He caught his bulging penis through his robes and held it, comforted slightly by the alien pressure.

He watched her hands. What hands, he thought. They moved fluidly, as if in the movements of oft-practiced caresses, over Cesare's back and buttocks. She obviously loved the feel of his skin. He watched her squirming and arching her body upwards. The sexy little bitch'll have an orgasm any minute now, he thought, and then she'll probably be coy and refuse to let him.

But, while his eyes began to bulge at the sight, he saw Cesare slide down on her and, feverishly but inaccurately, push his penis between her legs. At first he was too low. It was as if he intended only to get his knob in, if that. But then Lucrezia, eyes still closed, mouth open, snuggled down against him and brought his knob up against her crotch with a rush.

Cesare prodded uncertainly. Lucrezia in a sudden gust of passion opened her legs wide.

More vague proddings with Cesare breathing so heavily that the Cardinal wondered if his own breathing would reach them.

"That's it! Oh Cesare, Cesare!" The words exploded from her lips and she arched her back, thrusting her breasts up and back with the shock.

Cardinal Roderigo watched Cesare, trembling from head to toes, clamp his little buttocks awkwardly between her thighs as he uncertainly made a bridgehead in her vagina. Lucrezia, too, was trembling and whimpering and holding his shoulders with such force, that the

24

Cardinal could see the flesh white against the boy's tan, where her fingers were digging.

There, there, at last you little witch. The Cardinal's eyes gleamed with vicarious satisfaction. How does it feel, eh? But you won't really know until you've been screwed by your father's royal rammer.

Lucrezia's body was shaking with continual spasms. She kept her hips still, enduring the certain pain, excited beyond endurance at the thrill of Cesare's entry into her well-cared-for treasure. She moved her face against his, brushing his face with her lips, clasping his lips in hers, wanting to swallow his lips.

The Cardinal watched his son gradually advancing through his bridgehead, wriggling awkwardly up into her, squirming his hips up from their rather distant stance between her lower thighs until he was in the correct position for a full thrust.

After a time, as his hard little buttocks rose and fell above her, Lucrezia began to wriggle under him, too, moaning, kissing him passionately, mouthing his name.

Every so often Lucrezia would throw out her arms on the grass and lie there moaning in abandonment for several seconds before clasping them once more and with renewed passion around Cesare's back.

Cesare was panting furiously. His jerking was getting a smooth, more powerful flow, but the Cardinal could see that he hadn't sunk into her to the full and probably wouldn't before he came.

Lucrezia's thighs began to clasp Cesare's hips, rubbing them as she lifted her knees from the ground and twisted her loins in her passion.

When she lifted her knees and her thighs

rode up with them forming an angle with the grass, Cardinal Roderigo could see Cesare's penis pushing into her hole. It was in about two thirds of its length and her vaginal lips were sucking it voraciously. He noticed that there wasn't any blood. Cesare would enlarge her just enough to make the shock of his prick, when she got it, not too unbearable.

The sun shone down vividly on the bright green grass and the two passionately-fitted bodies writhing out their exquisite pleasure beside the pool. A fine picture of son and daughter with father watching from the bushes, the Cardinal thought with a chuckle.

Lucrezia's plump buttocks were flattening against the ground, oozing and spreading from under Cesare's hips. She was gasping, uttering his name. Her climax was near. Hot little bitch, her father murmured. What a delight you'll be to me.

"Oh Cesare, Cesare, my darling brother...!" Her words tumbled out in the whine of her breath and she sucked his lips again, straining her body at him. Cesare tried to utter something, failed, and gasped instead.

"Oh Cesare, Cesare! Oh, oh, oh!" She pushed against him so hard that she almost lifted him off the ground on top of her, her buttocks hollowing with the strain; her arms clasped him to her as if she wanted to envelop him with flesh. The breath exploded from her open mouth in a great whoosh as if someone had sat on her belly and expelled it as from a cushion. She gave several wild, self-concerned convulsions and then sank back under him.

Cesare had stopped his action, shaken out of his stride by her passion. She put her arms back around his neck, calmer but still loving and he resumed his hard, probing entry into her vagina.

How sweet — sweet minx, the Cardinal thought passionately. Lie there and wait for him to know the climax of pleasure you've just had.

Lucrezia drew up her thighs a little and the Cardinal could see again where Cesare's penis was still only two thirds in. It was too late now for him to learn the art of complete penetration. His head was rolling on his neck, tendons were standing out on that strong young neck of his and a vein pulsed in his forehead.

Lucrezia whispered, but more lazily this time:

"Cesare, darling Cesare!"

Cardinal Roderigo watched his son's body twist up into the culmination of passion as he pressed his sister into the grass. His breath was coming in a series of quick little gasps, he put his arms around her body hugging it to him, he gasped her name at last, the first time it had ever been gasped in passion.

"Lucrezia . . . Lucrezia . . . Aaaaah!"

He convulsed against her, lost control of his movements, actually drew out of her in his excitement and fear at what he was doing and spurted over the grass.

Lucrezia, breathing hard again, stroked his face and shoulders as his hips jerked in the air like a death spasm. She glanced down as he rolled immediately away from her, doubtful and half-ashamed now that it was finished. She saw the thin lines of sperm on the grass, his penis, deflated and small now, with the thin bubble of mucous liquid protruding from the little red nipple at its head.

"Cesare—we've done it," she whispered. She seemed astonished now.

Cesare didn't look at her. He lay on his stomach with his head in his arms. She rolled over to him.

"Cesare, darling, are you cross; do you wish we hadn't?"

He didn't answer and she put her arms around him in an almost motherly way and kissed his head.

"Cesare — don't wish we hadn't . . . because then I should feel terrible that I thought it was so wonderful."

At that Cesare lifted his head and smiled at her.

"That's better," she said softly. "You did like it didn't you?"

He nodded his head and she kissed him gently on the lips. She glanced around them and the Cardinal crouched softly back. His penis was still as hard and hot as a bar of red-hot iron.

"We'd better have another swim," Lucrezia was saying. She looked at her brother with her deep eyes. "We will be able to do it again before you go, won't we Cesare?"

Cesare nodded, jumped to his feet, helped her up and took a running dive into the pool.

Lucrezia followed, smiling. And the Cardinal slowly withdrew through the bushes. "The sexy little bitch," he kept repeating. "The sexy little bitch."

CHAPTER 2

Cardinal Roderigo's mistress, the beautiful Vannozza Cattanei, was sleeping in her room in a wing of the house when he went through to

28

see her later in the day. She was recovering from one of those ridiculous and unexpected summer chills.

He sat on the edge of her bed. She was certainly still beautiful although her youth was past. He still found her delicious in bed. But every so often he felt the need for a fresh body, words and whimpers of passion from a strange voice. He felt the need now. Not an abstract one, but the need for Lucrezia on whom his whole lustful attention had focused.

He leaned over the sleeping woman and kissed her forehead. She awoke and smiled sleepily at him.

"I'll leave you tonight," he said. "You still need rest. Is there anything you need?"

"Nothing, Roderigo, nothing. What have you been doing?"

"Watching the children. They're growing up."

"Yes, indeed," she said sadly. "I wish they could call me mother."

"Hardly becoming, my dear," the Cardinal answered with a chuckle. "The Pope would have the final fit to finish him if such a thing were openly admitted. Think of the disrepute the Church would fall into. Think of the Church, my sweet."

She pressed his hand with a smile.

"The Church is a hypocrite, Roderigo. You are the Church."

"Hush, dear, never let it be said. Now, if there's nothing you need I shall go and read for a while in the library, or perhaps I'll take a stroll in the grounds."

"Yes. I shall be better in the morning," she said.

He bent again and kissed her on the forehead

and she pulled his face down and kissed him on the lips.

"Good-night, my sweet."

"Sweet dreams."

He left her chamber and strolled through the wing of the house, meditating. He didn't head down the stairway toward the library, nor yet to the grounds. He directed his feet instead toward the children's wing.

Candles were burning in Cesare's room when he looked in and Cesare was sitting in bed staring vacantly at the opposite wall.

"Very pensive, my son. You'd better go to sleep now. I want you to be at your best for our little hunting trip tomorrow."

"Oh, yes, father. I was thinking about it."

Liar, thought the Cardinal with an inward chuckle. You'd forgotten it completely. You were dreaming of your little sister's breasts, reliving your first flesh-to-flesh liaison.

He went to Cesare's bedside and kissed him on the forehead.

"Good-night, my son."

"Good-night, father."

Cardinal Roderigo blew out the candles and retired from the room.

His heart beat faster and his penis was already at half-mast as he walked down the corridor to Lucrezia's room at the end. Anticipatory thrills licked down his spine at the thought of what he was going to enjoy. He hadn't decided exactly how to bring it about, but somehow or other he was going to have her tonight.

He opened her door softly, without knocking, and stepped inside.

Candles were burning in her room, too, but she was not in her bed. He glanced around the room and saw her sitting on a stool beside the window, gazing out into the grounds. She was clad in her thin nightdress, but the evening was warm.

She turned, startled.

"Oh, papa. I didn't hear you come in."

He came across to her and peered through the window.

"What are you doing, dearest, dreaming about the stars?"

"Oh, it's such a lovely night, father, and I don't feel a bit sleepy."

She had risen from the stool and stood beside him, looking out with him over the trees. He glanced down at her. Little did she know that he knew what she'd been up to. He found himself breathing nervously. Her breasts swelled out below the square neck of the nightgown, pushing the material out in a twin range of hills with just a slight indentation between them.

In spite of his years, the Cardinal felt quite nervous. Astonishing, he thought, after all my experience, to feel like a schoolboy with my own daughter.

He put his arm around her and she leaned against him affectionately. How often before I've put my arm around her without the slightest tremor, he thought. And now he could hardly keep his fingers from quivering on her soft shoulder. He wondered how she felt, now, with her new awareness. She'd been growing more and more provocative toward him, but, perhaps now, paradoxically, her experience had turned her mind on her brother Cesare; perhaps she could think of nothing and no one else.

"Have you had a pleasant day?" He tried to keep his voice normal.

"Oh, I've had a wonderful day, papa."

"Has Cesare been good to you?"

She looked up at him and he could see those deep eyes in the moonlight! They were not a bit apprehensive, but she was searching his eyes, as if wondering.

"He's always good to me, father. I sometimes think he'd die for me."

"A very romantic notion, my dear young lady. Maybe you mean you'd die for him, eh?"

He squeezed her shoulder and ran his hand down her arm, as if in affection. She moved her other hand onto his and pressed it.

"Perhaps that is what I mean, papa. I never feel I can hide anything from you."

"Ah, you'll learn, my sweet, to have admiration for others than your brother."

"Oh but I have, papa. I love you at least as much as Cesare."

Am I reading into those words what I want to read into them, the Cardinal asked himself? Are they as innocent as they could be — were it not for what I'd witnessed this afternoon? Or is she really being provocative again in a way that only a she-devil could be?

He bent and kissed the top of her golden head, moving his hand from her shoulder, under her armpit so that his fingers lay lightly along the outside bulge of her womanly breast.

"You speak like someone very old in years, my dear."

"I often feel very old in years, father. Much older than Cesare."

He laughed gently. The breast under his fingers was solid and sleek-feeling even through the nightdress. He longed to tear off that flimsy

32

garment and grasp her breast in his hands while he devoured her lips and felt his penis riding up between her thighs.

"Well, you'd better go to bed," he said. "Come, I'll carry you."

And with that he reached down and swung her from her feet, insuring as he did so that his arm rested under her thighs with his hand against the intimate, rounded crevice formed by the tops of her thighs and the beginnings of her buttocks.

He swung her playfully to and fro once or twice, enabling himself thus to let his hand slip, as if accidentally, between her legs where he could actually feel the slim flanges of her sex.

"Oh, papa!" she uttered sharply. And then she added quickly, to hide the real motive for her cry: "I thought you were going to drop me."

"Drop you," he cried jocularly. "As if I'd drop my beautiful daughter."

He swung her again, his hand slipping along her vaginal lips with every movement. She threw back her head over his arm and closed her eyes with a smile on her lips.

Got you now, my beauty, he thought. A little more of this and you're mine.

"Heave ho, heave ho!" he cried in a jolly tone, while his hand pressed and slid along her vagina which he could clearly feel through the thin cloth.

For a minute or two he swung her back and forth, turning in an occasional circle, raising her, lowering her, all the time his hand working on that newly-initiated core of her being. She remained with her head back, laughing nervously every now and then, saying "Oh, papa!" and flushing with ill-concealed excitement for the rest.

Suddenly, his intruding hand felt wetness through her gown. His hand slipped more easily against her vagina. She was getting really excited. The time had come where a facade of fun and games was no longer necessary.

He carried her to the bed and laid her out on it. He stood up then as if to go, eager to see her reaction. She opened her eyes. Her position was one of abandon, with her legs apart under the nightshift.

"Kiss me goodnight, papa," she said. And it seemed to him that even if he made no further move she would embark on an attempt at seduction.

He leaned down over the bed. Her beautiful young face with those full, indefinitely formed lips was very close. She put up her arms and caught his neck to pull his head down. He kissed her on the lips and it was certainly like no father-and-daughter kiss they'd ever had before. He felt those soft lips pushing hard against him, heard her body rustling, knew that she was rubbing her legs together.

Even now, for the last vestige of delicacy, he pretended to lose his balance as she pulled his head. He tumbled down beside her on the bed. She was still kissing him, but now she released him and laughed delightedly. Such a laugh, he thought. It was a mixture of amusement at his fall, of sensuality, of nervous excitement, of triumph — yes, perhaps, even triumph.

"You little minx," he said aloud.

"Why little minx, papa, darling?" she asked.

"I heard you 'darling' Cesare by the pool today," he retorted. "If I were a father like some I'd send you to a convent."

Lucrezia was obviously taken aback, but his attitude reassured her.

"Didn't you mind, papa? Was it very wicked?"

"Very wicked in the eyes of the world, my dear. But, in your father's eyes it was enviable."

"Papa — are you going to kiss me goodnight again?"

Her thighs were working together and the gown rising and falling from her breathing. With an ecstatic sigh he kissed her mouth, hard and then harder, forcing her lips apart so that his teeth grazed hers before he pushed his tongue through and into her mouth.

His hand went away, wandering over her body, trembling over the luscious, still-hidden flesh. He reached right down to the hem of her gown and slid his hand along her leg, up over the knee and up the thigh. He played with the thighs, teasing them with his fingertips, drawing his nails over the glossy, young flesh, right up to her vagina, teasing her without touching her cranny. She moved and slithered on the bed, eyes closed, in a heat of sensuality.

He too was fluttering inside. This was it. This beautiful, precocious daughter of his with her firm, fleshy body was his. His penis was taut with strain. He moved his mouth from hers and ran his lips over her slim, soft face.

"Put your tongue in my mouth," he murmured.

Her lips sought his and then he felt the soft, wet sliver of her tongue edge between his lips and push into his mouth. She flicked it in and out like a cobra; she breathed into his mouth, breathing her passion.

Good God, your mother would never believe it, he thought.

He sucked her tongue, his saliva mingling with hers. He forced it to retreat with his, filling her mouth with his, like a prick in a wide-open female orifice.

Her hands moved around his head and neck the way they had around Cesare's, but occasionally they jerked when his experienced technique gave her more of a shock.

Softly he began to brush her labia with his fingertips. Gently, gently, back and forth, until the moisture began to ooze out and trickle along her smooth, young thighs. Then he moved the lips apart and inserted two fingers, searched for and found the wet, hard little clitoris. This was something Cesare hadn't known. He'd have to tell him.

Gently he massaged it, feeling it thicken, harden in his fingers. Lucrezia began to squeal and jerked her head away from his and then back in little gusts of uncontrollable passion.

He caught the bud of flesh between two fingers and nipped it, drawing his fingers from its base up to the hard little point.

"Oh, papa! Oh, papa!" she squealed and thrust her tongue wildly into his mouth the way he'd instructed her.

The Cardinal, his face hot, perspiration beading on his almost bald pate, worked his fingers along the inside of the lips, easing them apart until he found the little hole nestling between them. He wormed his finger into it, pushing up through the tight, moist flesh which was as wet and smooth as sealskin. Lucrezia jerked and pressed her thighs tightly over his hand, hindering his progress. He felt the warm flesh of her thighs bulging around his hand. Gently he tickled her vagina with his fingers and gradually she relaxed again and opened her legs.

He leaned up from her a little and looked at her. Her face was flushed, she didn't open her eyes, her lips were open, quivering every so often. He looked down at her body. The night-dress was up around her hips, revealing the delicious proportions of her thighs, the soft bulges of skin between her legs, the little area of down at her thigh junction. The top part of her body was still covered. The hillocks of her breasts heaved in shapely unrest beneath the white material. Swiftly he grabbed the shift with his free hand and pulled it right up, exposing first the full roundness of her little belly and her hips, and then the bulbous symmetry of her breasts above with their slim, pointed nipples.

"Oh, you beauty!" he exclaimed aloud. "You beauty!"

He swooped down to her breasts. He kissed them, sucked the nipples, making her squirm with unbearable ecstasy. He ran his lips down over her ribs, her belly which yielded before the pressure. He covered her hips with hot, wet kisses, following the crease of her groin, licking the smooth, warm-tasting skin of her thighs.

"Oh, papa! Oh, papa!" She seemed incapable of saying anything but those two words as she wriggled her shoulders in the air and squirmed her hips and belly under his lips.

He took his fingers out of her vagina and moved his lips tantalizingly along the fleshy tops of her thighs.

"Oh, papa, I can't stand it!"

But she didn't close her legs and he thought —you'll have more than this to stand before I've finished, you lovely little minx.

Gently he pushed his hands under her buttocks. Oh, what delightful buttocks! They were tightened now, tense in his hands as she strained up toward his lips. He grasped a buttock in each hand and felt them, digging in his fingers, feeling them relax onto his palms, flood out in a sudden give of flesh all over his hands.

He gripped them, pushed her thighs wider with his bald head and licked the lips of her vagina.

She made noises of torment, as if she were gargling with water in her throat. He flicked his tongue into the aperture, which seemed to give way on all sides of his tongue. There was a taste of the inside of an oyster shell, soft and salty and indescribable.

The clitoris was there, seeming bigger to his tongue than to his fingers. He licked it, caught it in his lips and sucked it. She began to squirm even more, gripping his face between her thighs in convulsive spasms. Her breath passed through her lips in the form of a continuous groaning whimper. He hoped they would not disturb any of the household.

Her movements became more wild and uncontrolled and at this point he eased off and removed his mouth.

Reaching up he pulled her shift over her head. She stretched out her arms above her head and he slipped it over them and threw it on the floor. He got up from the bed quickly and began to slip out of his clothes. His penis still gave him cause for anxiety. When he came he wanted it to be right up in her.

Naked, with the warm air like a cool hand on his body, he turned back to the bed and saw her wide-open, anguished, desiring eyes.

His penis was sticking out like a pike. He was afraid she might run from the room at the sight of its size, but instead she fixed her fascinated gaze on it as if hypnotized.

He lay down on the bed beside her and kissed her neck.

"Oh, papa I'm frightened — it's so much bigger than Cesare's," she whispered.

"Don't worry, my darling — you'll find that after the first shock you're a match for it."

He ran his lips all around her neck and put his tongue in her ear until she shivered with the sensation and put her arms back around his neck.

For a few seconds he kneaded her clitoris again until she was moaning with pleasure, and then, his penis pounding as if it were a cannon discharging shot every few moments, he slithered onto her body.

Oh, the delight of feeling that warm, soft flesh meet his at so many points at once! It was as if she were gently kissing him all over. Oh, the joy of having that lovely body, that other personality waiting to submit to him, to join with him in an orgy of heart-pounding pleasure!

For several seconds Cardinal Roderigo just lay on his daughter, rubbing his fat penis on her fleshy lower belly, grating his hairy chest against the smooth silk of her breasts, moistening her lips with his tongue, licking her closed eyelids, stroking her golden plaits as he worked his loins into an unendurable state of dynamic tension.

"Lucrezia, my sweet darling," he whispered. "Now I am going to give you real delight."

In answer she gripped him with her slim arms and hugged him tight, murmuring simply, "Oh, papa, papa!"

Cardinal Roderigo slipped his hand down between their bodies, rough hair of his on one side, glossy, white flesh of hers on the other. He felt his penis, swollen and hot as the sum-

39

mer sun; he went beyond it and his hand was engulfed in a shallows of sticky moisture from the vagina. He found the vagina and moved his prick down for the entry.

Lucrezia's arms tightened around him in frightened anticipation, her legs hung limply apart.

"Now, my darling," he muttered.

The hot, wet knob of his cudgel slipped on the moisture of her thighs, encountered — deliciously cool — the soft, giving wetness of her vaginal lips and then, with a gasp from them both, moved into the opening of her aperture.

Inside his breast was a sudden rush of relief as he felt his knob clasped in that soft, soothing embrace. Inside his head, he thought, Oh, at last. Thank God, thank God!

. In the liquid clasp he thrust smoothly forward to a tighter region and Lucrezia uttered a stifled scream and jerked her hips backwards. But he followed them with his loins and jogged gently on her, probing in on farther, moving his prick in and out just an inch or so while she became accustomed to the pressure.

Gradually she relaxed and her thighs went limp again on either side of his hips. He put his hands under his chest, between their bodies and squeezed her breasts hard and she drew in her breath with a swoosh, and wriggled invitingly down in the region where his hot organ was waiting to advance.

He flexed his hips in a little more and Lucrezia gasped and drew back again.

"Oh, papa, papa," she moaned. "It hurts, it hurts!"

"We'll go gently, my baby," he breathed. "We have plenty of time. Soon it won't hurt you."

After a second or two she untensed again

and he screwed his loins in little circular motions on hers, pushing his penis no farther into her passage.

He turned her face which was pressing, sideways, into the bed, and kissed her, slipping his tongue into her mouth, licking the corners of her lips until she responded and thrust her own little tongue at his.

He screwed her gently, so gently, moving in a fraction of a centimeter at a time. Every time he moved in she tensed and he moved no farther for a while.

He found it excruciating not to be able to plunge right up her to the very hilt of his power, but it also inflicted on him a fresh innovation, a self-torture which was exquisite.

A considerable heat had been generated between their bodies and he saw that little beads of perspiration were bursting forth passionately on her forehead. No doubt she was sweating between her legs too. He slid his hands up the sides of her body, lingering over the rim of breast which oozed out from under him on either side. He moved his hands under her armpits. Yes, they were sweating, too. She was in a real answering fever heat.

Down at his loins a point of passion was growing, a thin pricking of red-hot sensation amidst the mass of indefinable loveliness which was her wet, excited cunt surrounding and eating at his prick.

The thin pricking of sensation seemed to be a bursting point; it seemed, of its own accord to be bursting up and up into her passage and it was only when she cried out again in anguish that he realized he was thrusting in with greater and greater force. Only this time he couldn't slow down, couldn't stop and mark time with his prick to allow her to recover.

Tightly he held her upper arms while he wriggled his hips in closer.

"It won't hurt, it won't hurt, in a moment it won't hurt," he wheezed through his leaping breath.

"Oh, it hurts, it hurts, oh, oh, oh!" Lucrezia moved her head from side to side, but made no further effort, realizing the futility, to jerk her hips away from her father's.

His great prick was like an elephant somehow got inside her body and barging in still farther. She felt as if her belly, her loins, were being purged in a painful, splitting scourging. And always, always as she thought it eased, the pain broke out afresh and the great object tearing and thundering inside swept up, impossibly, farther and farther.

She closed her eyes, trying to stop the tears oozing from them. She bit her lips and gritted her teeth. She couldn't stand it. She wished it had never begun. It wasn't like with Cesare. It was pain such as she'd never experienced. Was this how women were when they had a child? She would never have a child. Never!

But Cardinal Roderigo was in delirium. He moved his hands under her behind, pushed his fingers right around to feel his own organ crushing into that tightly-grasping pipeline. He squeezed her buttocks in a paroxysm of sensuality, thrust his fingers at her little rosebud anus. And all the time the fire in his prick was growing and growing, drawing oaths and obscenities from his mouth. He had nearly disappeared into her body now. There was little left to go. By the time of the explosion which was twisting his lips with its imminence, he would be crushing right in, stuffing her with the entirety of his penis. He pulled her thighs up to facilitate his last two centimeters.

"Oh, oh. What a delightful little hole," he choked. "Daughter — you're the best — the best — I've ever — had."

Lucrezia heard these oaths and mouthings with a slight chill of fear. This had got beyond expectations. But she was relieved to find that the pain had got no worse and that, apart from a soreness in her vagina, everything seemed to be much easier and she was actually recapturing some of the earlier sensation which had flattened in her as soon as the pain came. Papa had been right after all. It *would* only hurt for a while. In fact, now, as it became easier with every thrust he made and she began to wriggle her loins and thighs against him, it seemed impossible that a few minutes before she'd been ready to die from anguish.

"It's all right, papa," she whispered. "It — it doesn't hurt so much any more."

Her words spurred Cardinal Roderigo on as if she had suddenly bitten the blunt end of his rod. There was a sweetness, a submission about the way she told him that made him feel strangely sadistic.

He pulled her thighs up at an even more acute angle with her belly and pushed home the last length of pulsating flesh. Lucrezia gasped, but a gasp which was three parts pleasure, one part shock.

The Cardinal's loins were aflame. His penis was heavy and prickling inside her. It felt ready to burst along its whole length. His belly was heaving in and out enough to give him a heart attack, his hands rifled her bottom, pinching it,

43

grabbing it in paroxysms, digging at the anus which squirmed on his fingertips.

"Oh, Lucrezia! My darling!" he moaned.

"Papa, papa," she answered tenderly through her regrowing passion.

His lips moved, but no sounds came out except his choking breath. It was coming. He rammed smack into her, burying his staff so deep that his hairy surrounds cracked against her vaginal lips with force and made her squeal. In his belly there was a churning, a churning that was pure essence of sensation. Everything paled, he felt dizzy. The heat and solid pricking fury of the sensation was everything, but for dazed impressions of this beautiful body, this beautiful daughter lying under him, giving him this ecstasy from her lovely passionate flesh.

In the depths of his chest a long-drawn, choking gasp slowly followed the course of the long-drawn, loin-convulsing drawing of his fluid. He called her name through his moaning. He leaned up from her except for his loins. He gripped her waist just above the hips and squeezed it with more and more force as the fluid rushed inside him, fought its way to his penis and with a last rush shattered out and up into her writhing channel, inundating it as he jerked uncontrollably, inundating it until it rolled slowly out of her vagina between her wide-flung legs in the wake of his collapsed penis and he let go of her waist and slipped exhaustedly down onto the warmth of her flesh. Red marks were left on the tender white flesh where his hands had gripped.

Lucrezia had been aware, through her own passion, of the groaning and writhing around her as if a thousand demons were suddenly raping her body from all sides. She felt the hot jets of sperm spurt inside her, with a twinge of pleasure. And then, a few seconds later, she felt fresh twinges of disappointment when her father sank limply onto her and the solidity was withdrawn from her vagina leaving a sudden cool rush of air and the shadow of solidity in its place.

Her vagina was hot and a piquant burning remained. She was sore, but not so sore that she wouldn't have invited further entry to assuage her desire. She sighed and tensed her thighs against the Cardinal's hips.

He seemed to come out of the heavily breathing state of coma he'd fallen into and he stroked her thighs without moving from his position astride her.

"You learn very fast, daughter," he said. "I'm exhausted as a galley slave."

In answer she wound her legs around his and rubbed her cheek against his chin.

He lay on her, inwardly chuckling now, knowing her unquenched desire. It was warm and highly pleasant having her provocative body as a cushion. The wound which had just allowed his sperm to flow from him would soon be cured and then he would be ready for fresh action.

Lucrezia unwound her tightly clamping legs after a few minutes and slithered them in underneath his. He felt her soft little belly squirm against the rotundity of his and then the live pressure of her well-covered hips.

"Did I not hurt you, my sweet?"

"Yes, papa — but it changed halfway and I began to feel that I wanted to die in such happiness."

And she has yet to die in it, he thought, yet

to feel the soporific spread of satisfaction from her father's punishing penetration.

He rolled off her, at last. His prick, hot and tender, had half-risen again. He glanced down at it below the bulge of his belly and then he took Lucrezia's hand and placed it on the hot length of flesh.

Lucrezia looked down at the organ which had began to expand in her hand. She held it gently as if it were a hand, wondering at its great heat.

"Caress it, my love—particularly the knob," the Cardinal said, pressing his thighs one against the other.

His daughter obeyed, drawing her fingers gently, as if afraid, over the smooth, white skin from its hairy base to the fiery red knob at its extremity.

Cardinal Roderigo felt an explosion from him as if passion had broken out from a small cell, shattering the walls, and was now pervading the corridors, the antechambers of his entire body. He flexed his hips against the side of her thigh. He crossed one ankle behind the other, turning his body into an arch with the foremost point his penis. His heart began to gather speed in its pounding once again.

Lucrezia gained courage—or curiosity as the Cardinal became more and more impassioned. She allowed her fingers to slip away from the rigid, fleshy stem to fondle the hairy balls below. They, too, were hot and hairily smooth and she gathered them in her hand, weighing them gently in her palm, wondering at the strange makeup of man. The very feel of his genitals excited her, too, making her wet and exposed-feeling between her legs so that she closed her thighs and grazed them together achingly.

The Cardinal began to undulate his legs, breathing noisily through his hairy nostrils. He leaned his head over onto her, laying it against her breasts, brushing his smooth cheek from one to the other, sucking a nipple, descending the hill into the valley, climbing the opposite hill and kissing that other nipple which shot out like a flag on a mountain top.

Lucrezia felt overcome with a desire to kiss his whole body in return. She swayed over and lay her head on his chest as he relaxed backwards before her gentle pressure. She kissed his hairy chest, loving his breasts with her mouth. He placed his hand on her soft head and pushed her gently downwards. She let herself be pushed, let her head move down him, her lips moistly blazing a trail down his hairy flesh as they passed.

Her hand still held his prick which reached forth for the ceiling, trying to grow like Jack's beanstalk. As her lips crossed his lower belly, his muscles tautened, his prick became a shrieking urge. He wanted to bury it in her—in that soft, learning mouth which was moving toward it. He caught her head by the hair, roughly, so that she gasped and pushed her face down the last few inches which separated it from his prick.

She got the idea immediat␣ly and he felt her lips, tantalizingly ligh␣ and feathery, running up the stem of flesh. He cringed within himself, gritting his teeth.

He held his breath for what seemed an asphyxiating length of time and then he let it out in a long, gasping sigh as the mouth closed softly, like a vagina, over his radiant knob.

From what seemed a great height above him on the bed, he could hear her lips gently sucking. There seemed to be no correspondence between the noise which inflamed his ears and the actual pulling of her lips on his prick which sent chill after chill coursing through his body.

He had released her head as the mouth clamped over his penis, but now, wanting to plunge his rod farther into the tightness of sensation, he reached down again and forced her blonde head down against the rearing pikestaff. He felt his solid heat shoot forward, grazing her teeth. She gave a choking, muffled cry. He undulated his hips with the fury of a whirlpool and heaved them up at her face. He looked down at her slim, flushed face and the distended lips pulling on his prick which had been half swallowed in her mouth. The sight added to the sensation and his eyes narrowed, his lips broke apart, his hand tightened on her soft, fine hair.

In her mouth, his prick seemed to be thickening and thickening every second. His hand moved hard and violently over her head, pulling on those golden plaits, pressing the head with convulsive fingers. He wanted to bury his prick in her throat—but somehow the mouth and throat were not enough; the sensation was not consistent along the length of his rod.

He watched her sucking, her cheeks hollowing, her eyes closing and opening in her passion. Her slim, sleek back, white and without a blemish was presented to him, blooming abruptly into the luxury of her lips and soft, full buttocks that invited caresses, invited the pressure of another body.

He watched her buttocks. They slithered whitely one against the other, an outward sign of her inner excitement. They were smooth, lovely convexes of flesh. He longed to reach

48

out and touch them but he couldn't reach. He longed to press his loins against them, to feel their convexity in all its voluptuousness crushed against the elastic roundness of his own belly and loins.

He pulled her head sharply from his loins. Her mouth came off his raging prick with a sharp sucking noise. She looked up at him with her deep, blue eyes half open. His penis was tingling, the feel of her mouth still around it needing to be replaced.

He slithered down behind her, lying along her back, and put his arms round her to fondle her breasts with their erect nipples. The coolness of her buttocks exaggerated the heat of his penis against them. He pressed his prick against the soft mounds of flesh, biting his lips.

With his hand he reached down and explored her thighs from behind, pushing his fingers between them until he found the long portals of ultra-smooth moisture. He began to caress her vagina once again, kneading the hard, erect clitoris.

Immediately she began to wriggle in the most abandoned way and to moan in a manner which made him impatient to plunge his prick hard in and give her something to moan about.

His prick was down there between her legs, brushing against his searching fingers. He needed only to jerk forward and it would be once again between those milky thighs, breaking in with a strong, skin-rending pressure which would set her atrembling.

He eased her over onto her face. She went just wherever his hands guided. She seemed quite lost to anything but his touch.

Quivering with anticipation he lowered himself onto the provocative pertness of her but-

49

tocks, feeling them warm, soft and giving under his loins. His penis waved between her thighs which she had opened. Now he couldn't wait. Every moment was torment.

Swaying back onto his knees, he pulled her up onto her knees in front of him. Her bottom reared up at him, her face was pressed into the bed within the framework of her arms.

There, like a great cleft moon, her behind was juicily presented to him. Her thighs were spread, the lines between her knees forming the base of a triangle, the point at her thigh junction where he could see the red, wet opening of her cunt, its apex. She was kneeling before him like a sacrificial offering. She was his to do with as he wished.

He placed himself behind her. He eased her lips open with his thumbs and ranged his prick against the opening. Then with an all-pervading tremor of sublime pleasure he surged into her.

Lucrezia, her lips working, her mind confused with desire, knelt before the Cardinal, with her bottom right up in the air under his eyes. She felt his thumbs against the lips of her vagina and she squirmed against them, contracting her channel in concentrated passion. She moaned again—and the moan became a cry as, with the force and relentlessness of a battering ram, his great rod which had recently been filling her mouth to the choking point, tore into her channel and raced up with great momentum into the depths of her belly. This time it was easier and less painful, but these thoughts didn't occur to her at the time. She was aware only of the slight pain, the nakedness of her bottom, her whole body and her desire to submit, to be used, raped, hurt even

50

and to enjoy, to wallow in her enjoyment which transcended any other type of enjoyment she'd ever experienced.

She heard her father grunting behind the weight of his hips which pressed at her so hard that they edged her forward on the bed and made her push with her hands to keep her position.

His prick, which seemed enormous — she could still not believe that it could really disappear inside her — bludgeoned in and drew back and then thrust right up again.

On her waist his hands were cruel in the way they gripped her with such force. She felt his knees edging her knees apart. He seemed to want to embed himself deeper and deeper in her. It made the whole of her loins itch and flame. She was aware of the contraction and expansion inside her, the sensation that a regular wave of movement was getting faster and faster, deeper and deeper.

The Cardinal gritted his teeth as the tight sheath of flesh slipped back along his complementary dagger. Her channel was tight around his length, but his knob seemed to want to go farther, to be squeezed so tight that it hurt him.

He thrust in and out, up and up with a regular, strong flow from his hips. His stomach was fluttering, his thighs twitching. At the extremity of his inward stroke he gave an extra flick, feeling her buttocks give and spread under the weight of his loins, hearing her gasps and gulps. Every few strokes he would thrust his own hot organ right in and leave it there, tightly held in her body while he squirmed his hips against her cool buttocks, reveling in the brushing contact of their separate flesh.

He moved his hands from her waist, which,

it seemed, he could almost span, tracing them over her back, the lean, firm flesh. He pressed her shoulders into the bed as he drove his prick into her passage. He saw her shoulders shake and quiver, her bottom sway and rotate against him.

His prick felt like a trail of gunpowder rushing towards its annihilation in explosion. He ran his hands under her belly clasping her to him as he spread her thighs still wider with his knees. He clasped the flesh of her belly in small, elastic handfuls. He lowered his own belly onto her bottom, holding her in a close abdominal embrace as he smashed his loins against her, splitting her vagina with his ever-growing intrusion.

Subject under him, a willing slave, Lucrezia felt his prick filling her whole body. It seemed to surge right in up to her breasts with every thrust. And every thrust brought an involuntary explosion of breath from between her lips. Her hot face twisted in torment against the bed. Her hips waved and squirmed beyond her control. It felt as if his organ was as big as her entire belly and her belly was smarting and tingling and leaping with flame. In the middle of this overall sensation was a central channel of piercing stimulation where he surged into her channel, filling and spreading it as it tried to clasp him firmly.

Lucrezia heard her own groans as if they came from some other throat. She felt as if she were being dredged, all her entrails being dragged down into that channel. With a confusion of wild words in her head, many of them unspoken exhortations to him to fuck her to the last, to destroy her with his prick, she felt a great warmth spreading inside. It was a feeling she hadn't had before, an inexorable advance of nothing which shook her body and made her feel that the end of her life was near. She tried to say something to her father, to ask him something, but when she opened her mouth only muffled exclamations came out.

And the inexorable sensation went on and on and her hips waved as if they had their own delirium and her belly was afire with a burning-like snow. Snow rushing in an avalanche which was lovely and terrible, unbearable and all-desirable, unending yet moving quickly to an end. She groaned and cried out in loud, grating cries. Her whole body was moving downwards to pass out between her legs. She gasped and weaved her hips and pressed back against her father's belly, wanting his prick, loving him, loving the sensation, frightened of it—and now it was there, everywhere, a great bubble which was bursting, bursting and . . . "Oh, my God! Oh-oh-oh-oh-oooooh!" A great flowing through, an escape and a slow ebbing, ebbing slowly, slowly, back to normal which was not normal because it left a wash and a new feeling.

Cardinal Roderigo was inflamed with the sight and sound of Lucrezia's culmination. Her tortured face, pressing into the bed, remained in his mind even when it had calmed and the movement of her lips was nothing more than a muted recognition of the force of his continued penetration.

He felt a great outreaching for her, as if it were not enough to be screwing her here on the bed with all his power, as if he needed to destroy her to ensure a truly positive action.

His penis, hard and with the skin drawn back so tightly that it was often painful, pistoned into her, disappearing up to the very

53

hairs of his belly which became wet and stringy from her liquid outpourings. His penis felt harder and more solid as the moments rushed dizzily past and his mouth opened and closed with furious wheezings. When he gripped her he crushed her tender flesh sadistically, reflecting the force of his grip with a renewed vigor of his thrust. With every forward motion which tightened his buttocks into hard, male globes he crashed against her behind pushing her forward, pulling a little cry from her.

Within him he felt the curling up of the spring which would suddenly snap straight again at the point where it could curl no more. He wanted to push farther and farther into her body to some impossible point. Sensation gripped every hard, fleshy centimeter of his penis. His grip on her waist grew. He fixed his gaze on the little ring of her anus which he noticed now as she pushed her buttocks back at him. It was small and crinkly. He would have to have it someday soon. He watched it, the focal point of those revolving buttocks. He concentrated the whole force of his attention on its hairless contraction. The spring was winding up and up and up. He gritted his teeth. His eyes glazed over the little button. He moved his finger to it, prodded it, felt the cringing reaction. The spring was winding to breaking point. He felt he couldn't stand any more. He couldn't get any farther into her. It must come to an end now. He heard the murmurs of her breath. The anus was like an eye socket looking at him. He gasped, thrust forward in a long, hard stroke and then convulsed in a series of quick tremoring jerks as he spattered his fountain of sperm into the moist sheath which had held him so well.

Lucrezia wriggled a little, at last, from under his dead weight which had become too much for her. Her back ached a little where it had been curved in a concave while the Cardinal satisfied his passion on her.

Feeling her movement, the Cardinal rolled off her and flopped down on his back. He watched her nestle down beside him and wondered how long he had better stay. Then he thought of the sleeping household and decided he had time to show her a few more things yet.

CHAPTER 3

Cardinal Roderigo's thoughts were turned on his future as he sat in his big library which led, by a terrace, into the grounds. When he thought of his future he always thought back, first to Calixtus, who had given the family such a sudden rise to eminence. Don Alonso de Borja, as he had been before ascending the throne of St. Peter, had been a fine old man and Roderigo felt he owed it as much to him as to himself to fully recapture the family's previous office.

And such an aim appeared to be within his grasp. There were many amongst the pontificals who hated him, but he was convinced of his ability to buy them—with money or promises of estate—when the time was ripe.

The only slight stumbling block was the pertinacity with which Innocent VIII clung to his fading life. Already he had violently disappointed the Cardinal—among others—with unexpected recoveries from cataleptic trances after he'd already been taken for dead.

Under his lethargic rule, the Church had

again begun to lose much of the vigor it had possessed under his predecessor, Sixtus IV—a fact which filled Cardinal Roderigo with fury when it occurred to him that he would have the task of rebuilding its strength. What a stupid man he was. He had even openly acknowledged his children for his own, thus enabling his enemies to create open scandal about him. And in fact it often seemed that provision for his seven bastards was the only aim of his pontificate. Truly, Rome would be well rid of such a man.

Cardinal Roderigo idly flicked the pages of a book as he allowed his imagination to flow where his ambition prompted. As Pope he would immediately start a system of alliances which would increase the power of the pontifical troops; he would create fresh cardinals to insure his personal strength and he would force the proud barons to pay the taxes which for so long they'd ignored. That would be but a start. In the process, of course, he would clean up Rome of its lawlessness. It was indeed scandalous and dangerous for the authorities that the present Pope had allowed such lawlessness to scourge the streets. Every morning there were fresh corpses in the streets and it was dangerous to be abroad at night without an escort. Such a step should certainly gain him a certain immediate favor with the common people . . .

But then he realized that he was sitting in his library, that he was simply Cardinal Roderigo Borgia and that the Pope, weak and near-helpless, was still hanging stubbornly onto his life.

However, the possibility of ridding Rome of

the old man seemed rather nearer to the Cardinal today, for an idea had come to him.

He had in the past considered ways and means of doing away with Innocent, but a practicable method had never presented itself to him. There was always some snag either in the form of the Pope's vigilant attendant or the old man's own suspicious nature. Recently, however, he had been turning over in his mind the knowledge that Innocent was the toppling monument to grasping sensualism within himself. The only reason the old man was no longer visited by his courtesans was because his enfeebled state made him fear a fatal stroke if he indulged in the excitement of sexual intercourse. But, the Cardinal smiled to himself, supposing he were forced into it by a seduction he could not resist. In his present state that could well bring about the end of him—and then the way would be clear.

*   *   *

Several hours later Cardinal Roderigo was ushered into the Pope's chamber in the Vatican. Officially he was paying a duty call, to offer his hope of a quick improvement in the old man's health; in actual fact his thoughts were bent on quite a different path.

The Pope raised a weary hand from his bed. He was thin and pale. He looked worse every day.

"Ah, my dear Cardinal Roderigo, I am happy to be able to tell you I feel considerably better today." His voice belied his words with its thin, scraggy tone. The Cardinal sometimes felt that the old man divined his wishes and enjoyed

57

trying to annoy him with declarations about his improved state of health.

"That is very pleasing news, your Excellency. May it be God's will that you are soon risen from your bed and with us in body as in spirit without delay."

"Ah, you are too kind. But I trust your earnest hopes may be granted."

The Cardinal proceeded to sketch recent events within the Church as well as various communications which had passed through the embassy, notably from the King of France who had his eye on the acquisition of Naples. Finally he discreetly described items of scandal which had come to his ears. These he knew the Pope loved to hear most of all while pretending to be shocked and scandalized. Had he been hale and hearty he would have retained in his memory the names of women involved in doubtful intrigues in the hope of procuring them for his own pleasure at some future date.

"And that seems to be all that I can report at present. I trust that before I come again you will be even farther on the road to recovery."

The Pope made a sign of thanks and settled back in his bed when, as if in afterthought, Cardinal Roderigo added:

"Oh, by the way. I have a niece who has been with me of late—home from her studies—a very beautiful girl. She begged me to crave audience with you for her, saying that just to touch the foot of your bed would be a divine experience for her. For her, your Excellency embodies all that is great and of any consequence in any sphere.

"I told her that in view of your indisposition such an audience was out of the question, but

I promised to beg that you might receive her at such time as you felt able."

The Pope stared up from his bed, his dull eyes alight a little with interest.

"The girl is only a virginal eleven years old, but her mind and body are those of a mature woman," the Cardinal continued. He smiled. "So—if I might use a worldly term in a spiritual sense—infatuated is she with your holiness that she has said to me, 'Did he bid me go to a convent I would go without a thought, did he bid me sink into a slime of carnality, likewise I would obey him.' Truly a remarkable devotion in one so young—and so beautiful that a worldly career would be easily within her grasp. In fact I almost wonder if such passion in things spiritual doesn't go a little too far."

The Pope had sat up again, resting against his pillows. His eyes were sparkling more than they had since his illness had begun.

"Indeed she is a child of God by all accounts," he declared. "And is she really so much a woman at such a tender age?"

"Modesty forbids me to describe how lovely is her form and face," the Cardinal replied. "But Helen of Troy would have recognized her peer."

"Ah, you go too far, you go too far," the Pope chuckled. "But I should like to see her. Her audience is granted whenever she would wish it."

"I will communicate with her," the Cardinal said. "At present she is away from Rome in pursuance of her studies, but within a few days she may be again in the city."

"Excellent," the Pope murmured. "Tell me, what is the child's name?"

"Her name, your Excellency, is Lucrezia."

59

CHAPTER 4

While Cardinal Roderigo was meditating in his library, Lucrezia and her younger brother, Giuffredo, were on their way back to continue their studies in the Orsini Palace, Monte Giordano.

They rode on horseback, as usual, with their attendants and men at arms—for the highway could be a dangerous spot, particularly toward nightfall—strung out around them. They were both excellent horsemen. Giuffredo, who was almost two years younger than his sister, had shown particular promise almost the first time he was put on a horse some years previously. The horse had, for some reason, suddenly and unexpectedly bolted from under the eyes of the lad's teachers, but he had clung grimly on with his young, sturdy arms and, white as death, but determined, had still been seated when the horse was overtaken at the end of a furious five-minute chase.

Like his brother and sister, he looked older than his years and his body had been strengthened with continual exercise in archery, wrestling and swimming. His character was already taking a determined turn which brought him the respect of those elders who came into close contact with him.

He glanced over at his sister. He was very proud of her and her beauty and he hoped she would soon be tired so that he could take her in front of him on his own horse as was their established custom. Nothing made him feel more male and protective than to know that his sister was tired and dependent on him while he manfully guided their horse forward along the trail.

Lucrezia glanced back at him and smiled. He was rather like Cesare though his nose was slightly retroussé and his hair had faint tints of red in it. She had found, during the journey, that her thoughts, so much centered now on the sexual events of the past few days, wandered to Giuffredo and imagined what it would be like with him. Of course he was younger. But he was always so masculine that she was sure he'd be quite commanding if led. She rubbed her crotch along her saddle. The soreness had almost disappeared, but its traces left the strongly intangible memory of Cesare and her father, both with part of their bodies actually inside her body, crushing wetly, deliciously into her. The memory made her feel suddenly chill in her belly and she pressed down hard on the rough saddle.

It was dusk before she changed over to Giuffredo's horse. It always happened the same way; eventually she felt she couldn't keep her shoulders from sagging forward and her neck began to ache.

The lieutenant of the guard respectfully helped her up in front of her brother and then ordered his men to light the lanterns they carried.

The procession continued, slowly, with the lanterns throwing long, vague shadows on the road and dimly showing up the faces of the riders, glinting on the swords of the men-at-arms.

Lucrezia arranged her long, loose skirt around her. She still wore no underclothes but for her petticoats and she felt the cold leather of the saddle against her genitals with a shock of pleasure. She leaned back against Giuffredo, who put one arm protectively around her waist, guiding the horse with the other. Around them was the clip-clop of the horses, the shadows of the long barrows made weird and stark by the lantern-light. None of the attendants or the guards chatted around them—they were too tired after the day's ride. The procession had a slow, clip-clopping rhythm of its own which seemed to be lulling everyone to the brink of sleep.

Lucrezia's thighs slipped gently against the saddle. The movement of the horse jogged her in a gentle rise and fall. Once again, unconcerned now with the guidance of a horse, she let her thoughts dwell on the events of the past days. In cold blood she could hardly imagine herself prostrated in front of her father while from behind her, unseen, he screwed her with his unbearably big weapon. She wondered what she looked like to him in that position. The thought of herself stretched out with all her openings spread out before his eyes gave her a delicious little thrill of horror. She thought of his prick. How big it had been. How could it have gone in her? All of it! But how wonderful it had finally been!

Her crotch slipped on the saddle, bringing her back to the present. She was getting wet again with the thought. Now that she knew exactly what she longed for, knew the sight and feel of it, she felt she needed it every time her thoughts strayed in a sexy direction.

Up and down she jogged on the saddle. She wriggled her bottom slightly against it on the downward movement. Her breath was a series of small sighs in her throat as she leaned against Giuffredo. His presence and her feelings combined to make him seem the object of her desire. If only they were alone, she'd make him leap down from the horse and fuck her in the field alongside. She wondered if he'd ever done it and came to the conclusion it was out of the question. He was simply too young and they spent most of their time together.

Back and forth, up and down. She squirmed on the hard leather, flattening the slim wedges of her sex against it. There was really very little separating her from Giuffredo, she thought: just her tucked up skirt lying across the horse's back between them and his thin hose. His boyish prick was so close to her. She could actually feel the pressure of his legs against hers where he sat behind her on the same saddle. If only they could do it now.

She pushed her bottom back against his loins. She could feel the pressure of his body down there against the voluminous folds of her skirt; his free hand was still around her waist, her head against his shoulder.

Gently she edged her hips right back along the saddle, straightening her body imperceptibly, so that her bottom was tight against his loins. She held her breath and let the horse's movement jog her behind against his loins. With every pace forward, her buttocks crushed back against the point where his penis was hidden by his tight hose.

The main trouble, she realized, after a few minutes—in which her face became hotter and hotter and her vagina felt as if it were weeping—was that she couldn't feel what effect she was having on Giuffredo; the folds of cloth between them were too many.

She reached behind her, as if simply to arrange her skirt, and deftly drew it up a little above the point where her buttocks rose above the saddle. At the same time, she pushed her hips back again so that her naked flesh was in contact with the thin cloth of her brother's hose.

As she did so—and totally accidentally—her hand brushed against his loins and she knew what the effect had been. She had felt a small, but very definite bulge.

My sweet young brother, she thought. You're beginning to feel how nice it would be to possess your sister.

They jogged for a while and then Giuffredo pushed out his thighs along the horse so that Lucrezia was virtually sitting in his lap, with the point of his bulge pressed against the slit of her buttocks. Her skirt draped over them, falling over his legs quite naturally, so that their point of contact was quite hidden.

Now with every movement of the horse, her buttocks crushed back around the bulge in his hose, rubbing down it with a pressure which sent a spear of delight up Lucrezia's spine.

Giuffredo's hand had tightened on her belly, his arm surrounded her more tightly than it ever had before on their journeys. She felt his chest heaving and pressed hard against her back.

Giuffredo himself wasn't quite sure what was happening. He felt tight and prickly inside, particularly down at his reproductive organ. That was what his tutor called it in his advanced biology lessons. Giuffredo had never quite been able to believe in the process which it was alleged took place. He had never even felt any desire to masturbate, which he understood was a phase some boys got earlier than others. He'd always been rather frightened of the idea—as

64

. if something terrible would happen to him if he
' did.

But now Lucrezia, his beautiful sister of
whom he was so proud, was pressing against
him in a way which was having a strange and
exciting effect on his organ and his whole being.
And, what was more, he was certain she was
doing it on purpose. She'd deliberately pulled
her skirt over his legs and he could feel she
had nothing on underneath and her hand had
brushed his center of excitement, making it
jerk involuntarily against the tight hose he
wore and causing him considerable embarrassment.

He felt very strange, almost sick in a pleasant way—if that were possible. And every step
the horse made with consequent jog of Lucrezia's bottom against him he felt stranger and
sicker.

Guiltily he glanced at the surrounding horsemen. They were dim, unreal figures in the flickering light of the lanterns. They all appeared to
be asleep. They could almost have been ghosts,
following them, lit up in their own aura of
ghostliness.

He closed his eyes. His fingers on the reins
were clenched. He closed out everything but
the strong rubbing sensation of her bottom on
his organ under the skirt as the horse jogged
forward. He became aware of his hand on her
belly. He could feel the warm, firm arc of her
belly under the skirt and the feel of it made him
want to explore it with his hands, to feel it
naked.

Lucrezia, he noticed, was squirming in a
slightly unnatural way on the saddle. She leaned
back her head against him so that their faces
touched and for the first time in his life the

touch excited and embarrassed and delighted him. Her face was warm and her eyes were closed and their bodies were together from the saddle to their heads and the pressure on his loins was making him want to burst through his hose.

Suddenly he felt his sister's hand upon his leg, stroking his thigh—and moving up his thigh, reaching awkwardly under the skirt until her fingers lightly landed on the bulge of his penis. The touch sent a shock right through his body and he drew back his hips involuntarily. But her hand pursued and he let it fondle him there, with an excitement growing in his loins which he couldn't control.

It was at this point that the lieutenant of the guard coughed—and Giuffredo moved sharply, guiltily back from his sister again.

The cough was a preliminary for an announcement.

The lieutenant thought they should ride a little faster to reach the Orsini Palace at a reasonable hour. They had, still, rather farther to go than was wise on a night as dark as this.

Reins were tightened throughout the party and the pace increased to a canter.

The extra attention directed on horses and road and the greater noise of the canter seemed to Giuffredo to act as a cover for his secret activity with Lucrezia and he pressed the bulge of his loins back against the warm nudity of her backside. Her hand, which had momentarily withdrawn, also came back and rose and fell against his protrusion as they cantered forward into the night.

Giuffredo felt hot and almost dizzy with excitement. He kept having to control himself with an effort. Lucrezia, he saw, was breathing very heavily as if in the throes of some strong physical exertion.

Under cover of the noise she half turned to him and whispered something.

Now that she had spoken, reestablished with the sound of her voice, that she was his sister, he felt a new wave of embarrassment.

"What?" he asked leaning forward, blushing.

"I said put it in me," Lucrezia said brazenly.

Giuffredo was horrified and flustered—and then freshly excited. The actual thing! The hand came back and pinched and poked the hot mound of flesh which seemed bent on escaping from his clothing. He pushed his hips forward and pressed them against her flesh with a furious desire.

"It's not possible," he whispered back.

"Yes it is. Nobody'll ever notice with the jogging of the horse—it'll look natural. I can lean forward on the horse's neck as if I'm asleep."

Giuffredo was silent for a moment. He wanted to try it now to the point of desperation. He could never forgive himself if he lost this opportunity.

"But my clothes."

"Slit them with your knife," Lucrezia replied immediately. "You can change them as soon as we arrive and throw them away. "Nobody'll see in the dark."

Giuffredo's heart was pounding with excitement. It was all incredible. He couldn't think it out. There was something which would make it dangerous. It *was* dangerous. Riding through the night on the back of a horse in the midst of a crowd of men-at-arms!

But Lucrezia had suggested it and she sounded as if there was absolutely nothing to worry about. Her confidence was infectious. They were in it together and he was so wild with a frightened excitement now that he couldn't keep his loins still.

"Hurry!" Lucrezia whispered.

Giuffredo glanced around at the dim riding figures. Their lanterns illuminated them in little tents of light. He and his sister were in the central shadow. Besides, everybody was concentrating on the road.

Carefully he took his small, jeweled dagger from his belt. He held it in his hand and glanced around again. Then with a quick movement he inserted the tip in the stitches of the cloth and slid the knife downwards, between him and Lucrezia. He was very careful. He felt the flat of the blade, cold against the heat of his genitals. He withdrew it, shoved it back into his belt. His belly was frozen with nervous tension. Now he couldn't bear to look around him, sure that someone had noticed. But when at last he did, he laughed nervously at his own stupid imagination. It was unlikely that anyone would have been able to see clearly enough to know what he was doing even had they looked.

He sat against Lucrezia, who was still squirming on the saddle. His stomach was so churned up that he felt unable to move. And then she did it for him. He felt her fingers, cool and as foreign and strange as the knife blade, pull apart her skirt.

His organ shot out rigidly at her, short, but stubby in its adolescence. He felt as if he wanted to piss. He couldn't bear her touch. But there was nothing to be done. He couldn't pull back his loins more than a few centimeters and her fingers followed relentlessly.

He gasped aloud and tried to smother the noise in a cough. Her fingers stroked and then her hand closed around the fleshy branch and squeezed gently, and then harder.

Her hand went under his organ and in through the slit and he winced as it caressed his testicles. He felt he would die of the sensation.

"Oh, God—now," Lucrezia murmured. He felt her two bottom cheeks come back against his naked pin of flesh. Flesh against flesh! The thought as much as the sensation nearly made him swoon. His hand tightened on the reins, the other tightened on her stomach.

Lucrezia lay forward on the horse's neck, breathing hard against its mane. This position presented him with a half-full access to her genital region, while her skirt was still sufficiently long to cover them both.

Giuffredo felt suddenly very hopeless and incompetent. He wished the first time didn't have to be on a horse in full canter. But his prick was seething and it seemed that only the unknown thing would give a natural outlet to his feelings.

He pushed his penis against her, felt it nosing on the flesh of her buttocks, felt it rubbing into the rift between them and his chest was thumping all through with excitement.

Gently and then more firmly he pushed against her. He wasn't sure where he was or how to find out. The pressure of his organ against her flesh was enough to make him cough with stifled passion, but he couldn't seem to find the spot.

Lucrezia in her forward position would have made her movement too conspicuous by reaching back to guide him, and their position would have meant a dangerous disarrangement of her skirt, so she lay still, waiting for him to find the place.

Giuffredo edged his prick between the rift right down at its base near the saddle. He had to find the hole. He wanted desperately to find it. He pushed harder. His penis was pricking furiously and it felt suddenly moist. The horse cantered on and the echoes of the others surrounded them in the dimness.

He seemed unable to find the hole. He bit his lips in excitement and frustration. There was no feeling except a great, building pressure —and then suddenly Lucrezia gave a jerk which she controlled immediately and he felt a grip around the tip of his penis which filled him with a fresh wave of sensation. It gripped him like a claw and he tried to push straight in in his mad delight that he was fucking a woman that the unbelieved-in, impossible, was happening—actually happening.

Oh, that claw! Such an excruciating grip! He pushed and Lucrezia jerked and he heard her stifled gasp. Even in his desire he was frightened enough to look guiltily around. The horses cantered on, jogging up and down, gathering speed a little—a bustle of noise.

Giuffredo edged in farther, sliding forward on the saddle, jogging up into Lucrezia as the horse jogged, drawing out a little with the descent.

The hole was very tight. It was pulling back his foreskin with a bruising force which was painful and delightful at the same time. He occasionally heard a murmur from his sister. But she was controlling herself fairly well and pushing her bottom back onto him.

Lucrezia was in an agony of mixed pain and an excited desire to debase herself.

70

Lying along the horse, with her head so far from her extended bottom where she could feel Giuffredo's finger of flesh stiffly prodding, she had early realized that he was unwittingly probing her anus. She had been about to swing upright and back to tell him when something about the blunt exploration had stopped her. The point screwing there, not yet in the hole, but pushing hard into the cleft of entry made her strain as if she were emptying her bowels. It was a not unpleasant sensation and she suddenly wondered what it would be like to be screwed in her ass. She felt, too, a desire for a completely new sensation and there was something so wicked-seeming about the idea that she quickly resolved to let Giuffredo continue.

She even helped him by stretching back her behind and straining in an attempt to open the tiny posterior slit for him.

His prick was neither as big as his father's nor yet Cesare's, but when the first penetration came it gave her a nauseous shock of pain. She tried not to cry out and hid her face in the horse's thick mane.

From then on it was shock after shock becoming gradually less of a shock but always with the possibility of a relapse into an unexpected pain.

Her return was inflamed with pain which gave way to a sensation of being turned inside out, naked and debased but pervertedly thrilling. She tried not to wiggle and gasp, but she couldn't even be bothered to look up to see if anyone had noticed them.

His penetration, which became easier and easier, began actually to have an erotic effect on her normal sexual organ. She began to get more and more excited. It became more and more difficult to control both movement and sound. She was thankful that the canter of the horse hid her jogging to a considerable extent, making it seem quite natural.

Her anus felt as if it was a wide and deep hole, a gaping chasm into which Giuffredo was plunging his whole body in ravishment. Somehow she wanted more, even though she knew she could take little more. He seemed to be right up in her bowels. She thought of her inner tubes, wondered exactly where he was in them, felt the excitement growing in her vagina, knew she was going to come and pressed her head furiously into the horse's sweating neck and gasped out her fulfillment.

Giuffredo, quite unaware of his mistake, pushed his penis deeper and deeper into the unseen gulf which seemed to hold and suck it in like a whirlpool, refusing to let it withdraw without difficulty.

A million sharp pins seemed to attack his tender organ. It felt sore with the effort of penetration, yet the soreness was an exciting wonderful sensation. He kept his hand on Lucrezia's hip as she lay before him and he dug his fingers into her flesh, intense with his passion.

He no longer looked around him either. He didn't care. His movement was compatible with that of a horse-rider. His main difficulty as he jerked his hips sharply and surreptitiously up at the hole, which was sucking his soul through his body, was to prevent gasps and moans from breaking through his lips. The effort was as excruciating as the crushing of his prick down there under the skirt.

His jerking seemed to get naturally faster. He found that his penis seemed to lead him, working and throbbing with its own life. It was being swallowed in Lucrezia. He could feel the flesh of his loins around his genitals touching the smooth flesh of her bottom which wiggled ever so slightly and secretly against him.

The horse cantered on. Its loud clip-clopping drowning the scarcely controlled noise of Giuffredo's growing passion. Around their horse the men-at-arms scrutinized only the darkness on either side, watching for lawless bands of robbers.

Giuffredo jogged—a natural jogging with the horse. Lucrezia was still, lying along the horse's neck apparently asleep—except for that secretive squirming of her buttocks back against his prick under the sheltering skirt.

Gradually Giuffredo's loins became transformed into a mass of sensation such as he'd never felt before. So this was it! His loins were no longer flesh and blood but some strange, unearthly substance which glowed and burned in its own fire.

He felt himself becoming more and more helpless down in those nether regions. He could hardly disguise his audible passion and every so often a barking gasp broke through his lips and he tried to cover it with a cough. The burning sensation down there was carrying him along with it. He no longer guided, no longer had control. His loins were running away with him. It was excruciating delight and rather frightening as if he were about to have his blood sucked out of his body through his penis.

He felt ridiculously that at this stage he should stop before something terrible happened. But now it was too late; he was no longer able to. The mouth was sucking and sucking, drawing his blood into his prick, filling it, making it heavy and painful. His prick seemed to have swollen to enormous proportions. He heard Lucrezia give a slight gasp into the horse's mane. He jerked harder, harder. He felt as if his prick were splitting, peeling back in two parts from that small opening at its head, peeling back to let the blood shoot out. He gasped again, trying desperately to cover his noises. The horse jogged and his penis rammed up into the hole. Again, again, he gasped again, finally—and then he bit his lips smothering his groans in the depths of his throat as he felt the sudden release of a wet, sticky substance flowing from him, leaving him after a few moments weak and almost unable to hold the reins.

Now that it was over and Lucrezia sat up as if she'd just awakened from sleep, he felt acutely embarrassed. His embarrassment became wholesale confusion a little later when his sister confided in him what had happened. But she assured him it had been quite pleasant for her and was so open and provocative in her speech that his shame finally left him.

When they reached the Orsini Palace after another hour's ride, he managed to slip into his quarters and change his hose—under the pretext of caring for his horse. On the whole he felt glad, and excited at the new future the day had opened up for him.

CHAPTER FIVE

Innocent VIII lay on his back forming images in his head of his past loves and what he had done with them. That was what he regretted more than anything about his present illness: his doctors had strongly warned him of the danger of any exercise, which had cut out the possibility of having Caterina, his favorite courtesan, brought to satisfy his needs. In spite of his weakness, his sensuality had not left him. In fact, spending all day lying on his back imagining his lovers in all sorts of positions seemed merely to have added to that aspect of his being.

Every so often he thought about the niece that Cardinal Roderigo had told him about. It was so frustrating he could have wept. Now the most he could do was grant her audience and rue the fact that he had not been able to, and would not be able to enjoy her sexually. What a loss! The thought made his stomach turn over. A virgin, beautiful, had said she would do anything for him—even to the extreme of giving herself over to the lusts of the flesh. It needed only a word from him. Innocent felt like weeping, again. Was she as beautiful as Cardinal Roderigo claimed? Could she really have a woman's development at such a youthful age? Anyway he hoped it would not be long before she came to him and then he could truly wallow in self-pity at what he had missed.

For Innocent really doubted his capacity to recover from his present malady—his capacity to recover enough. He saw himself spending the remainder of his life in a continuous convalescence. He would, of course, be waited on hand and foot, and other people would take care of the running of the State although he would hold absolute power still. It was a not unpleasant existence, one that appealed to him. Again the one thing he regretted was his inability to drown himself in the delicious torment of sexual intercourse. But, after all, if he really took great care of himself, perhaps someday . . .

He clapped his hands and an attendant came around from a screen at the far end of the room.

The attendant bowed and withdrew to reappear almost immediately with a large silver salver piled high with fruit.

Innocent began to eat the grapes slowly, spitting the pips out onto the floor. His fingers caressed the taut, cool skin of each morsel. It reminded him of Caterina's breasts—her whole body. If only . . . He cursed suddenly to himself and flung a half eaten grape petulantly across the floor.

* * *

Cardinal Roderigo had lost no time in arranging for Lucrezia to return to Rome. The sooner he found himself in St. Peter's chair the safer he would feel.

He had spent a week or two sounding out his situation. It seemed a good one on the face of it. The Medici, who had long been friendly to the House of Borgia, were for him. Venice, Mantua, Genoa, Siena, the Orsini all were for him. Naples doubted him, rightly fearing the possibility of an alliance between him and Charles VIII of France, whose designs on the Neapolitan kingdom were well known. The French themselves favored Cardinal della Rovere as next Pope, but Roderigo was certain that with judicious gifts they could be won over and withdraw their strong backing of their candidate. Now seemed to be as good a time as any for dealing a death blow to Innocent, who, after all, was serving no good purpose lying sick in his bed with the anarchy of his misrule spread around him.

Lucrezia arrived back in Rome with a small cortege of attendants. The city was still given to the ravages of lawlessness and she made haste to her father's house.

There he had her stay for several days, instructing her in what she must do, explaining the necessity of Innocent's removal if the city and state were to survive—and enjoying Lucrezia's body himself the while.

With Lucrezia clear as to the exact—and fairly simple — nature of her duty, audience was arranged between her and the Pope.

Cardinal Roderigo had her dressed for the occasion in richly embroidered, but simple clothes which would show off the womanliness of her body. He had her plaits let out so that her hair flowed, long and silky to below her shoulders; he placed a string of sapphires set in silver around her neck where they gleamed and threw a blue sheen down onto the visible portion of her bosom, and reflected the bright blue of her eyes.

"My darling daughter—you are already the most beautiful woman in Italy," he declared when she was ready. "The old sensualist will have an orgasm at the very sight of you."

"Oh, papa, I trust all will go well," Lucrezia said anxiously. "I feel a little afraid."

The Cardinal placed a hand on her buttocks and kissed her gently on the neck.

"Don't you worry, my sweet. A beautiful creature such as you can get away with anything she wishes."

*   *   *

A little later, Lucrezia and her father were ushered into the Pope's chamber. He had propped himself up against his pillows and had his scanty remaining hair brushed and combed. He stared at Lucrezia with unabashed interest, hardly deigning to acknowledge the Cardinal's greeting.

"Truly you did not exaggerate," he said, not taking his eyes from Lucrezia.

Lucrezia curtsied and fixed him with her lovely, deep, knowing eyes.

"It is a great honor for me to be in the presence of your Excellency," she said softly as if in awe. "It is more than such a humble creature as myself could have considered in the realms of possibility."

"Ah, my child — if child you truly be — you are one of the lucky ones who in their natural goodness and humility deserve the highest honors," the Pope replied with an attempt at a winning smile.

"My niece is overcome in the presence of Christ's Vicar," Roderigo cut in. "Such an audience has been her life's object. She did not expect to achieve it so soon."

"I feel unable to speak," Lucrezia said in a hushed tone. "Your Excellency must forgive me."

"My child, come here and give me your hands," Innocent said paternally. "You shall not be afraid of me. Such beauty as you have, particularly if matched by the beauty of soul your uncle gives you, should fear nothing."

He took her hands in his skinny, cold fingers. He was amazed at her loveliness and the warm hands in his filled him with a yearning to be well and active. It had taken him but a fraction of a second to appraise her body as best he could see it under her dress and now he allowed his eyes the delight of fleeting anew and resting on the exposed portion of her bosom and on her neck, so young and smooth.

"I am afraid, your Excellency, that I cannot stay," Cardinal Roderigo said. "I have some important business to see to. I trust you will not find a while with my niece too wearisome. Send her away if she displeases you."

"My dear Cardinal," the Pope answered in sugary tones, "surely you forget yourself. As if such an infant of Christ, reflecting as she does the glorious emblem of early-gained womanhood, could displease me. Pray go your way, Cardinal Roderigo, and much as it grieves me to be deprived so soon of your company, I'm sure I could have no more pleasing visitor than your lovely niece."

Lucrezia wished she knew how to blush at will. But blushes came less easily than tears. She just dropped her head a little, as if overcome at his words. He still held her hands in his.

Cardinal Roderigo bowed and left the chamber. Even as he stepped over the threshold his thoughts were racing with plans for when the Pope was dead.

Innocent watched the exit of his Cardinal. The girl's hands were still warm in his. He didn't speak until Roderigo had left and the door had closed after him. Then he looked back at Lucrezia with eyes which he tried to make kindly.

"But tell me my dear, is it really true that you are only eleven years old?"

"I shall be twelve in a few weeks' time," she replied demurely.

"My child, you have matured far beyond your age. God has seen fit to prepare you for womanhood — who can tell what his wishes for you are."

The Pope's mind gloated over her. He could have given his answer to the question he'd just posed. He looked into her face. Truly those eyes were remarkable. There was . . . what was there? There was . . . yes, there was an aura of the devil about them. His eyes widened as this intuition came to him. But then Lucrezia smiled, as if in flattery at his remarks, a shy, innocent smile and Innocent dismissed the devil from her eyes. What nonsense!

"You are studying, I believe, my child. Tell me, how do you find yourself disposed to the acquisition of knowledge?"

"My studies are simple," she replied. "I find the knowledge of good and evil much more difficult."

In view of his own thoughts, the Pope was quite startled by her words. What precocious thoughts. And what, exactly, did she mean?

"Good and evil, my dear?" he echoed querulously.

Lucrezia suddenly spoke earnestly; she allowed tears to come into her eyes. She hoped she was sounding convincing.

"Your Excellency, I dared not tell my uncle, but I'm beset by problems. That is why I was so anxious for this audience. I knew that in the light of your holiness and wisdom, I should find guidance."

The Pope stared at her. The conversation had taken an unexpected turn which had almost thrown him out of his stride.

"My dear," he said at last, "you are very young and it may well be that the Lord will send you guidance through me. If you would pour out your heart to me, do so."

So far, so good, Lucrezia thought with an inward smile. She allowed a tear to slip over her cheek. The Pope responded to this display of femininity by pressing her hands.

"My child, my child," he said — rather theatrically, she thought —"I had no idea you were so upset."

"Most Holy Father," she blurted, "for most of my life I have known what is good and right — and indeed I still do — but recently things have happened which have made me doubt my strength and courage to continue along the path which I know is that of God."

"Tell me, child, tell me."

Innocent's interest was quickening. This confession from one so young and beautiful and now so obviously upset might prove very entertaining — on the other hand it might be dismally dull. He moved his hands on hers as if comforting her. He wished he could move them on her breasts.

"It is so terrible — I — I don't think I can."

"Now, child," the Pope made his voice slightly stern. He didn't want to miss this now. "You surely would not try to hide anything from God — and I am his representative on this Earth. You can confide in me without fear."

Lucrezia hesitated a minute, cleverly.

"You must forgive me, Holy Father," she whispered pathetically.

"Don't be afraid," he replied majestically. "God is love. All sinners may be forgiven their sins."

"Well, your Excellency, as I began to tell you, until recently my life was blameless. As a child, they tell me I was extremely good and always obeyed. I was brought up to understand the difference between Good and Evil — it all

81

seemed very simple. A saintly life did not seem an impossible idea." She paused, and another tear slipped down her face. She brushed it away and tossed back her hair nervously.

"Until — until a little while ago, I visited a friend's house and the friend put me in charge of her eldest son. I liked him very much . . . and he talked to me. He told me lots of things about men and women until my mind was all confused with what he told me." She stopped and hung her head, letting the tears flow more freely.

The Pope forced himself to fight against impatience. He thought he was beginning to catch on. What a delightful story. What an unexpected enjoyment this afternoon was providing him.

"Go on, dear. God and I are with you."

"And finally," Lucrezia went on brokenly, "he didn't stop with talk. He . . . took me in the grounds and he kissed me and . . . and . . . I believed him . . . it seemed right . . . it seemed right . . . I was all confused . . . until after it was over I knew I had been wicked."

The Pope's thought dwelt on the unmentioned, the undescribed. God, what a lucky fellow this friend was. The thought sent shivers up and down his spine. He felt a ripple in his loins which he knew he should smother or the frustration would be too terrible.

"My dear," he said, after a due interval for consideration, in which Lucrezia broke down and sobbed quietly and he paternally pulled her closer and put an arm around her. "My dear, you had a terrible experience and this man — he should be whipped — took advantage of your innocence in a most unscrupulous way. But, my dear, it often happens that young girls deceive themselves about the seriousness of what has happened. You say that he kissed you and then made advances. That is not too bad, after all."

As he had hoped, his dimness brought a protest from her.

"Oh, but . . . Holy Father . . . he did more than that."

"But he may not have done what I fear, my child. Tell me what he did. Don't be afraid or confused. We are in the presence of the Almighty Lord."

Lucrezia hesitated, as if overcoming a great reluctance.

"I was wearing only a long shift, because it was so hot," she said. "It was modest — it came down to my ankles. But after he had kissed me — it was in a tiny copse in the grounds out of sight of the house — he put his hands on my bottom . . . and — he — he pressed me against him so that I suddenly felt quite faint. And he put his tongue in my mouth and told me to do the same and he felt all over my body with his hands . . ."

She wiped away a tear. The Pope's hand had tightened around her. She had given him an erection. He couldn't wait to hear the rest of the story.

"Go on, my child. Forget nothing. I must know how far it went in order to pray."

"Well, first of all it was over my shift. He felt me all over and everywhere he touched me, particularly when he put his hand between my legs, he made me feel faint. And then I felt so dizzy and helpless that I suggested we sit down. We sat down on the grass beside a tree and, before I really knew what he was doing, he took my shift right off and left me lying there without any clothes on at all. I was . . . I was very frightened, but then . . . then he started feeling me all over again and I only remember the rest as if I were dreaming . . ."

"What do you remember, my dear? If you tell me you will be rid of it. You will have confessed."

"He . . . he kissed me all over — my mouth, my neck, my shoulders, my . . . my breasts and everything. And then he put his finger inside me . . . in between my legs. It made me feel as if I were swooning. I remember thinking that it was wrong, but then it seemed so strong and necessary that I even believed him and thought it might be right after all.

"And then after he'd had his finger in me for some time I began to get terribly excited — even though it was rather painful. I think he put more fingers in me then, because I . . . I felt more pain and I asked him to stop . . . but . . . he wouldn't and I hadn't the strength to push him away. He went on like that for some time until it wasn't painful any more . . . and sometimes he stopped and just kissed me and felt my breasts. And when he did that I wanted him to put his fingers back inside me again because I felt empty and naked as if I needed something . . .

"And then he seemed to leave me for a minute and I just lay there because I was too giddy and too frightened to move. But then he lay down beside me again and pushed me back and I could feel that he was naked, too.

"Then I became very frightened. Because I knew he was going to do something terrible. But . . . but one part of me kept telling me that it wasn't wrong and that I wanted it and that he was right and it would be all right . . .

"He put his fingers back inside me and he

84

told me to open my thighs wide. I must have done it although I don't remember deciding I would . . . because . . . because — oh Father, it's too terrible!"

The Pope, agog with ill-concealed excitement, had one hand on his erect penis under the sheets. He was inflamed by the story she was telling him about herself in her soft voice, with her head bowing against his shoulder in shame and agony.

"Go on, child," he said, with a great attempt at majestic calm. "You are bound to finish it now."

After a few sobs, Lucrezia continued, as if reluctantly.

"The next thing . . . he was . . . he was lying on top of me and he had my thighs wide open and he . . . he was pushing himself at me . . . pushing his . . . his . . . you know, Father, against mine until suddenly . . . oh . . . suddenly it was in and he was — he was making love to me completely . . . and he went on and on and he got terribly excited and so did I . . . I was almost fainting . . . and there was a little pain . . . and . . . and he began to gasp and groan and then . . . and then he made a great noise . . . and . . . and it was all over . . . it was finished."

"My poor child, my poor child," (oh to have been that young man! the Pope thought) "what a terrible time."

"Of course, afterwards," Lucrezia added, through her tears, "I was terribly sorry and ashamed at what had happened — and terribly embarrassed. But . . . but he laughed at me and tried to — what he called — reason with me. But I knew I'd done wrong."

The Pope was silent for a while, letting her

cry against his shoulder. He appeared to be deliberating. In fact, he was trying to live through what had just been described, trying to imagine every part of her body — the secret, intimate places, trying to imagine that enormous emotional chill that was felt at the moment of entry. Oh, he had been ill and unable for so long. He felt overcome with self-pity and defiance. His penis was hot in his hand, and aching with repressed longing.

"What you did, my child, was wrong in those circumstances," he said at last. "But you have little to reproach yourself for. We all sin — it is inescapable and some sins are greater than others. But you are only a young girl — even though you may have the appearance of a woman — and you were led astray by an older man who, obviously, well knew how to prey upon what, after all, are perfectly natural appetites. The fault is entirely his, my child. God will forgive you, have no fear. His mercy is boundless."

Lucrezia took a deep breath behind her veil of mock tears.

"But, Holy Father, the main trouble has come after the event. I told you I was having difficulty about Good and Evil. Well . . . I find, now, that I'm beset with overwhelming desires to repeat what happened. I do my best to overcome them, but I'm likely to give way at any moment."

"I see — I see."

Innocent's hand moved slightly on his prick. He felt very disturbed. This was better and better, but the thought that he couldn't take advantage of it was killing him.

"Have you seen the young man since?"

"No, your Excellency. I do all in my power to keep away from him. But I feel the desire with any man — oh I know it's terrible. You must think I'm unbelievably wicked."

"Not at all, my child, not at all," Innocent reassured her. That hand in mine is so near, he was thinking. I could just take it and put it on my prick under the sheets. It would take about two seconds in time and mean moving it a distance of thirty centimeters.

"You have had an experience," he said, "which was bound to shake you to your roots. It has opened up a whole new channel of experience . . ." He grinned to himself at his words. "And, naturally given you a desire for sensations and emotional experiences that you hardly realized existed. We all have these desires, my dear. Don't think you are alone."

"But what must I do?" Lucrezia pleaded.

She could see his erection through the sheets and the coverlets. So papa had been right. He would want to. So far, very good. But now she had to take what chances came to her. She rested her head against his shoulder so that her lightly perfumed hair was brushing against his face. Leaning forward toward him, she was able to expose much more of her bosom — showing him more than a third of their rounded fullness.

Innocent's head was in a whirl. Looking down on her, as if with compassion, he could see down the front of her dress. The cleavage of her lovely white breasts was agony to his loins. He could hardly restrain his hands. Her golden hair was against his face. It smelled slightly of lavender. He could see those full, ill-defined lips in the lovely, sad face. If only . . . he thought. If only . . . What did the doctors know about it? Half of them were fools and the other half scoundrels. Supposing he did — what then? His desire for life fought with his desire for her flesh. But the desire for life was weakened because he wasn't sure he'd lose his life if he had her. That could be all eyewash. And her flesh was here, so real and near and unbearably tantalizing.

"It is probable," the Pope said slowly, "that you've built up a myth around this one occasion when you made love. And because it seems so unholy and wicked to you, you therefore, in your deprivation, desire it the more — a very natural reaction.

"In very few cases would I suggest this course of cure. But you know, to overcome a greater, even God will allow a lesser evil. So it may be that if you permitted yourself intercourse just once again — and without any feeling of wrongdoing to add to the excitement — you would get the whole necessity out of your system. At least, you would rid yourself of its full power as you now feel it and would pave the way to a beginning at controlling it. This may seem a very strange recommendation, but reflect, my lamb, that the ways of God are often strange beyond belief — but always with the end in mind. If, by this means, you can help to overcome the acuteness of your desires and thus, eventually, overcome them completely, you will have taken the right and only course. If you go on as you are you will either go mad or give way again and again until you are no better than the lowest whore."

There was a long silence after his words. Lucrezia let her hand slip from his and flop against his thigh, as if accidentally, in weariness. She could feel his skinny thigh under the coverlet — and against the side of her hand she could feel the rising bulge of his erection.

Knowledge of his desire had given her course to be bold.

"I thank you, Holy Father. I'm sure your advice is good. And as it is your advice I'm willing to follow it with a glad heart — even though of my own willing the idea must have seemed wrong to me. I see that it may well be the only way. But there is one thing that frightens me still."

"What is that, my child?"

"Holy Father, it's just something I feel. It hardly makes sense. But I'd know that it was simply lust in the man with whom I made love. I'd know that although I was trying to purge myself, that he was on a different plane simply using me as an object of his passion. Although I could have holy aims and thoughts about what I was doing, it would shame me that the man would feel completely differently."

The Pope turned this over in his mind, gloating, playing cat with the mouse, unaware that he was being outplayed, that his thoughts were being directed along channels which would lead to the inevitable. Amidst his thoughts he was aware of her hand against his erection, the slight pressure making him involuntarily strain the mast up against her hand, trusting that she wouldn't realize what was happening.

"I think I could only do it, now, after what you've said, with someone who knew why I was doing it and sympathized and made love to me with the intention of curing my desires," Lucrezia told him.

"For that you would need the holiest of men," said the Pope innocently.

"Yes," Lucrezia replied from his shoulder, "the holiest of men."

She raised her head and stared into his eyes for several seconds.

The Pope felt her words sinking into his mind like a physical force. They startled and excited him — and her look heightened the effect. He was sure, now, that it would be a simple matter. The girl was very susceptible; she would really imagine she was ridding herself of evil.

Slowly he looked at her breasts again. How lovely they would look swinging free to the air. And her body! What would her body be like? And how would her face look screwed up and lost in passion. His hand clenched over his erection in a fierce surge of emotion. He couldn't pass up such an opportunity — even if it was the last thing he did. The last thing! He wondered. But doctors always exaggerated. It was part of their business to frighten the patient into submission. And surely he wouldn't feel so much like having intercourse with her if it were likely to do him any real harm.

Lucrezia had seen the lust in Innocent's eyes. She had very nearly won. She wondered what it would be like with such an old man, but the thought didn't appall her — in fact she rather liked the idea of being screwed by fatherly old men. The contrast between their balding heads, her golden locks, her young, firm body and their slack flesh added to her excitement, made the whole thing seem less permissible.

Without looking up she raised her hand to her cheek and then allowed it to drop back casually onto the bed — onto his stiff penis. She could feel the bulge under her hand and she felt him tense with her touch.

The Pope felt his breath rise up through his body, as if from his loins, strangling him in a weight of emotion. This was it; this was the moment of choice — but it was already too late to choose. Knowing the inevitable he nonetheless raced through a number of arguments in his mind against having her. But now her fingers were moving gently on his penis, stabbing it with needles of fire and she had raised her eyes to his again, was looking deeply into him as if she knew the depths of his soul.

"You are the holiest of men," she whispered. And her mouth opened gently and her eyes closed as if she were overcome at the awe the thought inspired.

He seized her then and drew her up to him.

"We will drive the evil out of you," he said with a voice he could hardly control. "Together we will prove the strength of the Lord." Inside he burned with excitement and laughed madly at his hypocritical words. He would do it. He would screw her young-girl flesh, fill her young-girl passage with his holy mace — if it was his very last act he would do it.

"I will do anything you think should be done," Lucrezia whispered, with a fine show of youthful, feminine weakness. So saying she pressed her breasts into him and pushed her young body alongside his in a sign of submission.

Innocent's lips trembled with lust. He tried to think clearly for a moment, forcing his thoughts away from a desire to rip her clothes from her with his ebbing strength.

"We are unlikely to be disturbed," he said softly. "My attendants wait in the antechamber when I have visitors, but against emergency perhaps you would go and bolt that door, my dear — and then you can remove your clothes — behind the screen if you wish — and come back here."

Lucrezia ran her hand along his hard tower and then obediently got up from the bed and went to the oak door. She slid the heavy bolt across, looked back to the bed, smiled nervously at the Pope and slipped behind the screen.

She took a fair time about undressing, flinging her garments one by one onto the top of the screen. She peered through one of the cracks at the join of the two panels and saw Innocent's eyes avidly taking in the items of clothing which had intimately draped her body. What a lustful old man he is, she thought—and with all that nonsense about the strength of the Lord. She sniggered to herself. She'd show him her strength and see how he stood up to that.

She pressed her hands down her buttocks. God, what a thrill he was going to have doing that—astonishing that her own body meant so little to her. She smoothed her belly and glanced down at the globes of her breasts. She felt a little nervous about what this was all leading to, but when she glanced for the last time through the crack and saw the Pope playing with himself so obviously under the sheets she took heart and walked around the screen, utterly naked, toward the bed.

Innocent's eyes goggled at her as she came toward him, with head bowed slightly.

"Don't be afraid of your nakedness—you have a rare beauty," he said in an attempt to sound pontifical. But his eagerness seeped into the words making them sound comic.

Lucrezia raised her head and fixed her eyes on him. She had adopted an expression of young and tender helplessness.

Innocent let his gaze rifle her from top to

toe. What beautiful proportions! If he couldn't have had her now he would have been willing to die rather than live with the memory of her body denied him.

Her slender neck ran into slim, sloping shoulders, well-covered with flesh; her breasts were firm and impudent, the sleek ovals begged to be cupped in a hand, to be squeezed. Her waist was very slim, which accentuated the sexy outward curve of her hips and the tapering into firm luscious-fleshed thighs. He could see the slight trace of blonde down on her lower belly and what was little more than a shadow of flesh at the nest between her legs.

Halfway toward him she turned and went back to the door to look at the bolt, as if afraid she hadn't fastened it completely. Her ruse to show off her body was effective.

Innocent strained up in bed, his old penis throbbing at the sight of her oval buttocks which shadowed into gentle hollows as she walked. Seen from the back her waist seemed even slimmer in comparison with her hips, filled out as they were by those incomparable buttocks. What a rump! His fingers itched to hold it in his hands.

Lucrezia came toward the bed once more, quickly this time, and the Pope stretched out his arms toward her.

"We must make it as if we were completely given to the lusts of the flesh," he said hoarsely. "If there is any self-consciousness about our lovemaking it will fail to satisfy and exorcise."

She slipped into his arms and threw back her head as he began, feverishly, to kiss her breasts. He released her and grasped a breast in each hand, sucking the points as if they were trumpets. Lucrezia felt cold shivers slide convulsively down her spine. She abandoned herself to his lips which ran all over the top part of her body, sucking as if he wanted to draw blood from her skin.

She put her arms around his skinny body and pressed his head against her breasts. He was quivering with excitement.

His hands began frantically to explore her body, moving down her back, smoothing her buttocks, gripping them, catching them in voluptuous handfuls of flesh; he ran his fingers along the warm ravine of cleavage between them, pressed the puckered flesh of her anus until she squirmed and whimpered; he stroked her thighs and sought her lips with his. His breath smelled of bad teeth and his tongue was rough. When she poked her fresh, little tongue back through his lips she felt spaces where some of his teeth were missing.

The Pope began to pant with a mixture of excitement and shortness of breath through his efforts. His heart was pounding unhealthily. But his penis was as stiff as a ramrod.

In a very short time his hands, which had savagely ravished her body, lingered over her most intimate parts with a dalliance which betrayed his utter sensuality, became insufficient instruments for his lustful satisfaction.

With each fistful of flesh he clenched—buttucks, breasts, belly, her vaginal lips, his hands showed a wild catholicity—his hips strained up under the sheets and his penis pulsated like barrels of heated gunpowder.

With a shock, sudden and overwhelming as if cold water had been poured on his loins, the Pope felt Lucrezia's cool hands slip under the sheets and enclose the burning heat of his prick in their soothing balm. He shuddered from head to toes.

Her fingers soothed and caressed with what he would have remarked as practiced excellence had he not been so immersed in his own feelings and satisfaction. Then, gently, they began to rub up and down the stiff, brittle-seeming stem of flesh.

The Pope's lips moved the way they did when he prayed.

"For God's sake get into bed!" he managed to utter at last.

Lucrezia quickly slipped under the sheets, with his clawing hands helping her in.

His body was cold against hers—the body of an old bloodless man—an astonishing contrast overall with the heat of his penis, the one part of him truly alive.

She pressed the warm overflow of her flesh against the chilly skinniness, warming him, exciting him so that his hands jumped over her body, unable to keep still on her.

Innocent's lips shivered an accompaniment to his quivering body. He had seldom come across such a completely rounded, filled-out delight of womanliness and his hands could hardly take sufficient fill.

He squirmed as her hand moved off his penis, running down it, skimming over its base and teasing his testicles and the growing nucleus of heat between his old thighs.

Lucrezia, too, was squirming with delight as his fingers brushed her vagina and pierced into its moist outskirts. She rolled over on top of him, infusing his body with her soft warmth. She pressed down on him and rubbed her hips voluptuously against his prick which she felt rolling like a length of doughy bread between them, a length of hot, newly-baked bread.

His skinny old arms encircled her, pulling her at him, his hips pressed up against her, indenting her slight, sensual superfluity of flesh.

Gently, for several minutes they pressed together, with his hands holding her buttocks, his lips sucking her open mouth. And then she wriggled up a little on him until his prick waved wildly between her slightly opened thighs, cleaving up so that she could feel its upper side against her labia and against her buttocks.

She broke from his ardent kissing and levered herself toward an upright position, sitting across his loins, one thigh on either side of his body. She caught his rod in her hand, gave it a last squeeze, knelt up and placed it against the open mouth of her vagina.

The Pope raised his head from its horizontal position and let his eyes augment the pleasure of his bodily senses.

He watched her hold his penis toward her poised aperture, lower herself gently and then flop down on it with a gasp of pent-up breath. Immediately he felt an abandonment of his soul; it rushed down through his body to the head of his penis which was caught in the powerful contractions of her channel. It made the rest of his body, his mind, seem so much putty, so much lifeless clay. It was only down there at that one slim tube of living flesh that there was any reason for existence. The rest of him could have died if only that would go on living forever and ever amen, living and feeling, being squeezed in her slim channel which descended and rose on it, tightly, firmly, wetly, deliciously, forever and ever so that his lips began to mutter feverish, delirious obscenities.

Lucrezia plunged down on that stiff pike, feeling it tear up inside her as if a pikesman had made a fierce homeward thrust. Her breasts jumped with her plunges, her thighs sank lower and lower, her knees slithered farther away from his body on either side until the whole of her crotch was pressed against and around the base of his organ and the staff itself was totally contained inside her juicy tunnel.

From time to time she opened her closed eyes or brushed the hair from her face. Then she would see the Pope lying back, only his hips tensed, moving up at her in slight undulations as she descended. She would see his lips moving and his white strained face. And through her own stimulation which wetly inflamed her trounced passage she had the double satisfaction of knowing that things were going according to plan.

The Pope, too, opened his eyes ever so often and fixed her with his gaze. Then—and it took very little acting on her part—she would screw up her beautiful face in passion, to excite him, mutter obscenities herself and let her hair swing forward over her face in abandonment.

His body began to writhe and twist as his penis sank deeper and deeper into her moist, hot body. It was frail and bony and covered now with a thin film of perspiration.

He could feel the pounding of his heart. It seemed to fill his ears and his whole body. He was panting wildly, but having difficulty in breathing. But these discomforts seemed to add rather than detract from the pure exquisite quality of his sensation. The physical torture of his body whipped up his senses to a fine point of receptivity.

Through half-closed eyes he watched her full breasts leap and sway in their smooth, glossy skin; he felt her thighs warmly press into his loins as she came down, impaling herself on the rod which had impaled so many times before her and which, in spite of the Pope's weakness was still in a state of perfect workability —the only part of him which functioned as always.

He was getting more and more excited. A thrumming in his loins joined with a thrumming in his chest and ears.

Lucrezia pressed harder and harder on him, giving him no respite, drawing herself right up above him, so that only the knob of his organ remained nestled in the warm pink portals of her sex and then crashing down again so that she felt that spear of flesh soar up inside her with a movement which made her stomach turn over. At the end of the downward stroke she ground her crotch and buttocks against him, squirming on him for a few seconds until gasps burst from his lips.

Occasionally his hands twitched out to her and managed to grasp and feebly squeeze her thighs or even reach to her breasts.

So furious was her youthful onslaught that she began to feel the excitement of culmination and forced herself to slow down the pace so as not to lose any ferocity of attack until Innocent was ready to come himself.

The Pope was no longer chill. His whole frame was flushed with a pink heat which was a frame between his legs. His prick felt bloated, aching and growing up to an ecstatic bursting point. His thighs and back ached with the upward pressure he'd continuously exerted at Lucrezia's bobbing crotch. The drumming in his ears was almost unbearable. He was trying desperately to force the explosion at his prick before there was an explosion in his head or in his chest.

His breathing had become a pitiful consumptive whine but Lucrezia showed no mercy at his tortured, pathetic state.

Innocent opened his eyes. In his aching head he suddenly felt a power of great emotion. She was beautiful, so beautiful and innocent and trying to do right. He would keep her after this day; he would keep her and look after her and any future intercourse she had would be with him and then she'd be able to enjoy it because she could tell herself always that it was purifying her, giving her a holy outlet for desires which would, of course, continue to beset her.

In that moment Innocent felt that he loved the child with the woman's body. He wanted to reach out and hold her to him, but he no longer had the strength and he had already closed his eyes and become acutely conscious once again of his prick which seemed to be swelling in her so that it seemed it might never come out again.

He writhed his loins against her. The desire to come was intolerable and yet he couldn't quite seem to manage it. It would happen, but his head felt as if it was splitting and his chest was constricted and he hoped it would hurry.

Feebly he tensed his thighs, felt a twinge of cramp and relaxed them again. He pressed his abdomen against her descending nether parts. He opened his eyes again and fixed her with a gaze which did not take her in clearly.

Lucrezia sensed from his writhing, his agonized expression, his gasps and groans that the end was approaching and she unleashed her body and began to pummel him for all she was worth, letting herself be carried away by her own momentous passion.

She could feel her loins swarming as if a thousand snakes were writhing inside. She released a stream of gasping cries which broke through the blackness in Innocent's head and revived in him a last flush of passion so that he thrust his loins up at her, mumbled painfully through dry lips, groaned agonizingly in an evident warning climax and clenched his fingers into her thighs with a last strength.

Dazedly he opened his eyes again. His loins seemed to be covered with a sticky wetness amidst Lucrezia's moanings. His prick felt grazed, beaten, full of something that must escape. He saw her face mistily, head thrown back—beautiful neck—lips moving. His fingers dug hard into her fleshy thighs in a last paroxysm of life. He felt the climax near . . . on him . . . there! He gasped deliriously, felt his penis explode as if in a thousand pieces, fought for breath, fought for consciousness, felt himself losing both, tried to appeal to her with his eyes and slowly slipped off into a painful darkness.

Lucrezia had echoed his feelings with precision. Her flood of sensation had swamped up in her loins with a dragging delightful pain, swamped up and over just as his prick had seemed to be at its biggest in her so that she felt it would smash right through her and up into her belly.

For some seconds afterwards, still excited and hardly knowing where she was, she had swayed about on his prostrate body and then she had flopped down on top of him.

It took her almost a minute to begin to collect her wits.

100

The first thing she realized was that Innocent was not just lying still through exhaustion. He had lost consciousness. Lucrezia wasn't dismayed: this was all part of the plan—except that it appeared to be succeeding almost beyond expectations.

Swiftly, methodically, she got up and dressed. With the inside of her dress she wiped away any tell-tale signs of the Pope's incontinence and then she rearranged the bed and his body. After that she collected herself for a moment, checked everything, quietly went to the door and unbolted it. She tiptoed back to Innocent's bed, let out a high-pitched scream and rushed back toward the door.

She hadn't reached it before it was flung open and two attendants rushed in.

Lucrezia pointed to the bed.

"God protect us," she cried. "His Holiness just passed out in the middle of talking."

CHAPTER 6

The news of the Pope's collapse spread like pillage through the city.

His doctors came forthwith and pronounced that the strain of receiving visitors had obviously been too much for his weak heart. There was little hope of his survival beyond a few hours.

His doctors stayed at his bedside and visitors from the Pope's circle were frequent. He got weaker and weaker at a very rapid rate. His physicians were agreed on their helplessness in face of his critical state.

The following day, Innocent, without having regained consciousness, was still clinging weakly to life and a Hebrew physician came to his bedside, claiming to have a prescription which would save the dying prelate's life. For his task, he said, he needed the blood of young boys. The Pope's skeptical physicians eventually found him two young boys, who, for a ducat each, were prepared to give him all the blood he needed.

But so complete was the failure of his remedy that the two boys died and the physician was forced to flee to save his own life from the wrath of those who had doubted him from the beginning.

For just one more day, Innocent lay in his bed breathing very feebly. In the early hours of the following morning he was found to be breathing no more.

*   *   *

Cardinal Roderigo lost no time in organizing the succession. Even during the prescribed nine days of ceremonies connected with Innocent's death, he was busy arguing, offering, bargaining, encouraging toward his own ends.

On the tenth day the cardinals assembled in St. Peter's to hear the Sacred Mass of the Holy Ghost recited on the tomb of the Prince of the Apostles. They swore upon the gospels to faithfully observe their trust and the Conclave was immured.

A few days later Cardinal Roderigo Borgia was elected Pope Alexander VI. He had bargained well.

Many were the cardinals who benefited from Roderigo's election. To Cardinal Sforza went the vacated vice-chancellorship and the bishopric of Agri; to the Orsini the Church of Carthage and the legation of Marche; to Colonna the Abbey of Subiaco; to Savelli the legation of Perugia; to Raffaele Riario went Spanish benefices worth four thousand ducats yearly. They, too, had bargained well.

Lucrezia, who had played the largest part of all, was rewarded with a beautiful diamond necklace and a passionate night in her father's bed during which he mounted her five times and both were completely satisfied. She was then sent off to continue her studies under the tutors who were shocked at her provocative display of bosom and would have died of horror had they known exactly what had been displayed to the Pope before his death.

CHAPTER 7

Cesare had been brought back to Rome on the news of his father's election. Cardinal Roderigo felt it only fitting that his son, whom he hoped would one day succeed him, should be present at the ceremony.

Ever since his adventure with his sister, Cesare had been in a fever heat to renew his relationship with her, but there had been no opportunity.

Over and over in his mind he had relived those furiously passionate moments by the pool, over and over he had thought of how next time he would be less embarrassed, more expert, more concerned with prolonging the pleasure. His incestuous lovemaking had given him a new awareness of women as well. In Perugia he had watched them walking down the street with their bosoms soaring, had imagined their breasts untrammeled by clothes. He had stared at the occasional traces of a round and protruding buttock under a dress such as the peasant girls wore and had longed to move up behind and place his hand on that undulating mound of firmness. He had longed for lips, for fondling hands, for the aching sensation of that body-grip on his penis—until he walked around with an almost permanent erection and a slight flush always on his face. At night he was haunted by dreams of his sister's passion-wracked body, images of other bodies. He masturbated with a new vigor. He almost wept with desire for a good screw. And on return to Rome he conceived of a daring plan to achieve the aided orgasm he so desperately needed.

The interregnum between the death of one Pope and the election of another was invariably filled with a furious outburst of lawlessness in Rome. Bands of lawbreakers would roam the streets. Murders were committed on an average of several a day, robberies took place on an unprecedented scale and rapes were so numerous that count was lost. It was this savage jungle state within the city that Cesare decided should cover his own fulfillment of his desires.

In the grounds of Cardinal Roderigo's house was a gardener's shed in which Cesare had previously noted some old, cheap clothing such as would be worn by the ordinary citizen. This, he decided, he would don one evening when his father was not at home. He would rub grime into his face, tousle his hair and, with his gold-hilted dagger in his belt under his doublet, sally out into the lawless streets in search of a woman.

It was a wild plan, he realized. It was full of dangers. He, himself, might be attacked; he might be caught in the act of rape; he might be beaten up by the city guard which functioned in a desultory fashion from time to time. But on the first count he hoped his old clothes would make him seem too worthless an object to make it worth anybody's while to assault him—and on the others he'd take a chance, so dearly did he need to plunge his dagger of genital flesh into a female sheath.

For a couple of days, while he awaited his opportunity, Cesare wandered through the city, which was calmer by daytime, watching the women who quickly came and went, or—in large bands for safety—washed their clothes down at the river's edge. He particularly frequented the poorer sections of the city as it was here that he was more likely to succeed in his plan without too many later investigations being made. And it was in one of these quarters that he found the sort of situation he had been seeking.

At dusk, he noted, at a particular spot, three goat-swains—two men and a girl—were in the habit of driving a large herd of goats from the city gates into their pen within the city. They all stayed together until a point near the Bridge of St. Angelo across the river where the girl would bid them good-night and slip across the bridge to her house which was close to the far bank. The two men would continue with the goats under the assumption that their companion was safe with only such a little distance to go alone.

Cesare made a survey of the area. His heart raced in anticipation of the deed. As he marked the spot—dangerously near her home—where he could drag her over the low parapet onto the shrub-covered, shelving bank, his breath came quickly as if he were already lying between her legs.

The girl, herself, was a peasant girl with a saucy, good-looking face and a strong, loose-limbed body with large breasts and a behind that was pert under the thin country dress she wore. She would be no easy conquest. Cesare was well aware. But he thought he could subdue her and the sight of her body, revealed in a way that only peasant clothing would allow, infused him with a nervous excitement that gave him butterflies in his stomach.

The day fixed for the crowning of the new Pope came nearer and Cardinal Roderigo spent more and more time away from his house fixing the details of the ceremony.

Cesare's chance came at last. In a sudden fit of trembling he donned the old clothes in the gardener's shed. The hose he slit between the legs—just enough so that another tug would give his organ free exit. The doublet came down far enough to hide the spot.

He stole out of the house, leaving a door to the grounds unlatched for his re-entry, hoping that no would-be robbers would discover it before he got back.

Along the main streets people were still passing in groups, sometimes singly. He avoided these more frequented places after a time and set out through the growing twilight to the poor quarter.

Narrow, cobbled streets led him down toward the river. Sometimes someone flitted quickly from one doorway to another, sending his heart into his mouth, sometimes a shutter would slam, making him jump and twice he brazened it past a group of men who peered at him in the half-light but made no move to interfere with him.

At the bridge across the river he stopped

and leaned on the parapet for a moment to calm himself and quell the thumping of his heart. He peered through the gloom. He was sure they hadn't yet come. Below, the river was a smooth, dark sheet, behind him odd noises rang out from the Castle of St. Angelo which towered up in ghostly form. In the distance he could still dimly see the outline of St. Peter's. There was nobody about, now. The majority of honest citizens who were able would now be safely locked behind their doors with the shutters barred.

Cesare listened. On the still air he heard the faint bleat of a goat.

Quickly he set off across the broad bridge. His heart was still pounding wildly. The seriousness of what he was doing crept over him and in the middle of his hurrying he wondered, without slowing his place, if he shouldn't just turn back and get home as quickly as possible. But in his head he had an image of the goat-girl with her loose-limbed walk and her body curves embraced in her peasant dress, and he hurried on.

By now the dusk was settling in; in a short time it would be completely dark.

He reached the point where the bridge ran into the far bank. He took a quick look around. He could almost see the girl's house to which he'd followed her twice already. Then he swung himself lightly over the parapet and crouched down out of sight.

The parapet at this point was only three feet high and there was a further six-inch drop on the bankside. From where Cesare crouched, trying to still his heaving breath, the bank, divided into patches of knee-high scrub and dusty sand, stretched gently down to the still edge of the river.

There he waited, not daring to look back over the parapet. He was so nervous that he ripped open the slit in his hose and urinated quickly against the wall of the bridge. He need still do nothing, he told himself. He could just let her go by and then go home. He still hadn't definitely decided he was going through with it when he heard her light footfall on the bridge.

He pulled the dagger from the belt under his doublet. His hand was trembling as he put it over his mouth to try and quiet his breath. In spite of his bladder-emptying, his organ was at half-cock with nervous excitement.

Suppose she was not alone today. Suppose someone came toward the bridge from the opposite direction and saw them. Suppose she broke away from him and screamed for the city guard. What would happen to him? What would his father say? A thousand doubts sprang in on him. But there was her footfall, unsuspecting and so close. He held his breath. There was no other noise at all. She was alone as usual.

Tense as a bowstring he waited. Now she was about ten paces away, now nine, now eight . . . now one . . . He put his hands on the parapet in the half-darkness, and with a spring he was up and over it just behind her.

The girl half-turned in horror before his hand clapped over her mouth and he flashed the dagger in front of her eyes.

"If you scream or make any sound I'll kill you," he whispered fiercely.

The girl stared at him with wide, horrified dark eyes. It was rather a shock to find himself so near her, touching her, the object of her terrified attention, after watching her from a distance for two nights.

Her body was very warm against him through her thin dress. She held herself taut, but didn't make a sound.

Still holding one hand over her mouth, Cesare, glancing nervously across the bridge, prodded her toward the parapet.

"Climb over and drop down the other side," he ordered. "And don't make a sound. I don't intend to kill you and I shan't unless you scream."

For a moment the girl wouldn't move and he thought she was going to resist. He prodded her side with the point of the dagger and she went in front of him to the parapet and swung over it, dropping down with him to the other side.

Cesare prodded her on down the bank toward the water's edge and away from the bridge. Behind them on the land side, the bank ended some distance up in a high wall. He was safe from that direction.

The girl made no sound as he walked with her, hand still on her mouth in case she tried to shout. It had all been very easy. Through his excitement he looked down sideways at the bulge of her breasts. It was really here at last —and so easy.

At a distance from the bridge they stopped. Cesare glanced quickly back. Nobody on the bridge could see them at that distance. He jabbed the girl with the knife.

"Lie down—and if you try to shout I'll slit your throat."

The girl looked around at him. She had long dark hair which was mussed up now around her dark face. Her eyes had lost some of their startled horror and were gleaming with anger.

"What do you want?" she said fiercely. "I am poor—I have no money."

Cesare was beginning to feel very sure of himself.

"You have something worth its weight in gold," he said softly. "Now lie down and I will show you."

The girl's sudden defense took him unawares. He had come to expect an easy victory. She twisted suddenly from his grasp and took a half step toward the bridge. But Cesare's reaction was quick. He caught her again before she had even the time to cry out. He clamped his hand roughly over her mouth and pushed her to the ground. She fell under him and he dug the knife at her ribs.

"I told you I'll kill you," he hissed.

But this time his warning had no effect. The girl probably thought he would slit her throat anyway when he'd finished with her and she resolved to sell her life dearly.

She twisted over and struggled furiously with him so that Cesare, who'd had no intention of using the knife and adding murder to his crime, was forced to drop the weapon and use both hands in an effort to overcome her.

His prick, which was erect as a raised draw-bridge, had flipped out of the slit in his clothing and was crushed and rubbed between them as they struggled.

He managed to stretch her arms out on either side, but her legs continued to writhe and buffet him as he lay along her.

Her face, wrinkled with dark fury, was directly below his. With a little gust of triumph he closed his mouth over hers as she struggled. He could tell he was much stronger than she.

When he took his face away she spat in his face. He released one of her arms and slapped her face with his free hand. She pushed with her released arm, jabbing him with her elbow and he fell off. The girl took full advantage of her gain and slithered out from under him, rolling over on top, clawing at him, reaching for his throat with strong fingers.

Surprised, Cesare decided that the time had come for stronger measures. He was afraid someone might hear their scuffling from the bridge—and apart from that he was almost coming against her wriggling body.

He pulled back his right fist, pushing her wrists away with his left, and punched hard and straight into her belly.

The girl collapsed on him, gasping with pain and he rolled her off and swayed over on top of her again. She was completely winded. She lay there helpless for the moment, with her dress halfway up her strong, naked thighs.

Cesare lost no time, now. He was very scared that somebody might have heard the noise. He ripped her dress up what remained hidden of her thighs, felt between her legs for the love-slit she was in no position to protect and guided his hungry prick at it.

He held the girl's arms with his hands once his knob was against her lower lips—and then he pushed in against her.

For several seconds he couldn't seem to make progress. He released an arm and reached down again, feeling for the opening. He pulled her flopping thighs apart to facilitate his entry and pushed again.

The girl squealed even through her lack of breath when his throbbing knob pierced into her. Automatically she swung her arm up and tried to push him off, gasping with the pain in her belly and the fresh pain down at her treasured vagina.

Cesare caught the arm and forced it down again. He was really in now. And it was tight enough to hurt. He was flooded with a great sense of relief, as if the frustrations of a lifetime had suddenly been put right.

The girl was squirming with pain. But his push had so hurt and winded her that she could hardly groan, let alone put up any serious opposition to his assault on her maidenhood.

Cesare breathed out his relief. At last he was able to quench his desire in a tight, loving, tender body. He thrust in as if he were ramming shot into a cannon and with each thrust he expelled a toe-shaking sigh of relief.

With his body quivering all over he wriggled his loins into her pelvis. He didn't want to take long now that he'd succeeded at last. His prick was heavy and prickling and the girl, her face creased in pain, had almost given up struggling under the fury of his attack.

Cesare lowered his face onto hers and kissed her lips. Her lips were unresponsive, tight together and she forced her face away from him. So he kissed her dark neck as his prick seared up into her clam-gripping vagina. He wriggled in and in until, for the first time, his whole prick from throbbing knob to tingling base was buried in a soft female passage.

He shagged her furiously with quick hard strokes. He couldn't take too much time, but he had to have that final world-shattering explosion; that had to take place in her soft, tight body.

The girl lay under him, still too wounded in her belly to resist. He let go of her arms and put his hands under her buttocks, scraping the backs of his fingers against the sand. Her rump was firm and springy. The feel of it sent a new zest winging through his hot ramrod. He pulled her belly up against him so that it seemed as if he was holding her vagina in a framework for his prick. He looked down at her belly which he could see, dimly white in the darkness. He could also see his weapon, dimly white, moving into the cranny at her thigh-junction.

He held her buttocks tightly. Each stroke now was as if he were bursting into her for the first time. His prick had grown tight, intense with sensation. It was coming. He gritted his teeth and fixed his eyes on her dim face, turned sideways, still creased in pain. She was a stranger, a total stranger. And he was joined with her here in this most complete of intimacies! They were one flesh—united by his bridge of penis!

As he felt the soaring mount in him he never took his eyes from her face. She moved her legs occasionally, but simply because she was uncomfortable. From start to near finish there had been little resistance.

He burst in and in and with each burst he felt the moment edge excruciatingly nearer. He was trying to keep his noises back in his throat. There he was, coughing and growling, trying not to lose control.

He felt the last movement in his loins. It was joy and beauty and savagery all combined in his screwing into this firm and beautiful unknown body. He squeezed the buttocks in his hands as he thrust, and his thrusts slowed to grinding heaves. He was losing control. It was heaven. It was hell. He couldn't keep it back. It was coming, coming, into the body of this strange, prostrate girl whose buttocks were in his hands, whose tight, clinging vagina was around his prick, whose face was there pressed into the sand in the darkness. It was coming, whirling, here, oh God, here . . . "Aaaaaaaah!" . . . the final cry groaned from his throat, forcing his lips apart and he flopped and bit her strained neck as he shot his sperm into her helpless, wide-open passage.

The girl lay as though dead and after a while he pulled his hands out from under her behind and rolled off her. Now that it was over he felt a flatness. It certainly didn't seem worth the extreme and violent measures he'd gone to to get it.

His thoughts, as he tucked his limp penis into the slit in his hose, turned on the difficulty of getting home, of getting away from the girl— it seemed too unnatural just to get up and walk off—of keeping clear of her in future, of avoiding recognition. It was chilly, too, now.

He glanced back at the bridge, wondering if anyone had heard the cry of his climax. As far as he could see nobody was there. But, by now, it was impossible really to see anything at that distance.

A slithering movement beside him brought his glance quickly back to the girl. He recoiled. Having had time, at last, to recover from her winding, she'd reached out and grabbed the dagger which he, so carelessly, had left lying beside them on the sand.

Now she had drawn herself up onto her knees and was glaring at him with eyes whose gleaming fury he could feel even through the gloom.

He drew back, without a word, slithering

back onto his knees, getting warily to his feet as she did.

"Now I shall kill you," she said with a quiet intensity. "Now I have the dagger and I shall kill you."

He didn't answer. He kept his eyes on her and the dagger, whose gold handle gave off a slight luster in the darkness.

Crouching, she came toward him. He faced her, arms bent out toward her like a wrestler, watching intently. There was danger in running. He might fall; she might overtake him on the rough ground and stab him from behind. He waited for her to come at him.

When she did, leaping forward suddenly with the knife upraised, his foot lashed out and caught her in the groin. She fell on one knee and he leapt on her. In spite of her pain, she clung desperately to the dagger. But he was too strong for her. Slowly he forced her arm down until the knife was between them. He brought up his knee under her elbow from his standing position and the knife fell from her momentarily paralyzed fingers.

He pushed her back with his foot and groped quickly for the knife. He was half aware of her body flying at him once more as he rose with the knife. There was a slight moan from her lips and she fell heavily against him.

He twisted and leapt away. But the knife didn't come away in his hand. Behind him the girl slumped heavily to the ground and lay face down without a tremor.

Cesare stayed stock-still where he was. A flush of horror washed over him. He waited for her to move, to groan, but she lay like a corpse.

Cautiously he moved back to where she lay.

He looked around for the knife, but he couldn't find it. He looked back at her still figure, chilled. He stood over her. He could see both her hands and the knife wasn't in either of them. Overcoming a sudden urge just to leave, to rush off into the night, he bent and turned her over. The cold sight of what he had known from her stillness petrified him. The dagger was buried in her breast almost to the gold hilt. Around it her brown, peasant dress was stained a darker brown. Her eyes were open, but unseeing.

Cesare's mind became a confusion of irrelevant, frightened thoughts. It was some minutes before he was able to think with any clarity. Then he forced himself to be calm and work out what to do. The main thing, he told himself tensely, was to be quick. The next, leave nothing to identify himself. He looked down at the hilt of the dagger and shuddered. He stopped his gaze from rising to the girl's face just in time and, closing his eyes, caught the handle of the knife and pulled. It came away with a smooth springy pressure and when he opened his eyes it was wet and dripping in his hand.

Have to wash it. He glanced around at the river a dozen paces away. He started toward it and then stopped and looked back at the body. He went back to it and put his hand on the girl's breast. No, of course she was dead. Steeling himself, he took her under each armpit and dragged her as quietly as he could manage to the edge of the bank. He swilled the knife in the almost still water of the river and wiped it on her dress. Then, very gently and carefully, he rolled her over into the water.

He stood up, breathing quickly. Now the city guard wouldn't see the body immediately if they came down onto the bank. He glanced back at the bridge which was like some great conscious presence, a witness to the drama. Suppose her people were out looking for her there, wondering why she hadn't got home. But surely they'd have come straight down onto the bank. Maybe there were a dozen reasons why she might be late on any particular day. He'd only watched her for three days in all—far from conclusive evidence that she followed an unchanging pattern.

Cesare stuffed the dagger back into his belt. He glanced at his hose and then pulled his doublet down as far as possible, hiding the slit as best he could. He didn't look back at the river.

At the parapet he heard voices. They filled him with a consuming dread. He *knew* they were looking for her. The voices came from people who must be standing on the bridge. There were several voices. He listened. A voice came out distinctly from the others . . .

"She came across the bridge just like everyday . . ."

And then another.

"Never should have left her. It was so near . . ."

Cesare didn't stay to hear any more. With his heart in his mouth, he crept down toward the river and slipped into the darkness of one of the great spans of the bridge. There he waited, quietly, hardly daring to breathe, hoping that the obvious wouldn't occur to them— to come down and scour the river bank.

For half an hour he waited, but nobody came down onto the bank and after a few minutes more he crept slowly back to the parapet higher

117

up. The voices had gone; there was nobody about.

Not much later he let himself into the grounds of Cardinal Roderigo's house. His clothes were still in the garden shed. He changed, rolled the others into an unrecognizable ball and went into the house to his room. He was there, reading, when his father came to see him much later and tell him the news of the morrow—it was to be the crowning day for Christ's Vicar.

CHAPTER 8

Cardinal Roderigo was crowned Pope Alexander VI next day on the steps of the Basilica of St. Peter. The streets of Rome were crowded with citizens, shouting, laughing, applauding.

Their common eyes were dazzled by the colorful beauty of the procession to the Lateran, the Pope's cathedral church.

Alexander, smiling and serene, completely confident and happy in the fulfillment of his aim, rode on a huge white stallion surrounded by banners including the arms of the Borgias —the Bull. The new Pope held his hand high, blessing the populace with the Fisherman's Ring which glittered from his forefinger in the sunshine.

The magnificent cortege included seven hundred priests and prelates, two thousand knights on horseback, three thousand archers and Turkish horsemen and the Palatine Guard with their flashing halberds and shields.

Watching the procession in all its blaze of color, listening to the music, smelling the incense and the flowers which heralded a night of festivity, Cesare could hardly believe in his adventure of the previous night. A desire not to recall the details of its ending denied him the liberty to enjoy remembering the beginning. It was an episode he preferred to forget.

One of Pope Alexander's first acts was to deal with the violence which had been rife in the city. To this end he used an iron fist.

His first decree was that the house of a murderer should be razed to the ground and the ruffian hanged for all to see above the ruins.

CHAPTER 9

Lucrezia was fourteen years old and a woman of great and varied experience before the Pope succeeded in arranging for her a marriage which suited his ambition. Such a marriage as would have been worthy for a daughter of Cardinal Roderigo Borgia was no longer good enough for Pope Alexander VI. He sought for her an alliance among Italy's princely houses.

It was thus that she became bestowed upon the Lord of Pesaro with a dowry of 30,000 ducats.

The Lord of Pesaro, Giovanni Sforza, himself no more than a youth, thus provided the Pope with much desired stronger relations with Milan — albeit Giovanni himself was no more than a bastard of the powerful Milanese house of Sforza.

The nuptials were celebrated with magnificence in the Vatican, and culminated in a supper party given by the Pope to which ten specially picked cardinals and a number of the ladies and gentlemen of Rome were invited.

After a meal of much good food and more good wine, the Pope announced a special attraction and following on his words some fifty courtesans were brought in and set to dance with the servants.

Many among them were of considerable beauty. They were well known to the Pope, the majority of them having already shared his bed.

The dances were stately and well-performed and the guests applauded politely, wondering what was so special about a spectacle which one could see at any Roman ball.

But, just about the time when those present were beginning to get a little bored with the dancing, Alexander clapped his hands. And at his signal, both courtesans and their partners stripped off their clothes and continued the dancing stark-naked.

There was an appreciative buzz of excitement at this unexpected novelty in the holy place. The men felt their pressures rise as they examined the stately sway of some of the most curvaceous bodies in Rome. The ladies, for their part, tried discreetly to hide their enormous interest in the flopping lengths of meat which dangled between the husky servants' legs.

The Pope, well flushed with liquor, stretched back in his chair and appraised the comparative qualities of various breasts and buttocks. To his nearest male neighbors he gave descriptions of the bedworthy qualities of many of the female dancers, while the ladies within earshot sniggered and replied with quips about the men's pricks, wagering on how big they would grow, which would be the longest under titivation.

Already having anticipated this argument,

Alexander clapped his hands once again and, continuing with their dance, the courtesans, each time they came into contact with their partners, gave a quick, expert rub or tickle to their organs until the latter were rising up majestically.

"Now you will have the answer to the problem," the Pope said with a chuckle to the Lady Manfredi who was his nearest neighbor. Her hand stole over to his lap and pressed him playfully at his genital region.

"I'm sure there can be no better than the holiest," she said with a grin.

The Pope leaned toward her with a smile.

"You flatter me," he said, "but modesty prevents me from comment. Perhaps you would like to join me in consideration of the possibility after the spectacle."

"You are very bold, Roderigo," she replied softly. "But a bold man usually gets what he wants."

She gave his penis a squeeze and withdrew her hand, smiling, to turn her attention back to the scene.

All the servants had big erections by this time. The great cudgels soared out from them like artificial fixtures. In spite of what must have been some turmoil in their loins, they contrived to keep poker faces as the Pope had previously ordered.

The eyes of the spectators were goggling. It was the first time most of them had seen such mass nudity and such mass sexual excitement so openly displayed. Many a prick and many a cunt, well hidden by clothes and the festive tables, was hot with desire at the sight.

Another sign from Alexander and more servants appeared with huge baskets of apples with the centers hollowed out so that only an outside husk remained. These were fitted onto the stiff rods of the nude dancers, so that they clung more or less closely to their reddening-to-purple knobs.

There were gusts of uproarious laughter throughout the great hall at the comic sight of the artificially bloated knobs which had changed color to green, yellow and rosy-apple pink.

Still with perfectly serious faces, the servants sank to their knees on the beautiful mosaic floor and remained kneeling while the laughter shook the chandeliers.

As the first wave of hilarity from the guests began to fade into a ripple of private titters, the naked women dancers knelt down on all fours with their backs toward each of their partners. There was a fresh craning of necks, goggling of eyeballs at the fresh views which were presented of juicy crannies and a frequent fuzz of soft, many-colored pubic hair.

Slowly, without looking backwards, the courtesans moved back until the apple-bloated pricks were touching the soft flesh between their thigh-tops. Then began a series of hip and bottom-wrigglings as they tried to work the apples into their vaginas. It became clear that the idea was for them to swallow the fruit in their orifices and then withdraw it if they could from the male organ it surrounded.

Cardinals watched with panting lips as vagina after vagina opened and distended and tried to ooze around a rosy apple as the woman it belonged to pushed gently back.

"It's a race," the Pope confided. "The first woman to get the apple off can choose the biggest penis to delight her in bed tonight."

The fascinating race was on. Some of the

women seemed unable to expand their holes sufficiently to get them around the large husk of apple. They were forced to rub against and around the fruit until their juices began to flow and they were able to slip backwards more easily. Others got halfways impaled but could get no further, while still others soon got the whole of the apple inside them but couldn't pull it off the prick, which had in most cases expanded within the husk.

The male servants were very excited and many of them gripped the hips of the woman kneeling against them, whereupon they were warned that they were not allowed to help her task in any way.

In some cases, careful watchers suspected that a woman was really making little effort to remove the apple, but was, on the contrary, trying to keep it in place while she jogged excitedly back and forth on it and the hilt of prick behind it.

In fact, the race appeared to be something of a put-up job for the benefit of the spectators' lustful instincts, for it certainly wasn't won quickly and soon every woman had swallowed the apple in her crevice. But each continued to push sexily backwards and forwards on her apple-crowned staff.

At last, however, one of the performers contracted her organ tightly and determinedly around the bulging apple which was killing her with its size and pulled it off its stem of prick with a fierce sucking 'plop' which was heard throughout the hall. There was an immediate, raucous round of applause and a number of the spectators stood up to get a clearer view of the winner.

She was a slim, dark girl with top-heavy

breasts, surprisingly slim hips and strong, unusually big thighs. She was kneeling with her head hanging as if in exhaustion, her lips apart, the apple spreading her vagina and presenting it as a large, fruit-filled cavern. Her partner's rod was red and chafed from the friction of the apple during her efforts to remove it. He, too, was panting and had fallen forward onto his hands, his stomach heaving deeply.

The Pope stood up and clapped his hands yet again. There was a gradual slowing down of the tempo in the hall. Reluctantly, the remaining couples recognized that someone had succeeded. There was a cascade of fresh 'plops' as one after another they followed up their achievement. Now they were in a hurry for the last to succeed was to be refused sexual intercourse for two months.

One by one the apples were swallowed in expanding clefts. At last all the apples had been confined in their moist and temporary dwelling-places. The servants stood up, showing off the extended proportions of their stimulated stems.

"Right, honorable gentlemen," the Pope addressed himself to the guests. "I'm sure you'll all agree we've just witnessed a delicious spectacle. What will happen to the apples? Well, gentlemen, it's not often that you can have tasted the finest fruit inundated with the finest love-juice. So the ladies will now pass over their delectable morsels for your gourmet taste."

With that, the courtesans divested themselves of their fruit as if dropping babies from their wombs. Some squatted and ejected the apples with a straining effort into their hands; others opened their slits with their fingers and pulled out the fruit that way; others still allowed their partners to spread their nether lips and pull out the slippery spheres.

Each of the women then carried her issue to the long banqueting table and presented it to a man of her choice—a cardinal, a knight, a baron, whoever took her fancy.

The apples were wet, slightly slimy. Each recipient eagerly took the fruit, raised it to the donor and then bit into it with relish, swallowing great mouthfuls.

The courtesans watched with gleaming eyes, smiling at the avidity with which the orbs from their crying orifices were munched in the mouths of the princes and prelates.

Alexander gave a fresh order and the woman who had first managed to suck the apple from her bloated branch looked around at the specimens of genital rigidity. They were of all lengths and thicknesses—little to choose between them. She walked among them, feeling them for heat and fleshiness and eventually she chose that of a handsome young man whose prick was so shaped that it grew thicker and thicker from knob to base. Thus she would be ensured of fresh delight and surprise through all its length.

At a sign from the Pope, the servant pushed the woman face forwards over the banquet table. He seized a banana from a cluster in a nearby basket and thrust it into her exposed channel from behind. In and in he jogged it while the spread-eagled strumpet wriggled against the heavily draped edge of the table in front of a hundred pairs of high-ranking eyes.

For some minutes the servant shoved the banana into her, holding it by one ripe, yellow end until it had almost disappeared. Then he withdrew it at last and with the first sign of animation he'd shown, rammed his tapering prick into her moist cleft.

The ladies present didn't know which to look at most, his handsome, passion-wracked face or his enormous, penetrating penis. They watched in a thigh-rubbing fascination as he thrust deeper and deeper and the woman, bent under him, her breasts crushed against the table, groaned and pleaded for more.

He had settled down to a steady, moan-drawing rhythm, gripping her table-flattened hips, pulling at the same time as lower down he pushed, before Alexander glanced at where Lady Manfredi was wriggling on her seat, a slight smile on her lips.

"It pleases you to see such a scene?" he whispered with a smile.

"I can think of only one thing to please me better," she whispered back, glancing significantly at the place where his organ was hidden by his robes.

"We needn't wait for the end," he said. "Cardinal Rovere will take over."

"Let's go then," she said. "I can't wait."

CHAPTER 10

Against the disturbing scene of national and international events which saw Charles of France claim Naples and advance with his enormous army down upon Italy, the domestic carnality of the Borgia family continued.

While the Pope was trying to gain time by refusing passage to the French troops, and then giving way when Charles, supported now by the unruly northern barons, made it clear

126

he would brook no refusal, Lucrezia, tiring of her young husband, had reverted to relations with her brothers whom she still found—with her father—the most sexually exciting of men.

Her two favorites were still her brother Cesare and, now, his younger brother Giovanni, the Duke of Gandia. She had seen very little of Giovanni in her youth as he had spent even more time away at his studies than Cesare. During his young manhood, however, he had been brought back to Rome and had been kept in close attendance on the Pontiff, while Charles of France, reveling too early in his victory on Naples, had been cut off from the north by allied States and attacked from the south by the Spanish under Gonzalo de Cordoba.

Charles had escaped from the trap somewhat precipitously by the skin of his teeth leaving King Federigo of Aragon to be crowned in Naples behind him.

Throughout this period, Cesare and—unknown to his brother—Giovanni, had been sharing their beautiful sister during a long holiday she was taking from her husband in Rome.

*　　*　　*

It was only two nights before the two brothers were due to leave Rome together to the crowning of Federigo that Cesare arrived, unexpectedly, at the apartment that Lucrezia had been given by her father. He let himself in, discreetly, with the key he'd had made for his own purposes, and walked into the apartment to find Lucrezia spread-eagled on a couch, her knees pulled up almost touching her breasts, urging her sweating brother Giovanni to greater efforts to satisfy her.

They were making such a bustle with their

squirmings and pantings that neither was aware of his presence until he spoke.

"I had no idea that we were all so in love with the family."

His cutting tones broke through their abandonment and brought them both to a standstill. They lay together on the couch, staring at him in confusion. Lucrezia slowly put her legs down from their exaggerated position. Both lay, nude and panting, in a momentary, shocked silence.

Lucrezia gathered her wits first.

"Cesare, darling, you surely didn't think your rights on me were exclusive." She gave a little laugh at the monstrosity of the thought and smoothed her round belly with her hand.

"I didn't expect to find my own brother sticking his prick in you." His tone was hostile, controlled but dangerous. Again it was Lucrezia who spoke.

"You're sounding very moral all of a sudden, dear," she said smoothly. "After all, Giovanni knows all about you and he doesn't mind." She laughed again as if she was thoroughly enjoying the situation. She swung her legs off the couch and came toward Cesare, her big breasts pointing out at him. His eyes flickered. He was furious. It had shocked him to find his brother with her. He didn't analyze his feelings, but his reaction was very simple: he was consumed with a sudden, hating jealousy.

Lucrezia reached him and put her arms around his neck.

"I'm surprised at you, darling," she said. "You sound jealous—anyone would think you were my husband." She laughed a third time.

Cesare caught her arms, holding the flesh so hard that she cried out. He pulled them from his neck and pushed her away from him.

128

"You're just a whore," he snarled at her.

Lucrezia colored, her eyes pinpointed, but she kept control of herself.

"You're being quite ridiculous, Cesare," she snapped. "I think you'd better go and come back some evening when you've got a sense of proportion and reality."

She looked around at Giovanni, who had slid slowly off the couch in front of them. "Besides," she added spitefully, "Giovanni and I have some business to finish."

For a moment it seemed that Cesare would strike her. His dark eyes raged furiously from her to her brother. Then he turned with a scowl and went out.

Lucrezia turned to Giovanni. Her eyes had assumed a wide, innocent look of wonder.

"Well, well," she said, "would you ever have believed that—from him of all people?"

"Amazing," Giovanni agreed. "I do believe he's really in love with you."

Lucrezia looked thoughtful. Her eyes softened. She had already forgiven Cesare at the thought. Her mind wandered off on one of her now frequent fantasies.

Giovanni came over and stood behind her. He put his arms around her and pressed her breasts. She turned her face sideways toward him as she felt his hips pressing her rump and his trunk growing fat again.

"I wonder which of you I'd choose if I had to," she mused. "Do you think Cesare's really angry?"

"It won't last long."

He drew her back to the couch and pulled her down on it. She seemed to come suddenly back to the present, to become aware again and she opened her legs and put her arms up

129

to him, opening her mouth and beckoning him with the deep, reawakened desire in her eyes.

She closed her eyes with the sharp sensation as he drove into her and she dug her nails into his shoulders. For the moment she had made her choice.

*   *   *

Cesare was not outwardly hostile to his brother when they met the next night. Their mother, Vannozza—the truth had been admitted to them at last—was giving them a farewell supper in her vineyard at Trastevere.

They dined in the rose-surrounded terrace with a number of other guests—including their younger brother Giuffredo. The conversation was easy and quite gay although a close observer would probably have noticed that neither of the two older brothers addressed each other directly and hardly once so much as glanced at each other.

However, the two left together in the early hours, accompanied by a number of servants, and set out for Rome on horseback.

Within the city, Giovanni reined in his horse and took his leave. He announced to the company in general that he was going elsewhere to amuse himself. With one attendant, he set off toward the Jewish quarter.

Again, a very close observer whose attention was on Cesare rather than his brother would have noticed that a faint smile which contained both vengeance and a shade of triumph, fleeted over the former's face.

After the Duke of Gandia had left, the company continued on their way for a time until Cesare in turn announced that he, too, was going in search of a little relaxation. He set off alone in the opposite direction to that taken by his brother.

*   *   *

Giovanni trotted his horse gently down the narrow streets toward the river. He had said a passionate farewell to Lucrezia last night. Now there was a little Jewish maid with a body like quicksilver that he wished to take his leave of in an equally passionate manner tonight.

He allowed thoughts of Cesare to interrupt his excited anticipation of the fleshly joys in store for him. He didn't relish the journey with his brother tomorrow. He was aware that he was still culpable in his brother's eyes and the knowledge disquieted him; he knew how ruthless Cesare was capable of being.

With a quiet clatter of hooves, the two horses crossed a little, deserted square.

From it they passed into the gloom of another narrow street with the deeper oblong gloom of courtyard doorways.

They were near the river. Giovanni decided he could soon tell his servant to leave him. He didn't want the man making use of his knowledge of the little Jewess during his absence.

He called to the man, who was riding a little ahead of him.

"You may leave me now."

The servant saluted, glad to be relieved at last of his duty, and cantered back the way they had come. Giovanni continued on his way down the narrow street.

Hardly had the sounds of his retreating servant died before something flew from a dark alley and hit him on the side of the head.

It dazed him, but he remained in his saddle

131

with an instinctive effort and drew his sword, turning wildly in the direction of the dark alley mouth.

Immediately he was pulled off his horse from behind in a sharp, muffled bustle of grunts and swishings and the sudden rearing of his mount. Flashes of silver flew rapidly in quick arcs and the next moment the body of the Duke of Gandia was being dragged into the alley, while his mount went trotting on without him.

"Is he dead?" a voice asked in the sheltering gloom of the alley.

"Aye, sir, he's dead all right," came rough answering voices in loud whispers.

"Right. Sling him over my horse — and then lead on to the river."

There was a bustling in the darkness, followed by a moment's silence and then three rough-looking men in the garb of sailors crept out of the dark passage and started off in a slanting direction from the path taken by the riderless horse. At the first corner one of them looked back and beckoned.

Another sailor came out of the darkness — and immediately behind him came a horse carrying a richly-cloaked figure with a mask. Behind Cesare on the horse, his brother lay dead with a dozen stabs in his back and chest.

The macabre little party continued cautiously and unchallenged toward the river at the very point near the Bridge of St. Angelo where Cesare had some years earlier disposed of the first of his corpses.

At a point where the narrow streets of the city emptied onto the quayside, Cesare reined in and motioned the men forward. He watched while they crept stealthily out onto the quay and surveyed the surroundings, including a number of timber-laden boats on the river. One of them turned and waved him on.

He rode carefully down to the water's edge, to a point where the scavengers normally tipped their refuse carts into the river.

There, he turned the horse's hindquarters to the river and two of the men seized the prostrate body behind him and flung it as far out as they could into the river.

"Is he well out?" Cesare asked softly.

"Aye — well out, sir."

Cesare strained his eyes through the dimness. The river was calm as usual, disturbed only by the disappearing ripple of widening circles where the body had gone under.

"Good work," he said, and turned his horse into the shadows of the narrow street again.

A little later, when he arrived at Lucrezia's place, he was completely self-possessed. He told her he was sorry for his previous night's behavior and that he had already apologized to Giovanni.

He found Lucrezia was delighted with him and she continued to be that way when his penis was shattering up to her cervix. Little did she realize that in his mind he was taking further delicious revenge on his brother.

CHAPTER 11

Rome had been deeply shocked at the murder of the Duke of Gandia, but not a soul dreamed of attaching the blame to his brother — not even Lucrezia. It was generally assumed he had been done to death by some political enemy of the Borgia House.

Cesare certainly felt no remorse and left Rome with a sense of considerable satisfaction to attend the crowning ceremony in Naples.

Lucrezia, robbed of the attentions of both her brothers, was forced to rely again on her husband for her nightly pleasures. As before she found him so comparatively frigid that, with her passionate nature, his very presence eventually became quite obnoxious to her. Some months later the Pope, on her request, dissolved Lucrezia's marriage to the young lord — on the grounds that he was *impotens et frigidus natura* — an impotence which was admitted by himself, and then became so widely published and lampooned that he became furious and in retaliation publicly accused the Borgias of incest. It was a charge which seemed so obviously designed to draw attention from his own comic state that nobody — not even the most gullible of the public — believed him.

After the dissolvement of the marriage, Lucrezia withdrew to the Convent of San Sisto in the Appian Way — partly to escape the various items of scandal which were rocking Rome, partly to appear to act with the decorum her situation demanded.

She was to spend a period of some six months in her own private quarters, taking part with the nuns in daily prayers, joining with them in much of their work.

For some weeks she lived with them, praying, making baskets, carving small figurines in wood, walking in the quiet grounds, feeding their dozen hens. She was happy for a time to be free of the world in which she always felt a little as if she was living on the summit of a volcano that was likely to erupt unexpectedly.

But, at the end of that time, accustomed as

she was to fierce and frequent intercourse, she began to feel an aching void in her loins, began to consider how to best soothe it.

During her walks in the grounds she had particularly befriended a young nun who had been in the convent only a short time before her. This young girl, whose name was Carlotta, was designated to show Lucrezia how to make the baskets and the little wooden figurines.

They got on very well and it soon became apparent to Lucrezia that the younger and unworldly Carlotta was quite fascinated by her.

Lucrezia managed, cleverly, to discover that the girl, who had never had a lover, was taking ill to her new and voluntary exile. She felt in her a need which she didn't understand, although listening to her confused explanations, Lucrezia was only too well aware of the trouble — the young girl needed a good fuck.

Carlotta was very attractive in her own way. She was dark, with a long face and slightly Jewish nose dominating long, well-defined lips. Her body was completely concealed under the shrouds of her long robes, but the melancholy attraction of her face was quite enough to excite Lucrezia in her present manless state.

Giving way to the girl's hinted-at curiosity, Lucrezia began, during their walks in the grounds, to tell her a few things about her sexual life. But always she exaggerated the brutality of the male, making him sound an utter, unbearable brute.

"I don't think I could stand to have a man using me in such a way," Carlotta said one morning as they sat staring at the water lilies in the little stream which ran sluggishly through the lower reaches of the convent grounds. "I should feel stripped of any sense of dignity I'd ever had."

Lucrezia took the plunge.

"Yes. If the choice was between man and this convent, I would choose a cloistered existence within these walls," she said. "But, fortunately there are other things one can do."

The girl raised her fine, dark eyebrows.

"What — other things in place of a man?"

"A woman, Carlotta. Women are much gentler and more loving than men. And they understand a woman's needs whereas most men are selfish and oafish in their lovemaking."

"But . . ."

"I think," Lucrezia went on quickly, "much as I respect the Mother Superior and the individual right of choice, that any woman who locks herself away in a prison is betraying her function as a woman and displaying a fear of the world which belief in God should not justify."

Carlotta stared at her, shocked. She had never dared to voice such sentiments, but they fitted well with her present mood of boredom and rebellion.

"You only have to look at the majority of the women here," Lucrezia continued, "and you see immediately that they're women who are too ugly or too witless to succeed in a competitive and natural world."

She took Carlotta's hand.

"But you don't belong among them, Carlotta. You are lovely and full of life which won't allow itself to be kept in check forever."

The girl was flattered and moved by the words which were spoken to her in such sincere tones. They sped her own unformed impulses along the channel that Lucrezia intended.

"I feel you are right," she said. She glanced around at the distant figures of the other nuns wandering in the upper part of the grounds among the trees. "I'm beginning to wish I hadn't taken my vows."

"You should make the best of things as they are," Lucrezia said. "We are both in the same cul-de-sac of frustration. We should help each other."

"But what can we . . .?"

"We can take the place of men for each other."

The girl dropped her eyes and gazed down at the lilies. There was a silence for some seconds.

"I — I wouldn't know how . . . and — and I'm not sure that it's . . ."

"We all have deep centers in our beings which others may never reach," Lucrezia cut in, "but unless they do, unless we try to help them to, we all live lonely, unsatisfied lives, lives which wrinkle us up with bitterness, the feeling of having missed what was essential."

Carlotta raised her eyes from the stream and found herself unable again to withdraw them from Lucrezia's deep, compelling gaze.

"Come to my quarters after evensong tonight," Lucrezia went on, "and I will show you what it means to reach that center."

The dull peal of a bell calling them in to prayer cut short any reply the young girl might have made. She stared at Lucrezia, dropped her eyes at last and walked away toward the building. Lucrezia smiled after her for a moment and then slowly followed her.

*　　*　　*

That evening, alone in her quarters — two

rooms at the far end of a wing of the convent — Lucrezia, garbed only in a dressing gown, waited for Carlotta to come. She was almost certain she would come although the girl had given her no answer. She knew how the possibility of sexual adventure could play on one's nerves, stimulating, frightening, exciting all at the same time.

For Lucrezia, too, this would be the first lesbian experience and the idea filled her with the same lustful chill of eagerness that her first fuck had — especially as she had been deprived of her conjugal and fraternal rights for some weeks now.

She found herself unable to keep still as the minutes went by following evensong. She rose time and time again and looked out of the sloping window down to the grounds. At last she sat on her bed and tried to concentrate on the pages of Boccaccio's *Il Decamerone* which she had smuggled into the convent with her.

As time passed she became more and more anxious. If Carlotta didn't come now she would die of frustration. She put down the book and stared out of the window again before walking into the next room where she studied herself in a small, silver-backed hand mirror.

Her heart leapt as there came a light tapping on her door. She ran to open it and almost clasped the young girl to her bosom as she drew her into her room.

Carlotta smiled at her briefly and stood uncertainly just inside the door while Lucrezia closed and bolted it.

"Make yourself at home," Lucrezia urged, turning around to her.

Nervously, the girl went to the window and looked out as if to reassure herself that the outside world was there, solid and unchanged. Lucrezia watched her pretending to interest herself in the exploration of the rooms, pretending to examine the few books, flicking pages over with a pointless speed.

"I was afraid to come," she said at last. "Wasn't that ridiculous — we are quite free to visit one another's rooms."

"We are quite free to act as we please," Lucrezia added.

"Yes," the girl said uncertainly.

"I have another gown — why don't you make yourself more comfortable and put it on," Lucrezia suggested.

She handed over the garment and Carlotta took it nervously.

Lucrezia turned away and studied *Il Decamerone,* listening to the rustle of clothes as Carlotta slipped out of them. She kept swallowing with nervous excitement.

At a well-judged moment she glanced around and caught her companion naked. Carlotta gazed at her with wide, embarrassed eyes and Lucrezia glanced back at her book immediately. But not before she'd had a glimpse of the girl's small, firm breasts, high up and dark, with the splodge of dark nipple giving them body, and her slim figure below it with the eye-catching fuzz of dark hair above her thighs. Lucrezia felt almost matronly beside the girl's small proportions.

She did not look up again until the girl came and sat beside her on the bed. Carlotta seemed to have lost some of her uncertainty. It was as if she'd reminded herself that she had, after all, come for a specific purpose and that there was no point in trying to pretend she hadn't.

Lucrezia replaced the book on a shelf over the

bed and lay back on it, looking at her companion. Carlotta looked even more attractive out of her nun's somber garb, and the long V-neck of the gown revealed a smooth stretch of her succulent-looking skin between her breasts. The beginning of their bulge on either side of the valley of flesh was heaving with a nervous emotion.

"You are really very lovely," Lucrezia told her. "It was a great mistake for a girl like you to get such a mad idea in her head that she wanted to pass the rest of her days in a tomb."

The conversation brought a sense of normalcy with it and Carlotta's voice hid a trace of relief as if a spell had been broken.

"If you hadn't come, I might never have realized it," she answered.

"Sooner or later you would have — but I'm glad it's through me that your revolution is to be achieved."

Carlotta had again, as in the afternoon, become lost in Lucrezia's eyes. They seemed to hold her hypnotically. She came, as if Lucrezia had commanded her, and lay down on the bed beside her. Lucrezia touched the girl's cheek, lightly.

"Remember that this is the only way to liberate yourself from the horror and monotony of a death in life," she said softly as her lips followed her hand.

Lucrezia was not very surprised to find that a relationship with a woman gave her as strong an erotic urge as with a man. It was as if it were something she'd always known, even when her conscious thought had included nothing but images of Cesare's, her father's, Giovanni's embraces. Now she felt the soft, smooth skin of the girl's cheek against her lips, a softness and

140

a leafy fragrance which were missing in a man, and she felt her spirit stirred with the upsetting excitement of a new and forbidden experience about to come to fruition.

She slipped her hand into the girl's gown and Carlotta winced. Then her hand was caressing the small, firm breast with the lightest of touches. Her lips moved over the girl's face without losing contact — and found her lips. The lips were still, slightly reluctant and unsure. But as Lucrezia's hand moved from one breast to the other and tweaked the nipple, as her tongue played hide and seek with Carlotta's lips, the mouth opened with a sound which was near to a sigh, the lips relaxed and then kissed back.

Lucrezia's tongue gave up its game and lunged right out to fill the mouth which opened and spread at its assault.

Gently, her hand untied the belt of the gown. The material slipped slowly down to the bed off the glossy flesh of Carlotta's hips and thighs.

Lucrezia's hand rested on the girl's waist for a moment, the index finger playing with her navel. She noticed the girl was trembling faintly, like a leaf in the merest zephyr. She let her hand float away over the glassy expanse of flesh, lingering, unhurried, exploring every part while her tongue continued to caress the moist, heavily-breathing lips.

As her advancing fingers encountered the silky van of pubic hair, she slowed. She let her fingers course through it as through money. Under it she could feel the flesh swollen in a little mound, like a slight rise in the ground covered with a fine grass.

Carlotta wriggled her hips very slightly. She

141

seemed ashamed of their movement, which was like an effort at escape.

Lucrezia sucked heavily on the lips which were trembling now in unison with the body.

With her free hand, she awkwardly unpulled her own belt and then pushed the plump flesh of her thigh against Carlotta's.

Slowly, as if stroking a timid animal, she allowed her fingers to continue on their downward progress. They moved down the rise and into the hot, little hollow between the oozing flesh of Carlotta's tightly-gripped thighs. Her path was barred for the moment by the instinctive inward pressure of those thighs. She stroked all the flesh she could reach and was rewarded with a sudden seepage of moisture around her fingers.

She moved her lips off Carlotta's and kissed her neck.

"Relax, darling," she whispered. "Open your legs."

"I can't bear it," Carlotta whispered back after a moment. "It makes me jump every time you touch me."

"All right — just let it go naturally. It'll come."

Lucrezia went on with her gentle fondling. The hollow was very warm now and Carlotta was letting out an odd "oh" every so often from deep down in her throat.

Moving her lips down the neck, over the slim shoulders, Lucrezia invaded the breasts which were taut and straining with sensation. She closed her mouth over a nipple and sucked hard and strong, bringing forth gasps of torment from the girl.

Carlotta's thighs relaxed and, awaiting her moment, Lucrezia was able suddenly to advance

142

her fingers so that the texture of flesh changed and she knew she was in the beginning of the wet ravine formed by those nether lips. Carlotta clasped her thighs together again, crushing the tormenting hand, but Lucrezia bore the weight and tickled the wet flesh with her fingertips.

She drew on the nipple again with her lips, sucking in as much of the breast behind it as she could.

Carlotta thrust her breast at the lips which seemed to be drawing milk from her shapely udders. She arched her hips and gave way suddenly, opening her thighs, relaxing them so that the raping hand was suddenly right between her legs, the fingers in at their target.

Lucrezia moved a finger in the suddenly conquered vagina. Carlotta groaned in submission.

Slowly Lucrezia titivated and explored the flood-washed well. She pushed in through the tight ring of flesh, to the accompaniment of a little squeal from Carlotta. She thrust up, and then up again, feeling the hips withdraw instinctively, pull up away from the hand and then ooze back as they became used to the exquisite pressure.

Steadily Lucrezia sucked the breast, gnawed it, remembering all the things she liked a man to do and doing them with that greater finesse which was born of her own intimate, subjective knowledge.

Her fingers could move more loosely, more freely now. The ravine had become a great river, like a dried-up wadi suddenly swollen with the seasonal rains, the channel leading from it had become bigger, more accommodating and the hips were moving and bobbing against hers, brushing her flesh with another's exciting, strange flesh.

Breathing hard herself, Lucrezia moved her finger out of the hole and fastened it on the hard little clitoris which had reared up with its first touch from an alien hand.

Carlotta cried out and then spread her thighs in complete, won-over invitation as the finger bit into that little stem of sensitive flesh. She was wriggling incessantly, her mouth wide open, gasping for air.

"Oh God, oh God!" she exclaimed.

Lucrezia worked furiously and delightedly on the clitoris which expanded at her touch, grew harder, longer. She could feel passion growing in it as her finger and thumb pinched it, tweaked it, stroked it, masturbated it. There was only one thing left to make Carlotta's initiating delight into utter rapture.

Lucrezia slid down her body, reveling in the tight, straining pressure of flesh against hers. Her wet lips followed the swells and hollows of the body in their descent. She withdrew down to Carlotta's thighs with them. She ran her lips down the thighs, kissing tantalizingly on their buttery, yielding insides. The thighs twitched, clasped her head, relaxed. She heard the fury of Carlotta's moans washing down upon her ears like the continual flow of waves against a reef.

Her thighs clasped and unclasped, tensed and untensed continually; her hips wriggled like fish on a hook and she was fastened to the bed with her own overwhelming passion which was no longer timid but demanding.

Sliding her lips up the thighs, Lucrezia met first the slippery ooze of fluid glossing the tops of the legs. She lapped it like a dog. It repre-

144

sented the passion of a lovely girl — nothing unpalatable about that.

Over the swamp and to the very brink of the ravine, a plunge of the tongue and she was kissing and licking in that inundated wadi which squirmed and pressed against her and squashed its side flat against her mouth.

She searched, her tongue leading her blindly in the wadi until she found that steep, stiff monument. She grasped it in her lips and Carlotta's hips went mad, writhing and twisting so that Lucrezia had to hang onto her prize as if she were on a wild horse. But she clung to it, sucking it voraciously while a thin whine of passion, broken often by a deep moan, crashed down on her ears from the tortured face high up above her.

Her hands grasped those slim hips. How slim they were compared to her own. They made Carlotta seem that much more girlish, innocent, helpless.

She slid her hands under the hips and ran them all around the firm, tense balls of bottom. What an excellent little bottom.

She squeezed and worked its pliable bulk as she sucked and licked. The buttocks tightened and relaxed in her hands, swinging wildly in torment. The girl had become a raging form of sexuality. There seemed nothing left of her except a moaning, writhing mass of sensual flesh.

Lucrezia pulled the buttocks apart forcibly. They were hot in the crack between them. There were a few young hairs and then a sweating smoothness. Her fingers slipped over it like little snakes.

The anus nestled there, unprotected now and she rifled it with her fingers they way she'd liked her father to intrude in hers. And Carlotta had no reticence any longer. She didn't even try to press her backside cheeks together. On the contrary she pressed them wide and back so that Lucrezia's finger actually penetrated the anus, the tight little ring of flesh, near to her sucking lips.

She used her tongue on the clitoris which seemed so big as to be unreal. There was a taste of salt and parsley in her mouth; the liquid was running over her face, growing into a torrent.

Above, out of sight, she heard Carlotta's sob.

"Oh, oh, it's here, it's here," she heard her cry, out of control.

She sucked even more furiously, jabbing her finger deeply into the tight, tearing hole. She was terribly excited herself. She got a vicarious pleasure from the girl's helpless passion.

Following on her gasped out words, Carlotta twisted first one way and then the other in a quick, shivering convulsion. Her mouth opened wide and a long, continuous moan of sound exploded from it as she clasped her thighs around Lucrezia's head and squeezed.

The grip on Lucrezia was strong and suffocating, but she bore it until it slowly relaxed and the thighs fell away.

She straightened up, realizing just how hot her loins had become. A little longer and she'd probably have come herself.

She looked at Carlotta. The girl seemed to have collapsed in a coma. She lay with her head thrown back dramatically, her arms wide out beside her head. Her eyes were closed, her breasts heaving in a great swell of emotion.

Lucrezia lay down alongside her and kissed her shoulder. After a while she spoke.

"Wasn't that worth a year in a convent? Isn't it worth anything on earth?"

146

Carlotta's eyes opened slowly, sleepily. She'd lost all trace of her early embarrassment.

"I feel purged," she said softly. "I feel satisfied and purged of all the frustration and not knowing that I've ever felt."

Lucrezia smiled at her and kissed her bare arm.

"You obviously enjoyed it," she agreed. "Your enjoyment was so infectious that I almost had a climax myself."

Carlotta opened her eyes again and looked at her. Realization had dawned that there were, of course, two of them, that Lucrezia had given her undreamed-of pleasure, that it was now up to her to reciprocate.

"I'm not at all expert," she said. "I shan't know what to do."

Lucrezia began to quiver with anticipation.

"Just do what I did," she said with a break in her voice. "And that will be wonderful."

"I have to get my breath back a moment."

They lay together for a few minutes longer. Lucrezia could hardly wait and she kept pressing her round belly again Carlotta's side and tensing her pelvis against her.

"God, I want it very badly!" she muttered.

At that Carlotta turned over toward her and she fell backwards on the bed. She lay there staring up at the ceiling concentrating on herself, looking inward at the sensation inside her.

She felt the warm face come down on her breasts. To Carlotta her breasts were enormous in comparison with her own. They just asked to be nestled against, to be used as a pillow in which to bury one's face.

The face brushed against the tight, hurting points of her breasts, piquing her with a spear-

147

point of ecstatic pain that rushed straight to her genitals. And then those cool, well-defined lips closed on her nipple in a soft, fondling grip that made her squirm already.

They began to suck, drawing her pear of breast into the mouth, drawing it in, in, swallowing it, sucking it, pulverizing it with sharp, needed pain.

Lucrezia's legs began to jerk in spasms and the unknown fingers slid down her body, the image of her own, and went straight to the spot which played no timid games with them but waited, wide open like a trap, thighs wide apart and squirming.

Lucrezia held her breath waiting for the contact, expecting it, but still jumping with delight when it came. Cool fingers caressed her long, deep cleft which was stinging as the juices were washed into it from her inner regions.

The fingers explored like timid animals—and everywhere they touched and slid they left a burning, a prickling sense of near-destruction.

Lucrezia groaned. She liked to groan. She let the groans escape from her mouth—not that she could really have controlled them—to show her appreciation of what was being done to her.

Then with a sudden jump she felt the fingertips find her little erection. That was too much. She squirmed her hips in a movement that was almost circular, that was wild, exaggerated.

And the fingers were relentless. They pressed there, loved there, pinched there, gave no quarter although her moans became helpless sobs of passion.

Lucrezia felt her hole growing wide. The love-juice was swamping, too, and her belly

148

was in unbearable torment. There couldn't be much more to go.

"Your mouth, your mouth!" she pleaded.

The fingers came out of her sultry cleft giving her a brief respite. But they were replaced immediately by a pair of cool lips which seized on her clitoris, sending a shock through her whole body.

"Oh, wonderful, wonderful!" she gasped. She could hardly utter the words. They tumbled out in a rush of sound which was mostly escaping breath, wheezing out like steam from a hot spring.

The mouth was working hard, giving her no chance to catch her breath. She was out of breath as if she'd been running hard.

And then the hands, remembering, slid around her hips and dug handfuls from her big buttocks, rummaging between them to find the anal orifice.

"Wonderful, wonderful!" she breathed again, lost and helpless.

She felt the heat like a great wood fire down in her passage. It was as hot as a lump of smoldering charcoal, felt ready to splinter into pieces at any moment.

"It's coming . . . it's . . . coming . . . oh!" she gasped, more as an outlet for her feeling than as a warning. She jerked her legs this way and that as if they were puppets and she held the strings. Speech was now impossible. The sounds from her mouth were animal noises, enlarging in abandon with every lick of that tongue on her erect little organ.

She clamped her legs around Carlotta's head and squeezed her loins up at her face, forcing, straining, arching. She felt the burst, the splintering and she cried out, stifling her cries with

149

her fist as the last suck drew her liquid passion through her channel.

A new and regular activity was begun in the quiet haven of the convent.

CHAPTER 12

While Lucrezia was still enjoying her quiet life in the convent, Cesare was pondering his future.

For some time now a marriage between him and Carlotta of Aragon, whom he had never seen, but of whose beauty he had heard, had been in the offing. To achieve this marriage, the Pope had been in contact with the new King of France, Louis XII, trying to enlist his support.

As was usual in these cases nothing was given for nothing, nobody gave his support if he gained nothing in return. So it was with Louis.

He chose this moment to apply to Rome for the dissolution of his marriage with Jeanne de Valois, daughter of Louis XI—an application which the Pope readily conceded to.

In the way that this sort of bargaining gathered momentum, the Pope freshly asked that Louis should confer the duchy of Valentinois on Cesare.

In this way he hoped to settle ownership of a morsel of territory in Dauphiné which had long been disputed between France and the Holy See. The claims of the Church would be given up — but Cesare Borgia would be in power.

Louis granted all this in turn, asking at the same time for a cardinal's hat for an old friend of his and a dispensation to marry the beautiful widow of Charles VIII, Anne of Brittany. So the wrangling, conducted in an aura of politeness and political courtesy, came to an end.

Cesare chose this moment to crave permission to doff the purple. He had long ago been made a cardinal, but Carlotta's father, Federigo of Aragon, would not have his daughter marry a priest. Her dowry, it was known, would be enormous—and Cesare prized money and territory above all at this time.

The only cardinal to stand out against this move was Cardinal Ximenes, the Spanish representative, who saw through the move and the proposed marriage an imminent alliance between France and the Holy See—an alliance which would not be at all in the interests of Spain.

Alexander routed these objections with the unanswerable pronouncement that he could not hinder Cesare's renunciation of the purple, as such a renunciation had clearly become necessary for the salvation of his soul. To appease Spain, however, he bestowed all Cesare's yielded benefices on Spanish churchmen.

Thus it was that Cesare Borgia, Duke of Valentinois, set out for the Court of France where Carlotta of Aragon was being raised.

His suite was enormous, with one hundred attendants, a dozen chariots and a score of mules for his baggage and presents for his future hosts.

In spite of the early hour chosen for departure, Rome was packed with people fighting to catch a glimpse of the newly-created Duke and to cheer him on his journey toward his prospective wife.

Cesare rode at the head of his retinue, following the Tiber along the Trastevere. He was mounted on a large white charger caparisoned in red silk and gold brocade—the colors of France. The Duke's doublet was of white damask laced with gold; a mantle of black velvet covered his shoulders, matched by a black velvet cap, studded with rubies.

Behind him his lackeys also wore the colors of France, as did his Roman gentlemen. The Spaniards in his cortege, however, retained the costumes of their native land.

The procession, hemmed in by cheering crowds, was escorted to the end of the Banchi by four cardinals. The Pope, his heart swollen with pride at the sight of his son so gorgeously arrayed, watched from a window of the Vatican.

At Ostia, the whole retinue boarded a ship, which, with a protective fleet of galleys Louis had sent to fetch the new Duke, set off for the coast of France.

* * *

Over a week later, they dropped anchor at Marseilles, where the Duke was met by the Bishop of Dijon, who had been sent by the King to meet him.

From Marseilles the glorious procession rode on to Avignon, everywhere watched by gaping crowds who broke out into cheers from the very awe of its color and royal appearance.

At Avignon, Cesare was met by Cardinal della Rovere, who was to escort him to the King's court at Chinon.

A month or so after leaving Italy, Cesare was welcomed by Louis in an atmosphere of pomp, ceremony and cordiality—a welcome he was not to receive from the lady he had come to woo.

In spite of Cesare's good looks and strong personality, Carlotta hedged and procrastinated until it became clear to all that she was not going through with the marriage. The background reasons were, of course, political and Carlotta followed the instructions of her father's ambassador. She also displayed a certain hauteur towards the Duke of Valentinois on the few occasions when they came into contact.

The final blow came when Cesare, who was impressed by the beauty and inaccessibility of the princess, sent word telling her in the most courteous of paraphrasing that he could not wait forever in the court of France and that he failed to see what was delaying her decision.

Carlotta sent back a message saying that her family was not in the habit of being pressed— even by Italian blood of noble ancestry. This was an open slight on Cesare's foreign origin and social history which cut him to the quick. He began immediately to plan his revenge, taking into his confidence his closest attendants and companions.

It was common knowledge that almost every day in the afternoon, Carlotta, a few ladies-in-waiting and a handful of male attendants went riding for exercise in the woods near the King's court. They would often be away for two or even three hours, cutting across the hillocks and hollows until the brush and trees became too thick for further progress. Sometimes they would descend from their mounts and continue their promenade on foot a short time—all dependent on Carlotta's whim of the moment.

Cesare had the movements of the little band

watched for a few days while he lingered on in the hospitality of Louis—who was somewhat embarrassed that his end of the bargain had not been fulfilled, through no fault of his own.

During the mornings, Cesare himself would ride discreetly out into the forest with a few of his men to explore, to scout out the ground on which he was going to carry out his plan—the rape of Carlotta.

At the beginning of an afternoon a few days after the princess's curt reply to Cesare's entreaty to make up her mind, the Duke and some twenty of his men rode out into the forest. In a clearing not far from the spot where Carlotta and her company usually began their jaunts, they all changed into a motley collection of clothing such as might well be worn by the bands of outlaws which infested the forests farther to the south. Several of the band then rode back to the forest outskirts and posted themselves to watch the approach of the princess.

Cesare had not long to wait before the first of the lookouts raced back to report the entry of Carlotta into the wood at a certain point.

For the next two hours the Duke and his men silently shadowed the unsuspecting party from the court. They kept well in the wings, only the lookouts keeping the party in sight. The laughs of the women would filter through the leaves and the sunlight every now and again, whetting the appetites of the stalkers who were soon going to enjoy their bodies.

A light breeze rustled through the foliage, conveniently covering the soft swishings of the horses, trampling through the grass and leaves. Nobody in the Duke's band spoke, communication being made simply through signs. The horses had been muzzled.

Deeper into the deserted forest the two bands made their way. Sometimes, from a ridge, they would have a view of the trees stretching out solidly in a great plain before them, at others they were almost enmeshed in a web of leaves and creepers as they advanced.

It was late in the afternoon and the sun was well down in the sky when a lookout came trotting gently back to report that Carlotta and her band had reached a spot near some rocks and had dismounted to pick some flowers.

At a sign from Cesare, his men donned rough masks of sacking which they had made themselves. They dismounted, unhitched bows and arrows from their horses, hobbled the animals and began to creep through the brush toward the spot indicated by the lookout.

They moved slowly, crouching, making use of every available cover, avoiding twigs with mathematical determination. As the sound of voices whispered through, they began to fan out, to surround the unsuspecting flower-pickers.

The wall of foliage became slighter and slighter, until Cesare, slipping slowly from tree to tree, could see the white garments of the women through the spaces in the low-hanging branches. He crouched lower and advanced a step at a time until the whole scene was clear to him. He stopped, a man on either side of him, and listened. There was no sound from his men, invisibly surrounding the small, rocky clearing.

The women, buxom wenches, were laughing and talking as they helped the princess gather

her blooms. The princess, herself, was in a gay mood which, for the moment, chased the haughtiness from her face, leaving only the tilt of her features to suggest her pride, her disdain of lesser mortals who thought themselves as good as herself.

Around the women the male attendants— less than a dozen of them—idled and wandered and exchanged a few words with each other.

Such a blissful, sylvan scene, Cesare thought with a grim inward chuckle. What a shock was in store for them. He watched Carlotta, laughing, unaware, bending to the ground. His lips curled in desire and revenge. He'd soon take that haughtiness from her, he'd soon debase her so that she couldn't lift her head again with that proud tilt. He'd provide the French Court and Society with the scandal of the decade— at Carlotta's expense. He'd have her haughty, inaccessible cunt so filled with prick that she'd never be able to close her legs again.

He straightened his bow in front of him, silently fitted an arrow. The two men at his sides followed suit. He took aim, slowly. He gave a sharp, piercing whistle and let fly. His arrow slashed straight through the neck of one of the men-at-arms. The man uttered a strangled, coughing cry and staggered to his knees before falling flat on his face.

The sunlight of the clearing was suddenly crisscrossed with a hail of arrows. All around the horrified women, their escorts crumpled up and ceased to exist. The attendants had no chance to escape. A few managed, pathetically, to draw their swords and start uncertainly toward the woods at their nearest point. They never got as far as the first thickness of foliage.

156

In the space of a few minutes the ground was littered with the still bodies of the dead. The women had gathered around Carlotta and were cringing in terror. The forest around them had relapsed into a temporary silence.

Cesare smiled his satisfaction and raised his bow once again. His arrow pierced the clothing of one of the ladies-in-waiting, stabbing through the hem of her dress and pinning it to the ground. There was a guffaw of laughter from his men on all sides at the sign—and then they moved into the clearing, a sinister-looking bunch with their rough masks.

Some of the women screamed as they were seized by the men. Their screams were stifled with rough and ruthless hands. Their clothes were torn from them, their eyes blindfolded with strips from their own undergarments.

Overcome with horror and a helpless indignation, some of the women struggled desperately, others yielded, sobbing and pleading for mercy.

Cesare watched while Carlotta was stripped. She was weeping, but more in rage and shame than fear. During her manhandling she continuously threatened and cursed the men who were denuding her. Her clothes were in rags by the time her captors succeeded in getting them off her and she stood between them, trying to cover breasts and loins at the same time.

Cesare's heart began pumping faster as they blindfolded her. She was small and slim, with a sinuous, perfectly proportioned body. Her breasts were not large, but they were high and firm with a luxurious curve which made him itch to run his hand slowly, gently around it; her hips were well-molded with a thrust of flesh on the peak of the bones; her legs were slim and rounded into light curves of muscle.

A delicate morsel, he thought, as his men began to march her toward the point where he still stood in the shelter of the surrounding bushes. If I can't have her legally, I'm sure I'll lose little by having her against her will. She'll still be warm, juicy flesh and blood. Her hips will still yield under mine, her breasts will still press hard against my flesh, her thighs will still ache from being spread so wide, her passage will still grow wet in spite of herself— and her hauteur. He clacked his tongue in satisfaction at the rape of her dignity, her reputation.

The strange trio had reached him while the thoughts wafted through his head. Close up she was more perfect than ever. He could see the moisture on her skin — the sweat of fear. He could make out the light down on parts of her body, a mole beneath her left breast, the puckered, corrugated skin around the base of her nipple, the slight quiver of her thighs as she approached.

He made a sign to his men and took her by the arms as they released her. Nobody spoke, no voices were to leave traces in her memory. With a wave, Cesare dismissed the men back to the clearing where the rest of his band were drawing lots for the order of ravishing the other women.

Left alone with her, he marched her in front of him, holding a slim bicep in each hand, away from the clearing.

She had a slim, straight back, a firm curve to her spine. The narrow waist rounded out into a fleshy dome of bottom which quivered sinuously as she walked. Her buttocks were like the heads on columns, rounded, well-fitting from the well-shaped, classical thighs. He put one hand down against her buttocks as she walked and the brushing of them, smooth as eggs, made his hand tingle, brought his penis crushing up inside his clothing, giving it that solid, blood-filled ache which only intercourse would relieve.

"Whoever you are I warn you you'll lose your head for this," she snapped suddenly, with a choke in her voice.

For answer he slapped each of her buttocks in turn. She squirmed and tried to break free but his grasp tightened on her arm so strongly that she cried out with pain and stumbled forward.

"If you get my clothes and put me on a horse I'll arrange a pardon for you personally," she urged with a sob. "You're all doomed—but you who are with me can be saved if you help me."

He jabbed his thumb between her quivering buttocks as she finished her desperate speech and she cried out and tried again to squirm away. He pulled her back toward him to control her and felt her buttocks writhing against his erection. He joggled against her, crushing his penis against her flesh, rotating it around the inner banks of the ravine between them.

"You beast, you swine!" She was crying bitterly again. He rubbed his hands over her breasts and sucked her neck as she struggled vainly. He had to get in her quickly.

Flushed and perspiring, he pushed her forward again. He ran his hand down her spine, let it swoop out with the lift of her buttocks. She kicked back at him and he slashed the flat of his hand across her rump anew.

At a distance from the clearing where he could no longer hear the scuffling of activity, he tied her to a tree while he cut four stakes with his dagger. The stakes he shoved deep into the ground in a rough square. He went back to the tree and looked at his victim. Now that she was in his power he tortured himself, gloating over her body, taking his time in the preparation.

He kissed her lips and she started at the unexpected assault. The lips trembled under his and tried to drag away but he pressed on them hard and bit them so that a muffled cry of protest tried to escape from her throat. He moved his mouth off her and nibbled her nipples.

"Oh, you swine, you swine! If you touch me I promise you you'll be tortured to death!"

He sucked the breast, letting it bulge right into his mouth like a perfect rounded fruit. He moved his mouth again and kissed her belly. She tried to fight him off with her legs, but emotion was exhausting her.

Cesare stepped back after a while and slowly began to undress. He stripped gradually, garment by garment, feeling the cool touch of air on his naked flesh. He revealed his loins last and a tremor of excitement ran through his body as his penis shot warmly into the cool atmosphere and soared there, tensed up, in a static thrust against nothing.

He went close to her and untied her from the tree. She felt his naked body as he brushed against her and she began to fight, weeping almost hysterically at the same time. She was no match for him. He held her easily in his arms while he pressed his hot joint against her loins, against her behind as she twisted. His knob was a deep blood-color; it had moistened over.

With a grunt of effort he pulled her to the ground and tied her wrist to one of the stakes.

She jerked against it while he held her other wrist and moved the second stake to a more suitable distance before tying the second wrist.

He smiled with lustful satisfaction at his work and pulled her left leg wide out from her body, as near a right angle with her hips as he could make it. She tried to kick him, gasping with pain and rage. That leg fastened, he caught the other and pulled it wide, moving the last stake over. The angle between her thighs was now an obtuse one. It left wide and unprotected that mass of delight between her white columns. He gazed down at her. The lips of her vagina were pink and fleshy, a muff of hair receded from their surroundings.

Cesare walked in between her legs and pressed her vagina with his big toe. She gave a little scream and tried to recoil.

"You can have anything if you'll get me a horse," she gasped, "pardon, money, jewels—anything you want!"

He inserted his toe slowly in her vagina. He felt it open and yield and he jogged his toe into her. His penis was sticking straight out from his loins like a handle; a drop of moisture dripped from it onto her belly.

He grinned and knelt down between her legs, staring at the opening he was going to fuck. He wanted to make her degradation complete. He lay down between her thighs with his face right up against her mossy opening. He pulled the lips wide apart with his thumbs and pushed his lips against her warm flesh. He kissed and licked and then he poked out his tongue into her hole.

Carlotta strained at her bonds and gasped out exclamations of horror and shock.

"Please, please!" she begged. "No, no!"

161

Cesare continued to lick. He had found the clitoris which was soft, unresponding and was sucking it hard, intending to hurt her physically as well as mentally.

At the same time he slipped his hands up under her behind, his fingers rustling on the bed of old leaves on which she was pinioned. Her buttocks squirmed tight and cringed at his touch. But so widely were her legs splayed apart that she couldn't hide her dark, little hole and he began to push it and pull it apart, so near to his lips.

"Oh, God, God, no, no!" Carlotta was almost in an hysterical delirium. But that only increased his thirst for revenge.

He released her anus after a while and caught both her wide-spread thighs, pulling her pelvis down at his mouth, pushing his tongue up into her passage as far as it would go. She was small, and obviously a virgin. He wondered if she'd bleed when he had her. He wondered if it would shame her more to bleed. Perhaps he shouldn't finger her too much for fear of making his passage easier.

He brought his tongue out of her and knelt up on both knees, looking at her body. She was a flesh and blood dummy there for him to use. There was nothing she could do or say to stop him from doing anything he wanted to in any way he pleased.

He lay down on her and slithered up her body. She gasped again at the horror of his weight on her and what it meant. Her breasts were firm and springy under him, balancing him up like two rubber cushions. Down at his thighs was a void, just the leaves under him, no thighs of hers, nothing. She was pulled too widely apart; there was just the almost horizontal line of legs and pelvis.

He put his hand down there and felt for her aperture. It was moist, but tight, difficult to open a little. He took his prick in his hand and aimed the knob at the small hole he'd found. She squirmed away, but there was no hope. She began to cry and to mutter a prayer. His knob was against the little orifice. He drew back his hips a little and then lunged forward and up.

A choking cry of pain burst from her lips as he smashed through a tight channel, right in and up, bursting the hole all the way until it was just too tight to take the rest of his thickening stem.

He drew his prick back a little. It was so tight in her passage that he felt a stab of pain in his organ, a pain that was exciting because it seemed to draw the fluid from him with his first thrust. He rammed up again, tearing farther this time so that his teeth gritted with the painful ecstasy of it.

Carlotta uttered a low groan which seemed to expand and contract as if she couldn't get her breath. She seemed to fade into a half-stupor, still crying and very white.

The sight of her pale, agonized face acted as a spur to Cesare penetrating her. He wanted to get up and up, right up into her haughty belly so that he could see that haughty face creased in the painful knowledge that a man was raping her, shagging that guarded treasure of hers so that it was numb with pain.

The pull on his penis was like the hug of a mountain bear. It was almost unbearable, but just bearable because it was so exquisite at the same time.

He flexed his hips at the horizontal bar of her legs and pelvis in sharp, powerful movements. His prick ran solidly up, bringing his loins against the fleshy undersides of her thighs with a bump. He was panting hard. There was such a tight pull on his organ.

He felt warmth and wetness. She had bled. It made it easier. He crammed it in short strokes, flicking up the last with an extra thrust until he could feel his knob right up in her as something separate from the rest of his penis. It seemed to make contact with something in its path in addition to the crunching pressure all around its hot, drawn-back length of skin.

This seemed to be the most pulverizing screw he'd ever had, and the sweet sensation of vengeance made it all the better, all the more sadistically exciting to grit his teeth and curl back his lips in passion as he seared into her squirming channel.

He grasped and squeezed her thighs in a grip that brought her out of her semi-coma and made her groan with a fresh awareness of reality.

He slipped his arms around her, grazing them on the leaves, and hugged her to him, crushing her in his strong arms. She was utterly in his power, crushed in his arms, crushed by his great, in-tearing mast. As a final possession he crushed his lips again on hers, forcing them savagely apart, feeling them yield and slip back on her clenched teeth. He bit her lips and the teeth came apart enabling his tongue to invade her mouth.

His prick and loins were boiling. With each thrust it seemed as if matter were being drawn from his penis with a hot poultice. His loins

164

were churned with chilling, twisting clasps which seemed to be tearing out his very guts.

"Oh, God . . . oh, wonderful!" he breathed—and then half-remembered that he shouldn't speak and fresh words merged into animal sounds of passion.

He leaned his body up from hers, pressing his knees into the leaves. Now he could exert more weight, more of a thrust from his loins. He slipped his hand down holding her buttocks, each oval of smooth flesh in his hands. At each stab he pulled her lower body hard against his loins, letting out a groan of pleasure.

Carlotta, her face wet with tears, could manage no more than a continuous whimper—the proud beauty was reduced to a sniveling, agonized toy. Her lips trembled, the bandage around her eyes was soaked from her weeping.

Cesare felt the end aproaching in a delicious agony. He pushed his prick ruggedly in to its full length and pressed there, trying to push farther than was possible, while he wriggled his hips against her pelvis, brushing her pubic hair with his, flattening the fleshy rims of her vagina.

He reached to her breasts with his hands as he felt the scorching helter-skelter from his stomach to his genitals. He grasped them, twisted them so that she cried out afresh with pain. He pulled her nipples. His face was a mask of lost, bacchanalian sensuality. His hips jerked and jumped, screwed and squirmed as if of their own volition while his hands trounced her breasts and his eyes glazed over.

"Ah, ah, ah!" He couldn't hold back the eruption of his breath. Carlotta cried out in despair, recognizing that she was soon to be filled with the polluting sperm of her tormentor, the final, cruel, inescapable indignity.

A rack seemed to be torturing Cesare's organ, pulling it, distending it, punishing it with a voluptuous, throbbing clench.

His hands moved off her marked, reddened breasts, clamped on her waist, jerked her hips at his prick. He slowed his stroke, surging into her to the very root of his pulsating tube. His head swayed back on his neck, his chest heaved with choking breaths, his buttocks clamped together as he flexed inwards, his hands made fresh marks on her waist. It was here, here, gathered ready to fly, gathered, gathered, couldn't be held. "Uuuuugh!" His head jumped, his teeth gritted and fell apart, gritted again as he pumped the full extent of his lust between her legs, discharging it into the slim, gripping channel.

The princess lay under him, her head turned sideways into the leaves. It was over now, over and done, an eternal, ineradicable shame. The tears dried on her face, her head ached, her vagina ached and throbbed. It felt swollen and inflamed and her breasts hurt. She wished she were dead.

Slowly Cesare climbed off her. He stood up, wiped his penis on one of her garments and looked down on her. There was nothing haughty or inaccessible about her now. Her body was marked in a number of places from the rough usage he'd subjected her to. And her gaping legs were divided by a red, raw-looking area of flesh where his prick had scourged her.

He looked down at his organ as he wiped it. It was red and hot and there were traces of her blood around its limp base. He wiped the blood off and threw the garment down beside her.

166

He dressed with a feeling of triumph and satisfaction and, leaving her fastened and spread-eagled, walked back through the trees to the clearing.

Most of his men had finished loosing their lust on Carlotta's ladies-in-waiting. Some were dressing, others still naked, yet others still bobbing on the nude bodies of their prey. Many hadn't bothered to seek the privacy of even a small bush in order to indulge their sexual appetites.

Cesare gave a loud whistle and after a few minutes lookouts rode in. They had taken up their posts as a matter of course although it was highly unlikely that there would be any wanderers at this depth of the forest.

The Duke indicated to the newly-arrived that they were to take the places of their companions, a task they fell to with gusto, while those who had worked out their passion moved off through the trees to keep guard.

Beckoning to three of his men, Cesare led them off toward the spot where Carlotta lay.

"Have her one after the other," he told them in low voice on the way, "and make her suffer."

The men grinned lasciviously. They considered themselves lucky to be offered the most noble lady of the group.

For a while Cesare watched his men tormenting the prostrate body of the princess as a preliminary to fresh rape, then he walked off through the trees to make sure the lookouts were well posted.

He felt highly satisfied with the day's events. He had taught Carlotta a lesson she would never forget. It was very probable she'd feel it necessary to leave the French Court. In any case he wouldn't have her now even if she suddenly agreed to his suit. She could keep her dowry.

Cesare had no fear of discovery. The coup had been well planned and executed. He was aware there was a slight possibility that in some quarters suspicion might fix on him. But he was not afraid of suspicion. And for the most part it would not be dreamed that such a dastardly crime could be authored by any but the crudest of brigands.

He and his men, he mused, would ride back —with suitable scouts—along the tracks made by the princess and her cortege on the outcoming journey. Near the fringe of the woods they would have to separate into pairs and ride off in different directions, getting back to their quarters at different times and from different directions. They would leave the women tied to trees with the dead for company. By nightfall the King's men would be scouring the woods in search of them and their cries would soon bring about their rescue. He'd have them left naked so that Louis' men would also have a very astonishing eyeful—an eyeful they would hardly be able to keep to themselves. And so the story would be quickly spread.

Whistling softly, Cesare finished the checking of the lookouts, and strolled back to the spot where Carlotta was finding over and again that her flesh was not inviolate.

The sun was still splaying through the leaves, though from a more acute angle. Perhaps he had time for one more act of revenge. Perhaps if he screwed his prick into her ass that would be the crowning indignity.

He skirted the clearing, avoiding the locked couples from whom gasps and screams emitted at intervals in a more or less regular accompaniment to their rustle of movement.

The last of his men was reaching the climax to which Carlotta's well-gripping passage had brought him and Cesare squatted down with his other two henchmen and watched the man from the back view, his balls dangling, his behind tensing as it swept forward and his rod widened her. Carlotta no longer showed any emotion except for an occasional gasp as an extra-hard thrust took her by surprise.

In a low voice Cesare gave orders to his men.

"When he's finished you can leave me with her for a short time. Go back and help the others lash the women to trees. Make sure that they remain blindfolded—and not a word if there's any chance you'll be heard."

The buttocks of the ravisher were whipping in faster and faster, the backs of his thighs trembling. He gave a staccato series of coughing barks in which his body straightened and jerked convulsively. Then he staggered back from her on his knees and rested, kneeling, with his head dropped forward onto his chest.

Nobody hurried him and after a minute or two he turned, grinned without embarrassment at his companions and began to dress.

Cesare waited until all three were disappearing through the trees and then he stood up and walked over to Carlotta. Her body exuded an air of crushed and beaten animal. She could go no lower—she thought.

He took his knife from his belt and cut through the cords binding her wrists. She lay there, motionless. He pushed her with his foot and she seemed to come to her senses. She

169

moved her hands up to the blindfold but he knocked them down.

Carlotta cringed in terror, completely subdued by the treatment to which she'd been subjected. He watched her, a cruel smile on his lips, until she moved her wrists and began to massage one with the other. She made no further attempt to remove the blindfold.

Watching her, ready for any movement to release her eyes from their confinement, he cut the bonds from her ankles and, painfully, she moved her legs together and wriggled her feet. She gave a little moan as she sat up and her vagina brushed the ground.

For a few minutes he allowed her to move her limbs and then he gathered the pieces of cord and knotted them into lengths again.

When he seized her, she made no effort to struggle. He turned her over so that she was lying face down on the ground. She lay pressed into the leaves, lifeless while he ended her brief freedom by fastening her wrists to the stakes once more.

He stood up and looked at her buttocks. They were like swollen buds preparing to burst into bloom—a little soiled from their contact with the ground—inviting a touch, to be fondled and held.

She had made no attempt to press her buttocks together or even to close her legs. She lay limp, exhausted, legs and arms slack, waiting for whatever was to come. She'll never be the same again, he thought with grim satisfaction; something in her will be broken forever—apart from her maidenhead.

He undressed for the second time that day. Desire was welling up in him again like a

170

dried-up river suddenly growing again with the floods.

His penis when it flipped into view was still pink, with veins standing out on it prominently. It was hot, too, and heavy, needing a fresh release.

It was still warm in the spots where the sun's rays crept through the tangled branches, but the air was cooling. He braced his wiry body. His penis was the hottest part of him.

Carlotta stirred and groaned. He bent toward her to hear.

"No more . . ." she murmured. "No more . . . have pity . . . please."

Her helpless throwing of herself on his mercy produced an opposite effect to the one she desired. It made a nervous throb pulse in his chest, a little crest of sexual excitement, which began to break over his body like the surf on a shoreline.

He kicked her thighs apart with his feet. She let them flop where he kicked them. She had no more strength to resist.

On her thighs he could see the layer of slight, fair down, but her bottom, so smooth as to be almost glossed with a sheen, held his gaze. He gripped his organ in his hand. It felt enormous. He wondered how women could take it all. It moved in his hand involuntarily, a little jerk over which he had no control.

He sank to his knees on the soft bed of leaves and stroked her buttocks with a hand that quivered. He caught each of the glossy hillocks and pulled them apart. She stiffened, tried to close them together and then gave up as he jerked at them rudely again.

Her anus was disclosed like the center of a flower whose petals are pulled apart. He gazed

171

at it. It was hairless, simply a small garden of the same slight, fair down leading up to its crinkled edge. From the crinkled edge, the little pouchy slit curved into itself redly.

Cesare ran his tongue over his lips. He settled down on her back, kissing her spine. He slid his hands between them and drew the buttocks apart like curtains and wriggled his prick between them. Alongside his prick he let his fingers glide, feeling the way. His index finger encountered the sudden rubbery point of her posterior opening and he nosed his knob after it, prodding tentatively.

"No, no . . . please, no!" he heard Carlotta's weak, muffled appeal beneath him.

He pressed down vertically with his stand of rigidity. He felt it come in contact with the spot and took his hands under her loins, gripping her tightly.

For a number of little strokes which were just rebuffed pressures on her anus, he jogged up and down, pushing his loins at the soft cushion of her rump. In, out, in, out, he sawed without any specific feeling but a growing sense of pressure, vague and ill-defined in his genital region.

The princess, who might have been his wife, lay quivering under him, knowing that he was about to sodomize her, not knowing what it would be like, only aware of the intense shame which burned in her like a disease.

Cesare pushed, pushed, levering his whole body on his stiff stem of flesh until it suddenly broke through with a great grip on his knob.

Carlotta uttered an agonized cry which sputtered into a gurgle.

He pushed down, thrusting into her, feeling his prick sliding in, now, the clamping pressure fitting tightly and strongly-defined along his inflated flesh.

Carlotta began to struggle, trying to press her thighs together under his, finding new strength to twist and fight against her bonds.

"No, no! I can't bear it!" she cried.

But Cesare held her in spite of her struggles and plunged more and more thickly into her with a slow swampy advance which seemed to be tearing his rod to shreds.

His victim couldn't keep back fresh tears. The pain forced them out of her eyes. The agony from her anus spread up into her throat and choked her. She felt sick and slightly dizzy. She continued struggling in her mind even when her body was not making movements, was taking no direction from the mind.

Her head was dazed, but through it all she was aware that his thick protrusion was entering her behind, spreading it, opening it up, making it wet and large, splitting it, making it ache, burn and protest with pain and indignity. She bit her lips until they were warm and wet. She didn't know it was blood on them.

The daze in her head was a mixture of pressure from her behind and noises from around her. It was only later that she realized the noises—which seemed impersonal—were those of her own groaning and his gasping on her back.

Eventually the pain meant nothing. It was simply a continuous, overwhelming cutting away of that opening between her buttocks, an enlarging which felt like the whole of her innards being pushed up into her chest and out of the way of the intruding pike.

There was pressure all around her, which

she also recognized later as the weight of his body on her back and backside.

For a long time the tearing, chafing in and out which was a wave of advancing and withdrawing torment, went on, until she was aware of herself performing certain actions which were dictated by his guidance. She was kneeling up with her head left on the leaves. Her thighs were widespread and pushed in under her. Her legs felt stiff and jelly-like at the same time.

She was aware of a greater edge to the continuity of pain, an extra pricking stab which her new position had enabled him to make. Now she was sure that her body was being ripped from that tiny point which now seemed so large, as if the entirety of her behind were just a gaping hole.

She became aware of another pressure on her waist just above the hip bones. That was his hands, pulling her back onto his enormous, indefinable mass of intrusion, pulling her back as his weight pushed forward and surged into her behind with a fresh shattering wave of pain every second.

Cesare skewered and screwed in from all angles, moving his hips at and across her bottom. His prick was burning again. It had never felt so deliciously crushed and pulverized —and yet so huge and swollen because the great pressure made it more acutely sensitive along the entirety of its throbbing length.

As he swept in, his belly smacked against her bottom. The well-fleshed buttocks provided a buffer from which his body recoiled with a spring before flowing in again with a smooth, agonizing fluency.

His penis was undergoing the most voluptuous torture. He wished it could go on forever —but he wanted it to gather momentum as well, to sweep to the inevitable climax which was such sweet torment.

In and in he surged, his prick tearing right in until it was completely swallowed and his hair squashed against the down on the inner crack of her buttocks.

He felt the liquid of climax growing in intensity and his mind reeled with the pleasure of it. His mind took in the groaning of his soft-fleshed victim, the abandon of her posture, her helplessness, the fact that she was crying again through her groans. He gripped her waist like a vise as he felt the thin, fluid movement right up to the base of his rod.

The moment of oblivion, wonderful oblivion was almost on him. He gasped for breath, his chest heaving in great, gasping sighs. His prick was crushed and squeezed beyond endurance. He couldn't keep on at the same pitch. It was too much.

The fluid blocked into a great, pricking weight at the base of his penis. He couldn't hold it. His mouth twisted into a multitude of ungovernable shapes. Her buttocks were there containing his penis, glossy and smooth, lovely and exciting and her prostrate back and her thighs like a tripod under her and her groans and her sobs. He couldn't hold it. It was rushing suddenly along the thick length of his staff, terribly clear and acute like scalding water. And it flowed straight through and burst from his knob with a force which dragged a long, grating cry from his mouth. Twisting his mouth under the cries he smashed his prick home again and again, ridding himself of a great weight of sperm, letting it shoot up into

175

her, hearing her cry out sharply every time he shattered in.

By the time he felt sufficiently recovered to dress and return to the clearing, the sun had gone down and the twilight was on its way.

His men were waiting for him. Their naked victims were already grotesquely attached to the surrounding trees in positions which were at once revealing and comic.

CHAPTER 14

It was close on the following dawn before Carlotta and her women were found by the search party the King sent out a couple of hours after dusk.

The captain who led the party was hard put to stop his men from committing too many indiscretions with their wandering hands as they untied the unfortunate women. And many a lady-in-waiting had her breasts and behind slyly stroked in the process of being set free. But, so relieved were they after a chilly night in the woods at the mercy of any vagabond who might happen upon them, that the women didn't even notice that they were being rather unnecessarily felt as hands fought with their bonds.

Carlotta was too ashamed and exhausted to be indignant about the fate she'd suffered. She mounted a horse with difficulty and conserved all her energy to prevent the physical pain she felt from showing on her face as, surrounded by their fresh escort—bodies of the dead flung over the horses' rumps—they headed back to the court.

By that time, Cesare and his men were sleeping soundly in their beds—a sleep of exhausted passion.

The following day a large band of men-at-arms, including many of Cesare's retinue, set out to scour the woods in search for the villains who had attacked the ladies of the court.

But, although they spent the whole day, they found no trace of any possible aggressors—in fact the forest seemed to be totally deserted and uninhabited for many miles around the spot.

There was much discreet talk about the dastardly fate of the ladies, but nobody seemed even to think of Cesare Borgia as the possible dispenser of the treatment. The King was restrained by Carlotta from offering a large reward for information leading to the capture of the unknown rogues. The less said the better, she decided. As it was she felt unable to leave her chambers for shame.

His Majesty, after a few more days of searching and interrogating, called off the hunt. But not before half his kingdom was aware of the story—often in a grossly exaggerated form. Some even suggested in the countryside's inns that the King himself had already tired of his wife and desired the haughty Carlotta, who had enhanced her desirability in refusing to accept Cesare's suit. Certainly many were the tongues which wagged over the Duke's part in the plot. But they wagged only among the peasants, who loved to talk about things connected with nobility, and the more scandalous the better. In the court itself, Cesare, who had always conducted himself in a manner of the utmost courtesy and delicacy, was considered beyond reproach. Besides, he had never had a definite refusal to his plan for marriage from the princess.

*   *   *

Such a scandal, however, certainly put
Carlotta out of the marriage market for the
time being, and Louis, still wishing for a firm
alliance between the Pope and himself, presented Cesare with two fresh possibilities for
a wife. He was offered either one of the King's
nieces or the daughter of the Duc de Guyenne,
Charlotte d'Albret.

Charlotte was only seventeen, beautiful and
she was a sister of the King of Navarre. It was
she that Cesare chose.

For a short time her father appeared to oppose the proposed marriage. But the King of
Navarre needed the friendship of France to
withstand any possible attack from Castille
and pressure was brought to bear on the girl's
father so that he eventually consented.

The marriage was politically sound, uniting
both sides as it did at the time when Milan was
noticeably belligerent over disputed territory.

Cesare was able to spend a few months only,
consolidating his reputation in France and
enjoying his duchess. For the trumpets of war
with Milan were soon sounding forth and the
Duke of Valentinois was riding south in Louis'
train to chastise the Italian kingdom.

In the Vatican, Alexander breathed a sigh
of relief that his son had thus consolidated the
alliance with France, and began to prepare
celebrations for his homecoming.

Lucrezia, to whom news of her family came
once in a while, also began to make preparations—to leave her little love nest in the
convent and give herself once again into
Cesare's arms.

LUSTS OF THE BORGIAS

VOLUME TWO

CHAPTER 1

Cesare Borgia sat still and straight on his horse smiling wryly. Across the green plains of Romagna which surrounded the river Po, the city of Imola was humped behind its great, protecting wall. A siege would have meant a long delay in his campaign, possibly into winter. But Imola, like all the other towns he had taken since Louis had gone back to France after the fall of Milan, was coming over to him without pressure of arms.

He watched his lieutenant, Ramiro de Lorqua, in earnest conversation with the little delegation from the city. They had met to parley in a little group some several hundred yards in advance of Cesare's army which stretched in an ominously broad arc across the great valley. Away to the south the Etruscan Apennines shimmered and misted in the blue haze of summer. The weather was as satisfying as the campaign.

It was with the psychological cunning which Machiavelli was to take as example for his book, *Il Principe*, that the Duke of Valentinois had contrived to triumph so easily everywhere he went. Romagna was, in fact, noted for its tyrants and it was merely habit and tradition which had brought citizens loyally around their despotic leaders in times of crisis. With the capture of his first city, Cesare had pardoned all the citizens who had fought against him and had forbidden his men to indulge in the usual postcapture assuaging of their lusts. There had been no pillage, no killing, no rape, no disorder. This he had enforced with the severity for which, when occasion demanded it, he was notorious.

The effect had been miraculous. Word had been allowed to spread of the good treatment received by the beaten populaces and, as if Cesare possessed some new and irresistible weapon, the common folk of all the cities in his path had denounced their tyrannical lords and flung open their fortresses to the Pope's son.

In front of the great army, Ramiro de Lorqua and his subordinates reined round their horses and sped back across the intervening space toward their chief. The councillors of Imola remained in a motionless group—a helpless, hopeful band almost surrounded by the mass of Borgian troops.

De Lorqua reined in beside the Duke. A grim smile of triumph flickered across his normally austere visage.

"The gates are open, Sire," he said quietly. "Imola is ours. They will lead us across the moat into the city."

"Good," Cesare replied, briefly but with satisfaction.

He spurred his mount forward and the great army came to slow life behind him, following patiently in his wake.

"If it please God, no soldier of mine shall have to raise his right arm to fight again. He will be received like a visiting monarch and have to find his exercise in the brothels."

De Lorqua laughed, a quick, unbelieving laugh.

"There is yet Forli to come," he reminded.

As the towers and campaniles beyond the tall buff walls of the city became clearer, Cesare reflected on his advance. If all went well he should, in time, succeed to the title of Duke of Romagna, a pleasing thought. His campaign, which had begun as a war to recover the temporal power of the Holy See in these areas where the barons refused to pay their taxes, had developed into a personal triumph, which —intelligence had it—was being talked of throughout Italy and beyond. Already the subjugated people—if one could give that title to a people liberated by an alleged enemy from despotism—were demanding that Cesare be made their permanent master and that they enjoy his protection forevermore. His ambition was fired and seemed likely to be rewarded.

But there was, of course, Forli, with that amazon of a Countess, who would doubtless defend it to the last, crying death to the enemy even as death shattered her heart—or, as was very likely—rapacious lust shattered another part of her anatomy.

Crowds were thronging the streets and the squares to cheer the invading army; flags and kerchiefs fluttered in the air and women of doubtful character hung their half-naked bosoms from the windows of establishments of doubtful reputation in a surge of welcome.

But the battle was not quite over. A councillor of the city joined the vanguard to warn that a captain of the guard with a body of troops had withdrawn to the almost impregnable citadel, swearing to surrender only when death claimed him.

Even as the populace waved and the women flaunted their waiting breasts before the eager arrivals, a cannon boomed out from the citadel and sent the crowds screaming and scurrying for shelter.

Cesare immediately trained a number of his cannons on the stark, scarred walls of the citadel and returned fire until the challenge had petered out for a while and he was able to direct the billeting of his troops and arrange a siege of the inner stronghold which still resisted him.

CHAPTER 2

Cesare stretched himself at ease on the red plush couch which had been put at his disposal. Around him, his principal officers shared with their leader the privilege of being the guest of the Chief Councillor of the city. Outside, the cannon was quiet, the citadel comfortably besieged. Full-scale assault operations could wait until tomorrow. The army needed rest and a little entertainment.

Throughout the city the brothels were doing fine, wine-flushed business. And any woman who showed herself willing was feeling the full pent-up strength following days of abstinence on the part of the visitors between her thighs. But, as usual, Cesare had forbidden violence. Any man reported stealing a citizen's unwilling wife or raping a reluctant maiden would be made an example of for all the town to see.

Within the mansion of the Chief Councillor, gypsy music was playing. A band of well-dressed nomads were strumming their guitars and tambourines. There was controlled passion in the music and in the dark, gypsy faces. There was ill-controlled passion, too, in the loins of Cesare's officers. This man, their host, had promised them, later, the full benefits of the high-class brothel which was virtually his harem. They were anxious to relieve this ache of longing in their lower regions.

Cesare toyed with his glass, sipping the

rich, sweet wine with which his host had bolstered a magnificent meal. He was thinking of Lucrezia, wishing she were here, now, so that they could retire to a quiet nook and enjoy each other with the furious abandon of the days before he had left for the French Court.

"How do you like my gypsy orchestra?" his host asked, leaning across from his neighboring couch.

"Excellent, excellent, but they look a little domesticated."

"You mean they are well dressed, well fed? But of course. They have become quite famous these last few months. Everybody is paying big prices to have them play and dance. Their days of dirt and rags are over."

He swallowed a glass of wine in one long draught.

"But if you talk of domestication, wait until you see Maria. Domestication! I'd like to see the man who could domesticate her. Violence, passion, sensuality! They ripple in her limbs when she dances, they reach to you from her breasts, they writhe in her buttocks. And yet she's not for sale. Oh, they've tried to rape her —many a man in torment. But she carries a stiletto and knows how to use it, they say. She's a proud one. I have to rush to my mistress in excitement after she's danced, and then I try to imagine she's the divine Maria who won't be bought."

Cesare listened, idly swishing the wine in his refilled glass and letting the music flow in him. The old dotard, he was thinking; the thought that he couldn't have her would make him pay groveling homage to the ugliest old whore.

185

"Well, when does this proud creature deign to appear?" he asked.

"Immediately if you so wish it."

The host clapped his hands and gave orders to a servant, who disappeared, gliding over the rich carpets which covered the tiled floor, into the other rooms which led off from a portico at the far end of the main dining hall.

After a few minutes, he reappeared, gave a few whispered instructions to the leader of the gypsy orchestra and withdrew.

The music changed suddenly to a wild, passionate flamenco in true Spanish style, the notes hurtling and gyrating one after the other in a loud, fiery torrent. There was a sudden strumming of chords and then a lowering of tempo and pitch. The guest officers glanced up from their conversation and wine. There was a foreboding in the music which immediately attracted all attention. While they stared, not knowing quite what to expect, but certain that something was going to happen, a figure danced slowly in from the shadows of the portico, a shadowy movement at first, growing into a flame of red and black, becoming a beautiful girl who swayed sensually in before the gypsy band which accompanied her.

There was an instant tension in the assembly. Men who had been engaged in, at least, the semblance of war for more than a week or two, flushed over with the tightening of desire. Cesare put down the glass with which he had been describing circles in the air.

"You hardly exaggerated," he said quietly and in some surprise.

"Almost worth a stiletto in the ribs if one could be certain of achieving one's fill before the death blow, eh?" chuckled his host.

186

Cesare Borgia didn't reply. His thoughts were away on the hips that revolved gently, the breasts that were taut from her upstretched, slender brown arms. Her face seemed to spark and blaze with pride and a controlled sensuality; her dark hair swept back, dropping, long onto her shoulders; broad brow over dark, almond eyes, a straight nose which flared lightly at the nostrils, long, full lips which opened often in intense concentration as she danced, a good, clear chin which was round and smooth under her mouth; and then the neck, long and unexpectedly well-developed as she came forward into the light, full and with the slight ridge of a vein; below the black lace frill of the tight-bodiced red dress she wore, the breasts which forced out the yielding stuff in strong, taut lines, the slim waist which moved and writhed inside the dress, the skirt tight over her hips, enclosing her buttocks in a tight embrace and then flaring out loosely around her thighs to permit her freedom of movement.

"Superb, superb," Cesare murmured aloud and his host smiled with a pleasure that conflicted with his mask of almost miserable longing.

The music gathered in crescendo and the girl made a full, twirling tour of the room, skimming the tables of the spectators with her flying skirt. She seemed to see nobody. At times her face was serene and ethereal, at others working with passion as if she were in the throes of sexual intercourse. The men seemed to come to life, out of the still, electric petrification her arrival had induced. They slithered forward on their couches the better to see. There were odd comments of coarse appreciation uttered without a withdrawal of the eyes watching her every movement, every crease and tension of every part of her body under the flaming silk dress.

The Duke of Valentinois watched with the others. He felt his heart pounding and that empty sucking in his stomach. She was as beautiful as Lucrezia, this Maria, the gypsy; as beautiful at the other end of the scale, each of them perfection of their own kind.

His eyes ran over her avidly. As she swayed toward his end of the room, slim arms flowering in the light of the candles around the walls, he watched her breasts, full and alive under the slender covering. They bulged and moved in unison with her movement. The points of her nipples jutted, large and voluptuous from the summits of the warm mounds of flesh behind them. He let his glance fall, taking in the slim waist, so slim that it moved all by itself inside the dress as if it wanted no part of these protecting clothes. And then the tight containment of those hips, the rounded belly, which could be cupped with a hand, the protrusion of hipbones, well-fleshed and bulging against the silk, the lines of the strong, sexual thighs and then the slim, lightly-muscled calves that twirled below the whirl of the skirts.

"Beautiful, beautiful," Cesare whispered.

His host leaned toward him, hotly.

"You must forgive me," he muttered. "I can't bear to stay. It is a mistake for me to be here at all and I must take my leave in a few moments. If there is anything you or your officers require of me, you have only to ask my servants. They will show you to your quarters and to the source of your future enjoyment."

His breath had come with difficulty and when Cesare looked at him he saw that his

188

face was almost crimson and his eyes drawn in anguish.

"My poor Chief Councillor," he whispered sympathetically, "I understand your predicament. To have such a delight within your house and be unable to sip of the ecstasy she promises is hard indeed. But I crave one boon before you leave—that I may be permitted to try my gallantry with the lady."

There was a note of envy in the Chief Councillor's tone as he gazed into Cesare's handsome, commanding face.

"By all means," he said, "and I wish you success. Perhaps a conquest would soften her heart toward others who would give their souls to share her bed. I will see that she joins you alone after the entertainment and that you are not disturbed."

With that the Chief Councillor rose, not waiting even to hear his guest's thanks, and slipped from the banquet hall as if he were afraid he would in some way disgrace himself if he delayed his exit a single second.

Grinning to himself, Cesare turned back to the spectacle. The music was throbbing, drugging the room with its heavy insistence. The girl had her back to him, arms high above her head, hips swaying, heels tapping on the marble floor. The outlines of her buttocks pressed and relaxed in firm ovals against the seat of the dress. Each seemed to move of its own accord, rounded and naked, inviting lustful attack. She whirled and flitted forward with flying, little steps, toward Cesare's table. Her eyes seemed to catch his for an instant. He held them and they bored back at him until slowly he dropped his gaze and stared meaningfully at the triangular crease of her dress between her thighs.

189

When he glanced up again, her eyes were still on him, but flicked away immediately, her head bowing to the ground in concentration.

A hot glow consumed Cesare, slowly, from his genitals. He had no thought of failure. The meeting of their eyes had established the beginning. He would, as always, win.

For a moment, he took his eyes from the scene to witness its effect. His officers were hypnotized. Some faces were scarlet, others white with desire: a band of civilized men, suddenly naked and primitive in the face of elemental sexual passion. The difference between most of them and himself, Cesare knew, was the difference between himself and the Chief Councillor: that he would not give his soul to possess this woman. It was, also, this very aloof quality which communicated itself even in moments of intimacy, which gave him his extraordinary power of attracting and, if desired, maintaining the interest of the most difficult and independent of women. Cesare had learned from his sister, Lucrezia, the intricacies of intrigue and attitude that women were capable of; he had, perhaps, been fortunate in learning from her the necessity of keeping himself beyond the snares which they set, of keeping himself whole in mind and emotions, of being always the master.

Now, catching again the eyes of the beautiful gypsy girl as she danced toward him, letting his eyes rove insolently over her breasts as if he were stroking them with his eyelashes, he felt certain that she was his. He could hardly wait to hold those buttocks naked in his hands and drive his strength and mastery between her naked thighs into the conquered lips that waited softly to receive him.

CHAPTER 3

It was very warm in the banquet hall — as if all those who had left had jettisoned their heat before departure. Not all the candles still glowed smoothly into the gloom, only a few at odd points around the walls cast deep and slightly moving shadows. There were two red candles flickering on the table and they threw a warm, flattering light on the faces of Cesare and the gypsy girl.

"A little wine," Cesare was saying, as he filled her glass again.

She took her long-stemmed glass and sipped, looking at him over its rim. Her eyes were warm, and so friendly that they would have turned over the Chief Councillor's heart had he been there.

"They say that you will soon be lord of all Romagna—perhaps of all Italy," she said softly.

"Gossip," Cesare said. "But it may be true." He smiled. "My chances would be greater had I your power of reducing men to willing slavery."

"Gossip," she retorted, "if we speak of men. I can think of many I would not put in that category."

"Our poor Chief Councillor is slowly dying of suffocation—suffocation of his desires."

"He is like a cow," she said. "He chews his food and watches me with great, gawking eyes. When he desired me he had to send a servant to try to procure me so afraid was he that I might spit in his face."

Cesare took a long gulp of wine.

"Are all as unlucky as he?"

"Did he not tell you I'm not to be bought?"

"I'm not talking of buying."

She raised an eyebrow at him over her glass and smiled. She gave no answer and Cesare put his hand on hers on the table, gently but firmly.

"You remind me of my sister Lucrezia," he said.

"But isn't she blonde?"

"I mean that you are perfect in your particular beauty as she is in hers. I am told, too, that she is perfect in bed. As for that, I would never be able to compare you."

He watched her closely. But she didn't take his words amiss. Clearly he was not in the same class as the Chief Councillor, nor had she removed her hand from his.

"What happens when you want to give—and not be bought?" he asked.

"These are very personal questions—I had heard you were very direct," she said, still smiling.

"It's the only way to know people," he replied. "Hedging and social protocol are all very well in their place."

"Yes," she said and she turned her hand in his and entwined their fingers gently. "I have given very rarely,'" she went on. "I only give when I'm moved, otherwise it's not worth the pestering which would follow from all those who assume that because a woman gives she is free to all."

She had leaned forward slightly and Cesare could see deep down between the swellings of her breasts. The skin was a tawny flame-color and as smooth looking as parchment. He let his eyes run from her breasts up over her shoulders and that strong, voluptuous neck. When his eyes reached hers she was looking at him without the smile. It had been replaced by a look he recognized—Lucrezia's look of desire. In those few seconds he thought with amazement that she must always have looked like this. That even in rags, running the streets of the slum quarters in her youth before she joined the gypsy band, she looked this same lovely, haughty, sensual woman who might, at that time, have given herself to anyone who was prepared to make her rich, to give her the life of a lady. He wondered that no rich merchant, straying on his horse through the poor quarter, had caught a glimpse of her—probably with half a breast naked through her rags and tatters, or a side view of a straining buttock. She could, by now, have been at the court of kings.

"What are you thinking?" she asked softly, the desire still heavy in her eyes. "Why do you look at me like that?" He looked at the dark shadows below her high, smooth cheekbones, his glance lingered on those full lips which had hardly moved as she spoke.

"I was thinking that you are, perhaps, more beautiful even than Lucrezia," he said quietly.

"She would not be flattered to hear you say that."

"She would probably retort by claiming that she was far superior in the boudoir."

"But even after tonight you would have no way of comparing us—you would never have slept with her."

Cesare stood up, slowly, not taking his eyes off the girl. Mingled with his unexpectedly easy triumph was a sly amusement at her peasant assumption. He was tempted to tell her, but the moment was not to be spoiled and, in any case, her tongue might wag.

He walked around the table toward her and

she stood up with her lips parted, waiting. When he reached her and caught her face in both his hands, her body swept in and wriggled against him. Sparks seemed to fly in his body. God, he thought, it's almost as if she divined and were determined to prove herself the better. The flesh, smoothly, glossily almost, covering the fine bones of her face was hot under his fingers. There was a delicate perfume of roses about her hair. Her lips were moist and gave like a sponge, opening under his. They seemed to swallow his mouth—and then her tongue, smooth as milk was panting into his mouth, exploring it, brushing against his own. Along his whole length he felt the warm slender solidity of her body pressing and moving slightly—the weight of her breasts protruding, the smooth roundness of her thighs brushing and clinging to his, her hips and that excruciating abdominal area which pressed against his confined genitals and slithered against them hotly. He pulled his mouth from hers and she let it go reluctantly. Audible little pantings breathed through her lips, now released, as he moved down her neck, sucking it, biting it, drawing a pattern of little red marks on the velvety skin. He reached her shoulders, the top halves, naked halves, of her breasts, which bulged and wanted to escape and soar forth for him in their entirety. As he bit her breasts gently, her abdomen, that triangular section between her strong thighs, squirmed furiously against the mound of his genitals which she could feel in an erect hump beneath his clothes.

"Let's go through to the private chambers," he whispered.

"No, now—here!" she said passionately.

He pushed her gently back toward the divan from which he'd watched her dancing earlier in the evening. The Chief Councillor had promised they would be alone—and what did it matter if a servant did tumble onto them? Guilt and fear were for the weak and subordinate.

She fell back onto the couch and he lowered himself down with her. She put her hand on the covered heat of his penis and he felt its trembling, demanding pressure with a wild surge of immediate desire. He began, quickly, to slip off her clothes and she helped him, breathing heavily, looking at him with deep, fire-filled eyes, concentrating on ridding herself of the garments that hid her body from him.

In a matter of seconds she was stretched out on the couch, more naked than in the days of flimsy rags and Cesare's mouth was avidly sucking her large, erect nipples, as his hands flared over her body, exploring its firm, beautiful contours while his penis seemed to throb and hum like a hive of bees.

Her breasts were taut and high in spite of their size. The nipples that he sucked crowned them in a dark, hard summit which seemed to epitomize her desire; the hard bosses yielded and flipped back in rubbering resilience and seemed to reach out to him in pleading desire for assuagement. Below her breasts her hard, narrow waist was the pivot for her writhing hips. No bones showed in her hips, the flesh was full and rounded, the little bulge of her abdomen heaving in and out with its crest of fine, dark hair. Her sensual, well-holding thighs pressed and slithered against each other, opening wide from time to time as Cesare's hands moved over her flesh. Between them, dark rose lips, moist and ready, were crushed with her movement.

Cesare's penis felt wet inside his clothes and the throbbing was unbearable. When, without opening her eyes or stopping the convulsions of her lost body, the girl put her hand again on his penis and began to squeeze and caress it, he stood up quickly and began to tear off his clothes.

She lay there, her breath exploding from between her parted lips, her thighs tight together as if to keep the sensation locked tightly in. She opened her eyes after a few seconds and watched Cesare baring his body. Her eyes were in anguish and her hands, which had moved up to the breasts on which the heat and fury of his lips remained, twitched gently.

Feeling the warm air strike his suddenly naked flesh with a cooling draught, Cesare looked back at the girl's body as he stripped. She was beautiful as a Greek statue and burning with sexual life. He could worship a body like that—except that he didn't worship bodies. He had a sudden irreverent thought of the envy the Chief Councillor would feel when he knew. What that man would give to be here now in his shoes—or rather in his skin.

Nude at last, with his penis soaring ruggedly out and up at an acute angle with his belly, Cesare moved toward the couch. She watched him come, her eyes flowing over his face and from it down over his lightly haired and muscular chest to the slim hips dominated by that great boom of penis with its narrowing, fiery tip. As he reached the divan she reached up and grasped it and icy darts shot through his belly and clashed in his genitals.

He lay down beside her and she stroked and

caressed his prick and smothered his lips with hers, flicking her tongue in what seemed an almost involuntary spasm of sensuality.

Cesare pressed her dark head back onto the couch. The rose perfume was all around like an ethereal cushion and her dark hair brushed softly against his face as he sank into her lips and sucked them and her tongue into his mouth. Her flesh was hot and receptive, trembling against his as he slid his hand down over those firm, reaching breasts and the belly with its little indentation and then over the fine hair which was warm and soothing to his fingers, and so between those hot and slightly sweating thighs, right at their topmost point where they merged into the hot arch containing the point of desire.

She gasped as his hand reached the lips of her cunt, gasped into his mouth and was unable to keep her lips against his with the sudden sensation. She dragged her head away and turned it so that her cheek lay along the divan, pressing into it as if she were resisting some torture.

Through the loose, wet flesh, his fingers wandered and into the suddenly tight and opening hole which he found.

"Oh, oh!" she gasped and bit her lips under his passionate, watching eyes as he lay with his cheek against hers. Her hand on his prick redoubled its activity and she began to stroke him gently, moving her fingers lightly on the hot, stiff flesh.

He felt her thighs moving and then opening widely and her crotch rose up slightly toward him, facilitating and demanding the entry of his searching fingers into the moist channel at whose entrance they dawdled. He pressed in, wiping a finger around the elastic rim and plunging on into the depths of the cavern beyond.

"Oh, oh, oh, oh!" Her face on the couch swung back at his and she released his prick and held him tightly with both arms as she kissed him wildly and rubbed her face all over and around his.

Cesare could feel his prick, hot and waiting, pressing up against her hip, the cool, yielding flesh of her hip. He moved in against her, crushing it against that flesh, rubbing his loins against her, moving one of his thighs half over hers.

His finger, now, had penetrated all the way and he could feel the smooth, viscid roof of the cavern. Her thighs alternately clamped his hand in the pressure of a vise and released it, sweeping apart in a wild, passionate gesture. She was panting continuously and punctuating the panting with little moans as he moved his fingertip gently against the roof of the cavern.

Her lovely lips were trembling and her nostrils were slightly flared the way he'd noticed them as she concentrated on her dancing. She had closed her eyes and the long lashes made tremulous shadows on her cheeks. Her long, slim hands ran convulsively over his body, not seeming to be controlled by her at all.

Cesare moved another finger into her vagina and she cringed away and then pushed back on the double prong which filled her. He allowed his fingers to roam all over and through the moist channel of her sex and then slowly withdrew them and searched for the tiny stub of her passion. He found it, hard and erect. It evaded him from time to time as he caressed it, slipping away into the fleshy folds of her lips.

The touch of his fingers on her clitoris had sparked even greater depths of passion reaction from her. She had caught his penis again and squeezed it hard. She ran her fingertips over his balls as far down as she could reach. She brought up her head and bit his neck and lips. She was like a tigress.

Caressing her, tantalizing her, bringing her to a pitch of excitement, with his own thunderous, growing passion as a controlled background, Cesare felt her thigh slipping and digging under his trying to get him to mount her. Her arms pulled his face onto her chest over against her breasts which strained up, digging him with erect, large nipples.

"Now, now," she murmured. "Do it now."

Overcome with a nervous excitement, now that the moment had come, as if afraid of the power of his own passion, Cesare hesitated, drawing his fingertips up her hard, little clitoris for a few seconds longer until she was groaning with ecstasy.

"Please, please, now, now, now," she begged, hardly able to utter the words, squeezing blindly on his rod of flesh.

Cesare slithered over onto her. She made a superb, warm cushion for his body. Her thighs swung wide apart as she felt the knob of his penis tickling against the lips of her vagina. She gripped both his shoulders very tightly with her hands which quivered with emotion.

Cesare wriggled on her, longing to plunge in but enjoying the sight and sound of her passion and desire.

He felt her release a shoulder and then her hand came down under her thigh and felt for and found his penis. She held it gently, seeming to hold her breath, too, at the same time, and guided it at her wide-open cunt.

Right, now, at last, Cesare thought in a sudden, fierce, violent joy. He thrust in with a long, excruciating grind, all the way in one long, agonizing movement. She drew up her thighs with his penetration and her hands bit into his shoulders.

"Aaaaaah!" The ecstatic groan dragged out from between their lips at the same moment. With her it continued on a slightly lower key, a continuous, gentle, lost groaning. With Cesare it broke down into a shunting accompaniment of groans and pantings for breath as he drove in and in, crashing and plundering, right to the soft, giving wall of the cavern's roof.

Her thighs which had opened, giving him wider access, and moved back toward her shoulders giving him depth, came down and clasped his hips, moving and slithering against them as he pistoned in and out. Her breasts flattened and rounded under his varying pressure and her eyes opened to look abandonedly into his as her groaning lips sought to touch, to bite, to kiss his face, any part of his face.

His loins aflame, consumed in the ecstatic relief of her moist, claiming containment, Cesare felt her passage plucking sensation from his prick along its whole length. Her channel fitted him like a glove, smooth and with a gentle pressure which became stronger as the tip of his organ coursed right through to its end.

Already he could feel pressure building up in his pulsating staff. All that preliminary titivating had prepared his prick for a quick release.

Under him, squirming and mouthing noises, the gypsy girl, too, was building up to the intense final pressure. Her arms moved around him, over his shoulder, down his back, to his buttocks which she could just reach. She pressed on them exhorting him into her and her legs swung up suddenly and entwined his thighs and then up further and gripped his waist.

Cesare slipped his hand under her full, soft buttocks which strained down firmly in his hands and then relaxed, soft again. He reached underneath, feeling her thighs from behind and she gasped anew as his fingers entered the long slit of her vagina, pulling the lips gently apart, brushing in with his hard length of penis.

Her head began to move from side to side on the divan. Her legs released his waist and swung down, flattening into the couch and then gripped him again before falling away, almost at right angles to her body.

Her crotch was running with moisture. Cesare's fingers slipped from it and ran up the crease between her buttocks. He pulled the buttocks apart and she gave a start of passion through her moaning. He plunged a finger against the tight, warm, puckering of her anus and felt it give and his fingertip break through to soft, tender flesh.

"Oh, oh, oh!" she gasped again and again.

She began to writhe as if in a paroxysm. It must be now, Cesare was able to think as he drummed into her, pulling back and then thrusting in his whole length in a slow, grinding crush.

She opened her eyes and looked at him desperately. Her eyes seemed to be speaking to him, loving him, wanting him, abandoning herself to him. Her mouth opened and her tongue came out—a long, point-tipped, moist and perfectly smooth tongue. Cesare lowered his lips to hers and bit the tongue gently. He ground in with slow, strong strokes. He could feel his penis swelling in a hot tingling expansion. He couldn't keep his mouth on hers and drew up, his hands under her buttocks, pulling them up off the divan, against his loins.

She wriggled furiously, her shoulders quivered, and her breasts under his eyes. She groaned and looked at his eyes in a last gleam of passion and then her mouth opened in a great circle, her head dropped back, her thighs clasped him and she emitted a loud, aching gasp and another and another, dwindling away into body-racking sighs.

Still holding her buttocks in his hands, fired by the sight of her fulfillment, Cesare, himself, trembled on the brink of release. His penis was chafing against the flesh of her passage and his loins were screwed up in a turmoil of pre-explosion. Her beautiful body, heaving with passionate sighs, was in his hands. He looked down and saw her thighs hanging over his hands as he held her bottom, and saw his prick, inflamed and wet, disappearing into her red, loose lips. Her breasts swayed and heaved below him and that narrow waist was heaving too, above the hips that he held up slightly off the bed.

He thrust savagely in and felt his knob growing and growing as if it would burst into a thousand pieces. He ground slowly, slowly, extracting every iota of sensation from the long, slow stroke. His breath was rising up from his chest, rising up through his throat at the same time that his knob was expanding in unbearable torture. He felt the quick fire dart in his loins and come racing through. His mouth opened wide as the breath finally, suddenly, reached it. He shattered his sperm up, up into her belly as the breath broke from his throat, twisting his mouth out into an agonized explosion. He felt the pressure of her thighs renewed, fleetingly, heard a faint gasp echoing a recognition of his orgasm.

For several seconds he pumped into her, seeming to loose all the juices of his pent up body into that lovely, waiting receptacle. Then, slowly he collapsed on her warm, cushioning flesh and felt her arms encircle him gently and her lips, light and tender on his cheek.

Later, nude still, she preceded him as they walked to the private chamber Cesare had been allotted off the banquet hall. Watching her buttocks swaying and rounding under the slim, taut waist, Cesare wondered if the Chief Councillor meant it when he said it would be worth getting a stiletto in one's ribs if one could be sure of fulfillment first. Looking at her thighs, slenderly moving under the rounded volptuousness of the buttocks, he felt pretty sure he meant it.

CHAPTER 4

It was a very cheerful Cesare Borgia that directed his forces for the storming of the citadel the following day. He was to have the delight of Maria's company for the remainder of his nights at Imola. She had fallen for him and was his to do with as he wished. In his mind he was even turning over plans to establish her near him when he finally settled in a permanent headquarters after the campaign.

So touched and pleased by his success had Cesare been that he'd even refused himself the satisfaction of giving the Chief Councillor an account of his conquest.

"She is, indeed, a fiery one," was the only comment he would make when discreetly pressed by his host.

With a concentration equalling that of his lovemaking of the night before, Cesare set about the quelling of the citadel.

His lieutenants had suggested a storming of the walls immediately a breach appeared. But the Duke, with some acute questioning, was able to establish that munitions in the citadel were not very plentiful and were likely to give out in a very few days.

Content with his host and his companion of the nights, and ever sparing of the lives of his men who would have to cross a deep moat in order to reach a breach in the walls, he settled down to a siege, maintaining a steady bombardment, producing a breach from time to time, which, those inside, panic-stricken at the thought of a resultant assault, rushed rashly to repair, exposing themselves to a deadly fire from the Borgian troops.

The Borgian army, after a week of womenless nights, were very happy, in turn, to remain in a town long enough to win over those maidens who were conserving of their reputation in the first encounters.

For four days the siege continued. The last breaches in the walls were not repaired and it was doubtful whether Dionigio di Naldo, the rebellious captain of the guard, could risk losing any of his dwindling number of men to see to them.

Those days of constant cannon fire from outside, dwindling ammunition and men inside, wore down the defenders with an inescapable psychological inevitability. They had little hope of relief from Forli which was too busy preparing its defense as the next on the Duke of Valentinois' list and they were surrounded by a vast sea of Borgian troops. There was no hope of victory and very little hope of holding out until Cesare tired and moved on leaving just a covering force which might afford some hope, at least, of escape.

At the end of the four days of concentrated pressure, during which he was able to profit from no risks taken by his besiegers, di Naldo begged for a parley.

Within a few hours he had made a formal surrender of the citadel, Cesare having, generously and not without political acumen, granted a safe conduct to his garrison.

Joy at yet another triumph was tempered in the Borgian ranks with a reluctance to leave what had proved to be such a sexual haven. But lusty men will find lusty women no matter where and Forli was likely to prove as welcoming as Imola once the amazon Countess had been removed.

CHAPTER 5

Countess Caterina Sforza-Riario was often described as a virago. She was certainly beautiful, severe and of a fiery independence. Life had hardened her. She had seen her father murdered by patriots in Milan Cathedral and her husband, Girolamo Riario, butchered by a mob in the very city she now defended. Her second husband, too, had been killed by a band of rebels. She had ordered a massacre of all who lived in the quarter from which the rebels came and had ridden, herself, at the head of her men-at-arms, to see that her orders were carried out.

A third husband had died of natural causes. It would be true to say she had, in spite of her terrible revenge for her second husband's death, not been floored by the loss of any of them.

Caterina Sforza-Riario was one of those unfortunate women unable to find her place. She didn't like to be alone, she wanted men, a husband, a lover. But she also wanted independence and was totally unable to make any compromise by which she surrendered any or part of it. She had finished by despising each of the three men she had married. Fascinated by that very independence, their devotion to her had grown in proportion to which hers for them had diminished. They had been unable to lead her as she really needed to be led and consequently she had found herself doing the leading—and that was the way the world saw her, as a severe, often cruel and totally unbending woman.

Like most women in Italy, she had heard of Cesare Borgia. She had, in fact, wondered what manner of man it was who, finally, was coming to attack her city under orders from the Pope. Talk had it that he was handsome and of iron will. She thought of her poor, weak husbands and the thought made her sick. Who knew what Cesare Borgia really was? Certainly she would have little opportunity of discovering now as he ranged his enemy troops in preparation for the assault.

The citadel in which she was ensconced, within the town, was well provisioned. She could and would resist this man of iron will, this "monster" as some preferred to call him. For weeks she had had outworks thrown up all around the city and built in nearly all the gates as a fortification. Now, with the Borgian troops a few hours' march away, she had another trouble: as in Imola, there were rumblings among the townsfolk to whom she had never been overly-generous, rebellious rumblings, which talked of handing over the city, her city, to Cesare Borgia, the upstart son of an upstart cardinal who had bargained his way into the papacy.

Even now, the Countess' brother Alessandro had left the citadel with a strong body of men to exhort the council of the city to stand by their overlord.

The Countess, standing with her guards on the ramparts of the citadel, shielded her eyes to gaze down into Forli. Her ample bosom was heaving slightly. She had heard of the turn of events at Imola and she was well aware of the heavy hand with which she had long ruled her people.

Down in the city, lost in the mass of winding streets and the old, uneven buildings there was noise and shouting. It was impossible to tell whether this was simply excitement and fear at the imminent arrival of the enemy or whether harsh words were flying between her brother and the council.

Below, under the shadow of the citadel's walls, the heavy drawbridge was still down across the moat.

"What's happened to them," she muttered fiercely.

"There, Madam!" a captain of the guard called from a point some distance along the thick crenellated rampart.

She squinted in the direction indicated and her blood boiled with anger. Her brother and his men, surrounding a couple of the leading citizens of Forli, were fighting a retreating action against a rabble of the townsfolk. While she watched, she saw a couple of her hard-pressed men fall under the sword and stave-blows of their attackers.

"Turn the cannon on them," she yelled.

But it was impossible to scatter the townspeople without risking injury to her brother and she ordered a couple of shots to be sent among the houses in the rear of the mob and a body of soldiers to go to the aid of her guards.

The portcullis was raised within seconds and a crowd of soldiers ran across it as the cannon crashed. Seeing the reinforcements and hearing the shot flying over their heads, threatening to cut off their retreat, the mob of townsfolk began to break off, to disappear in ragged, hurrying groups along the cobbled streets in all directions.

Caterina Sforza-Riario climbed down from the ramparts to meet her hard-pressed troops. Her brother was wild-eyed and there was blood from a flesh-wound on his wrist.

"They are handing over the city!" His voice was choked with venom and he motioned to the two city elders who stood, surrounded by his men in the center of the courtyard.

The eyes of the Countess sparked with anger. She was not used to having her authority flouted. She walked up close to the two men. She knew them well, Ascanio Guicciardini and Galeazzo Ferrante.

"Do you dare?" she spat. "Do you dare to assume authority for what is mine?"

Galeazzo Ferrante did not flinch from her blazing eyes. He was known as a fearless man.

"It is a time to see reason, Madam," he said. "There is no hope of survival if we fight; if we lay down our arms the Duke of Valentinois will show the generosity he has shown elsewhere."

"You cur!" She moved closer to him. "Have you no loyalty? Would you thus defy the order of your rightful sovereign?"

Galeazzo Ferrante hesitated for half a second and then in tones which rose loudly on the still air inside the citadel's courtyard, as if he were ringing his death knell, he said:

"When, Madam, a sovereign has lost the confidence of the people and must rule them by oppression, she has forfeited her right to be obeyed by her subjects."

The Countess' hand slashed across his face and a dozen lances pricked at his body as he made an involuntary movement toward her.

For several minutes she stared at him, eyes afire, hardly able to believe that this common vassal had spoken to her in that way.

"When we have chased this brigand back to his churches in the south," she said slowly, "you will know what right I have forfeited. Long before then you will wish you could have forfeited your life rather than face what is meant for traitors of your caliber."

Ferrante made no reply. So hard had been her blow that a ring she wore had cut his lip and blood oozed thickly down his chin.

"Take them down and put them among the instruments," she said after a short silence. "They can have time to consider what is in store for them."

CHAPTER 6

Later on the same day that the two elders of the city council had been taken to the dungeons beneath the citadel, Cesare Borgia rode into Forli at the head of his army, to the vast wave of cheering from the inhabitants which welcomed him as deliverer from the warlike Countess.

He began immediately to make preparations to take her stronghold. This was the time to make an impression of invincibility, against this warrior lady whose reputation of fearlessness and martial ability represented the last hope of most of Italy against the threatening papal army. He wanted quick results to prove that his campaign was not won by diplomacy alone but could equally be carried on force of arms if the occasion arose.

By early the following day his siege guns were in position, trained on the citadel above which the Countess' flag still ruffled bravely in the slight breeze. Her men could be seen from time to time moving along the ramparts, and she herself appeared occasionally as if to inspect the measures that were being taken toward her downfall.

Cesare, well aware of her determination to fight, nonetheless made a cunning gesture to prove beyond all doubt to the people of Forli that he was a fair and generous man from whom they need fear nothing if they stood with him in the future. He rode out from his surrounding troops toward the broad moat of the citadel and offered to parley with the Countess on the terms of her surrender. He did not, he said, enjoy the thought of such a loss of life which her blind obstinacy could only assure.

There was silence behind the ramparts at his offer and, smiling to himself, Cesare reined his horse away to be pulled up short by the shouted intimation that the Countess would descend from the ramparts to talk with him and that he, well covered by his men, should meet her on the broad drawbridge.

There was nothing to be done. She had a nerve this Countess, but, decided Cesare, it would make his gesture all the more spectacular if he met her on her own drawbridge. He turned on his horse and waved to his men, at which a posse of some sixty men rode forward and ranged up a little behind him with swords ready.

Slowly the drawbridge creaked down and the portcullis went up. At its far end Cesare saw, for the first time, the figure of the Countess with an immediate impression of an austere beauty which was there, although she did nothing to enhance it.

She was on foot and Cesare got slowly down from his horse, felt for his sword hilt and walked with measured step to the drawbridge.

He stepped forward, feeling the heavy wood under his feet and then, instinctively, hesitated. There was a sudden creaking of winches and with several times the speed with which it had been lowered, the drawbridge swept up as cannons boomed out from the ramparts.

Cesare's hesitation gave him the seconds to fling himself clear; another step or two and he'd have been too far advanced on the bridge to do anything but be swept forward into the citadel's gate where the Countess and her men were waiting to receive him.

He landed heavily on the side of the moat, grasping at strong plants to prevent himself from slipping into the deep, muddy water. His advance guard were with him immediately under the very walls of the stronghold to help him clear and, under the orders of his lieutenants, the Borgian cannons and falconets were replying, like thunder drowning the roar of a rapids.

"Are you hurt, Sire?"

He pulled himself up and, with heavy vengeance vowed in his heart, waved aside his men's concern.

"She shall be paid for this treachery," he said.

For the rest of that day and well into the next, Cesare's cannons cracked and thundered and the citadel shook and lost pieces of its scarred old stone. The recruited citizens stood eagerly by with great cartloads of faggots, waiting for the order which inevitably grew nearer.

They were firmly for Cesare Borgia, now. Talk had raced through the town of his offer to parley—an offer to parley when he had the strength to crush all resistance almost before it had begun. And hadn't she dealt with that generous offer in just the way one would expect from such a mean-hearted tyrant? And hadn't Cesare Borgia given out the usual order to his troops that no woman of Forli was to be molested under pain of death? And weren't their two most respected councillors languishing in the citadel, probably being tortured even now if they hadn't been killed already? There was hardly a man in Forli who would not have risked his life for Cesare and for revenge on the oppressor of his life's years.

The Borgian cannons, concentrating on forming a breach, soon had dangerous cracks zigzagging down the walls of the citadel and the citizens stroked their bundles of faggots as if they were lovers, waiting and ready for the order.

The obvious approach of the end seemed to fire Caterina Sforza-Riario with madness. As the walls began to crack under the furious onslaught of the attackers' cannons, she had both the elders of the council brought out and hanged from the ramparts before the eyes of their fellow citizens. Their bodies were left swinging over the breach which was rapidly forming in the walls, while cries of hatred and revenge burst from the lips of the townsfolk gathered in a vast mass behind the lines of Cesare's ready troops and the busy cannons.

Cesare watched the gap in the walls with a grim smile. He saw the vain attempt of the defenders to fill it in with earth and stones, watched them scatter or be blown to pieces as his cannons continued a relentless punishment.

"Tell the citizens to move forward with their faggots," he ordered. "Another dead hit and the time is with us."

The carts, swaying and creaking, with the Borgian army advancing slowly just behind, moved slowly, ominously, toward the moat, while the cannons redoubled their fire to keep the defenders at bay.

The bodies of the two hanged councillors had fallen and were lost somewhere under the debris.

"They shall be well revenged," Cesare muttered to one of his lieutenants. "This misguided woman shall learn that it is not for her to meddle in men's affairs and oppose the foremost army in Italy."

The gap in the wall had broadened and the defenders had given up attempts to seal it as more and more sections were swept away under the unceasing bombardment. They could be seen, beyond, forming a wall of falconets ready to hotly receive the invading forces. There was activity too on the ramparts, where the smaller, more wieldy guns were being swiveled in an effort to cover the impending attack.

The citizen army moved like an exodus across the intervening space, slowly covering it, approaching like death, the grim defenders of Forli's suicidal stronghold.

Soon they had reached the broad, murky expanse of the moat and although some carts had been overturned by the guns on the ramparts and some of the citizens floated facedown in the waters, they set quickly and determinedly to work, piling both carts and faggots into the depths.

Cesare had ridden forward to be in the vanguard of his forces, just behind the first spearhead which would take the brunt of the defensive counterattack. The cannons, which had moved nearer, played over the heads of the bridge-builders, aiming with greater and greater accuracy, shot after shot through the gap in the wall beyond which the ranks of the defenders were trying not to break but to organize and reorganize as death took its toll of their lines.

Steadily the rough bridge forged across the moat. The citizens, volunteers to a man, worked with vigor and courage. Cesare's men stood waiting for the word to storm over the light, rocky pathway which was being made and hurl themselves through the waning fire of the defense whose ranks and guns they could clearly see in some confusion through the broadening gap.

Almost before the bridge was completed, Cesare gave the command for which his men had been waiting. The first lines of the attack had to jump the last four feet to the debris of the citadel's wall. They were met with a scattered fire from within and rocks and missiles from above, but forged on and in, pressed forward by those from behind until they were all over the courtyard and spouting up into the ramparts.

The faggot bridge was finished. The army pounded over, the citizens seized the arms of the dead to fight against their Countess, Cesare crossed and joined in the hand-to-hand fighting in which the weight of his men's numbers was a crushing advantage.

So quickly had the invasion of the citadel come that the defenders had had no time to withdraw across the smaller inner moat and into the tower where munitions and provisions were stored. Attack and defense together in a great, struggling mob, swept over that small moat, preceded by a few paces by the Countess and her personal guard.

"The tower, the tower!" Cesare roared, seeing the danger. Locked in there they'd be able to hold out for a week or two.

Behind him came his fresh body of men through the gap. Nobody to engage them. They swept in his wake over the inner moat, through the struggling dogfights and up into the tower.

The fighting was short and bloodcurdling. One by one, giving their lives with a devotion which flamed an aura of death around them, the Countess' guard fell until only she was left, knocked to the stone floor, a point of steel at her throat and one of Cesare's Swiss mercenaries grinning with lustful delight over her prostrate body.

CHAPTER 7

A great wood fire had been made in the dungeons. Its red and sparkling heat was fighting to keep the chill of the thick, stone walls at bay. Along one wall a couch had been placed on which Cesare was lying eating the meat from a leg of chicken. On mats on the floor his four or five principal lieutenants were quaffing wine, filling their glasses from a barrel which had been brought from the stores, and themselves devouring pieces of fowl which they were roasting on spits over the fire.

"When are we going to get up this beauty, Sire," one of them asked with a slight slur to his speech as he rose and crossed the dungeon. Cesare followed him with his eyes and his glance took in the defenseless form of the proud Countess. She was naked, stripped of all her austere covering. She was stretched out on the great wheel of a rack to one side of the gloomy, shadowed room.

"When I've finished with her," he said, swigging a draught of wine and passing his glass to one of the men for a refill.

"Seems such a pity to keep her waiting," the man replied. "She obviously loves us."

A gust of laughter greeted his words.

The eyes of the Countess were still able to give a feeble reflection of their earlier glitter although by now she was hurt and exhausted and thoroughly humiliated.

Cesare looked at her as his strong teeth pulled at the chicken flesh. Would any of her subordinates have expected quite such a physical beauty? When she lashed them with her tongue would they have pictured those glossy, firm breasts, high and perky with their small impudent nipples? When she scowled and barked an order would they have thought of that tight waist with its rather sinewy, muscular stomach? When she ordered men to the dungeons and had them hanged from battlements would they have thought of those soft, feminine buttocks, that bottom which asked for caresses? When she rode through the town to order a massacre of reprisal, supervising its execution, would they have considered those warm thighs and those fleshy hips with the moss of pale hair and the heavy overlap of flesh between those white, tapering columns? She was really a beauty. She could have taken her place in an elegant court as one of its prime beauties at any time, except that her attitude had decided that lines of severity were to be drawn between her brows, that her mouth was to be hardened into grimness and her eyes, which could blaze and spark like any insulted courtesan's, should grow to contain the disgust for her fellow creatures which gleamed constantly in them.

They had watched her writhe on the rack—and it had to be admitted she had borne her punishment like a martyr. They had humiliated her, her eyes wide with horror had revealed just how much, with their mauling of her breasts and the supple contours of her naked body. But Cesare had reserved her principal humiliation for himself. He had yet personally to repay her for the near loss of his life on the drawbridge and also he was impressed with her looks and hauteur.

He grinned as his lieutenant took the leg of

217

fowl he was munching and with a quick movement thrust it up between her straddled thighs into her cunt. The Countess gasped and swore. The lips of her vagina opened and then closed over the knobby, half-chewed meat.

"You wouldn't think a chicken would have enough guts to do that to a Countess," his lieutenant jested, and there were fresh guffaws from the spectators. The man moved the fleshy bone around in her for a few seconds and then, tiring of the game—or perhaps being made too hot by it—withdrew the leg and flung it across to a corner of the room.

"Well seasoned," called another. "Why didn't you eat it."

"By the look of her Ladyship it might have poisoned me."

Cesare swung himself off the couch and crossed to the rack. He stared at the inert body spread-eagled across it. The Countess glared back at him. All she wanted was a dagger, her eyes seemed to say, and he'd regret these humiliating tortures and liberties to which he'd subjected her.

Cesare lowered his eyes over her body. He could see the small blue veins on her white breasts and on the taut flesh where her thighs ran into her hips. He reached out his hand and stroked it softly over her breast, gently savoring the butteriness of the firm skin beneath his fingers. He could feel his lust rising in confined warmth at his loins. His eyes glittered and he looked up at hers again and saw something like fear in them for the first time.

"Leave us," he commanded.

His men ceased their jesting immediately and began to gather their belongings prior to departure.

"Later, perhaps, we too may pay her out for her treachery to you, Sire," murmured his principal lieutenant as they passed the rack on their way to the steep stone steps that led up the wall to the dungeon exit.

"Did you not know it was an offense to have any kind of intercourse with a corpse?" Cesare asked.

His lieutenant roared with laughter, laughter which was taken up by the others and followed them up the steps and beyond the citadel, leaving only a wan glinting echo of itself in Cesare's ears.

"They tell me, Madam," he said softly, "that you have had three husbands. I wonder were they afraid of you—such a woman as could hang from the battlements two of her most respected citizens in the face of a besieging army."

Her eyes blazed at him and she made no reply.

"Difficult to think those husbands were ever permitted to mount you," he mused on, "but I'm told you have some fine sons safely out of harm's way. Were you afraid I might take them and train them for my army?"

Caterina Sforza-Riario moved her lips in a grimace of fury and loathing. Her voice was soft and a little strained and hoarse.

"Your army," she mocked. "Your rabble, a horde of barbarians like their leader, an upstart drunk with power."

Cesare almost raised his hand to strike her, but instead, with unerring instinct to humiliate her further, he stroked her breast instead and pinched her nipple between his thumb and forefinger.

"Were those husbands of yours allowed to

see the body they entered?" he went on. "Or were they allowed only shamefacedly to slip their pricks up under your skirts and do their best to produce children for their lord and mistress?"

"They were weak and wretched—but each was a better man than you," she spat.

Cesare sighed and let his fingers slide down over her muscular belly to dabble in the hair around her crotch.

"Madam, your desire to be brave seems to have injured your reasoning capacity."

"Take your hands off me you vile beast," she flared.

For answer Cesare bent and kissed a nipple and his fingers slipped into her crotch and penetrated her vagina which he tickled, grinning into her eyes.

She turned her face away from him. He saw a light muscle twitching in her cheek.

"And your body was so meant for spending days and nights in the throbbing heat of bed," he went on, knowing that his words and attitude were making her desperate with fury and humiliation. "You have such a moist and ready cunt. I do believe you'd like to tryst with every man in my army."

"Beast . . . swine . . ."

The words were faded echoes of her recent outbrust. She was exhausted, physically and psychologically.

Cesare gloated over her helpless body. Now, he felt just like it. But a mere fuck wouldn't be sufficiently humiliating for her. He could feel his penis, large, hot and pushing to escape. With an image of soft, juicy entry into her and the relief it would bring to his lusting loins, he began to unstrap her legs.

She turned her face back to him, her eyes questioning.

Her legs flapped freely in a few seconds. She seemed to have lost the use of them. He untied her wrists which were stretched out above her head and she slid down over the wheel and crumpled to the floor, her eyes open and alive, but her weakened body refusing to obey her.

On the cold stone floor, she tried to move and stand up, but her ankles were stiff and dead, her arms numb, so she lay there where she'd slid, moving her hands weakly to restore the circulation.

For a few minutes, Cesare allowed her a little respite. He wanted her to recover so that nothing was lost on her. Then, when she was able, rather stiffly, to move her limbs and sit up, he pulled her to her feet, letting her stand a moment to get used to the pressure. She leaned on him, helpless to pull herself away. He breathed heavily with the touch of her flesh along him and moved her over toward the rack again.

She began to struggle weakly and with little gasps of pain as she realized that he was going to attach her once more to that instrument of torture, but, especially in her enfeebled state, she was no match for him and he pressed her face forward against the wheel while he tied her hands to it high above her head once again.

Her body moved fleshily against him as she tried to escape and he felt the spongy warmth of her buttocks squeezing against his organ as he pressed into her to hold her fast.

With her wrists firmly attached, he moved and caught one of her ankles, drawing it up around the side of the great wheel to attach it to the hub. She lost balance with the other foot and sagged down to the floor, held up only by her wrists as the wheel swung around with her weight.

Dexterously, Cesare fastened one ankle to the hub and then moved around to the other side and fastened the other. Then he pulled the wheel back to its original position, fixed it with a prop of wood and stood back.

The Countess was now in more or less a sitting position against and around the rack. Her body was held in against it, her legs spread wide and wrapped around the wheel at an angle of something more than 60 degrees with the floor. Her hanging behind was the lowest part of her.

"Now we'll see what your husbands should have done to teach you a little obedience and your place as a woman, wife and mother," Cesare said.

Her eyes were closed, all the weight of her body on her fastened wrists. She was white and subdued and said nothing.

Quickly, Cesare pulled off his clothes until he was standing naked on the cold floor. His prick was tingling and the foreskin had drawn back to reveal the ardent, almost purpling knob. A little seminal fluid was already moistening its hot expanse in anticipation. He held it with his hand for a moment and he could feel its throbbing desire. Its heat was like an aura of red-hot lust around his genitals.

Around the fire, still blazing merrily, were the carpets and rugs on which his lieutenants had been reclining. He arranged them rapidly near the wheel under the Countess' behind which hovered a couple of feet above the ground.

222

He knelt down on the thick rugs and ran his hands down the smooth lines of her back until they flared out over the soft cushion of her buttocks. The skin was smooth and sweating slightly with the strain she was undergoing. He ran his fingers between her buttocks where a few fine hairs straggled and the skin was suddenly softer, more tender feeling, like a raw steak. He dug his finger gently against her anus and felt it tight and denying like a pursed, puritanical mouth.

For some minutes he played with her anus while she sagged, seeming almost lifeless, then he felt it give and she gave a repressed squeal as his finger penetrated the tiny hole and moved like an animal in the soft portals of her rectum. She gasped again as he dug farther in up to the first finger joint and then the second. He squeezed in another finger and she cried out and her head fell back from the rack and then swung forward against the wood again.

Cesare moved his fingers around in her bottom, pressing out and up alternately, broadening, preparing the nether hole that was to receive the issue of his lust. The Countess wriggled her ankles against the hub of the wheel, but was unable to escape. Her widely spread legs and widely spread buttocks prevented her totally from escaping that foreign invasion of her private domain.

Easier and yet more easily Cesare's finger slipped and explored in the softening, yielding depths of her anus. His two fingers had easy access now and he thrust them right in to their full extent. In front of him, his prick carved the air like a sword, hard and ready for action. His balls seemed to ache and in his loins there was a ferment of sharp, spiraling coils of sen-

223

sation. A drop of seminal fluid had dripped to the floor and he felt he could wait no longer.

Carefully he lay down under her and moved into position so that her dark, little hole would descend onto his rearing mast. Then, with his foot he deftly kicked aside the prop, reached up to catch her hips as she swung down toward him and pulled her down onto his prick.

The trembling arm of flesh battered in at first thrust and he felt her buttocks tense and try to close the slit to him. She cried out in pain and struggled with her bonds, but could do nothing.

Cesare pushed her upwards gently and the wheel swung back so that all the weight was on her wrists again. Then she fell slowly back with the turning wheel onto his prick once more.

The breach was made and broadened. Cesare felt her tight, rasping back channel tearing at his penis as he surged into the squeezing depths. He gritted his teeth and flexed his hips upward, sighing with the excruciating sensation. He heard her moan and pushed up again with his hands. Her anus slid off his prick and she swung up a little and then wheeled back again, her bottom meeting his hands and the spread crack between the buttocks enclosing his penis once again.

Her anus was becoming easier. He was already half buried in her and encountering no resistance with the exploring forepart of his rod. Only around the entrance, with the thickening dimension of his sex down to its root, was the pressure still enormous and every further tearing inch thrust into her drawing fresh groans from her open lips.

The great squeezing pressure, the tight contraction of her unused back passage around his long arm of violation began to draw panting gasps from Cesare. He had never felt such over-whelming pressure before. He wriggled as his prick thrust in and pulled her right down so that she yelled out in exhausted pain.

Now he didn't push her up very far each time, but allowed the rocking movement of the wheel to do it for him, simply guiding her gently with his hands.

Every time she came down and her behind rested for a moment on his belly its elastic entrance crushed the base of his penis. His loins were in fiery turmoil and his knob seemed to itch with desire to rid itself of his load. He wanted to get farther and farther into her and he spread her buttocks wide with his hands and screwed in for all he was worth.

The strain on the Countess' wrists when he pushed her up was so great that she was relieved each time she sagged back. She began to resist his efforts to push her up away from him and he let her rest on his loins while he wriggled his prick around inside her and she gasped and moaned and began to feel a strange, unanticipated tingling.

The Countess hated herself for this unexpected reaction on her part, but she couldn't help herself. In her exhausted condition there was little resistance left and it was easier to let herself be carried away on a sexual tide, to allow this creeping in her loins to crawl forward and farther forward, tingling her inside and pulsating in her vagina. His great invasion of her backside no longer seemed so vile nor yet so painful. It was producing these sexual feelings in her which she more normally associated with ordinary sex. She could hardly believe that it could happen, but it was.

She knew that he filled her behind like a spear, not sparing her at all, shagging her pitilessly, but she almost wanted more. It was such a relief on her wrists to be able to rest on his hairy stomach and to feel that fleshy wand digging into her.

She felt his hands clasping the fleshy rotundities of her buttocks, clasping them so hard that his fingers dug into her deeply and must have made deep weals in the soft flesh. His action was becoming more and more rapid; he was virtually pummeling her with thrusts and she could feel his hard belly, rising up, straining up to meet her downward rush so that they met in a clashing embrace and his spear tore in making her shriek with the shattering advance of it.

She heard him grunting and gasping, heavy masculine grunts with a certain savage brutality in them. With the growing desire in her belly she felt an outgoing to him, to Cesare Borgia, who had dared to submit her to this fantastic experience, who respected her not one jot and was not afraid to use her as he wished.

She heard his gasping become a heavy whine of exploding breath, felt his body tense along her buttocks and press there.

Then, with a sense of disappointment and the reality of her captive situation, she felt him relax on the floor under her and she rested, sagging on his stomach as he lay for a moment, motionless, breathing heavily.

When he slipped from under her and got to his feet, she became aware of the ache at her anus. She felt sore all the way up inside her; her back passage seemed to be burning and around its portals she felt wet and open and exposed.

She had slipped down to the rugs and hung there, trying to take the weight off her wrists, with her legs up in the air toward the hub of the rack. She opened her eyes and looked sideways at Cesare Borgia. He had climbed to his feet and was looking at her with a smile of satisfaction. Her eyes dropped to his long, limp, white prick which swung down between his hairy thighs.

"How was that, my proud Countess?" he asked.

She didn't answer. She looked away from him back to the wooden slats of the rack. The desire in her loins was still there, albeit ebbing. She could not remember having felt so sexy before. It was like confession under torture only this was sexiness under torture.

She heard him pad away to a corner of the dungeon and she opened her eyes which she'd closed for a moment in an attempt to clear her head. She saw him, still nude, returning through the flame-stabbed gloom. He was carrying a short-handled whip with a dozen narrow thongs. Her eyes opened wider in fear and her throat felt constricted. She felt as if there was nothing of her left that was real; she was exposed and helpless in a way she'd never been before. She could only hope that this man would eventually spare her.

Cesare replaced the wooden prop and she found herself again hanging in midair with the straps biting into her aching wrists, the muscles of her back aching under the strain. She could hardly move at all, only press her body into the wooden wheel as she prepared for the punishment he had designed for her.

227

She heard the thongs swishing in the air, but nothing happened. He was tantalizing her. There was silence. She bit her lips and rested her head against the slats which were hard and unfriendly.

Suddenly she cried out and flattened involuntarily into the wood as the first lash of the dozen-thonged whip wrapped around her body, stinging it and leaping away again to leave an unbearable stinging in its wake.

Her chest and stomach cringed under the pain and then she flattened into the wood a second time as the lash flicked all over her back and buttocks. No sound would get past her lips but a deflated "Ouff."

The next lash was around her thighs, curling in a weal-tracing embrace with a pain that sickened and made her bite her tongue.

Tears of pain forced their way from under her lashes, her belly felt like a void and down in her loins was a strange, frightened, tingling, tickling, sick, sexy reaction to the beating. The humiliation of being whipped like a slave was lost in a horror of the pain and her reaction to it. She began to sob softly as the lash rose and fell, stroking her back, buttocks and thighs in flesh-cutting caresses.

When he'd stopped and she slowly became aware of the fact, she felt the individual strands of pain across her body and that unfinished symphony of aching in her loins which craved for fulfillment. In an unreal world of pain and longing and humility she was capable of strange reactions.

"Well, Madam, now you see how it is to be a slave, to be a city councillor who can be tortured and hanged from the ramparts of your citadel."

"Fuck me," she croaked.

There was a brief silence and then Cesare broke into peals of astonished laughter.

"A disguised pain-lover of the first order!" he exclaimed. "Such ardent wishes should never be spurned—even though the spurning would make the torture greater."

The act of flagellation had sparked off erotic feelings deep in his core and his penis had risen once again and was jutting out toward his prey. The proud Caterina was begging him to fuck her!

He walked over to where she sagged with the thin pattern of weals across her back. She looked exhausted. It was difficult to believe she would have the energy to make love. He untied her hands and then her ankles and she fell back onto the rugs to roll over immediately onto her stomach away from the pain of the lashes.

She lay there for some minutes with him standing over her, looking down on her pink-grooved flesh. She moved her hands and feet gently and groaned a couple of times. Then she raised her tear-washed face and looked at him. There was no hostility in her eyes, nothing but desire and her eyes dropped meaningfully to his ramrod of a prick.

"So you desire a good length of male strength inside you, my proud Madam," Cesare mocked.

His taunting brought no reaction but a nod of almost desperate agreement. She climbed painfully to her knees. The ache of anticipation had shifted from her loins and seemed to flame all over her.

Cesare helped her to her feet. If her citizens could see this, he thought, their proud, haughty

229

tyrant begging to be upthrust by the enemy chief!

She pressed hard against him and his prick ran up between them, crushing against the soft flesh of her hips and the sinewy mound of her belly. She joggled against him and he felt the prickling of reciprocation swimming about in his long length of rigidity.

He began to lead her to the couch. Her eyes showed no reaction to him, no feeling, but that of an inturned yearning. It was as if she were drugged.

As they stepped slowly toward the divan, she stroked his penis tenderly as if she adored every inch of it. He made way for her to lie down on the couch, but she intimated that he was to lie down himself. Her back was too sore.

Cesare stretched out, tensed his buttocks and jutted his organ massively up toward the gloomy roof of the dungeon. The fire had begun to diminish and the glow was now a centralized one, surrounded by a half-pierced gloom.

When he tensed his behind, a live desire moved like a solid thing along from his loins to the base of his reaching rod.

For a moment the Countess looked at him. She ran her fingers softly up his hot tube of flesh and then swung herself painfully astride him, poising above his prick, arranging her vagina directly above it. She leaned forward, resting her hands on either side of his face while she positioned herself. Her knees brushed his ribs. And then with a long-drawn moan of deliverance, she sank down onto the prick that seared up into her belly like a jet of oil.

Her head rolled on her neck and she felt giddy and out of control as it raced up inside her and she sank down, until her buttocks met his thighs. Her movement was mechanical, dictated only by the feeling brain in his loins. She rose up and sank again with a broken sob of relief. She began to squirm and skewer her buttocks on his thighs, feeling the point of his prick at its summit pressing and poking at her cervix. She rolled about on his body like a puppet, a puppet crazed with human desire for the orgasm which was so agonizingly slow in coming.

Cesare brought his thighs up from the horizontal and contained her buttock and hips in them. He reached down with his tingling hands and grasped her thighs in which he could feel the light muscles flexing and unflexing with her movement.

My God, he thought, this woman was made for one thing only and all her life by all accounts she's lived a lie.

Her breasts swayed and jumped over her heaving belly and her mouth hung open, under flared nostrils and closed eyes. Her long, fair hair swung across her face each time she descended and with her uprise she shook her head so that it swung away.

Cesare tensed his buttocks and felt sensation tremble and palpitate at the base of his prick. All the way up, his organ was alive with pinpricks and the knob almost hurt with the treatment, the ferocity she was subjecting it to. He knew he wasn't far off and he dug his fingers into her thighs so hard that he brought a murmur of shock from her puppet lips.

As she bobbed on him, the Countess tensed her loins, aching for the sensation to flee. She couldn't stand it much longer, that yearning,

bursting ball of flame inside her. She had to
have release.

She clasped his hips with her thighs and
squirmed her bottom from side to side as she
fell. She had forgotten the pain of her thrashing, all sensation was in that long, wet channel
in which his prick was like a great, drumming
barge-pole. His penis was spreading and battering her belly. It hurt, it was wonderful, it
was hateful, it was necessary to be over or she
would die.

As if she were drowning, her past life
seemed to mist into the sensation that racked
her. This moment seemed to be what she had
always lived for, this moment when thinking
was painful and the only thing that mattered
was the prick in her quim and the manflesh
consuming her in its embrace. If there were
only this moment it was all that she had ever
desired, this acuteness of sensation, this be-
yond-reality that she had never truly experienced with her tired, frightened, fawing,
subservient husbands of before.

The name of the man who had subjected her
fused with her gasps of pain and love: "Cesare
Borgia, Cesare Borgia . . ." It was inevitably
this man that everybody had said was just the
way he was — and she had thought to feel differently from everybody else.

There were times when she'd wondered what
it was that would tie her to a man so that she
felt no longer free and strong. It was no physical beauty, it was not intellectual strength—
both those had been embodied in various of her
husbands. It was—what could one say?—a *je ne
sais quoi* which was nothing more than an animal force in a man, an understanding in a man
that he would lead, a lack of fright in a man,

232

of doubt, of hesitation in his certainty that he would stand by his acts.

These thoughts moved through her head like a phantom, not clear, felt rather. In a feeling connected like cause and result with the wide, scourging opening of her loins which was beginning to happen now, now, now. In a maze of wild, swimming confusion in head and loins, she heard, like a distant train, his breath growing under her, recognized his climax trembling. With a great giving thrust down in which she contracted her loins and concentrated them on the pole down which she slid, she felt the fire within her burst out into a great conflagration as she moaned in delirium and seemed to die and die and die again . . .

She was aware after some seconds which were like darkness, that he had held her up with his strong arms and that his staccato gasping was flailing the cooling air of the dungeon as his prick jerked quickly into her in its fading heat.

Her last thought before she flopped exhausted along the length of his hot, strong body was that she was his for as long as he wanted her.

CHAPTER 8

It goes without mention that Cesare Borgia, Duke of Valentinois, carried more than military glory back with him to Rome. Maria the gypsy was already established in Imola, well provisioned for his return in a few weeks or months, and in his train, strangely changed to anyone who knew her, the Countess Caterina Sforza-Riario dressed in stark black and white, sat her horse, impressive and emotionless but a willing captive.

All those cities which had refused to pay their fiefs to the Holy See had been subdued and Cesare's fame—as much his personality as his achievements—had spread throughout the whole of Italy.

Small wonder that on his return to Rome, the city was the scene of wild enthusiasm. There is nothing the crowd will take to its heart more than a strong man who has a reputation for magnanimity.

Alexander, himself, overflowed with pride at his son's victories and the glory of his reputation. He dispatched a deputation, which included two cardinals and a number of dignitaries, to meet his son on the road beyond the gates of Rome. A huge reception was prepared for him within with prelates, ambassadors, generals and officials of the city waiting eagerly to receive him.

When he made his entry through the northern gate, wave upon wave of thunderous cheering filled the air above the seven hills; people threw garments and flowers into the air; there was a salute of cannon fire.

His train was splendid enough to inspire awe and devotion. In the van were the baggage carts, splendidly caparisoned, and immediately followed by several thousand foot soldiers in full campaign apparel preceded by trumpet-blasting heralds in the livery of the Duke and the King of France. The Duke, who followed next on horseback, was surrounded by a guard of fifty mounted men simply clad and with the Borgian bull emblazoned on their breasts.

The Duke, plainly dressed in black velvet with a gold chain about his neck, was followed by several thousand cavalry, with halberds and banners. A posse of trumpeters, blowing hard enough to reduce the walls of Jericho, brought up the rear in a fine flourish . . .

With Cesare, within his protecting body of men-at-arms, rode the deputation which had met him, broad smiles on their faces, happy and proud to share in his glory for a brief moment.

And not far behind him rode the Countess, unsmiling, severe, but hiding deep thoughts of unbelievable incidents.

Around this vast cortege, the city was *en fete*. Guns continuously thundered salutes, banners floated from the Castle of St. Angelo.

The Pope, tears of joy in his eyes, watched from the loggia above the portals of the Vatican as his son approached. He remembered that son of his, that athletic, gawky boy who had been initiated in the art of love by his young sister Lucrezia, he remembered that panting embrace, guilty and half-afraid beside the pool in the grounds of his mansion. And he thought: This is my son, Cesare Borgia, riding in triumph through the streets of Rome with the whole world as far as the French Court listening to tales of his exploits and success.

It was only a couple of nights ago that Alexander had, himself, stuck his prick up his daughter's cunt and fucked and fucked her until they had both been paralyzed with inertia —and Cesare had, indirectly, shared in that. It was with him, under the Pope's guidance, that the young girl had lost her virginity and started on that path which made her such a bone-shaking joy to men.

Alexander brought his thoughts back to the present with an effort. Later tonight, Cesare, if he had no other plans—and who could possibly have other plans—would be able to enjoy his sister in a nude-entwining embrace. This would be a fitting reward for his achievement and richly deserved.

He watched as his son dismounted at the steps and his bright army ranged itself behind him. When Cesare began to climb the broad flights with the two cardinals and the ambassadors who accompanied him, the Pope, his heart overwhelmed with pleasure, descended to the comfortable chambers below and arranged himself on his throne.

Cesare, his eyes alight with pleasure at the sight of his father, advanced through the marble-pillared chamber and fell upon his knees before the throne.

As Alexander, tears in his eyes, placed his hands upon his son's head, prior to embracing him, he thought what a fine and imposing figure his son had become even in the months since he'd departed. Every tiniest period of time seemed to add to his stature. Lucrezia would be overjoyed; indeed, the juices would start to run between her legs at the very sight of her brother, whom she still adored.

CHAPTER 9

With the departure of Cesare's army from Romagna, it was not long before the physical absence of troops began once again to cause rebellion. News filtered through that the town of Faenza, which had once enjoyed the protection of Venice, was arming itself to the teeth prior to proclaiming itself independent of the Holy See. Thither, after a period of recuperation, Cesare marched again at the head of his army. With winter fast approaching and the town much stronger than had been expected, he settled down to a blockade, cutting off all entry and exit. He had plenty of time.

In fact, leaving his troops in charge of one of his lieutenants, he repaired with the others to Cesena with the idea of a little light relief.

At this time of year, late autumn, there were many rustic sports held in the villages of the northern part of Italy where the village Hercules and Appolos were able to show off their prowess in such different arts as wrestling, running and archery. It was to one of these villages, dressed as peasants, incognito, that Cesare and his lieutenants laughingly made their way.

Each of these sports days was the great local event of the year. The local dignitary, duke or count, with his ladies and retinue, would have the place of honor in a temporary stand at the edge of the sports field, from which he would present the awards when the day was done. The people, drinking and making merry all day, would explode into a carnival of conviviality as darkness fell. There would be dancing in the streets and fireworks, people would get lost, there would be necking and an occasional robbery or rape. Often, long-bored wives would choose this occasion to get caught up in the crowd away from their half-drunk husbands and join in a furious and desperate copulation with any stranger who caught hold of their long hair and planted a kiss on their longing lips. In the morning, their husbands, who, perhaps, had not been particularly virtuous either, would find their wives sleeping a sleep of the dead in a bed it appeared they'd never left during the festivities. At this time, too, young maids, in sober times so careful of their virginity, would, under the influence of a glass or two of wine, allow themselves to go far enough in their lovemaking for there suddenly to be no return. They would find themselves, startled and helpless, tumbled on their backs in the corner of some field, with their skirts around their waists or perhaps on the nearby hedge and their thighs unbelievably wide as a masculine rigidity brought them pain and then relief from their days of fear and wondering. Many a bastard owed his birth to the abandon of carnival time in the villages, many a maiden found herself the following day, or in the days that followed, wondering which of the many men she passed in the streets had deflowered her while she lay in half-drunk ecstasy beneath him. If it were not that so many were in the same boat and everybody knew it, there would be great embarrassment. And, of course, some of the one-night affairs developed into liaisons of a more permanent nature so that many a wife on a shopping expedition, would take to wandering through the fields and woods on a sunny morning, to return, rather late, with crumpled dress and a guilty expression, to the family bosom.

It was to join in such ribald and licentious gaiety that Cesare and his party left Cesena in high spirits one morning.

CHAPTER 10

"Who is the lady next to the Duke of Alfaro?" Cesare voiced the question to Rossano Erfredi, one of his followers. His eyes gazed up to the nearby stand where the Duke, a pompous, condescending old fellow, was surrounded by his wife, a band of men and ladies-in-waiting and a very attractive, fair-haired girl with pale, blue eyes which sparkled occasionally like sun-flecks on a shallow, Mediterranean sea.

"I've never seen her before, Sire—but I can find out in no time."

"She appears to be alone—she's a beauty, isn't she?"

"Indeed, Sire, worthy of any gentleman's attention, grinned Erfredi.

"I'm glad our views concur," smiled Cesare. "Go and see what you can find out."

With Erfredi gone, Cesare turned back to where the village champion was in the act of eliminating yet another of his wrestling challengers. The man was stocky and over-muscular, probably the village blacksmith. So far he had won all his contests against his fellow villagers and foreign rustics by sheer brute strength. He was certainly dangerously strong, Cesare reflected, but he'd have to use more than brute strength if he wanted to keep his title this year.

The crowd was excited, as much by its own effervescence as the spectacle and the cheering and encouragement was considerable. It had not escaped their attention that there was a stranger in the field this year who looked a force to be reckoned with, but their money was on their local celebrity.

"A moronic mountain," one of Cesare's lieutenants whispered at his elbow, "but one would have to be careful if one got in close with him."

"I have his measure — I trust."

"If he looks like breaking one of your bones I'll put an arrow through his arm."

"You want us to be lynched from the trees over yonder—no, I have his measure, I say," Cesare replied.

While his bulging adversary had been breaking bones and spirits in dealing with his challengers, Cesare had, himself, come gently through the earlier rounds, with well applied pressures, to a less spectacular but just as efficient entry into the final bout which he was destined to have with the champion.

Already, the ladies had remarked his tall, slim-hipped figure with its supple muscular chest and arms which were in such contrast to the bulky power of the favorite. Many a feminine heart had already felt a twinge of desire and of curiosity as to who this handsome young man might be.

"There should be fun tonight," Cesare said to another of his lieutenants. "The whole place is swarming with pretty women and you can see their eyes gleaming with hope for a bit of freedom."

"Aye, Sire, I've made up my mind to have four in turn tonight—at least four."

"What a gourmand, Enrico, you'd better mind you don't break your neck in the races."

"It's something else I have to mind I don't break."

Cesare chuckled. "Well, Enrico, I'm a gourmet, and I've made my single choice already."

"Indeed, Sire—might one ask . . . ?"

"Over there in the stand. There's only one I could mean."

Enrico gazed discreetly towards the aristocrats' shelter.

"Ah, yes," he sighed. "I'd reluctantly put thoughts of that away. She's much too well chaperoned by the Duke and Duchess—might even be their daughter."

"The better she's chaperoned, the more determined she'll be to escape them once the idea's in her," Cesare said, with a grin.

"Well, good luck, Sire—perhaps the result of the wrestling will be an omen."

"Ah, Rossano, you must have intelligence in every village in the north to be so quick—who is she?"

Rossanno Erfredi was a little out of breath with hurrying to obey his chief's command. He spoke quickly, his words punctuated by little gasps which seemed, somehow, to enshroud the object of his inquiries in an exotic urgency.

"Her name, Sire, is Dorotea Caracciolo. She is the wife of Gianbattista Caracciolo, a captain of foot with the Venetians. She's here as a friend of the Duke and Duchess of Alfaro."

"And her husband—where is he?"

"In Venice, Sire—the lady is quite alone."

"Well done, Rossano—I'll save you a piece of the lady's garter for your pains."

There was a gust of laughter which died away as one of the sports officials came to say that the champion was ready for his final challenger. Across the greensward, his muscles more extended than usual from his limbering efforts with earlier adversaries, the champion strutted in an orgy of self-congratulation from which it was clear he saw no likelihood of losing his crown.

"I wish you'd let me take him, Sire," Rossano Erfredi said quietly. "He's an ugly looking brute and I could more easily afford to break a bone or two than you."

"You don't trust my strength, Rossano?

Come, is that worthy from a lieutenant to his captain?"

"Oh, Sire, forgive me, no!" Erfredi was covered with confusion. "It's simply that . . . if there were any risk—and I don't suppose for a moment there is—I'd sooner it were me than that you should risk a strain . . ." He was embarrassed now that he'd said anything which could be taken ambiguously when it had merely been an automatic statement of his devotion to the Duke of Valentinois.

"Yes, Sire," another lieutenant added. "I wish you'd let any of us take him. He's not worth your trouble."

Cesare laughed.

"It's no trouble, Enrico, I assure you, and it's only reasonable that I should lead our spearhead into the sports. Rossano, I don't forget a man's concern for my skin. It's the highest tribute anyone could ask."

A slight hush, broken with odd shouts, guffaws and other noises of movement and early tipsiness, had clouded over the green. Few doubted that the champion would be champion yet again. But the stranger provided a little more interest than was usually taken in a foregone conclusion. The fact was, that Cesare's victories had been so easy that they had lacked the impressive cock-strutting dazzle of his opponent's.

"Here's to the omen for the fair lady," Cesare said, as he moved out, away from his little band of disguised officers, and walked alertly toward the approaching champion.

Both were dressed in tights. Cesare in shoes and the champion in boots. The muscles in their torsos contained no shadows from the dying sun, but veins stood out on them like marks

242

traced heavily around the highland on a map.

They approached each other slowly, cunningly, surrounded at a distance by a crowd of several thousand villagers and countryfolk above whom the Duke of Alfaro's party looked on from the height of their perch.

Both men reached a point just beyond each other's reach and circled for a moment, sizing each other up. Then the champion, a man of uncomplicated reactions, who wanted a quick and spectacular victory to make him the undisputed wrestler of all time in his village, rushed in. Cesare caught his fist as he came, ignoring the other arm which reached out triumphantly for his neck. As the champion's fingers, all in a second, grazed his skin, he gave a quick twist to the fist he held. With a gasp, the champion jerked over off his balance and landed with a breath-shattering thud on his back. It was not for nothing that Cesare had had a Turkish instructor during his student days.

Quickly, Cesare was in with a full nelson on his opponent. The astonished referee counted according to the village rule, while the champion fumed and strained at the vise-like pressure on his neck, trying to jerk his shoulders from the ground. When Cesare released him at the end of the count, he got up slowly, easing his neck. The cheers of Cesare's lieutenants hailed over the green, followed, rather uncertainly, by cheering encouragement from the crowd.

The champion was furious, his eyes were the sparking color of red-hot coal in his blacksmith's furnace. He had not yet realized his danger. This was an accident. Some insolent, quick-moving stranger had taken him off his guard. Perhaps he'd been just a little too confident. But now he knew what his opponent was up to he'd crush his insolence out of him —but quickly before he lost face in front of his countrymen.

He came in again, caught Cesare's arms which came out to meet him and felt vague astonishment that his progress was completely checked. Those arms were as stiffly strong as the barrel of a cannon. For a second or two they stood there, leaning forward slightly, arms on each other's biceps and then the blacksmith swung Cesare and felt him going, sideways, apparently off-balance. He moved in to get his bear grip around the man's neck and suddenly, Cesare seemed to have righted himself. As the champion came to close quarters a sharp ankle blow knocked his legs together painfully and an even sharper jab under his chin sent him crashing on his back for the second time. There were fresh cheers and sounds of triumphant merriment from Cesare's little band of lieutenants. The rest of the crowd was hushed in something like awe.

Cesare leapt onto the heaving, almost deflated chest of his opponent, bent over him, so that their faces were close together and slipped a stranglehold around his neck with both arms.

The champion flailed for a moment, grabbed at Cesare's shoulders, arms and then his hair, but sudden, sharp tightenings of the asphyxiating grip on his neck made him release his hold each time with squeals of pain.

"Lie still or I'll strangle the life from you," Cesare gritted. Half-conscious only, with tears of strain in his eyes, the champion lay back, hardly knowing what had happened to him. The referee counted, slowly, it seemed, as if he could hardly credit the possibility of the title-holder being out for the second time in such a tiny space and with so little resistance.

When Cesare sprang to his feet, lithe as a gymnast, his opponent lay where he had fallen for a moment. Then he rolled over on his side and looked dazedly at Cesare with something like real fear in his eyes. He didn't move and the crowd began to shout for him, a shouting which slowly turned into a barracking as he turned a white face around the field as if he'd like to run for it.

"Had enough, my friend?" Cesare taunted. "Do you want to hand the title to me on a platter?"

A momentary gleam of hatred chased the fear from the blacksmith's face. All his dominance, all his respect in the village was dissipating. He had held a sure place in the set-up in this part of the world. Everybody knew who he was, what he was, how strong he was, what he could do to a man who questioned his position. And now, this fellow, this devil incarnate had arrived from nowhere to make what should have been a splendid, strength-displaying sports day into a farce in which he couldn't even seem to get near his opponent.

He struggled to his feet. He would make this effort. One more throw and hold and he was finished. The fellow was slippery, but he must be stronger. He *must* be stronger. Nobody could question that. If he could get the fellow before he had any chance to perform one of those dirty conjuring tricks, he'd have him crying out for mercy and then they'd see if they hadn't decided a little too early to flout his authority, to decide that if this fellow could beat him he wasn't so strong and wonderful after all.

On his feet, he moved slowly, carefully. His neck hurt with a searing pain when he moved it, but his eyes had cleared and the breath had come back to fill his big body. This time he'd keep hyper-alert for a nuance of a movement, ready to counter it.

Cesare knew, he knew what was going on in his opponent's mind and in his own the little warning that always came when things seemed to be going almost too much his way, spoke out. "Don't relax for a moment," it said. "Don't assume that you've won just because if you keep your head it's a cakewalk. First you have to keep your head."

So Cesare, too, moved slowly, hyper-alert, rather than dulled into carelessness by his near-victory.

Silence had come on the crowd again. They seemed to sense the desperate plight of the local champion, for whom no love was lost, certainly, but for whom there was a certain feeling of kinsmanship in that he was born and bred in the village in which they all lived and worked and made love.

During several seconds they circled each other, hands taut and moving slightly, arms taut and waiting. The blacksmith was unwilling to rush in this time and waited for Cesare to make the first move.

It came, suddenly. Cesare moved in, catching his opponent's fist again. But this time, the blacksmith flung himself in at the Duke's waist, not quick enough to avoid the knee which caught him a searing blow in the chest as he came in, but quick enough to get his great arms around his adversary's body so that, like a boa constrictor, he could slowly squeeze the life out of him.

There was a gasping rustle of excitement in the crowd. Cesare's men fidgeted, hands on the daggers in their belts.

Cesare was too late to resist. He felt the backbreaking grip around him and let himself go limp, suddenly, reaching behind at the same time with both hands. He found the little fingers as the breath began to heave and choke in his chest, and tugged at them sharply. The blacksmith gave a cry of pain and released his grip, his hands hanging limp as Cesare seized an arm, levered with his hips in the man's groin and threw him heavily again to the ground. There were gasps which resounded all over the field as if every member of the assembled multitude had had the breath knocked out of him by the fall.

Although strained, the blacksmith's fingers had not been broken. Cesare had not applied all the pressure he might have done. After all this was not war to the death. But in the mind of the champion it might have been. Winded, his fingers smarting, he nonetheless managed to seize Cesare's foot as he came in and twisted him off his balance so that he in turn slipped onto his back. He was up in an instant, however, and the blacksmith, slow, cumbersome and opening his mouth to get his breath, was not able to follow up his momentary advantage. The two men faced each other again, circling, chests heaving, muscles sliding in their arms and shoulders as they moved.

Cesare knew he would be wise to exploit the other's temporary exhaustion and injury quickly, but, having felt the strength of those great tree-trunk arms around him, he was cautious. The champion's eyes were afire, but mingled with the fire was a recognition of defeat staring him in the face. When his gaze met the cool, unyielding look of his unknown adversary he felt that he was up against some strange presence against whom he could do little.

Suddenly Cesare moved in and the blacksmith's arms went out in mingled defense and attack. But with a speed which took his still half-winded opponent completely by surprise, Cesare had ducked under his arms, seized his widespread legs with each hand and pulled upwards as he thrust up with his shoulders in the man's crotch. The blacksmith was bewildered by the lightning thrust and unable to do anything but flail his arms in the air as he found himself flung into the air and then crashing on his face. He had not time even to roll over before Cesare was on him from behind and gripping him in a leg hold which brought tears of pain to his eyes. He scratched at the ground with tensed hands and tried to unseat his opponent with his buttocks, but Cesare was unmoveable. He simply applied more pressure until the blacksmith was bellowing in pain and beating on the ground in surrender.

A great roar of appreciation went up from the crowd. Their champion had been well beaten by a man who was immeasurably his superior. There were no hard feelings and it would take the cocky blacksmith down a peg or two.

Among Cesare's officers nobody could understand how they'd ever even considered that he was running a risk in taking on this adversary. Their chief was invincible.

*   *   *

"Who is that man?" Dorotea Caracciolo's pale blue eyes were sparkling in their depths with admiration.

"Don't know," said the Duke of Alfaro indifferently. "Some lout from one of the villages, I suppose."

"He doesn't look much like a lout, does he?"

Dorotea had caught his tone and she knew what he was thinking. Since the beginning of her stay, the old man had been trying hard to seduce her, a fact that didn't cause her much concern. Except that last night in a flush of desperation he had come into her boudoir in his underclothes, while his wife slept. She had been bathing and had time only to cover herself with a towel before he had seized her and was begging her to yield to him or his life stood for nothing. In half earnest, half bravado he'd actually managed to lay hold of her and pull the towel from her breasts. She'd felt his hand on her buttocks, his panting breath on her neck and his fat body with its hot penis crushing against her before she'd managed to fight him off, threatening to tell his wife if he persisted. Really, such conduct wasn't to be tolerated and she'd informed her hosts that she thought she should leave in two days' time. Although she was more amused than offended. After all, all men were the same at heart and she recognized that he had a genuine heart-aching lust for her which was not unflattering. However it was too boring to have to be subjected to invasions of her boudoir and, who knew, he might take her unawares some time, get her at some disadvantage and actually screw her—rape her. That would disgust her. His hot, fat flesh. Now . . . if it were the young man on the field . . .

"Looks a typical country bumpkin to me," the Duke persisted in a disgruntled tone. "Eh, my dear," he added a little more loudly for the benefit of his wife on his other side.

"I think he's glorious—looks like a prodigal prince," his wife said.

Dorotea laughed to herself. Now he was going to be as jealous as hell if he thought she admired this young man.

"How beautiful he is compared to that ogre of a man he's just beaten so soundly," she went on. "I think he has one of the finest bodies imaginable."

"Well, you can guarantee he'll have no brain," the Duke said, eyeing his guest with annoyance. "A beautiful carcass and nothing whatever in his head — probably can't even read or write."

"Oh, but I thought he used his brain very well during the match," Dorotea teased, "and I'd sooner take a body like that than what passes for brains any day."

She pulled her hand away as the Duke tried to hold it on the bench on which they sat.

"Any woman would be proud and happy to have a man like that," she added, maliciously.

Pangs of envy and frustrated fury skewered through the Duke's breast. He knew how she was tormenting him. But she couldn't be serious —give herself to a common rustic like that when she could have a man of quality. But tomorrow she was leaving. Oh those delicious little white breasts with their pert, pink-rimmed nipples, high, firm, cheeky almost. He had a picture of them ever before his eyes. And the feel of the smooth skin of her buttocks and the animal warmth of her body behind the towel against him. Oh heaven and hell! He

250

would live his life in a dream of what might have been if she didn't yield to him before her departure. Tonight was the only chance. If only he could drug her with wine or something. It wouldn't matter not to feel her responses if it had to be that way. Just to enter in up that moist, warm creek would be salvation. His eyes glanced sideways at her lovely profile, that tremulous, sexy, jutting lower lip, that small nose and firm chin, that high forehead with the sweep of long fair hair back from it—and most of all those pale, mysterious eyes, sphinx-like half the time, dancing with animation the rest. Oh to have that face close to his as her body wriggled—or just lay dead—under his. Better to see those eyes dancing with passion, that jutting lip trembling with emotion and ecstasy as he drove her and himself to fulfillment. Oh, darling Dorotea! A country bumpkin with muscles and straw in his hair! How could she be so ridiculous—or so cruel!

The sports continued, with their closing events. Cesare and his lieutenants had entered separately in only some of the events so as not to attract too much attention. They had won everything they'd undertaken and Cesare closed the day by walking off with the archery contest.

"It was as well, Sire, that we didn't enter for everything or they'd have nothing to show in the village except a mass of long faces tomorrow," Rossano Erfredi said.

"Oh, they'd have had time to recover their good spirits in the dark corners tonight," Cesare said with a laugh. "Nothing like a good orgasm or two for a relaxed view of life."

It was the Duke of Alfaro's privilege and duty to present the awards—hogsheads of wine, great hams and sides of bacon with little silver cups—and the successful competitors, donning jerkins, lined up in the last rays of the sun, with a cool night air beginning to freshen, at the foot of the stand.

Cesare took his place in the queue, smiling at his role of prizewinner in a local fete. And when he looked for Dorotea Caracciolo, he found her eyes were on him.

She was standing next to the Duke of Alfaro, helping him to present the trophies, but her glance had risen from the immediate presentation and traveled along the line of waiting men to Cesare. With a twinge of pleasurable excitement he met her gaze and smiled slowly at her. She pulled her eyes from him and he suddenly remembered that he was a simple rustic. Hardly the thing to be making advances to the wives of captains in the service of Venice. But maybe she liked country pleasures. He chuckled quietly.

The line dwindled and Cesare found himself face to face with the aristocrat of the district and his lovely guest. Now that he saw her close up he felt a flush of eagerness to get on intimate terms with her, to get in intimate postures with her. Her figure, well draped in her dress, was nonetheless visibly exciting and her face was alive with a vivacious fire which sprang out of her eyes in twin points like mischievous children. What an excellent carnival companion she would make.

Solemnly the Duke of Alfaro handed him two cups: one for the wrestling, one for the archery. At his side were a ham and a hogshead of wine, the supplementary, gastronomic prizes.

The Duke had not meant to address this rustic. It seemed quite enough to him that the man had already given rise to some conversation—rather uncalled for. But when confronted by Cesare he was reluctantly impressed by the man's presence—and made hostile by it.

"Tell me, my man—you don't belong to the village?" he asked.

"No your Grace. I'm an infantryman with the Duke of Valentinois' troops—on leave at the moment, so please your Grace."

"You see—he speaks," Dorotea cut in, laughing lightly and looking first at Cesare's muscular, uncovered forearm and then raising her eyes to his handsome, commanding face.

"Did you think me to be a deaf mute, Madame?" he asked.

The Duke of Alfaro began to expostulate, but Dorotea cut him short.

"We were simply wondering whether such a splendid physique could really be crowned by any brain at all," she said, with another little laugh.

"It's not unknown for the two to go together," Cesare said with a smile. "You, Madame, are, I'm sure, a fair example of such."

"Why you . . . " the Duke of Alfaro began to splutter, but Dorotea put a restraining hand on his arm while her eyes continued to smile at Cesare.

"I thank you for a very nice compliment," she said. "I have heard that the Duke of Valentinois is an iron-willed man of great physical strength. If he could out-wrestle and out-shoot you, it would be worth the seeing."

"Madame, I owe all I know to His Grace," Cesare replied. "A finer man never lived."

"Yes, indeed, they say all his men would die for him. Are you visiting all the carnivals and sports you can reach on your leave?"

"No, Madame, I have a feeling that this area has something really delightful to offer. I shall probably stay for a while if I and my friends can find a suitable inn."

"Well, I hope you are able fully to enjoy the delights of which you speak."

During their conversation, the Duke of Alfaro had not hidden his annoyance and his obvious irritation that Dorotea should talk so easily with a mere infantryman. But he had restrained his anger not to appear ridiculous in front of the villagers who had gathered in a great throng around the stand, and some of whom could hear the words which were being spoken. Also he didn't want to offend Dorotea, although he was certain she was doing this just to tease him. He still wanted to fuck Dorotea. Fuck Dorotea! Fuck Dorotea! He repeated the words to himself, fiercely and then blushed with desire at the images and sensations they brought forth in his mind.

He refused to have anything further to say to the lout, however, and simply began to lift the hogshead.

"Your Grace," Cesare said, "if it would not displease you I'd like the village to have the hogshead and the ham—a gesture of friendship from strangers in their midst."

This sign of gentle manners somehow annoyed the Duke even more. There was something disturbing about this stranger. He actually felt a little afraid of the man although he wouldn't admit it to himself in such terms.

"All right," he said curtly, "as you wish."

"Come Benvenuto—a very fine gesture, too," the Duchess chided from his side.

The Duke of Alfaro was about to add a reluctant word in agreement when his voice was drowned out by a great gust of cheering which thundered out through the quietening night air. The word had been passed back that the carnival victuals of the village were to be reinforced through the generosity of this stranger who had fought so well.

Cesare bowed slightly to the Duke and Duchess and then to Dorotea, whose eyes, glinting with what might have been a light amusement, or something else, continued to watch him as he withdrew.

"What a charming fellow," the Duchess whispered to her companions. "He hardly seemed like a peasant. Manners and speech are improving in the country."

"No, he didn't, did he?" Dorotea mused.

"Well, I think he was damned insolent speaking that way to our guest."

"Oh come, Benvenuto, he was just paying a bold compliment. No lady really minds. Yes, he struck me as a bold man—quite strange."

A bold compliment? the Duke was thinking. What could have been bolder than my compliment? God! I nearly had her. Just a towel between us—and not even that between parts of us. His loins cringed at the thought of what had been so near and now seemed so far away.

CHAPTER 11

Night had now fully fallen. The stars were on a high, dark, mellow ceiling and there was a reflection below from a huge fire which had been built in the center of the field. It cast a broad, bright glow over the faces of the nearest rank of the people who were gathered in a great, loose mob around it. It was hot, too, and those who had sat, cross-legged on the ground near it, had, several times, to get up and move back a little.

Over the fire on an enormous spit an ox was slowly roasting. The deflated hogsheads of wine were lying in the small clearing formed by the crowd and illuminated by the fire. The wine was now either smoldering in lustful bellies or swishing in the water-bottles which the villagers had brought with them. Bread had been distributed and bits of it, broken and dusty, lay around the field. The hams, the sides of bacon had already been privately eaten or taken home to fill the larder for a few days. Now everyone was waiting for the distribution of the ox which the Duke of Alfaro ritually provided for this occasion.

The Duke, himself, was basting the animal with ponderous, self-important deliberation, drawing back from the heat of the fire every so often when it became too much. For the moment, concentrating on his official task, he had allowed lustful thoughts of Dorotea to slip into the recesses of his mind. Which was just as well. For Dorotea, standing with the aristocrats' group, a little within and away from the main sprawling mob, was gazing at Cesare, who, from the front ranks of the crowd, was returning her look just as meaningfully.

It was nearing Dorotea's time to conceive and she was feeling the lack of intercourse which her trip had deprived her of. She was full of honest, animal appetites. Her husband would have done, although in truth she was not in love with him. But this athletic rustic who didn't seem to be a rustic had captured her imagination and would do much better. He was the only *man* she could recall having come

256

across since her arrival. What a pity he wasn't one of the Duke's entourage. It would be so much less complicated.

She saw him smile at her and gave a sideways glance with the corners of her eyes before returning his smile quickly, briefly. He was so handsome and he had a sort of fire in him, a controlled fire that was quite obvious. She just knew that he hadn't been the slightest concerned about the Duke of Alfaro's ill-concealed anger. She believed that for two pins he could have snapped his fingers in the Duke's face. There was something very strange somewhere.

"Done, done, I think," the Duke called, red-faced and sweating beside the crackling, delicious-smelling ox.

The distribution began—a hunk of ox for everybody and bread and wine flowing liberally. The power of the grape was, indeed, stalking in the crowds and with the fireworks and main carnival to come, some young couples were already so fired that they were creeping off for a quick, ecstatic embrace before the public displays. Before the night was out there were going to be some very exhausted, very satiated bodies in this corner of Italy.

The Duke of Alfaro had rejoined his party and was now looking once more at the object of his desire as he munched a fat piece of meat. Cesare saw his look and understood. It was very understandable, after all. His own feelings were identical.

Dorotea, unable to go where she felt inclined to, unwilling to put up with the Duke of Alfaro's verbally amorous advances, engaged one of the Duchess' waiting women in conversation. The Duke withdrew, hurt and cross, to watch her curvaceous movements from a slight distance. Cesare took a long swig of wine from a bottle passed by one of his men and settled down to wait.

While the big fire was still blazing there was a fizz of color and noise from the direction of the village and a long-tailed rocket swooped into the air, scattering a confetti of varicolored sparks and stars through the dark sky and fizzled away into darkness and silence again.

There was a short hush of surprise which was shattered almost immediately by whoops and roars of delight from the crowds. The sign for the festivities had been given. As the crowds began to stream away toward the village a whole cluster of rockets soared into the air with tails like birds of paradise and then exploded into a rainbow of colors which filtered into a disappearing rain of particles of color.

The skeleton of the ox was left gently charring over the still blazing fire. The field, littered with pieces of discarded food, began to clear. Caught in the crowd, trying to remain dignified aloof from it, the Duke of Alfaro's party also made its way toward the lanes which led from the field to the village square.

Cesare, with his officers, followed close in their wake.

Outside the field in the narrow lanes with their crumble-walled cottages and houses and cobbled surfaces, the crush became severe. People pushed, some fell and struggled to their feet shrieking, women were felt by men they couldn't even turn to scold, many a pert buttock was pinched and held, many a masculine loin rubbed and ground impudently against feminine asses as the mob, like a single moving entity, hustled toward the square from which more and yet more rockets were being launched into the still air.

Cesare, who had kept close to the local dignitaries' party, elbowed his way still closer as the mob became less and less controlled. There was a great din of cries and a great strife of falling and pushing and fighting and protesting. Every man for himself, and nobody was very concerned about what his neighbor was doing.

The Duke of Valentinois was slowly separated from his lieutenants, who tried in vain to keep up with him. Shortly he had pushed through to the fringe of the Duke of Alfaro's party which was trying to maintain a semblance of decorum in the crush. Peasants flocking around were trying desperately and often vainly to stop those behind from shoving them into the ladies-in-waiting.

Dorotea was in the midst of the party. Often she looked around until at last she was able to see Cesare. They both knew what they were up to, both accepted that they were working toward each other.

Gradually Dorotea fell back, imperceptibly at first and then more boldly, until she was at the very fringe of her group, all occupied in keeping their own feet, and only a pace or two in front of Cesare. He battled and elbowed a fraction more and he was next to her and had taken her hand, his movement hidden in the crush of bodies. Her fingers clasped and interlaced with his immediately, although she didn't look at him any more.

Gently, but as swiftly as possible, before her disappearance was discovered, he edged her through the crowd toward the side of the line. Nobody noticed them. *Sauve qui peut.*

As they approached the main square, narrow,

259

arched alleyways gave off from the lane, corridors between rows of large houses. It was into one of these that Cesare eased Dorotea and then quickly through another archway into the deserted gloom of a mansion courtyard. There he pulled her to him and kissed her fiercely on the lips, feeling her response, her lips which softly opened and her hands which moved and dug against his shoulders. He released her a little later and saw her pale face looking up at him in the gloom.

"Who are you?" she whispered.

"The champion wrestler and archer of the Duke of Alfaro's lands," he replied with a chuckle.

"You're no infantryman—you don't look like one, you don't speak like one."

The noise of the crowds, interpolated with the fizz and bang of the rockets and fireworks came to them from a little distance. Within the walls of the empty courtyard it was quiet as if in a glass house. At frequent intervals the flame of a rocket seared the sky, lightly dispersing the gloom surrounding them for a few seconds.

Cesare stepped back from her a little and bowed, a vague shape in the darkness.

"Allow me to present myself, Madame," he said softly. "The Duke of Valentinois."

He heard her sudden intake of breath in the darkness. A short silence followed in which he heard her breathing heavily. Then she came in toward him and he felt her whole body fuse along his own as he put his arms around her.

"One might have known," she whispered. "They say he's the most handsome man in Italy."

He kissed her again, forcing her lips apart,

edging them away from each other with his own. Her tongue darted into his mouth, smooth and slippery and enticing.

"My disguise is not very good if you almost saw through me so easily," he whispered.

"No disguise would hide you," she whispered back. "Even my pompous old host noticed. I think he was afraid of you and certainly envious."

"He obviously desires you."

"Yes—he's an old lecher."

"Then I am a younger lecher."

For answer she laughed softly and kissed him again, running her hands through his hair. Her breath came heavily and he could feel her breasts heaving crazily against his chest. She pulled away from him suddenly, a little wildly.

"Not here," she whispered. "Not now. They'll find I'm missing in no time and search the whole place to find me."

He ran his hands over her breasts, richly draped in her velvet dress, as he spoke. Her body shivered under his touch.

"Where then—when?" he asked.

"I leave tomorrow," she said. "Must you stay here?"

"No, I can take my titles with me."

"We could meet on the road—although it will be difficult to give my retinue the slip. They're sending an armed band of men-at-arms with my ladies-in-waiting."

"I'll kidnap you," he whispered, stroking his hand over her velvet-covered bottom.

"Such a scandal," she chided, not taking him seriously.

"It would be simpler," he said. "Then no blame can be attached to you whatever. You were simply being held for ransom, but managed later to escape."

"But . . ."

"Leave it to me." He kissed her again and she twined her body passionately with his, her tongue searching and probing in a way that made him hot and desperate to have her. He kissed her neck, feeling with the direction of his genitals that perhaps they could take a chance now and find some spot in this courtyard where he could taste her treasure. She was breathing thickly and gasping softly, seeming to come to the same view, for her hand strayed over his body and pressed his buttocks into her loins, while her thighs opened and rubbed against him. But in the midst of their mounting passion there were cries and the sound of footsteps above the dull, distant rumble of the crowd, more incisive. Her name was being called.

Swiftly they drew back into the deeper gloom of the courtyard and, against the lighter patch of gloom which was the arched entrance, saw a band of men with pikes and drawn swords run past.

"They're looking for me. We have no time," she whispered fiercely, as if furious that they had no time now to make love.

He left her and crossed to the archway. Outside all was dark and deserted. The men had passed but they would be back and doubtless there were more. He called to her softly and in a moment she was at his side, her hand on his arm.

"Until tomorrow then," he said. "You can join the crowds quickly now."

"I wish it were now," she said, with a sudden fierce streak of desire. She caught his hand

and put it on her breast. And she kissed him once again, fiercely. He ran his lips over her face: the high, warm brow, the animated, pale blue eyes, the short, straight nose, and he bit at that sexy, jutting underlip which told such an accurate story.

She broke away from him with a little cry.

"Tomorrow," she said and ran off into the gloom.

He followed, slowly, watching her dim figure round the corner. By the time he had reached it, she was swallowed up amidst the stragglers making their way to the fringe of the crowds in the square.

Cesare wandered down to the square where in a roped off space around the pump and an old statue, the fireworks were being exploded. Rockets were still scarring the sky and on the ground a trelliswork of Roman candles, Catherine wheels and other specialities were popping and whirring in profusion and hurtling sparks into the shrieking, joyful crowds. There was no sign of Dorotea, nor yet the Duke of Alfaro's party. Many people were drunk and there were several necking sessions being carried on openly in a way which would have shocked everybody to the core on a day which was more realistic than the present.

Soon the crowds began to waver back to make room for the grotesquely masked figures, many several times life size which marched into the square, followed by great floats and carts with tableaux from which more fireworks were being hurtled into the flame-scratched sky.

Men were swigging back wine from flasks and couples were dancing, alone and in groups.

There was singing, shouting and, doubtless in some dark doorways, there was fucking too.

Cesare began to get into the mood of the crowd. He was disappointed that he'd not managed to possess Dorotea that very night. It had left him hot and frustrated. She had an impish animation with her loveliness, and her obvious desire for him increased his own for her. Now his penis was hot and unsatisfied and his face still flaming from the passion which remained unrequited in his loins. He held out his hand for a flask of wine which was readily passed to him by one of the merrymakers and took a long draught. He joined the group from which he'd received this beneficence and took stock of its members. Among them was an attractive and rather young girl whose cheeks were flushed and whose skirts swished in abandon as she danced and sang. She appeared for the moment to be with nobody and Cesare joined the dancing group next to her.

"You're so beautiful," he whispered to her as they swung around each other in the dance, and her laughing, tipsy eyes laughed up at him and she pouted her mouth as if she wanted to be kissed. A young bud ripe for the plucking, he said to himself as he kissed her lightly on her rosebud lips.

The group raced toward the edge of the crowd for a better view as more floats and carts rumbled into the square. Cesare caught the girl, who was about to run with them and waltzed her into a dance. Laughing and leaning back from his arms, she allowed herself to be danced away from the crowd, until they were almost lost in the gloom at the edge of the square. There Cesare kissed her more ardently and she responded with a similar, but innocent ardor.

"Let's go and salvage the remains of the ox," he suggested.

"But I'm not hungry."

"I am—we can dance all the way and be back in a moment."

She threw back her head and laughed at the thought of dancing through the streets and they moved off with one accord through the gloom of the lane which led to the field where the skeleton of the ox was sagging over the dying fire. On the way they were passed by a group of armed men, who stared at them closely as they passed. You'll find her when you join the throng, Cesare thought with a twinkle. His thoughts roamed for a moment over the face and body of Dorotea. He put his arm around the girl at his side, who was laughing and chattering. A good second best, he thought.

When they reached the field, the fire was a small, flickering spot in a distant point. It was dark and he led her away from the fire. She didn't seem to notice and when, near a clump of small bushes he pulled her around and kissed her again, she closed her eyes and threw back her head. The soft lips on his enveloped him in flame. Her dark hair was lavender-scented. He caught her neck in his hands and crushed his body into her. He stroked her breasts over her dress and drew her down onto the grass in the gloomy shadow of the bushes. She did not resist while he roved over her breasts, but when his hand moved away and traveled up her leg, lifting the hem of her dress and moving up a soft bare thigh, she pulled her face from his.

"No, no," she said.

He ignored her protest, held her tightly and moved his hand right up until he could feel the concave heat of her crotch and his fingertips brushed against a soft down.

"No, no, no," she said softly but desperately. She tried to pull away and closed her thighs over his hand. As she struggled he held her tighter and then his fingers were brushing the soft, hanging folds of her labia. When he dug inside she cried out and began to whimper. She was evidently a virgin. But tonight was revelry night, the night for deflowering, and Cesare was at boiling point from his earlier encounter.

Holding her struggling body he pulled, tugged and tore off her undergarment and stretched her back on the grass. He slithered from his own undergarments and felt the cool night air on his rigid prick.

"No, no, please, no . . ." the girl begged. But the caress of his fingers in her vagina which was moistening rapidly seemed to have subdued her. It was now herself she was fighting as much as him.

Cesare wasted no time. He swung onto her and jabbed his prick at her hole.

"No, no, no—Ooooooooooh!"

His penis had coursed into her wet flesh, in pain and excitement. Her mouth screwed up. This was it. This was the point of waiting finally reached on a dark carnival night in a cool field with a strange man. It hurt, but it was exciting and after a while it began to give pleasure. Cesare, thrusting deeper and deeper into her body which quivered like a frightened animal's imagined to himself that it was Dorotea, with whom he looked forward to emulating today's performance on the morrow.

CHAPTER 12

Dorotea had rejoined the Duke of Alfaro's party, explained her absence due to being lost in the crowd and then wandering in curiosity, and had finally left the carnival early. Drunks were already lying around the streets and the Duke and his entourage, who returned to his chateau with her, saw some scenes which the Pope could not officially have approved of.

The Duke, with lovesick, desire-jaundiced eyes seized every opportunity to catch her hand, to press against her, to look down the front of her dress. He seemed to her really like a child. But she could forgive him. If she hadn't come to stay at the chateau she would never have met the Duke of Valentinois, with whom her thoughts were overwhelmed. She wondered how he would execute the daring plan he had decided on for tomorrow. They said he stopped at nothing. That was what thrilled her—the thought of being in the arms of a man who stopped at nothing, to know that even as you felt his organ filling you he was a strange, iron-willed man who stopped at nothing, would take from you whatever he desired and there was nothing you could do about it.

Back in the chateau, she retired to her own suite of rooms, undressed and stood by her window, staring out over the empty grounds to the distant glow of the village. She had been violently frustrated, but now she could wait until tomorrow. But if only he were here with her in this room, if only he could see her from the grounds and find a way in. She might have suggested it . . .

But down in the grounds, hidden among the trees, another figure was watching her win-

dows—the Duke of Alfaro. And when he saw
her slim, tight, curvaceous form appear in its
fleshly state at her window he nearly died from
apoplexy. His gaze became transfixed, his eyes
bulged, he hardly breathed during the several
minutes that she stood gazing dreamily out
over the hill and her body was there for him to
see, vaguely, at a distance, but well silhouetted
by the lights in her room.

The Duke nearly fainted from desire. His
prick felt as if it would burst and he took it
out from the robe he was wearing and fondled
it, while he watched her. He had to get in the
bitch!

*　　*　　*

Dorotea lay on her bed, naked and cool,
thinking of her night's activity. She pressed
her hands down her body. Tomorrow he would
be doing that. Tomorrow her body would have
no secrets from him. It would be his to do with
as he wished. She smiled, her fingers touched
her thigh near the lips of her vagina and she
turned on her side and lost herself in a sleeping
maze of thoughts and images.

*　　*　　*

The Duke of Alfaro walked softly through
corridors of his castle. He did not creep
stealthily in case he met any of the servants,
but he walked more quietly and quickly than
was usual with him. He still wore his robe
under which was nothing but his fat, shaggy
body. He had waited outside for some time,
hoping that his erection would deflate and not
push out the robe in a great protuberance. But
his turmoil of sexy thoughts somehow just

refused to let it go down, so now he was walking quickly and quietly, hoping he wouldn't meet a soul.

In the pocket of his robe, his clenched hand, against which he could feel the silk-covered, horizontal tower of his ramrod, rested against the cooling metal of a key—a skeleton key, a *passe-partout*, a gateway to heaven and perhaps hell, the key to the suite of rooms that his young, luscious guest was occupying.

The corridors were dark, with an occasional candle at the dark corners. There were old, dusty pictures on the walls and old suits of armor stood, chill and austere, at respectable tilting distance from one another. His feet made no sound on the thick carpet; the slight swishing of his robe and the grating of his excited breath, which he tried to control, were the only sounds.

He reached the door of her suite without seeing anybody, and fitted the key quietly. The first room was a salon. It was doubtful that she would be there. When he'd witnessed her nudity it had been at the large, balcony windows of her bedroom.

The key turned in the lock of the heavy door and his heart thumped furiously and he felt as if the color had drained out of his face. It certainly hadn't drained out of his prick, for his pride stood up stark and stiff still—and tingling with hope eternal.

Inside it was dark, but a vague, diffused light misted through the open archway which connected the salon with the boudoir.

Softly, his heart in his mouth, the Duke closed the door behind him. Just as softly, he locked it and slipped the key back into the pocket of his robe.

For a few seconds he leaned against the door, listening, hearing nothing but the beating of his heart, seeing nothing but the misty light from the next room and the mixed images of her that he carried in his head, the feel of her buttocks and the sight of her uncovered breasts from the torn-off towel, the outline of her firm body from the grounds below.

He tiptoed carefully toward the arch, moving with a nervous skill between the tables, chairs and other objects which sprang up in the twilight to waylay him.

He peered, on tenterhooks, around the edge of the archway. Candlelight was flickering around her huge, four-poster bed and what he saw turned him hot and cold and made his prick give a sudden throb.

She was lying on her side and the vague outline of her showed that she was still utterly naked. He moved in, almost gliding on the carpet, until he stood a few feet from the edge of the bed. She was asleep. Her regular breathing came clearly to him in the still room. Her body was still and vulnerable. The slim shoulders—he was viewing her from behind—curved down into a tight slender waist and then rounded out into voluptuously proportioned hips and buttocks. The flesh was real, alive, would yield when he touched it.

Softly he walked around the bed. His robe had fallen back from his prick and the great tower stood up and out now like a white cannon through an aperture in some battlements.

From the other side he could see her face, with some of the long, fair hair falling over it. Her lips were slightly apart and the lower lip looked ready for eating. Her breasts were not large, but, as he remembered them from

270

his briefest of glimpses before, well-shaped and firm with those pert, pink nipples that looked like lollipops ready for the sucking. Her hips were warmly-fleshed, her thighs, rounded and superb and the hair above her vagina formed a matching triangle with that which swept down to her shoulders.

The Duke was trembling from head to foot. He moved unsteadily back to his former viewpoint, feeling, somehow, safer for the moment behind her. He took off his robe and stood, gross and naked, over her, gloating over her body with his eyes.

Gently he began to fondle and massage his prick, gazing intently all the time at her ass. His gaze tried to see through her buttocks, to feel them through sight. His penis was hot and throbbed furiously in his fingers. He rubbed the skin back and forth, pressing his legs together, pushing sensation through his loins to the aching protuberance which reared over her sleeping form.

His breathing was difficult and he opened his mouth, emitting a gasp into the room. She stirred and he froze—he hardly knew why as he had been willing for his presence to be discovered. She rolled over onto her back and raised one thigh in her sleep. It flopped outwards, revealing the fluff-shrouded mass of flesh around her vagina. Now her breasts stood out, straight and round above her ribs and the flesh of her hips seemed to reach out toward him. He shuffled nearer, with his hand still gently squeezing his knob.

The knob had flamed red and he felt a boiling in his rod as he pulled the foreskin back and forth. His chest was heaving, his eyes roamed over her as if they were physically invading her body.

He moved his other hand down past his massive boom and stroked his balls with his fingertips. He imagined she was stroking them and the tickling sensation in the twin sacs became all the more intense for his imaginings.

I must have her now, he thought intensely. I must have her now—I could be in her with any luck before she realized what was happening.

Strangely, he now felt nervous. His breath seemed to be stifling both his stomach and his chest and he found himself trying to hold his breath. But the turbulence in his loins, reaching up to its zenith in the reddening flower of his passion, was his only *raison d'être* for the moment and he had to have his passion slaked in her body. Nothing less would do.

He moved up still closer so that his knees and thighs touched the coverlet of the bed and he was looking directly down on her prostrate nudity, her sleeping face. That was the face which taunted him. The eyes, of course, were closed and he was deprived of their sudden fluctuation from sphinx to wildcat, but the other features remained to view, the same, voluptuously the same as usual. But she didn't know he was there. He was leaning over her studying those very same features which looked at him with scorn, every detail of which he knew—and she didn't know he was there. Now was the point of crisis. Before now was peace and the sleeping body and features. Beyond now was unknown wakefulness and fighting and . . . who knew? He felt the impulsive importance of this moment on the brink—and then, with a little intake of breath, he fell on her, knocking her other thigh away as he lay between her legs.

*   *   *

Dorotea was lying in a huge bed with the Duke of Valentinois. He had pulled her close and was stroking her buttocks. She was bathed in a light dew which was the faint sweat of her passion breaking out like a rash all over her body. He was beautiful and warm and she desired him more than she had ever desired anyone or anything. She could feel the warmth of his great weapon of manhood against her hips and she wanted it inside her. But he only went on stroking her buttocks until she was quivering with excitement.

She wanted to show him how much she desired him and she rolled over onto her back and opened her thighs ready for him, inviting him to mount her and fill her with his lust.

But he seemed to hang back and transferred his stroking hand to her aching breast.

When she moved her lips, slightly, and opened her lips to him he moved at last and kneeled over her ready to lower himself and ride her body like a stallion riding a mare, riding, riding in a euphoria of sexuality. His face came down to her and suddenly his body.

But his body was heavier than expected and seemed to be scrabbling, there was confusion and unexpected sensation . . . she awoke with a start and a low scream. A face was over hers, its eyes dilated with lust—that of the Duke of Alfaro's and it was his heavy, fat body which covered hers.

For several seconds she didn't know whether this was dream or reality. And in that moment or two in which she lay, petrified, wondering where and who she was, a great, fat prick had thrust roughly into her cunt, finding it moist from her dream, and torn up toward her cervix, while its owner gave a cry of ecstasy.

She began to struggle. She beat him with her fists, lashing his fleshy face. She twisted her legs and writhed her body. She felt his penis drubbing up into her, wider and wider. He was gasping little gasps of pain at her blows, of agonized joy at the tight contraction of his penis in her Dorotea, of the teasing face, of the blue eyes, of the jutting lip, into her firm, slim body.

For several seconds they struggled together. He thrust several strokes into her. But she was stronger than he was, in his fleshy decay. Her firm, athletic body was more capable of tension and thrust than his limp flabbiness and she realized that with a strong effort she could wriggle away from him.

But the Duke's preface of rubbing over her body, his palpitating excitement of getting in her cunt at last, raced him to a record climax.

Even as she gathered her strength, he gave a grating, grinding, heart-shaking groan of a gasp and came in the channel he was spearing.

As she pushed him roughly off her, a stream of viscid liquid streamed after his knob out of her vagina and splayed across her thighs.

"You beast, you beast!" she shouted.

He lay back on the bed, slightly frightened, sorry in many ways that it had been so quick, feeling slightly cheated, feeling that he hadn't really enjoyed her, would remember only with regret the time when he'd snatched at her body only to lose need for it almost immediately.

But she had seized a candelabrum and bashed

it down across his chest. Her eyes were blazing and she looked dangerous.

He rolled off the bed, grabbed his robe, dodged her, winced with the pain of a blow on his shoulder and rushed into the salon and out into the gloomy corridors.

He spent a sleepless, regretful night, wondering if she would complain and wishing he could have had her long and languorously, with her cooperation.

CHAPTER 13

It was on a road through the woods north of Cesena that Cesare waited for Dorotea Caracciolo and her retinue to come on their journey back to Venice.

He waited on his horse in the shadow of a huge tree which blocked him from the view of anyone riding along the narrow road from a southern direction. Around, in the bushes, his half-dozen officers waited with swords drawn, hidden themselves by the trailing, autumn-leafed undergrowth.

The road through the woods was deserted. In the half hour they'd been waiting, nobody had passed. It was unlikely that anyone would.

Cesare felt welling in his breast the daring delight he experienced at being in dangerous action again. That his officers had entered enthusiastically in his plan was as much their sharing of his audacity as their devotion to him. Soon, soon he would be holding the naked body of that lovely, sphinx-eyed girl in his arms. He thought of her substitute of the night before, who had cried at first and then lain passive and groaning and then become animated at approaching orgasm. For a virgin, she'd really been quite a bundle of abandon eventually—and then she'd run off into the darkness after his limp prick had come out of her as if she was ashamed of what had happened and couldn't bear to look him in the face. It wouldn't be long before she took other lovers.

"I hear them, Sire!"

The voice of one of his lieutenants hissed through the light rustle of the breeze on the dry leaves. Cesare's mind became a straining ear to catch the slightest sound. He heard them too, some distance off—the steady thud, thud of approaching hoofs.

"Everybody ready," he called softly.

Whispers echoed through the woods and an answering affirmation came back from his nearest lieutenant.

"They have to think we're a score of men, at least."

"Aye, Sire."

Cesare's horse quivered under him lightly as they waited in a heavy silence, listening to the loudening thud of the hooves until the thud had split up into individual horse-sounds: snorts and jangling of bridles and rustling of dead leaves underfoot. There were voices, too, female voices and male commands to animals. Cesare waited. The sounds spread, seeming to stretch into the forest on either side of him in an eerie echoing. They must have passed the first of his officers. He let them come, judging the moment, holding his quivering horse into the shade of the tree. And then, of a sudden he spurred forward onto the road, arquebus in hand.

There was a startled, astonished pile-up of the leading men-at-arms. Cesare had just a second in which he glimpsed the lady of his desires in the midst of her handmaidens before he shouted immediately:

"Lay down your arms. You're surrounded."

As he shouted these words, there were rustlings in the trees and bushes around the road, everything half hidden in leaves and foliage. The front-quarters of horses eased into view, the extended arms of standing men, there was movement all around, seeming to come in mysterious volume from all sides.

The men-at-arms stared around them fearfully, hands petrified halfway to swords and guns.

"If you try to resist, you'll be shot down on your horses," Cesare cried. "Lay down your arms and you'll not be harmed."

There was still a hesitation and Cesare fired his arquebus into the air: a sign for his men, half hidden in the surrounding bushes, to fire volleys over the heads of the ambushed cortege. Horses shied and nearly threw their riders. The men-at-arms began to throw down their weapons, which thudded softly into the leaf-mold which covered the road.

"Dismount—and the ladies," Cesare ordered.

He watched them obey him, smiling to himself at Dorotea feigning terror with the rest of her women.

"Three men to secure them," he called. "The rest keep them covered."

Three of his lieutenants, still, like Cesare himself, dressed as peasants, but fully armed, stepped out from the bushes. It was the work of a few minutes to secure the handful of men-at-arms, an even shorter period to tie up the women—all except Dorotea who was left aside.

When all was done, Cesare's men came out of

the surrounding trees—all three of them, leading their horses who had served to indicate greater numbers.

Cesare rode up to Dorotea and commanded her to mount, which she did with every show of reluctance. He cast a last look at the trussed men-at-arms and the ladies. It would be some time before they were discovered or managed to break free. He directed his arquebus at Dorotea, sitting woodenly on her horse beside him.

"You will ride with us," he said in a loud voice, "and if you don't attempt to escape, no harm will come to you."

She made no answer. Her eyes, when she looked at him, twinkled for the briefest of seconds.

Cesare gave a sharp command and he and his band spurred their horses away up the road in the direction of Cesena from which the ambushed party had come. Once out of sight, Dorotea's face lit up and she reached across to clasp his hand at full gallop, Cesare grinned broadly and around them his men were chortling with mirth.

For a mile they rode south and then wheeled abruptly into the forest. They pushed and battled their way for a mile or so and then turned again, toward the north. When, at last, they reached the road to Forli, the trussed party were still trying to shake free of their bonds prior to riding south in pursuit and to raise the alarm.

Some distance from the city which Cesare had captured some time before, they dismounted in the forest. Dorotea retired to a discreet distance. Cesare and his officers changed into their own attire—and when

Dorotea returned she, too, was dressed as a soldier, a young and very attractive soldier, but a soldier nonetheless with her long, blonde hair hidden and her soft, woman's curves disguised.

Thus they rode, a merry band of men, saluted by the guard at the gates of the city, into Forli.

CHAPTER 14

When Cesare turned, having stripped off his clothes, Dorotea was naked. She came toward him with her eyes smoldering and her lips apart. He had time only to glimpse the firm, high breasts, the waist and hips devoid of an ounce of superfluous flesh, the way the thighs tensed as she walked bare-foot across the few feet of boudoir between them, and then she was in his arms, her naked flesh grazing warmly against his, clinging to his like rubber.

His prick rode up between their warm bodies and he felt her hips moving against it, surrounding it hotly with the flesh of her hips and loins.

"Oh, darling," she whispered. And for a fleeting instant her dream came back to her and the memory of her awakening horror. It seemed unbelievable that that beastly old man, after all his vain advances and insinuations, his daring to enter her room and pull a towel from her breasts so that he saw them, his fighting with her and feeling her buttocks, it seemed unbelievable that he should actually have got his prick in her and fucked her for at least a minute. She quivered with outrage at the thought of his effrontery. And that he should have had an orgasm in that time, shooting his load into her reluctant body. That was the most infuriating thing of all. Anyway, she'd caught him a sharp blow or two with the candlestick. He'd have a few bruises to remember — but she wished he didn't have the memory of the feel of her quim to remember as well. It was an insult.

But Cesare was kissing her neck, sucking up the flesh and his hands were roving down her spine, stroking her buttocks, caressing her shoulders, reaching under the buttocks, cupping them and pulling them up and in toward him. This was the man she'd dreamed about and now it was true. She tensed her thighs, sighed a deep sigh of passion and gave herself to their union.

Cesare's fingers seemed to burn as they coursed gently over her flesh, tasting its firmness, its often softness, its roundness, its glossy texture, its warmth and responsive trembling. Her body rubbed and squirmed against his and he dug his fingers deep into her, seizing the flesh in a handful until she squealed and bit his neck.

He lifted her and carried her to the bed.

Light of a watery autumn sun streamed in through a large window which overlooked the rooftops of Forli. They were above and far from all eyes in the citadel where the Countess Sforza-Riario had submitted to him less willingly at first.

Cesare lay her down on the bed and stood over her. He reached down and caught her breasts, easing them up toward him, elongating them with his hands. He knelt beside her and, bending, kissed her fiercely, invaded her sweet mouth with his tongue and bit that sexy lower lip, which in answer enveloped his mouth.

He pulled his mouth suckingly from hers and caught her small, pink nipple between his teeth. He sucked at her breast, drawing as much of the solid, malleable flesh into his mouth as he could. Her nipples hardened in his mouth and she gave a gasp and, taking his hand, put it on the little raised mound of moss-covered flesh at her thigh junction.

Still kneeling, he moved down the bed and raised her thighs, spreading them wide. Her pale, blue eyes watched him with a deep look of concentrated passion.

"Kiss me!" she said.

He looked down at where the raw, pink flesh of her cunt was open and then he slithered down and put his lips to it. She gave a little shriek as she felt his sucking pressure. He began to suck the moist, rain-tasting flesh. He poked his tongue as high as it would go and moved it around against the walls of her vagina. He licked the insides of her hot thighs and found and seized in his lips, the hard, little clitoris.

Dorotea had flung her thighs wide and was wriggling and shrieking with tiny helpless explosions every second. Her hands clenched and unclenched beside her head on the bed and her face, drawn in harrowed passion, swung from side to side with jerky, involuntary movements. Her eyes were closed, her mouth wide open, gasping warm, suffocated breath into the room.

Cesare buried his face between her thighs and put his hands under her buttocks, levering them up.

"Oh, oh, oh, oooooh!"

Her gasping moans assailed his ears, her

moist, warm, slipperiness assailed his mouth, the sweet rain-taste lay on his tongue.

His prick was a long, trembling mass of excited, jostling particles. It was heavy, too heavy, needed to throw off ballast, but when he drew his mouth away, she tried to catch at his head and pleaded desperately.

"Oh, don't stop, please — not now!"

He bent back to her and her loins leapt up to meet him. Her mouth was emitting a long, drawn-out and continuous whine. He could sense her whole body twisting and turning in ecstatic torment. He wanted to get in her, but the fury of her excitement was exciting him even more than if he'd rammed into her at this point.

He heard her gasp, felt her scrabbling on the bed, churning up the covers and then she gave a short, low scream and a sticky heat surrounded him.

She continued to writhe and moan for some time after her climax and he continued to kiss her gently, to bring her back to a tensity of passion.

"Oh, God," she exclaimed at last. "I thought I'd die."

He came away from her loins then, up her body, tracing its light bulges with his lips. He knelt up, astride her, and she reached down and took his rigid, pulsating penis which stuck out horizontally over her breasts.

She put it between her breasts, which she pushed up into a ravine of cleavage and for several seconds he rubbed up and down in the ravine formed by the warm, firm flesh of her teats. He felt a tingling deep in his loins, deep, perhaps, in his bowels and moved forward on her again.

She reached up, her eyes sparkling with depth, and took his organ in both hands. He leaned forward on his hands and she covered the flaming knob with her lips, enveloping it with that sexy lower jut. She took him into her warm, wet mouth and he felt, with streaks of fire, her tongue licking and nuzzling the passionpoint of his knob.

She began to suck as she licked, sucking on the rest of his rigidity, biting gently from time to time. Her eyes watched him, held his, matching his look of furious passion with her own. He held her face with his hands, guiding it, feeling her cheeks hollowing, rhythmically, around the long length of flesh which filled her mouth.

"Harder," he gritted.

He felt her answering response — a greater pressure on his knob, a tighter embrace from her warm lips. He felt his culmination growing in hell-fire in his loins and he wanted to get in her, but couldn't resist the idea of coming into that lovely, sexy mouth, of watching her face hollowing, her eyes recognizing his orgasm even as he came.

He began to rock slightly, flexing his loins forward as she sucked. She had released his prick with her hands and was stroking his buttocks with them. She was breathing heavily, passionately through her flared nostrils and he could feel her hips moving again under him.

Her hands couldn't stay still on him and he felt them, suddenly, drawing lines of loin-convulsing sensation across and around his balls which hung down against her breasts.

He gasped aloud at the new attack and shoved his prick into her mouth so hard that for a moment she fought for breath and nearly choked before reorientating her embrace.

He gasped again, tensing his loins. He could feel himself starting to come, slowly at first in a sort of smoldering ember. The ember grew. He flexed his loins at her hard and held her face, looking into her eyes, which seemed to gasp into his in a strange visual voice.

Inside him the ember burst into a flame and roared from the pit of its sensation along and along . . . he looked deep into her eyes, owning her, subduing her under him, wracked with passion. The fire raced through him, quivered in his penis, trembled at the knob and shattered out of him, as he cried out with the agonizing joy of it.

*   *   *

Later, after a glass or two of wine, from which his passion flamed again to meet hers, already kindled, they stood at the foot of the bed, embracing fiercely, brokenly.

They were both alive with the desire of at last joining as one. There was no necessity for preliminaries.

Her thighs were open against him as she clung around his neck. Her warm flesh rubbed up on him, catching his penis between the tops of her thighs, so that it reached right through, rubbing against the lips of her vagina.

Cesare caught her under her rump, holding a buttock in each hand, and lifted her off the floor. She put her arms firmly around his neck and brought her legs up on either side of him, hanging around him as he held her.

He moved to a table in one of the corners of the room. He sat her on its edge, reached under

284

her upraised thighs with his hand and guided himself toward her vagina. He needed to bend his knees a little to get down, and when he straightened, his penis rushed in up to its hilt in one long movement.

"Oh-oh-oh-oh!" she cried out in a staccato chatter of gasps.

His knob felt the softness of flesh up at her cervix. The walls of her channel were tight but moistly prepared against the huge expansion of his desire-bloated organ.

Panting, he pulled her right onto the edge of the table and drove up into her with a pressure that came up from his toes and made his abdomen flop against her crotch. His hairs mingled wetly with hers.

She clung, gaspingly, to his neck, her breasts brushing against his chest, her hair swaying across her face, touching his. She bit his neck and moved her trembling lips around his face to fasten them on his, with her searching tongue flopping out in willing surrender into his mouth, keeping her eyes open for a moment and then closing them as his penis crushed up into her so hard that it brought a spasm of pain into the joy.

She groaned in an orgy of passion, her hanging, floating tongue in his mouth was a symbol of the way she gave herself for him to do as he wished, to hurt her, to give her pain, pleasure, ecstasy, to take her body, her life in his hands.

He slid his hands under her buttocks, so that they rested and flowed around his hands. He lifted her in ecstatic fury off the table and walked away around the room, jogging into her, feeling her rise and fall on him, the two of them working together to produce that white-heat which would blaze out and smother them both in the end of everything.

He flung her down on the bed, coming down heavily on top of her and she twisted in masochistic fury under him, swinging her legs up to her shoulders as if she wanted him to pierce her through, right up to her neck.

He straightened up from her, leaning at an angle, pulling her behind off the bed so that her hips were the highest point of her body. He crashed in and in and up and up, tearing her moist flesh with his great rifling cannon.

"Oh, oh, darling!"

She gasped and the gasps became meaningless words and then sometimes crude, filthy words which were pulled out of her in the effort to express what she felt and which couldn't be expressed.

He flopped onto her and bit her neck so hard that she screamed and a little perforation of the white skin exploded and drops of blood oozed through.

Her body was a live animal, active and straining. She opened her eyes one second, looking at him in a smoldering agony and then closed them as if the upthrust of his great prick had forced her to do so from sheer weight of sensation.

Cesare could feel his climax approaching again. It was that much more agonizing the second time. It would be relief to unload his store of sperm. A relief that he didn't want to come because he wanted this agony to go on forever.

"Darling, darling," she screamed. "Now, nearly, now, nearly . . ."

He felt her thighs squirming and wriggling, enclosing his hips in their heat. He felt her little belly brushing hotly against his. She caught his face again and thrust her tongue into his mouth, pushing it out and out as if she wanted to transfer it totally from her own body to his.

He bit it and felt her scream rather than heard it. His prick seemed loaded down with the weight of thunder. The thunder was preparing to burst. The relief was coming.

"Now, yes!" he barked and heard her answering gasps.

The thunder grew into a great, black cloud and suddenly burst so that the liquid, hot rain came thundering down and burst through and up into her belly as she screamed and jack-knifed her legs up and down several times.

This was merely the beginning of their night of love.

CHAPTER 15

The winter sun had watered away, black skies had held bruised dominion over the northern plains and spring had come again with a great flowering of oleanders. By the time young men's fancies had led them into woods and dales to suck the nectar of their loved and lusted-after ones, Cesare was sufficiently lord of the northern provinces to be able to declare himself Duke of Romagna and return again to Rome in even greater pomp and glory than before.

But greater campaigns were afoot and it soon filtered to the Vatican, to be followed by official notification from the ambassadors, that by the Treaty of Granada, both France and Spain had come to agreement about the division of a long disputed territory — the Kingdom of

Naples, to which both claimed the right of sovereignty through heritage.

The two claimants, it was revealed, had agreed to undertake the conquest together, sharing the spoils between them. Puglia and Calabria would go to Spain, and Naples and the Abruzzi to Louis.

Pope Alexander immediately declared Federigo of Naples deposed for disobedience to the Church, a charge which was not difficult to fabricate under a number of pretexts.

Cesare, it was decided, should join the French troops, marching through Italy from the north, taking with him a fair proportion of his own troops.

At the same time Gonzalo de Cordoba, the great Spanish soldier, landed a Spanish army in Calabria. Resistance was put up, strong in places, weak in others, but the territory was ravaged and stamped underfoot by the two mighty armies moving inexorably to meet. Within a few weeks they had met at Naples and the days of the House of Aragon were over. Nevertheless, Naples itself put up a stiff resistance and with well-directed cannon fire played such havoc with the lines of the Spaniards who, in enthusiasm to finish the campaign in record time, had permitted themselves to approach too close too soon, that Gonzalo de Cordoba swore a terrible vengeance when the city was taken.

The inevitable breach was made and the waves of the invading armies stormed through. Carnage followed. No quarter was given. The defenders were driven back and back and if they lay down their arms or fled they were slaughtered. This would have been against Cesare's policy. But for once he commanded only a small section of the attack and commands could be issued over his head by the generals of the two main forces, French and Spanish.

Every human being was butchered. The streets of Naples ran with blood as if an animal sacrifice of unheard-of magnitude had been offered for several days running.

But it was with the women of Naples that the invader took the most sadistic vengeance. Women, fleeing, screaming, were seized and raped and massacred. While soldiers ran, searching for victims through the streets, they would pass prostrate huddles of women, their clothes ripped from them by the sword, screaming and weeping, while shaggy soldiers thrust their pricks brutally up into bodies whose thighs they held wide by force.

Gonzalo de Cordoba had some of the most noble families of the city rounded up and saved from the slaughter. He had them taken to the center square of the city where the men were tied so that they couldn't move. He then had the women stripped, surrounded by soldiers wielding whips and forced to dance in front of their menfolk and his army of gawking soldiers to the accompaniment of light lashes around their legs, which grew stronger and stronger and rose around their hips and breasts until many of them fainted and blood had welled out from under their tortured skins.

Cesare, with the situation out of his hands, was indifferent to the suffering. He watched and felt a chill of sensuality course through him as he watched the women pathetically trying to dance, being savagely tickled as soon as they lagged by those stinging lashes. What a variety of breasts and buttocks. And as they fell one by one into a swooning helplessness under the agonized gaze of their helpless husbands and sweethearts, each was seized at the Commander's orders by a rude soldier who proceeded to bury his prick according to his taste, right there on the square in full view. Some of the women remained unconscious throughout the whole proceedings, unaware of the brutality with which they were being shagged or their menfolk's crying fury.

CHAPTER 16

By the time Cesare returned to Rome, richer in money and in French favor, an event of some importance in the Borgia family had taken place: his widowed sister, Lucrezia, had become betrothed to Alfonse d'Este, young son of Duke Ercole of Ferrara. It was a marriage of convenience, although it is probable that the young Alfonse nursed an infatuation for the beautiful Lucrezia.

Into the midst of celebrations, salvoes of artillery, and after dark illuminations, Cesare arrived, crowned with fresh glory from the war, fired still by memories of the spectacle in Naples, desiring the orgasm, coveting his sister.

"Darling, Cesare," she greeted him, when he went to her temporary rooms in the Vatican to invite her down to the supper which was being prepared by the Pope for intimates. "Darling, Cesare," she said, "are you never going to make love to me again? I think you prefer fighting to fucking."

Cesare pulled her to him. He kissed her fiercely on the lips and felt her tongue slide like a snake into his mouth.

"I want you tonight!" he snapped.

"But, darling — I'm married. I have to offer what I have to my new husband. It's his right you know."

She laughed long and merrily and Cesare couldn't help but laugh with her.

"You mean you'd prefer that stripling?"

For answer she sank to her knees, seized his erection which was pushing hard through his clothing and bit it. She got quickly to her feet again and he forced her, panting, back into the room.

"No, Cesare," she said, "not now. I'll come to you tonight — you'll see."

"Do you promise? How can you? Will you leave him on the wedding night to finger his own, unloved cock?"

"He's very young, my sweet, and I think if he's fed a little wine he'll be in no fit state to benefit from the delight he might expect. After all, I don't want to get to bed with him and then find I've only a limp piece of rag trying to squeeze into my vagina."

Cesare laughed. He was delighted with his sister and she still excited him as of old — and he was always certain, absolutely certain of a skillful, satisfying, entrail-tearing fuck with her.

He bent down quickly and lifted her skirt. She wore nothing underneath, which made her feel more natural.

"One kiss until later," he whispered.

"Oh, no, Cesare — you're just trying to excite me!"

But he'd already whipped up her skirt, thrust his head under, pushing aside her thighs and licked his tongue all along the powdered, perfumed folds which hid her sweet tunnel. He felt her thighs rub against his shoulders and pulled the folds aside with the tips of his thumbs. He kissed the moistening flesh hard and heard her gasp.

She broke away from him with a stifled cry.

"Oh, Cesare, stop!"

Kneeling, he grinned.

"I bet you'd love it now," he said.

As he escorted her down the stairway toward the banquet room where they were to dine, she said, softly, looking into his eyes with love: "You are a devil, Cesare, you've made me all wet."

As they descended, she added: "Perhaps he'll go silly with the first glass."

"One can always hope," Cesare answered, smiling.

* * *

But it took more than one glass to put young Alfonse in a stupor. As soon as his glass was half-empty, Lucrezia had it solicitously refilled. The meal progressed; there was music and talk and laughter among the dozen or so guests. There were toasts and good wishes and sly winks from the Pope at his daughter, as if wishing her fun in bed tonight.

Throughout the evening, Cesare's eyes met those of his sister. Sometimes he would nod at her husband's glass to indicate it might be topped up just a shade. Over the dessert, with Lucrezia almost in despair, Alfonse became very talkative — he was usually rather silent — and the sign gave her hope.

Servants carried away the debris of the meal and Alfonse suggested quietly that they retire, but not so quietly that some of the surrounding guests were not forced to suppress grins of amusement to say nothing of more embarrassing indications of envy.

"Oh, but we haven't heard the other orchestra, yet," Lucrezia insisted smoothly. "It's a beautiful orchestra. It will make a fitting goodnight."

Alfonse sat back, slightly disappointed, but prepared to wait for something that he knew was inevitably his.

Lucrezia filled his glass again.

"What excellent wine," she said, and took a sip.

The suggestion produced the desired effect. Alphonse automatically picked up his own glass, sipped it and then emptied it in three long gulps. It was quietly refilled.

As the "other orchestra" began to play — in a manner which hardly justified her description — Alfonse seemed to grow silent. A little later he made a slight effort at conversation with his neighbor, but then his head sank down, he gave a little belch and his eyes glazed over slightly.

Cesare smiled to himself. His clever sister. No difficulty at all.

But Alfonse came drunkenly to. He caught hold of Lucrezia's arm and stood up, lurching a little.

"Well . . . we . . . must . . . retire," he said, slurring each word and waiting for long concentrated pauses.

Those other guests who had heard stood up politely and Lucrezia, so as not to make a scene, found herself obliged to stand up, make her excuses and retire with her drunken husband who hadn't once released his hold on her arm. She was quite taken aback by the sudden reversal of her plan. One minute he'd looked as if he'd have to be carried to bed, the next he'd made a comeback like some punchdrunk fighter who won't go down.

On Cesare the effect was even worse. He saw the image of his night's exhilaration slipping away. No other woman would do. He loved his sister, had more feeling for her than for any other woman, and he had to unite with her tonight.

Thinking furiously, he waited for them to reach the doors of the banquet hall. None of the other guests seemed inclined to leave so early.

Cesare stood up.

"If you'll excuse me father . . ."

"What, my son — we have some saucy dancing to follow. Why, it's not yet midnight."

"I'm sorry father, but I have a bad head. I got a knock in Naples, you know, and they've been recurring, these headaches, ever since."

"My poor boy. We'll have the physician in first thing tomorrow . . ."

"Oh, it's nothing serious, father . . ."

"And you'd better have one of the servants get you something."

The Pope called to an attractive female servant, who had ceased to be a virgin the moment he'd discovered that she was one.

"Carlotta, the Duke needs a brew for his head."

The woman moved off to obey and Cesare took his leave of the guests and followed her. The plan had fallen into his lap if the drink had caught up on Alfonse as much as he thought it should have done by now.

He caught the girl, walking through the corridors, and took her by the arm. She turned toward him, smiling. She was a well-known libertine and Cesare remembered that he'd yet to try her.

He talked to her quietly for a few minutes, explaining that his sister did not want to sleep with her newlywed in his drunken state but could hardly refuse. He outlined a brief plan and slipped an emerald ring into her hand. She held his fingers suggestively and he whispered in her ear that he would like to see her the next day. That seemed to satisfy her more than the ring had, and she followed him as he walked quickly through the various chambers and up the broad steps to Lucrezia's temporary apartment.

At the top of the stairs, Lucrezia was almost supporting Alfonse, whose eyes were half closed, but whose arms were mechanically mauling her while his face nuzzled at hers.

Cesare slowed down and motioned to the servant, Carlotta, who grinned as she moved up. Lucrezia saw them coming and, at a sign from Cesare, pushed open the door to her apartment and moved in, rather awkwardly as Alfonse was trying to kiss her breasts and get his hand up her skirt at the same time.

When Cesare and his companion reached the door, Lucrezia had already maneuvered her part-conscious husband into the bedroom. He had succeeded in getting his hand up her skirt and was rummaging between her thighs as they staggered toward the bed. He pulled her onto the bed as they reached it and her skirt fell up over her hips as she landed beside him. He began to kiss her passionately and she pulled away saying, loudly, to ensure that it got through to him:

"Wait, darling. Let me undress."

He didn't seem to hear. His hand mauled

between her legs, exposing all that was there to the eyes of the two watchers at the door. Lucrezia pulled away from him by main force and he rolled onto his side and lay there muttering to himself, reaching blindly toward her figure which he could probably only vaguely see.

Cesare gave his companion a push and she slipped into the room, pulling off her clothes. As she moved in, Lucrezia moved out.

Brother and sister waited long enough to see the unabashed servant stripped — and very comely, Cesare thought, reserving his true appreciation for the morrow — and settling down to undress Alfonse who slobbered over her naked body. She was hoping he was just conscious enough to get it stiff and stick it in her. She liked the idea of being rammed by young gentry and her hands skillfully teased his prick up to more than life size as she undressed him.

Cesare and his sister made their way quickly to his own apartments. When he had locked the door behind them they both burst into helpless laughter which shook them for several minutes.

"How brilliant, Cesare . . . brilliant!" Lucrezia gasped at last. "But supposing he sobers up?"

"If he does he'll find himself in bed with a maid who'll tell him he dragged her there. He'll be so confused he won't even dare mention it to you. You can say you put him to bed and told the maid to look in later to see if he was all right." He paused. "If he doesn't come to, you'll have time to join him before the morning, and he'll think that he had you before he passed out."

"Brilliant, brilliant — but I'd hate him to

296

have had a servant girl and think that it was me — a poor level of performance."

"I'll let you know how you compare tomorrow," he said.

"Why you *diablo*, you've got her into your bed for tomorrow night? What about me?"

"You'd better make peace with your Alfonse."

"Cold-hearted brute. You don't care for me one jot."

She came toward him, mock-pouting through her smile and he grabbed her and kissed her as if he wanted to push her mouth through to the back of her head. She opened her mouth under his pressure and, squirming at him, began to undo his doublet.

"I can't wait, darling. God he got me all excited for you with his mauling!"

Cesare stripped rapidly and Lucrezia tore off her astonishingly few garments.

"You should have been a gypsy," he said, and the thought reminded him of another liaison not yet exhausted. Doubtless he would be returning north before very long.

She twisted around for him, moving her limbs in a wild pirouette, showing off the almost exaggerated curves of her highly voluptuous body.

"Do you remember the day you chased me around the pool?" she asked breathlessly, falling into his arms and stroking his penis underneath from base to tip. "What did you think when you saw me running naked, for the first time, in front of you."

Cesare kissed her ear and quivered with the feel of her lovely nakedness against his.

"I thought you had a bottom more beautiful than the moon," he said.

"Oh, darling, how poetic. Is it still?"

She broke away from him and turned her back coquettishly.

He looked down at the bottom. It was perfect, not too much flesh, slightly oval — shaped with the buttocks billowing out, smooth and shiny as a cannon from her tiny waist.

He moved up behind her, so that his prick pressed up along the crack between the buttocks. He put his hand under her armpits and held a bulbous breast in each. She pushed her behind back at him and felt behind her for his prick as she rested her head back against his shoulder.

"So beautiful I could possess that little crevice between them and imagine myself sailing around the moon on a magic carpet."

Lucrezia laughed breathlessly.

"Why not?" she said. "If you do it'll make me so excited by the time you've finished that I'll cut off your penis with my scissors if you can't come up again within half a minute to satisfy me — that is, if I'm not satisfied already."

He pressed hard against her. That tight little posterior hole was just as delightful as the other. It didn't matter which he had first. He pushed her toward the bed and put her hands around behind his back, pushing his buttocks at her as if she were propelling them both along in their movement.

From a table beside his bed she took some pomade with which, in times of peace and pomp, he treated his hair.

"Use a little of that," she said. "It's a long time since I've felt an invasion in that quarter."

She climbed onto the bed and lay on her stomach, holding her thighs together, pressing them into the coverlet, grunting with expectation.

Cesare knelt over her and pulled her buttocks apart as if he were separating the quarters of an orange. Between was that dark, puckered, very bald-looking crack, seeming so tiny that it was impossible to believe his battering-ram could possibly force its way in.

He took the pomade and gently massaged the little hole with it, smearing it around the bald, puckered flesh, gently tickling her tender spot with his fingertips.

Lucrezia wriggled under him so that her buttocks tensed around his fingers and held him in a light grip.

"Oh hurry, darling," she said, her voice coming up, muffled by the coverlet into which she was pressing her face to control her passion.

Her anus was slippery with the pomade and he pushed his index finger at the clinging little hole. It gave without much difficulty and his finger slipped in and was held. His fingertip found soft, loose depths and he waggled his finger around a little and then pushed in another finger.

Lucrezia pressed her hips into the bed, squealing.

"Darling, darling, don't torment me!"

Cesare looked at his prick. It was red and angry looking. He pulled his foreskin right back and smeared a little of the pomade on so that it glistened.

"Spread your legs," he ordered.

Lucrezia, as if she too were hungry and opening her mouth for food, spread her legs in a large, obtuse-angled V, pressing her legs hard and quiveringly into the coverlet. She loosed her buttock-tension and lay there, her mouth

299

open, heart and loins pounding for the stiff entry.

Cesare leveled himself over her, caught his prick in one hand and aimed it as he stretched out on her, feeling at first the gentle brushing of their skins from chest to loins as he positioned himself and then the full, hot weight of flesh against flesh as he lay heavily on her body.

"That's it!" she grated. "Go on darling. I can stand it!"

Cesare pushed down harder, practically pivoting on his vertical stand.

She groaned out a long exclamation which at first was formless and then managed to transform itself into a stifled "Daaarling!"

His penis was pinched and contracted in her deep passage. It felt as if sparks were being squeezed out of it, as if it were being squeezed into little sections, each with its own burning light.

Cesare moaned with the tight excruciating excitement of it and put his arms around and under her, grasping her breasts, slightly flattened against the bed, and began to squeeze and pull them.

Lucrezia uttered a little scream and he felt her undulating under him, her buttocks rising and falling, wriggling and squirming against the hairy flesh of his loins.

The relief he'd felt at shoving his penis at last into the soft receptacle of his sister's body began to fade and its place was taken by a gnawing pressure which was growing agony.

He rose and fell on her with long deep strokes, pushing right up in a tearing invasion of her posterior passage.

His mouth opened of its own accord and his

breath barked out. Under him, muffled in the coverlet he heard Lucrezia's little screams of passion and he strengthened his grip on her breasts which seemed to expand and resist him.

Up and down, in and out he sawed into her, feeling his organ rasp against the warm walls of her fleshy channel. He wanted still more of her and, without coming out of her, he struggled up onto his knees, pulling her up with him so that she was kneeling with her buttocks in an arc towards him, their bodies joined by the single erect bridge.

Her body curved away from him, her head still resting on the coverlet. She arched her back like a stretching cat and rolled her buttocks in all directions in abandon. He caught her buttocks in each hand and pinched up the flesh, holding it in handfuls, squeezing it furiously as he drove in, wanting to hurt her, to communicate to her the ecstasy of pain and delight in which he was plunged.

He rammed his penis in and then waggled his hips around against her stretched, naked buttocks, feeling the warmth of the friction spring up between them.

To Lucrezia it seemed that there was nothing to her body but loins and buttocks. Her loins were afire and her behind was a gaping cavern into which all of Cesare seemed to have plunged. It seemed that all her entrails had been pushed aside to leave only a great empty, palpitating space in which he moved thickly and expanded with more and more fury.

Ramming in, Cesare was caught on a rhythmic tide of movement in which there seemed to be no thought, no mind, only wild, orgiastic movement and loin-tearing sensation. His penis was chafed and burning and seemed to be still growing, thickening in its every particle, stiffening still when it had seemed utterly stiff before.

His gasps came with rhythmic regularity. Every in-stroke pulled breath from his mouth.

He leaned forward, grasping her tiny waist which seemed so fragile under the voluptuous hips that it looked as if it might snap. He held it on either side, gripping it fiercely, revelling in the feel of the tight flesh and the power that he felt in having her body completely at his command. He pressed her waist down against the bed, forcing it to yield. He drew back and rammed into her with shattering force so that her head grazed forward along the coverlet. He drew back again and shattered in again, tearing into her brutally, savagely, hearing her cry out, losing his whole rigid length in her with a single long thrust. As he drove in he pulled her waist toward him so that her round buttocks crushed back to meet his thrust and helped his searing entry.

He varied his stroke, giving short, quick little thrusts in a quick series and then he reverted to long, slow strokes, bringing from her a fresh gasp or groan with every variation of pressure and movement.

"Oh, oh, oh — I'm coming!"

Her wailing moan came up to him and he gritted his teeth in the brutal ecstasy. His fury had produced her orgasm.

He hurried himself, tensing his loins, grinding his inside, with mental and physical aid, feeling the knot of sensation tighten and complicate in his genitals.

He heard her gasp several short, furious emissions of breath. She rammed back at him as if he couldn't penetrate her enough and then she gave out a long, wild wail which slowly choked and faded into a background of groaning whimpers.

Now, now, now, he told himself as he heaved and bucked over her buttocks which still undulated around him.

He gnashed his teeth, feeling the climax upon him. He pushed her waist flat down toward the bed, wanting to destroy her in the sadistic urge which his near orgasm sent quivering and tumulting through his whole body so that even his toes seemed to tingle with it.

He wanted to split her right apart. He couldn't tell what he wanted. He wanted to go further to achieve some end to his thrusting which he had not yet achieved.

Almost crying with the excruciation of sensation, he knew the end was coming up. It twirled and spun in his genitals, growing into a great, inexorable force. And with a great, hot, slippery outrush it spiralled through his depths, raced like a sharp pain along his pounding rod and broke out in a wild mob of scattering sperm which lashed up and around deep inside her.

He collapsed over her and after a while they rolled over and lay exhausted in each other's arms.

"Darling, I don't think dear Alphonse would have been quite capable, somehow," Lucrezia said softly at last.

Cesare smiled and began gently and expertly to caress her breasts.

CHAPTER 17

When some days later Lucrezia Borgia rode north with her young husband it was as if the lucky star of the Borgia family had left with her. Ominous clouds were gathering to change the fortunes which never seemed to have been so high as at this moment with Cesare, Duke of Romagna and the Pope on good terms with Louis and Ferdinand and Isabella of Spain.

Cesare's dreams at this time were centered on the consolidation for himself of a kingdom which would comprise all of central Italy. Vaulting ambition was already beginning to o'erleap itself in his heart. He glimpsed in those dreams of his a conquest even further which would eventually drive both the Spanish and the French from Italy, leaving the whole peninsula in his hands. And then perhaps? Who could say that the glory of the Roman Empire was dead forever . . .?

At first it seemed that his campaign might succeed. He accomplished what amounted to almost the total subjugation of the Camerino in the space of a very few weeks. But the very fact of his growing power was breeding him more and more enemies — and more and more powerful enemies. Tuscany, Venice and Florence were all worried by the enlarging weight of his mailed fist and agreements were come to between them in preparation for future action. Milan, too, joined the league and rumor had it that the only thing that kept Louis XII himself out of Italy and a containment of the Borgian realm, was that he still needed the Pope's favor in connection with Naples — where the spoils of war were being violently disputed, between the victorious contestants.

Rebellions were provoked among Cesare's mercenaries, by his enemies, for offered reward. He found himself moving hither and yon over Italy crushing first one and then another, growing weary and uncertain in the process.

Although he returned eventually to Rome with a semblance of order in his territories, he knew that powerful Venice was stayed from attacking him only by doubts as to which side the King of France would take in the event of war.

A short time after his return to Rome both Cesare and the Pope fell ill of a mysterious fever which, it was thought, may have been the result of poisoning deliberately designed by their enemies.

The beginnings of their sickness could be traced to a dinner given in the Vatican by the Pope for a number of his cardinals.

So corrupted was the Church from earlier ideals that it was not beyond the bounds of possibility that one of his own ambitious and envious cardinals had contrived to slip some poison into the wine that was drunk and had intended Cesare to be affected also as his temporal power was sufficient to "arrange" the next papacy should his father die.

Father and son both lay for a week between life and death in their rooms in the Vatican. The old man, being of less robust constitution, fought vainly against the inevitable.

Late one evening, with Cesare still tortured by the fever in an adjacent apartment, Pope Alexander — the Cardinal Roderigo that was — feebly summoned his cardinals to his bedside. For a long time they stood in his presence watching his deathlike face, waiting for words which did not come.

When his voice broke through lips which hardly moved, his words seemed to come from some other place than the room in which they stood.

"For years," he murmured — and they

moved softly forward the better to hear — "I have bargained with the devil." He raised his half-closed eyes with an effort to take in the faces of those around his bed and a trace of a smile flickered over his visage.

"A full . . . and devilish . . . life and I'm not afraid to pay. The devil is not unkind to his disciples . . ."

There was a deathly hush in the room. All were aghast, but none dared interrupt this voice coming from the verge of death. There was a flutter-like movement among them as, with a superhuman effort, the old man raised himself up and gazed beyond his bed, but the flutter died into petrification.

"I am coming," he breathed. "I am coming . . . it is just . . ."

He lay back on his pillow. He was dead.

Those present crossed themselves. Nobody said a word. Each was thinking of his own end, his own life, strayed from the paths of righteousness.

It was only after they'd left the quiet room and were on the broad marble steps which led down, that one whispered to another: "Whom was he talking to? What was just?"

"It was not God in the room with him," the other replied.

Within a few days, the body of Alexander, after exposure on a catafalque in full pontificals in St. Peter's, was removed to the Chapel of Santa Maria delle Febbre.

It was a sweltering day and the poison in the Pope's body aided his obesity in the quick decomposition of his body so that his face had become almost black and looked like some macabre creature from the underworld.

Those who gathered to watch the corpse pass

saw in the blackened, grotesque features the entry of the devil himself into the body.

"That's what happens when you fuck your daughter," declared some peasant bystander, who'd heard the rumors which had sounded all over the kingdom and beyond.

"Then you'd better have your carcass burned as soon as you go," retorted his neighbor.

There was a roar of laughter which seemed to infuriate the first speaker. It was true he had a reputation for initiating his 11-year-old daughter in the rites of love and he was touchy on the point. Rounding on his tormentor he dealt him a lusty blow on the jaw. This brought the intervention of another of the crowd and in no time a battle royal was being waged along the side of the road.

The bearers of the body tried desperately to keep a straight and steady path, but as the crowd swarmed and fought around them, one of them lost his balance and the catafalque, body and bearers found themselves rolling in the dust amidst a mob of flailing legs and arms.

It was the lot of Pope Alexander to be embroiled in violence right to the very coffin.

CHAPTER 18

Cesare recovered slowly, becoming conscious and clear in mind long before he'd regained sufficient physical strength to leave his sick-bed.

The northern allies took quick advantage of the absence of both a Pope and a general to lead the Holy Forces. Venice came out in her true colors, sallied across the border and helped to reinstate half the tyrants whom Cesare had driven from the Romagna.

In Rome itself, the powerful Orsini, enemies of the Duke, proved so strong that he was forced to recall a thousand men from the northern provinces for his personal protection in the vulnerable Vatican.

So many of his troops, under treaty obligation, were engaged with Louis of France in checking the Spaniards in Naples that Cesare could do nothing but chafe in his bed and wait for reverse after reverse of his forces, weakened as they were, in Romagna and Camerino.

Meanwhile, in the Vatican, the Sacred College assembled to ask for Holy Inspiration in the election of a new Pope. Whatever divine guidance was expected, due regard was paid by the various factions to letters from Venice and France in which — through the medium of the ambassadors — the cardinals of each of those nationalities were ordered to vote for the favored of the particular power.

Three candidates — any of which would have been hostile to Cesare — appeared, however, in almost equal strength and a compromise had temporarily to be made in the election of someone entirely different — weak and doddering Cardinal Francesco Piccolomini — while the factions canvassed and manipulated to improve their positions *vis-à-vis* one another.

So a feeble, illness-tormented octogenarian became Pius III.

The new Pope was with Cesare, not against him, indicated his displeasure to Venice and issued briefs to the reinstated tyrants commanding their obedience to the Holy See. The Venetians also received a command from France that they desist in their activities under pain of Louis' displeasure. It was the least he could do now that the Borgian power was broken and while he still needed Cesare's troops in Naples and clear passage through Rome.

Cesare, at last able to rise from his bed and buckle on his sword, found Rome so dangerous, with emissaries from the tyrants and even from Venice hidden in the city with orders to kill him, that he had to pass from the Vatican to the Castle of San' Angelo by the way of a secret underground passage connecting them.

There he summoned his captains, planned to withdraw some of his men from the banners of the King of France and prepared to attempt the arduous task of reestablishing his power and his dukedoms.

Even while plans were under way, a further blow shattered the Duke's hopes. Pius III, for whom excitement of succeeding to high office had, perhaps, proved too much, died suddenly overnight. And with his death came a fresh wave of attacks in the north. It seemed that even the voice of France — tied up as the French were in Naples — had little weight in checking the violence which lost Cesare city after city of his old territories.

* * *

The strongest candidate for the Papacy was a life-long enemy of the Borgias, Cardinal della Rovere. This was the man whom Roderigo Borgia had defeated in the Conclave of 1492 and kept out of the coveted throne for 12 years. This was the man who for a number of years had nursed his hatred under a mask of friendship and flattery toward the Pope and Cesare Borgia.

Cardinal della Rovere's election was certain but for one thing, the possible non-support of the Spanish cardinals with whom Cesare wielded considerable influence. A bargain was struck: for the votes of these Spanish cardinals, della Rovere would confirm Cesare in his office of Gonfalonier and Captain-General and support and preserve his title to Romagna.

Cesare felt the ground of his influence with the Spanish cardinals and then agreed to these terms. The election of the longest-standing enemy of the House of Borgia was ensured. For once, and fatally, Cesare's political brain had allowed him to go astray.

Giuliano della Rovere took the name of Julius II at his election and a few days later issued briefs to the Romagna towns that Cesare was to be obeyed. But insurrection and invasion continued in the north and Cesare prepared to go himself into the Romagna and raise a fresh army from loyal subjects in the once liberated cities.

The new Pope asked that Tuscany and the enemy city of Florence should grant Cesare a safe conduct through the territory he would have to cross, but intimated in private dispatches that he quite understood the disturbances in the north were against Cesare Borgia and not against the Church. With this indication of the turn of events were likely to take, no safe conduct was forthcoming.

Out of patience, Cesare asked for the escort of the Pontifical navy by sea to Genoa from which point he would travel into the Romagna via Ferrara. The Pope acquiesced and Cesare set out.

While Cesare was still at sea, news came that the Venetians had captured Faenza and were massing powerful armies in the Duke's lands. Pope Julius came out into the open at last and sent a message to Cesare suggesting that he surrendered the pontifical fiefs into the Pope's hands in an effort to bring law and order into the Romagna.

Cesare, smelling a rat at last, refused and was immediately arrested by the captain of the navy on the Pope's orders.

Julius broke his agreement blatantly and appointed a bishop as new governor of Cesare's old territories. As it was against Cesare that the enemy was moving, he speciously held the only way to bring peace was for the territories to come directly into his own hands under the Church.

Cesare was brought back to Rome and virtually held a prisoner in the Vatican while the war in the north, in spite of the Pope's argument, continued.

While, Cesare, stripped of his titles, property and power, was being treated with an outward show of friendliness in the Vatican, news came of the resounding victory of Gonzalo de Cordoba in Naples. French power was smashed south of Rome. Ferdinand and Isabella, became monarchs of Naples. Spanish influence with the Pope rose like a sudden heat wave.

Not wishing to make a wrong move which could endanger his position, Julius allowed Cesare to depart by sea to the north where he was to enter France. It amounted virtually to deportation.

But, not far out from Ostia, Cesare, with his few loyal men, had his ship turned about and made full sail for Naples to seek asylum in the Spanish camp where he was assured of a friendly welcome.

There, he found other members of the Borgia family, rallying around Gonzalo de Cordoba in an attempt to escape the antagonism of the Pope, and he was made very welcome by the Great Captain with whose troops he had fought in the original quelling of Naples.

Encouraged by the success in the south, Spain was, in fact, considering an invasion of Tuscany — which was allied to France — and then Milan. It was confidently hoped to drive all French power and influence out of the peninsula which for so long had been dominated by a Spanish-born Pope; Cesare was such an obvious choice to lead an expedition into country that he knew well and which bordered areas where he still had friends, that he was chosen a few days after his arrival to lead the Spanish troops north.

This choice gave Cesare fresh hope for his dreams. With the peninsula subjugated to Spain he saw himself in the role of pro-consul, wielding a complete power, divorced from the distant Spanish Crown. But it was not to be.

Nothing could go right for the Borgias after so many years of everything dropping into their laps.

A few days before he was due to depart at the head of a sizeable army, Cesare was arrested by the order of Gonzalo de Cordoba himself.

In the wings of action, diplomatic exchanges had been passing from Julius to the Spanish monarchs and back. The Pope in these exchanges had complained bitterly and with skill of Cesare's refusal to hand the Romagna to the Church in spite, he alleged, of the desires of the local populace, and of the Borgia's designs on an all-powerful state which he would try to expand againt Spanish and French influence, coveting for himself the lordship of all territory south of the Alps.

So successfully did he plead his cause — which, indeed, was not without a basis of fact in its latter hypotheses — that Ferdinand and Isabella took fright. They had heard distant echoes of the determination and ability to succeed with his projected plans of Cesare Borgia and they had no desire to risk a future colony by placing its formation in the hands of a ruthless man who would use their power for his own ends.

Word was sent to Gonzalo de Cordoba and — reluctantly — he complied with the order from his monarchs. Cesare was held in close confinement.

In vain did his friends and his sister Lucrezia write to the new Gonfalonier of the Church to exert his influence with the Pope in securing Cesare's release; the very ardor of their pleas seemed to frighten Julius into renewing his persecution of Cesare's name.

All his former officers were rounded up — some of them fortifying towns they still held in his name and giving bitter resistance — and brought to Rome where they were tortured in an effort to make them sign statements as to the selfish aims of their former chief.

In August of 1504, Cesare Borgia was once again on the high seas. But the bright Mediterranean sun and the loveliness of the azure sea afforded him little joy. He was bound for a Spanish dungeon in the fortress of Medina del Campo where his power would have no hope of revival and his dreams of glory fade into memories of what used to be.

CHAPTER 19

Lucrezia was riding south on what, so she had assured her husband, was a sentimental journey to see her father's grave and visit the places of her youth. In fact, she had come to plead and use every means at her disposal to persuade the Pope to use his influence in securing her brother's release from the Spanish prison in which he was languishing, and from which an occasional letter arrived telling her of his boredom and depression although he was not treated unkindly.

Lucrezia had little to offer. But one trump still remained with her — the undecaying beauty of her flesh. Della Rovere was accounted just as much a libertine as his predecessors and Lucrezia in a moment of sarcastic humor had declared that to have been the source of gratification for three Popes should open the gates of heaven for her without fail.

She traveled with a small retinue of ladies-in-waiting and a posse of men-at-arms. Her passing occasioned no apprehension in territories which once would have regarded her as a potential spy. Her brother was being forgotten. Some people were no longer sure whether he was dead or alive. Talk was centered rather on the possibility of Spanish invasion, which, since Cesare's departure, had come to nothing so far.

Lucrezia and her party were received with mock cordiality by Julius and accommodated in the Vatican for a short stay. Della Rovere could guess why the beautiful Borgia had come and he was interested to see what her pleading and encouragement would be.

Over a luncheon which the two of them had

alone in the Pope's private quarters, Lucrezia had broached the subject.

"My dear lady," the Pope said, thinking at the same time what an exquisite creature she was and wondering just how true were all the stories he'd heard, "your brother is a remarkable man, but remarkableness alone is not enough to allow a man pardon for misdeeds."

"But what did he do? Didn't he recapture for the Holy See lands that had long been lost?"

"He dreamed himself another Caesar, dear lady, but Caesars depend not only on personal qualities. They depend upon propitious circumstances at the right time. The world has, perhaps, become more complicated than in the days of Republic and Empire. Too many powers are equal, so much more depends on compromise, alliance, knowing when to change allies and how to maneuver a man out of favor with his superiors."

"A cynical outlook."

"One that your brother practiced well enough in his day, but failed to maintain to the bitter end."

"But if he were permitted to return to Rome, Capua — anywhere — and undertook to take no part in political or military life. What would you say to that?"

"I would say, my lady, that a man's word is a reed which will bend and bend and eventually snap."

"Do you think me beautiful?"

The Pope was startled by this change of flow in the conversation. But he replied with a smile which contained a hint of lechery.

"Your beauty is well-known, madam, and likewise your accomplishment."

He placed an impudent emphasis on the final

315

word and his eyes moved down to her neck and the low bodice which revealed the rising swell of her breasts.

Lucrezia's heart beat rapidly. This thought of giving herself to a lifelong enemy, of having his prick gouge her where her dear father's and beloved Cesare's had been before, was a bitter pill. But she had nothing else to offer.

"My accomplishment is admirable," she said brazenly, "but it demands that return be made."

"I see. If I don't mistake you, you are offering to be my mistress at the price of your brother's freedom — as far as my persuasion can achieve it."

Julius' penis had moved and staggered up at the thought. This would be sweet vengeance, indeed. The old man dead, the son in prison and now the daughter to lie under him while he made her a harlot, punishing her body with his bludgeon to push home the subservience of the Borgia family to his will in the most sadistically dominating manner. And why need he keep his word. She had no way of enforcing it. She was completely at his mercy. She had to take him at his word.

"Your brother would be unable to resist trying to avenge your family's honor," he hedged, feeling for how serious her proposal was.

Her hand came under the table at which they sat and rested on his thigh, a warm, foreign pressure, harbinger of things to come.

"He shall never know," she said.

His eyes moved over her. The whiteness of her soft skin at the half-bulge of her breasts was a spur. It was so little of that beautiful body to see and it made the hidden remainder superbly exciting.

He leaned forward and kissed the white, soft

316

patch and Lucrezia closed her eyes to hide her shame. She felt his lips glide over the revealed bulge and his fingers pull her dress away at its top so that he could look down the front. The man was a piggish brute.

But while her thoughts were those of hatred, her actions belied them and her hand moved up his thigh and pulled at the hard core of flesh she could feel under his robes. The Pope drew back his head and looked at her. She opened her eyes and smiled, forcing her look to be one of invitation.

Julius was suddenly hot with desire. To know that this famous beauty would be his, all naked in a bed, her whole body at his disposal. It was too much for a man like him to resist — particularly as he was not bound to make any return.

"I agree to your terms," he said.

She took her hand off his erect penis and he felt naked and filled with passion.

"How shall I know you will keep your word?"

"I will draft out the letter and send it off immediately."

"Very well."

Lucrezia was well aware of the probability of trickery, but her bargain was a long shot. She had to take a chance if anything was to be done for her brother.

Julius, now, could hardly keep his hands off her and as they stood up he took her in his arms and pulled her to him. He crushed his lips hungrily on hers and she fought down her anger and opened her lips so that she could flick her tongue into his mouth.

She drew back as his hand began to fumble with her body.

"Later," she said.

He laughed fiercely and rang a bell for his servants.

Lucrezia watched while the letter was written. When it was powdered and signed, she took it in her hands and read it with a glow of hope. It explained that due to new information which had come to light, Cesare Borgia was, in fact, no longer considered guilty of the motives which had previously been ascribed to him. It asked, on behalf of the Pope, that he be returned to Rome as soon as possible as his services were needed.

The letter was sealed, a courier summoned and then dispatched to Ostia that the document might leave on the next ship setting sail for Spain. He had hardly left the Vatican when he was intercepted and the letter taken from him to be burnt to ashes within minutes.

Lucrezia, all unaware of the promptness of the treachery, feeling that there was a good chance of Cesare's rejoining her within the next month or so prepared to fulfill her side of the bargain.

The Pope excused himself for a few minutes to give her time to undress. While she stripped herself of her few garments, bitter and almost tearful at preparing to be ignominiously used by the oldest enemy of her family, the Pope was inviting one of his nearest cardinals, Cardinal Rimini, to secrete himself in the papal rooms and witness all that followed. For so overjoyed and proud was the Pope that the beautiful, luscious daughter of his old enemy was to open her legs in subjection to him that he could not keep it to himself. Only by having a witness could he be sure that he would be believed if ever he told the story. The thought of a voyeur—and how that would further humiliate Lucrezia—added to his own lecherous expectation of enjoyment.

So by the time Julius returned to his bedroom, where Lucrezia lay on the bed, naked, not looking at him, Cardinal Rimini had slipped into the papal apartment and was peering through the crack of an open door at the beautiful and unexpected sight.

"So this is the luscious Lucrezia Borgia," Julius said, with a slight break in his voice as he saw her curved nudity. He flicked his tongue over dry lips. Her buttocks and breasts were the most superb he'd seen in his life, full and juicy but with a firmness which indicated a power in the act and a luster which made them look as smooth as he was to find they felt. Her shoulders were slim, her waist tiny, which accentuated the voluptuous quality of her rotundities. Her thighs were soft and full, with muscles hidden under the surface which could work like a Trojan when her body was afire.

"A bargain well made," he added, with theatrical hypocrisy.

Lucrezia turned her eyes toward him as he stripped off his robes. He had an ugly narrow body, with a rough, pockmarked skin. His prick which pointed out at her like a cannon seemed out of proportion to the rest of his body. It looked wicked and capable of producing pain and desecration.

"How do you find that?" he asked, taking it in his hand and holding it toward her. Obviously he'd been told by other conquests that he had a prick second to none.

"I have seen its equals," Lucrezia lied with a haughty irritation.

"Never its superior, however," he chuckled. He came toward the bed and the sight of his prick almost frightened her. Belonging to a desired friend she would have regarded it with a trembling anticipation. It promised a brutal and therefore ecstatic penetration. But, belonging as it did to an enemy, she felt it had the power to humiliate and destroy her.

The Pope stretched out on the bed beside her and his hands trembled as they began to feel her body. She shivered with repressed antipathy as she felt his hated hands foraging her breasts and buttocks, stroking her thighs. She hated him more than ever now that the moment had come and she saw in his eyes as he bent and ravaged her lips, a gleam of triumph mingled with his passion.

She felt no answering passion. His body, his face, the whole hostile idea of his position repelled her. He was the master. She had sold herself to him. He was not lost and reveling in his passion, he was owning her—with passion —but cruelly, knowing that she could not escape him, had no option but to submit to what he demanded from her body.

"Ah, I want you, I want you," he whispered hoarsely, as if the very sound of the words increased the power he felt over her.

"You're mine, mine. Lucrezia Borgia, you're mine!"

She uttered a little cry at the wanton ring in his words and the cry was muffled in her groan as, with a quick movement he mounted her and thrust into her dry vagina.

The dryness, unresponsiveness of her flesh tore at his prick, drawing a hoarse cry from his lips.

"Oh, oh, you beauty—you slave!" he shouted, his voice broken with ecstatic fury.

Lucrezia, pain shooting between her thighs,

winced at his words. She had never been taken thus. She was virtually being raped. She hated the man who was joined in one flesh with her.

Her passage was so dry that his penis scraped and drubbed it so that it seemed to her he must be drawing blood. She relaxed. It was too painful not to, and gradually her channel moistened a little and his progress became easier and with it her comfort greater.

Julius was determined to be brutal. Watching the old man die and going to the devil, breaking Cesare's power and getting him imprisoned were not made of the same physical revenge as this—this flesh-to-flesh punishment and chastisement of the living body.

He saw the disgust and self-hatred in her face and the hatred of himself and it increased his appetite for savagery so that he crashed his prick into her with all the force of his loins, so that their crotches met in a smack which was bruising and made her cry out.

He pushed her thighs out and up so that they were waving at first out over the bed and then crushed back against her shoulders. She was doubled up under him, twisted and pain-racked, with her naked toes against the sides of his hips and the whole pressure of his upraised body meeting hers at the out-curved point of his loins, culminating in the stiff tree of organ that rammed into her with increasing force and vigor.

Forgotten, out in the next room, with his fine view of the proceedings, Cardinal Rimini was beside himself. He had never in his wildest dreams hoped to see even the breast of such a woman as Lucrezia Borgia. And now to be seeing all—and to be seeing it in operation. It was too much for a man to bear.

321

On the bed, Lucrezia felt as if she were suffocating under the narrow, bony body of her invader. His prick, digging to its full depth in her, seemed to be splitting her passage, to be tearing away layers of it in a painful, sickening, widening process.

He was mouthing oaths and wild expressions of his power over her. He called her names, harlot names and spat words like "fuck" and "cunt" at her as if they would physically hurt her.

Hurt and seared with pain, Lucrezia moved her head from side to side, biting her lips. His words humiliated her and in conjunction with having her legs cramped and defenseless as she lay naked on her back under him and felt his penis filling her loins with a persistent, drubbing, dominating rhythm, the humiliation was overwhelming.

His hands pulled and twisted her breasts as he undulated on her. He made them into weird shapes and she cried out with protest at the pain and tried to wriggle free. But she seemed to be pinned to the bed as with a spear by his enormous fleshy weapon. Her body was being ransacked, torn and turned inside out for the savage pleasure of an old enemy who had her at his mercy.

She opened her eyes and saw his eyes on her face, taking in her fear and horror. His eyes were mad with lust and triumph and his mouth twisted into an ugly gash of sadism from which burst roaring explosions of passion as he speared her.

Lucrezia closed her eyes again to keep the sight of him away from her, but its image followed her eyes, creeping under the closed lids, making a picture in the darkness, which the physical touch of his rapacious taking of her body seemed to hold in position no matter how she tried to thrust it out.

She heard him growing frantic with excitement and her crotch and lower buttocks were aching where his loins around that protruding sword rammed at them. There was pain and aching and hatred all contained in a melting pot which was her vagina.

And suddenly there was something else. Her head had been caught by hot hands and, while Julius still drummed into her with frenzy, a hot, pliable-feeling penis was wormed into her mouth which opened in astonishment.

The excitement of watching had become too much for Cardinal Rimini. The soothing touch of his own hand on his prick was not soothing enough. He needed something cooler, something more foreign, some part of the luscious fruit of a woman on the bed to coax his juices from him.

For several minutes he had stood, trembling, fondling his organ in the doorway in full view of their unseeing eyes. He had gone through fear and desire in quick succession, alternately several times, until he could stand it no more. He would risk the Pope's displeasure. The woman was obviously in no position to resist.

With a guilty, scuffling movement, he had rushed to the bedside, seized her face and thrust himself into her mouth.

His eyes took in the Pope as he did so and the Pope nodded and he said through his gasps: "Take care of him Lucrezia, or I'll recall the letter."

Infamy, infamy. Lucrezia felt a tear roll from her eye. She was helpless and chastened. To be doing this against her will and with these men who had brought about her brother's downfall. The tears were rage and humiliation, with the rage suppressed of necessity.

She began to work. The sooner it was over the better.

On top of her still, the Pope had slipped his hands under her buttocks, raising them slightly off the bed and was squeezing them so hard that it made her cry out. He was gasping and groaning in a wild excresence of sound and his loins were not only pummelling at her but undergoing contortions in every direction as well.

The object in her mouth had bloated until she could hardly breathe. She bit it with a sudden supreme fury at what was being forced on her and the bite brought a wild, wavering cry from the lips of Cardinal Rimini.

Lucrezia, still struggling for breath, looked up at the Pope. Her pelvis was numb with its buffeting and her quim was a raging area of pain. She saw his head go back and then come forward sharply so that his eyes could look at her. The eyes dilated and he emitted a shrill gasp as he came into the pain that he'd caused her. There was savage conquest in his eyes and the thought that this man's sperm was a great lake in her belly was the final humiliation.

CHAPTER 20

"Mate!" said Cesare, as he moved his knight, exposing the clear path between his castle and his opponent's king. Count Benavente sighed and then smiled.

"I begin to understand why your enemies

find you such a redoubtable opponent," he said. "May I never be among them."

"Come, your mind wasn't on the play."

Count Benavente, who had been a frequent visitor to Cesare's confinement quarters these last few weeks, pushed back his chair from the table and stood up, looking not at Cesare but at the chessboard. He walked away after a second or two and stared out of the narrow window to the flat, green land a hundred or more feet below. Cesare watched him without speaking.

"I was thinking," the Count said, "of the matter we mentioned a few days ago."

Cesare glanced quickly at the door and then back at the Count.

"It's too well guarded," he said quietly. "You'd need an army."

"For once I believe I'm right and you're wrong," the Count continued. "But of course I know the place and the people in a way you couldn't possibly."

Cesare didn't answer. It was clear the Count had been mulling over some plan. Best let him speak. He liked the Count, who was a good, upright man and one of the most powerful lords in this part of Spain. He was aware, too, that in some way he fascinated the man, who had lost no opportunity of visiting, talking to and playing chess with him once their acquaintanceship had been made.

"I think, in fact . . . " At this point the Count, too, turned and glanced at the heavy wooden door which was closed. "I think you could be away from here within a few days."

Cesare quickened with interest. This sounded like something concrete. If he could get out of this fortress he'd start immediately to find ways and means of getting back to Italy for the re-conquest of his realms — and then death to anyone who tried to stop him. He had many accounts to settle.

The Count played idly with a pawn, his brow creased in concentration. When he looked up at Cesare, his eyes were intent with purpose.

"I have bribed the guard two nights from now," he said softly, "and we have the help of one of the governor's servants. At two in the morning a rope will be lowered from the battlements. It will pass your window . . . "

The Count took several quick steps across the room and studied the window.

"Yes . . ." he said. "There's just room for you to squeeze through — but you must be careful. You will climb down the rope — preceded by the servant who will make sure that everything is safe — and my men will be waiting above the castle ditch."

Cesare got up slowly, his eyes shining. He moved over to the Count and took his hand, pressing it in both his own. The Count returned the pressure with a smile.

"Some men were meant to be hermits," he said, "but not you."

"But the risk to you . . . "

"Little enough and worth the trouble. My men will escort you at all speed to Santander. I will provide you with money and you should be able to get a boat immediately to France." He smiled wanly: "My only regret is that I shall be deprived of your play and your conversation—but we shall meet again."

"I hope I shall live to repay you," Cesare said.

"Oh, come, it's a small enough thing. Any man with blood would do such for another were

326

it in his power. But . . . " he became practical again, "it must be done with no noise for only the two guards on the western battlements are in our pay."

He shook Cesare's hand again.

"My dear Duke, I must take my leave. I'll come again on the day to assure you that everything is unchanged."

When the heavy door with its fastenings had grated shut and been bolted behind the Count, Cesare sat down at the chessboard. How long had he been here? He'd lost count of the months. He'd had odd contacts with the outside world beyond the Spanish frontier. His sister Lucrezia had written saying that she had pleaded with the Pope and that Julius had sent off a letter of reprieve. Whatever had happened, Cesare had not been released. He wondered what machinations had gone on to account for Lucrezia's certainty and then the lack of results. Certainly to get even with the Pope and then with Gonzalo de Cordoba would be two of his most desired objectives. He would offer himself to Louis. At the head of a French army, he'd soon have the whole peninsula falling over itself to make terms with him.

Smiling, he lifted a knight from the board and with it, triumphantly took a bishop.

CHAPTER 21

Through the narrow embrasure was the free, sleeping, peaceful world. The stars were out. It was a clear, moonlit night, which was a pity.

Beside Cesare was the Governor's servant, a small man, with quick intelligent eyes who kept his gaze fixed on the oblong of light.

"There!" he said suddenly.

Cesare felt a needling in his stomach as he saw the thick rope snake down across the window, swing away out of sight for a second and then float back again to be grabbed by the man at his side.

Quickly he helped his companion up onto the still of the embrasure. The man squeezed the top part of his body through and looked back.

"Better wait until I'm off, Sire," he whispered. "It would be wise not to put too much weight on the rope."

"Yes, yes. Off you go!" Cesare said quickly.

He watched while the man took the strain on his arms and pulled himself through the opening. He swung out high over the ground and the rope swayed away from the sheer wall of the battlements and then back, grazing him along its stone surface.

In what seemed like agonizingly slow time he began to go down the rope hand under hand, his feet twisted around it, helping to take the strain.

Cesare climbed onto the sill and knelt precariously, peering out. Down below he could see the servant descending, growing smaller, just the top of his head a vague black mass. He looked down to the distant ground. He couldn't see Benavente's men but he had no doubt they'd be there, waiting in the shadows and that above the guards were watching, cursing at the time it took for the prisoner to escape, risking their skins a little more with every second that passed.

He shifted his cramped position on the sill. Hurry man, hurry! He could see the black dot, but it was impossible to tell now whether it was going down or had stopped. At any rate the

328

man was still on the rope, holding him back
from launching himself in the void.

Cesare strained his eyes into the moonlit
darkness. It was gloomy in the shadow of the
walls, which cut off the moon. What was the
matter with the man? His head was still there,
a tiny, indistinct point far down, surely not far
from the ground. He seemed not to be moving.

And then the point moved and even from his
height Cesare heard the thud. A groan rose on
the still air and vaguely he saw shadows moving in a flurry down in the deep, empty ditch.

The fool, the idiot! What had he done—got
tangled with the rope? There was another
groan, sounding like thunder in the motionless
night.

Cesare caught the rope which swung in loosely towards him. He heard challenging shouts
from somewhere down near the gates of the
fortress and cursed. What a bungling farce!
He could have spat with rage, but he kept his
head, swinging out from the embrasure and
back against the rough wall as he began to let
hand under hand and slide his feet with the
rope between them.

He felt the chafing on his hands, but speed
was essential, he had not time to lower himself
in correct, comfortable fashion.

Lights were flashing a way off on the ground
and he slid faster. Up above there were shouts
on the battlements too. The bribed guards could
not pretend to be blind for so long without risking their necks.

Down, down with a blank face of wall, a
turmoil in his stomach, a long drop to the ditch
and noise and light growing off on his right.

"Hurry!" He heard the single, sharp shout

from below and slid so rapidly that he could feel the skin being torn on his hands.

And then another cry—of warning.

"The rope is short—take care!"

Cesare glanced down into the gloom which had cleared sufficiently to enable him to see several of Benavente's men, with the Count at the head of them, and to see the dangling end of the rope some fifteen feet short of the ground. Along in the ditch he saw some of the men trying to lift the servant, who was still groaning audibly.

He swarmed down the last few feet of rope, measured the dangerous distance to the ground and jumped—just as the rope was cut from above. It came hurtling down on top of him, heavy and painful. But he landed with nothing more than a shaking and probably a bruised arm and knee as he fell sideways.

With furious haste he was pulled from the ditch by Benavente's men as shouts from the castle barked out close by.

From further along the ditch one of the men called.

"He seems to have both legs broken—it's difficult to move him."

Cesare, slightly winded, his ears singing, was pulled onto a horse as cries of recognition sounded from the corner of the wall down which he had crawled. A small crowd of guards were racing toward the group. Behind them was commotion and sounds of horses clattering over the lowered drawbridge.

The Count thrust a sword into Cesare's hand.

"Take that my friend—you'll have to use it yet."

He called back to his men in the ditch.

"Leave him!"

There was no hope of escape with an injured man. And it was important that the Count was not recognized.

They could see the light of the moon glinting on the pikes and swords of their pursuers as they wheeled and set their horses at a gallop away from the fortress. There was a crash of gunshot from the castle turrets and then they were outdistancing the guards who faded back into anonymous shadows, calling and shouting to the horsemen who were yelling for direction.

Cesare's head cleared as they streamed through the night air, setting up a wind from their rapid motion through its stillness. He could feel the irritating pains in his arm and leg, but they were worth nothing compared with the exhilarating vigor he felt in freedom.

They rode at all speed until there was neither sight nor sound of any pursuit.

"A narrow success," the Count called against the wind as he galloped beside Cesare.

"A little spice to give it perfection," Cesare called back, laughing into the wind.

CHAPTER 22

"I tell you, you can name your price," Cesare said.

The ship's master with whom he spoke turned a steady searching gaze on him. There was no compromise in his hard eyes.

"I tell you that my route is not to France— and I know of nobody else who has such a direction."

He stared hard at Cesare.

"Besides, from what you sound there's danger in it—and I'll not risk my ship for any money."

"As you wish," Cesare sighed. "The loss is yours."

He bade the captain goodnight and left the tavern.

Throughout the small town, the Count's men were plying all and sundry with similar questions. Meeting at pre-determined times in an auberge down near the seashore they discussed their latest lack of success. All efforts so far had been in vain. Nobody was able or willing to take the risk of going off his route with a man who was obviously in some way an enemy of the State.

The Count himself had taken his leave of the party earlier, to return to his domain, leaving several of his men to aid Cesare in Santander. He had not anticipated such difficulty as the party was now encountering.

Meeting for the umpteenth time to quaff ale in the little inn within sound of the waves breaking on the shore, Cesare and the Count's men were glum with failure.

"We'll have a last attempt," Cesare said at last, downing his liquor and rising. "If it fails then there's one thing left—I'll have to cross the frontier into Navarre."

"You run more risk on land than on sea."

"I run more risk still stuck here without hope of escape."

They began, for the last time, to scour the bars and inns of the town, cutting it into sections, working methodically.

It was in a little tavern where everyone seemed to be slightly the worse for drink, that Cesare got what sounded like a hopeful tip. He had sat himself in a corner to take stock of those in the place, which was alive with noise and the clatter of tankards.

An old seadog, talkative with wine, flopped down on the bench beside him.

"I say that we're the freest of 'em all," he said fiercely, not looking at Cesare, but apparently speaking to him as there was nobody else very near.

"If we don' like our wives we go on a long trip, if we do we go on a short 'un. We got fresh air and good pay an' all the world to see. What more?"

He turned to Cesare, beetling his thick brows, as if he expected argument. His eyes within their crinkled, sunburned lids were bright blue and ringed with little red veins and the yellow wash of age and liquor. His tankard sagged in his hand and there was a beer stain on his old black neckerchief.

"Quite right. Let me fill 'em up on it," Cesare said, taking the tankard from his hand and calling to the skivvy who hopped around and tripped over sprawling feet.

"You'm a stranger. New face around here."

It was a question and the man suddenly seemed soberer than first appearance would have suggested.

"Yes, looking for a boat to take me to France."

"To France?"

The old man gazed reflectively as their filled tankards were set down on the rough table in front of them. He raised his, glanced over Cesare's clothes which were well-to-do although a disguise.

"Your health, sir."

"And yours—and to the free life."

"Aye. You'll get no boat going to France at this time."

"I can pay well. It would be a good bargain."

The old man looked at him again, with his eyes narrowed slightly.

"You'm very anxious to get there."

"A matter of urgent business," Cesare snapped. He was irritated at the man's irrelevant interest in his activities.

"Could be done, I suppose . . . could be done . . . "

"What can you tell me?" Cesare demanded. "It's very urgent."

The old man considered, glancing around the tavern with eyes that seemed to have awakened completely from the half-stupor of liquor.

"Don't know as I ought," he said. "Don't sound legal to me—what you're up to."

"I'll thank you to keep your opinions to yourself," Cesare snapped. "I'll make it worth your while to give me any useful information."

"How worth."

Cesare opened a pouch on his belt and threw some gold pieces on the table. The man's eyes glistened and he stared, fascinated, at the money. He put out his hand to pick them up and Cesare's hand closed on his wrist with a force which made him start.

"Not before you tell me what you have to say."

The man stared at him. He was beginning to wonder with whom he was dealing. There was an authority about the stranger which, even in this familiar seaman's bar where every strong arm would be with him, made his spirit yield.

"All right. Take them off the table."

Cesare grinned and swept the pieces off the table and onto the wooden bench between them.

334

"She's a ship-owner's widow," the seaman explained. "Lives just on the outskirts o' the town. They say she likes a 'andsome man though she's nothin' to look at 'erself. There was some young duke came through here three year ago with a price on 'is head. 'E went and offered isself to her for work on one of 'er ships and she told him he could 'ave a job if he was nice to 'er." The old man laughed coarsely. "Least thats 'ow the tale goes. Ain't nothin' can 'appen in a place like this without folks get to know about it afore long."

"Where can this woman be found?"

But the old man had warmed to the lechery of his story.

"They do say she's real frustrated—her husband been dead for six year and none as she thinks are suitable as'll have 'er. They do say . . . " he grinned lasciviously . . . "as she likes a little tickle with a rope afore she has 'er cranny stuffed."

He guffawed suddenly in a tone which made the nearest people turn towards him and then grin before resuming their own conversation.

"But o' course if you was goin' to pay, anyway, you probably wouldn' 'ave to pander to 'er every whim."

"Where can this woman be found—enough of your prattle!"

The seaman sobered down although his eyes were still alight with mirth at his humor. He picked up the golden pieces and slipped them quickly into a pocket as if he were afraid to be seen looking at them.

"For another such, I'll show ye."

"Right, but quick about it."

They left the inn and ambled at a pace which exasperated Cesare, through the narrow streets near the seashore. At last the man pointed out a large house on the corner of a narrow street, with a porch and steps over which shone a lantern.

"There—an' I hope you'm feelin fit and 'earty."

Cesare caught him by the arm and held it with a grip which made the old man wince.

"Not a word about this to anyone," he said, knowing that his words were probably useless. "I have men here and if you start shouting this around it'll be the worse for you."

There was real startled fear in the old man's eyes.

"Aye, aye, sir," he said. "I wouldn' want 'em to know as I'd got rich, anyway."

He ambled off into the darkness and Cesare knocked at the door of the big house. Shortly Cesare was being ushered by one of what seemed to be many servants into the presence of the mistress of the house.

After he had explained his business, the woman relapsed into thought, toying with a cushion. He judged her to be about sixty or a little under. She had a commanding face and had probably once been quite beautiful. But now she had grown stout and flabby and the skin hung on her fingers like plain rings.

After a while she looked up at him, lightly studying his face and figure.

"It is a risky thing you're asking," she said.

"I'm offering a good price."

"But I'm not poor. I'm not in great need of money so your price isn't all that interesting to me."

So the town gossip was true. How impossible these small towns were. He decided to make things easy for her.

336

"But what else can I offer, my dear madam?"

She smiled and stood up. She began to move slowly around the lighted room as if thinking. She stopped in front of a painting, small painting above a grate where a log fire was burning low. He watched her, her stout bottom and belly rustling in her skirts.

"This is a picture of my husband," she said, staring at it.

Cesare moved across the room and stood beside her and just a little behind.

"A good-looking man."

"Yes, he had many virtues and I miss him—particularly in bed."

Cesare smiled. So she was going to brazen it. She didn't look at him. She had crossed the bounds of decorum and was waiting with bated breath to see how he reacted.

"I'm sure the loss is more his."

"Ah, you mustn't say such blasphemy," she said—but quite disarmed at his reply.

She moved away again, leaving him standing beside the portrait. When she turned, her eyes dropped to his loins and then rose to meet his.

"I long for people to take his place—just for a while," she said in a tone which, Cesare was surprised to find, made him feel rather sorry for her.

"Madam, there can be few could resist such an open-hearted admission from such a fine woman as yourself."

"Oh tush!" But she smiled again and moved toward him. "A beautiful person like yourself has no need of elderly women but . . . " she hesitated . . . "that is my price."

"My dear lady you overestimate me. You offer me delight and disparage yourself at the same time."

She was pleased with his gallantry even if she hardly believed it. She came toward him and put her hands on his shoulders, her head against his breast as he pressed her body into his.

That it should come to this, Cesare thought with a sardonic humor. But bargainers can't be choosers.

"My husband was so good because he knew my quirks," she said softly, rubbing her loins gently against his, so that in spite of his reservations he found his prick responding.

"Your quirks—you like to be excited in some —abnormal—manner?"

Gallantly he helped her, saving her embarrassment. Besides he was in a hurry.

"Yes—he used to whip me. But I no longer have the whip and, besides, now that I'm a little older, I prefer the more intimate touch of the hand and then perhaps a few strokes from a cane I keep in my boudoir."

Better get it going, Cesare decided. He pushed his hips back at hers and tried to get his hands around her big buttocks. She looked up at him with her mouth open and he lowered his face onto hers as if going into a dungeon. Her skin was rather dry under her powder but she had kept herself well and he was surprised at the keenness of passion with which she responded.

"I'll send the servants to their quarters," she whispered.

She disappeared for several minutes and when she was once again in the doorway, he saw she was dressed in a silk gown which hid her stout flabbiness and gave a certain silken luster to her appearance.

She beckoned and he followed. She led him up a flight of stairs and into a tasteful boudoir with a large bed to one side on which was a long, whippy cane.

"Will you undress?" she pleaded.

He began to slip out of his clothes and she watched as if she would eat his body. When he stood in front of her, naked and with his upstanding penis rearing toward her, he could hear the rustle of the gown where she was trembling. She stared at his body in admiration and desire.

"So young—so strong," she whispered.

She came over to him, opened her gown and enclosed them both in it, crushing against him. He could feel the sag of her breasts, low down on his chest and the bush of hair around her cunt. The fat thighs were hot and met his like bastions.

"Kiss me—and then beat me until I scream," she said fiercely.

He kissed her and she held his prick, squeezing it gently so that he felt the blood running into and expanding it. He was surprisingly excited. It occurred to him that she'd be the oldest woman he'd ever fucked.

She dragged him to the bed, pushed him down, flung off her gown and threw herself face down, sinking into its soft depth. For a moment he gazed at the fat, flabby buttocks which quivered like jelly, so fleshy were they. He glimpsed her breasts, large and hanging down toward her waist. There were rolls of fat at her waist and lines across her thighs. He could see the fringe of a tuft of black hair protruding between her buttocks.

Well, she should have her money's worth. He'd make fine play with that fat, soft body.

He knelt beside her on the bed, holding her down in the small of the back with one hand.

He brought his other sharply down across her buttocks, feeling it sink, stingingly into the flesh, leaving a red and white mark as he lifted it again. She winced and muffled her gasp in the bed. Her buttocks quivered with that jelly-like helplessness and she winced with her whole body.

He raised his hand again and smacked it down in the wake of the first blow. Again she smothered her gasp in the sheets. Again and again he brought down his hand, until she was writhing and squirming and her buttocks were fiery red. Sometimes he stopped, thinking from her stifled scream that she'd had enough, but then she'd raised her smarting bottom up toward him to indicate that she needed yet more.

When her rump was glowing in a single smoldering flush, he took hold of the cane, swished it once in the air and then brought it down with half-force across her backside. It made a single deeper weal across the blush of her puddings. She cried out, made as if to escape, and then pushed her loins hard into the bed, remaining where she was.

Cesare held her firmly with his left hand and brought the cane down with all his force. This time she shrieked with pain and the weal came up immediately, bruised and angry-looking. Three more times, holding her fast as she squirmed and struggled and screamed with the pain, he lashed the flickering stick down across her fat behind and then she cried out in a loud voice.

"Screw me now! Stuff me up, quickly—oh now!"

He pulled her up onto her knees and slipped between them. His prick was stretching and in excitement, invigorated by the thrashing he'd

340

subjected her to. He eased back, directed his organ and surged forward into her, pushing the walls of her vagina aside like earth under a pick.

She quivered and screamed. And he caught those tender buttocks in his hands and began to punish her with his prick, ramming in and in with strong, rough thrusts which jerked her forward on her face every time he reached the extremity of her passage.

She cried out again and again and at last she was laughing and sobbing with joy at the same time. He wondered through his teeth-gritting labor how long it was since she'd had a young man's prick up her cranny.

Every time he jabbed it in a long, breath-sucking stroke, the friction of his loins against her fat pink behind set off her buttocks wobbling furiously. He separated them in rolls of fat and plunged his fingers between their great curves. He pulled on the tuft of black hair he found, making her shriek with ecstacy and skewer her unsupple body against him.

He reached right under her with his other hand and felt through the sticky juices which were beginning to flow. Her clitoris was as hard as a nut, and big, too. He pinched it, hurting her and then held her fat wobbling belly in handfuls, feeling it heave and jump under the emotional and physical turmoil through which she was passing.

"Oh, oh," he heard her cry. "I can't . . . can't bear . . . it."

He slashed her buttocks with his hands, making them roll and squirm and drubbed her harder and harder, pulling his lips back from his teeth in the bone-splitting fury of it.

He could hardly feel anything now, just a

light slippery stroke as he thrust in and up.
Only at the very end was there sharp sensation
for him. But she was racing to a climax. A climax, it seemed, such as could hardly be imagined.

He had difficulty in holding her upright on
the bed. She seemed to have lost all control, was
emitting lost, soul-rending cries, which made
him realize why she'd dismissed the servants,
and was swaying and pitching on the end of his
penis like a wild young horse.

Of a sudden she shrieked out:

"Oh, love, love—uuuuuuuugh!"

And her body seemed to petrify in a tense
pushing orgasm and even Cesare could feel the
added warmth surround his prick. Having controlled himself to some extent to the point
where he was waiting for her to be satisfied,
he now let himself go and within seconds was
discharging his venom into her wide, van-
quished quim and subsiding over her gross behind, which gradually lost its quiver as she
calmed.

* * *

On the way to the tavern with one of the
woman's servants who carried a message from
her to the master of one of her ships, Cesare
was waylaid by one of the Count's men.

"Quick, Sire, off the road."

The man took hold of him by the arm and
dragged him into a doorway while the servant
stood uncertainly, watching them in astonishment.

"What's up?" Cesare demanded. "Quick man
—I've got a boat."

"Too late, Sire. Someone's talked out and the
King's men are scouring the town. They have

342

the port under close surveillance. It would be impossible to get through."

Cesare cursed furiously. He could hardly believe in such shocking luck.

"I'd like to get my hands on that old dog!" he snarled.

"Sire, our horses have been brought to a stable a little way from here. The men are waiting. Your only chance is to ride for the frontier as you foresaw."

Cesare lost no further time with his fury. He dismissed the servant, telling him to say to his mistress that circumstances had arisen which made the passage unnecessary but that he considered himself, taking everything into account, not to be at such a great loss.

He smiled grimly as they ran through the streets toward the stables. The experience had been more amusing than he'd expected and she'd practically abased herself before him on his departure, even offering him a permanent pension if he'd stay in the region and visit her no more than once a fortnight. He had been forced to explain the urgency of his leaving this part of the world.

In the stables the horses were ready, champing at the bit, and they made no secret of their departure as they clattered full pelt through the streets toward the open country. For once it was more haste, more speed.

CHAPTER 23

So it was to Navarre that Cesare managed at last to escape from Spain, to the court of his brother-in-law, King Jean. His arrival threw the kingdom into confusion and as far off as

343

the Vatican, hearts were quaking at news of his escape.

He was given asylum and every attention and wrote to the King of France offering his services in any capacity which would provide him with an army in the service of Louis.

After some weeks he received the cool communication that as he had for a period joined the camp of Gonzalo de Cordoba he could no longer be considered a friend of France. Just that and no more. A bitter pill, which retarded, it seemed, indefinitely his hopes of reconquest of his former territories in Italy.

Cesare champed and chafed and wrote to friends and his sister to seek intelligence of the situation in his homeland. He wanted action and instead he had to remain, tucked away in Navarre eating fruit and drinking wine all day long while he listened to interminable lute-playing.

It was at this time that trouble grew in the teacup of Navarre, a small storm in which Cesare would have taken not the slightest interest had accident of circumstance not held him in the country at the time—a gratuitous, irrelevant involvement which, it seemed, by some prank of destiny, making a mockery of man's aims and ambitions, was to cost him all.

The country was suddenly torn by opposite factions which had long been snarling at each other. The Beaumontes, principal of these factions, refused to be brought to heel and surrender to the King. Into Cesare's lap fell the offer of the Captain-Generalcy of Navarre with a force of 10,000 men. He was to lay siege to the main Beaumontese fortress of Viana and make the name of the King absolute throughout his realms.

Seeing in this, the possibility of an ally and material assistance at some later date, Cesare agreed and led the army into its siege position.

The fortress was strong, but its provisions were running low. It stood fair to be starved to surrender in a short time.

But Beaumont, who gave his name to his faction, conceived the risky and daring plan of creeping through the enemy lines at night and getting supplies from a nearby, friendly town.

The attempt—a complete surprise to the besiegers—would have been completely successful had not a party of reinforcements coming up to join Cesare's army bumped into the retreating Beaumontese with the first light of dawn preparing to break through.

The alarm was given, and Cesare, who had been unable to sleep, was one of the first in pursuit, leaving his men to follow the obvious trail of the Beaumontese through the hillocks surrounding the fortress.

He was full of fury at the trick. This would mean weeks more for the siege and he could not be involved in the petty disturbances of a petty kingdom for that long. Such troubles, as he rode in pursuit, unaware of his start on the men of his own army, blinded him to the risk one could run equally in petty kingdoms.

At a turn in the track he was ambushed by a score of the Beaumontese who, seeing a lone rider well ahead of the main body of the pursuit and being so near safety themselves, had turned back for the sake of the kill.

Cesare was surrounded, realized for the first time that the pursuit party of his army was not yet even in earshot and tried to break free from the encircling horses. But he was hemmed in and although he dispatched several of the enemy he was dragged from his horse at last and there on the road near the lonely fortress of Viana in Navarre in a cause which was not his own and of no real interest to him, Cesare Borgia was cut down under a rain of blows.

The thunder of the hooves of the pursuit came into earshot as those of the retreat died away and Cesare lay dying beside the road, stood over by his horse.

His army was dismayed and Navarre stricken by the gratuitous death of this man who had been such a fine leader in his day. There were few, even among his enemies, as the news raged over the border and into the surrounding countries, who did not feel a pang of regret that he should have met such a strange end.

There were many who said that God had finally decided that this creature of his creation who had murdered and schemed and raped and dallied with incest, had done enough; that he had made him lose his reason just at the moment when there had been no cause for him to risk his life.

Of Lucrezia no more was heard after her brother's death. It was rumored that she was so stricken with grief that she never again left the walls of her quarters in her husband's palace. Others again insisted that she was seen no more simply because she continued to indulge in practices for which she needed the secrecy of a screen from the public eyes.

Centuries later, it was said, Italian mothers would occasionally use the names of Cesare and Lucrezia or Roderigo Borgia to frighten their naughty children and send them scurrying, subdued, to bed.

THE END

LUSTS OF THE BORGIAS

POSTSCRIPT

POSTSCRIPT

Throughout history, humanity has given birth to many monsters. From Caligula to Hitler the names roll off the tongue and doubtless there were many before and others yet to come.

But the world has never known, and probably never will, an evil quite so peculiar as that synonymous with the name, Borgia.

True, the mores of 15th-century Italy—or the many separate states which then made up the peninsula—were what is sometimes euphemistically described as "robust," but the excesses of licentiousness, treachery and murder perpetrated by this notorious family are heightened beyond parallel by the fact that one of their number reigned supreme over the Roman Catholic world while such depravity was indulged to the full. As Pope Alexander VI, Roderigo de Borja not only condoned the rape, murder and incest committed by his progeny, but joined them in the airing of their infamous appetites.

Roderigo, in fact, already had a number of children by a Roman girl, Vannozza dei Cattanei, when he was elected Pope. Two of them, Cesare and Lucrezia, both of outstanding looks and intelligence, were, with the Pope, responsible for the family reputation.

Cesare, idealized by Machiavelli in his book, *Il Principe*, murdered his brother to improve his position in the Church and was himself a cardinal before he stood down to take an army on a mission to subdue a large part of the peninsula to the overlordship of the Holy See. He is described by one historian as "handsome, brave, talented, a brilliant soldier and a just and able administrator," but we also know him

as a man of cruelty, avarice and sexual preda-
toriness, who would stop at nothing to satisfy
these appetites. Like his father, he gloated over
his lovely sister and there is little reason to
doubt that he enjoyed her charms to the full,
sharing her in this respect with Roderigo. So
pronounced was his incestuous passion that he
was responsible for the murder of one of Lucrezia's three husbands, the Duke of Bisceglie.

Lucrezia herself was a born seductress, who
enjoyed the game of ensnaring men, even to
the point of alluring her own son, and was only
too willing to give them outlet for their lust to
ensure the achievement of her purpose.

There are many apologists for the Borgias,
but the wealth of evidence concerning their
sinister and all-embracing corruption is overwhelming. Theirs is a fascinating story whose
details beg to be laid bare in an attempt to
understand the full motivation of their actions
and the depths of perversion to which they
jointly sank.

When I first read a book on the Borgias as
a 17-year-old schoolboy in the sedate provincial-
ism of the English West Country where I spent
my adolescence, I was unaware that the notorious family differed only in degree from so
much of society. To someone raised in a moral
atmosphere of Victorian dimensions, the idea
of sex used not only to gratify appetite, but as
a currency to gain ends, was exotic in the extreme.

It was not until I became a journalist, working at first in those same provincial back-
waters, that I discovered the barely-disguised
libidos running abrasively through the most apparently placid areas. In the courts I heard
tales of Borgia quality, from the tenements to

350

high society; local politics and cultural life were rife with this subcutaneous ferment.

At the age of 23, I uprooted myself and went to Paris to write and—perhaps partly through that process—to find some meaning in things. What, in fact, I found was more Borgia evidence everywhere. While working for the expatriate literary magazine, *Merlin,* writing for the Olympia Press and teaching English to classes of air personnel at Orly Airport, I viewed at first hand the naked use of sex to gain other than sensual satisfaction: writers sleeping with publishers to ensure they were published; publishers going to bed with writers to secure their next novel; impecunious artists getting sexually involved with heiresses to acquire funds for their creative activities; wives of airline pilots trying to seduce the English teacher as a guarantee of language tuition.

After four and a half years of this—with periods in Spain and Italy, where the predatory youth emulate their infamous forebears for gain from rich tourists—I returned to England to a job in Government publicity. In those Civil Service corridors of power, too, I found the phallus reigning supreme: career ladies sleeping with their directors for promotion; sexual jockeying for advantage; nepotism; above it all a well publicized case of a middle-aged woman colleague allured into an affair by an Eastern European diplomat and, in no time, providing him with confidential and secret papers as security against the loss of his prowess in bed.

All this we come to accept as part of the pattern of "ordinary" life. To each protagonist his activities seem completely understandable and even inevitable expressions of personality produced by pressures of environment, both material and mental. Doubtless the Borgias would have felt the same way about their own excesses. For the question of evil is relative. It has many levels and it is in all of us. Like Eichmann, we seldom recognize or accept it for what it is.

The Borgias do not stand alone, extreme though their story may be. They are a monument to the world today—and a warning.

Marcus van Heller
London, July 1967

MORE EROTIC CLASSICS FROM
CARROLL & GRAF

☐ Anonymous/SATANIC VENUS	$4.50
☐ Anonymous/SECRET LIVES	$3.95
☐ Anonymous/SENSUAL SECRETS	$4.50
☐ Anonymous/SWEET TALES	$4.50
☐ Anonymous/THREE TIMES A WOMAN	$3.95
☐ Anonymous/VENUS DISPOSES	$3.95
☐ Anonymous/VENUS UNBOUND	$3.95
☐ Anonymous/THE WANTONS	$3.95
☐ Anonymous/WAYWARD VENUS	$4.50
☐ Anonymous/A WOMAN OF PLEASURE	$3.95
☐ Anonymous/WHITE THIGHS	$4.50
☐ Cleland, John/FANNY HILL	$4.95
☐ Perez, Faustino/LA LOLITA	$3.95
☐ Thornton, Louise, *et al.*/TOUCHING FIRE	$9.95
☐ van Heller, Marcus/THE LOINS OF AMON	$3.95
☐ van Heller, Marcus/ROMAN ORGY	$3.95
☐ Villefranche, Anne-Marie/FOLIES D'AMOUR	$3.95
☐ Villefranche, Anne-Marie/MYSTERE D'AMOUR	$3.95
☐ Villefranche, Anne-Marie/SECRETS D'AMOUR	$4.50
☐ Von Falkensee, Margarete/BLUE ANGEL NIGHTS	$3.95
☐ Von Falkensee, Margarete/BLUE ANGEL SECRETS	$4.50